Twelve Deaths of Christmas

Twelve Deaths of Christmas

JACKSON SHARP

PENGUIN BOOKS

PENGUIN BOOKS

UK | USA | Canada | Ireland | Australia
India | New Zealand | South Africa

Penguin Books is part of the Penguin Random House group of companies
whose addresses can be found at global.penguinrandomhouse.com.

First published 2015
001

Set in 12.5/14.75 pt Garamond MT Std
Typeset by Jouve (UK), Milton Keynes
Printed in Great Britain by Clays Ltd, St Ives plc

A CIP catalogue record for this book is available from the British Library

ISBN: 978–1–405–92028–5

www.greenpenguin.co.uk

With special thanks to Richard Smyth

Prologue

15 May 2014

A muggy, fly-bitten day. A reach of colourless scrubland under a sky of shifting clouds. DI Kerry Cox climbed from the car.

'You all know who Warren Boyd is, you all know what he looks like, but I want to take another look. Be sure.' Detective Chief Inspector Peter Naysmith had to bawl to be heard over the roar of an aeroplane tracking overhead along the Stansted flightpath. He walked from officer to officer – there were six of them, four uniform, two CID, all armed – passing out prints of the man's mugshot: a beaky nose, close-set eyes, a sulky, sour expression. Boyd.

'He's a slippery bastard,' Naysmith went on, handing Cox the last print, propping his hands on his hips. 'He's resourceful, he's cautious and he knows the area.'

Cox looked around, took in the layout, which she'd already memorized from an aerial printout. A poorly maintained chainlink fence separated the scrubland from a bare earth track and a row of three concrete lockups, each the size of a double garage. Beyond that, a stretch of boggy fields straggled west towards an ex-council estate a mile or so away. Naysmith had wanted a chopper, but Cox didn't want to spook Boyd. It would have been a nightmare with air-traffic control too.

Her gun felt heavy, awkward in her hands. Wasn't her first time on an armed op, but it never felt right. They'd got new vests since her last, though – not quite so bulky.

'The GPS says he's here,' continued Naysmith. 'One of the lockups. Now, these lockups, far as we know, have been disused for years: the company that owned them went bust, and there's been no registered owner since – least until Boyd bought one for peanuts earlier this year. Bottom line, there could be fucking anything in there. So be ready.'

'Do we know if he's armed?' One of the uniforms, chewing gum, trying to hide his nerves.

'We know he's got no firearms licence,' said Kerry. 'Beyond that, no idea. He might come out shooting. He might try to run, he might try to negotiate with us. Like I say: be ready.'

Naysmith nodded: 'Okay.' Made a gesture. The seven of them began to move purposefully towards the lockups.

They didn't need the bolt-cutters to breach the tatty fence; there were holes where the wire had been hacked before, or had rusted away. One by one they picked their way through. The lockups, squat and grey, waited for them.

Naysmith and two uniforms moved warily left, circling in a line around the back of the buildings; Cox and the rest made their way to the front. Beyond the farthest unit Cox saw the front end of a parked bottle-green car, a dusty old Vauxhall – Boyd's.

Her pulse quickened. She glanced at the GPS; the tracker was showing in the last lockup in the row.

They moved anticlockwise, filing between the car and the lockup's westward wall. Cox was hoping for a side-door. The corrugated garage doors to the front, rust-streaked and spray-painted clumsily with NO PARKING and KEAP OUT, would take too long to break open – she didn't want to give Boyd even a half-second more than she had to.

And there it was: a windowless, peeling uPVC door, no padlock, halfway along the wall.

To her right, Naysmith and his guys were edging around the far corner of the lockup. Cox caught the chief's eye; he glanced quickly at the door, gave her a nod.

She stepped forward, gun heavy in her right hand, and tried the door-handle cautiously with her left.

It was unlocked.

Took a breath. Pulled the door open.

The seven officers surged inside, torches flaring in the darkness; fanned out swiftly into a semi-circle around the door. Their torch beams raked the bare walls, the ridged concrete floor.

Dust. Cobwebs. A hank of bindweed growing through a flaw in the iron roof.

'Nothing, guv,' someone said.

There was relief in his voice, she thought.

Where the fuck was Boyd? He couldn't have known they were coming – and even if he had, he couldn't have just *vanished* . . .

Cox turned her torch on the wall to her right, the back wall of the lockup. Doors – four vertically folding shutter-type doors, steel by the look of them, all locked at the bottom with heavy D-locks. Behind, she calculated, a space of – what – three feet by four feet? Wardrobe-sized. Room enough to stash a bike, say, or a couple of filing cabinets, or a decent haul of drugs or guns, or . . .

Again she looked at Naysmith.

'Guv?'

'The car,' Naysmith said, eyeing the locks. 'Find a key.'

Cox went out, blinking in the muddy May light. A passenger jet howled by overhead. Tried the car's passenger door – it, too, was unlocked. Wasn't like Boyd to be so sloppy, she thought, as she pulled it open – no, wasn't like Boyd at all.

Opened the glove compartment, rifled quickly through a clutter of odds and ends: a pocket *A–Z*, an open packet of boiled sweets, an in-car mobile charger – and a key, attached to a plastic tag.

31, the tag read.

Back into the lockup, the dust and darkness, the confusion of torch beams. 31: the third shutter along.

A lockup within a lockup. A paedophile's hiding place. *There could be fucking anything in there*, Naysmith had said. Well, she wasn't exactly new to the job – whatever was in there, she was ready for it.

She crouched, broke open the D-lock, heaved up the shutter door. Shone her torch into the darkness.

She wasn't ready. She wasn't ready at all.

I

26 December 2014

Dead white skies over London and low, cold mist clinging to the lawns of the park. Black rooks in the leafless trees. The wires and railings of the zoo enclosures glimmered dully with beads of rainwater. It was busy, despite the weather: kids restless, parents weary at the dog-end of the Christmas holidays. Kerry saw the ennui in the other parents' eyes and wondered if she looked the same. Perhaps they'd just wanted to get out of the house after being cooped up the previous day, with the heating on too high and the kids coming down from another sugar rush. She felt like an impostor.

The polar bear enclosure was gloomy, an angular pattern of grey water, weak shadow and dark, wet concrete. By the waterside a female bear pawed at her cub. She played roughly, tumbling the cub down the concrete slope. The ball of fluffy white fur yawped.

At the rail, wide-eyed, togged up in scarf and hat, a young boy watched intently. Rapt. The mother bear ambled heavily towards the cub, nuzzled it, batted it with a paw. Every movement showed her strength, her weight – the damage she could do.

'I'm not sure he ought to be up there. It doesn't look very safe.'

A youngish mum, her own toddler held in the crook of her arm, leaning across with a look of concern.

Cox blinked.

'Sorry?'

'That's your boy up there on the railing, isn't it? I'm not sure he should be climbing on the railing.'

'Yes. No. Of course.' Mustered a brief smile. 'Thanks.'

Matthew had stepped on to the first rung of the railing to get a better view. What was he, eight inches off the floor? He didn't respond when she called his name. Too busy watching the bear. She could feel the woman with the toddler watching her – judging her.

There's more dangerous things in the world than climbing on a bloody railing, she wanted to say. *More dangerous than polar bears, even.*

Tried again: 'Matthew. Get down.'

This time he looked around, glowering at her under his patterned woolly hat. Grudgingly stepped down. Turned back to the bear.

Cox sighed. Six years old, and giving her attitude already. Growing up fast. She had a good few years of that to look forward to, she thought wryly.

At the same time, she heard the counsellor in her brain, doing that infuriating cocking of her head – *maybe 'attitude' is the wrong word, Kerry. How do you think Matthew is* feeling?

She wondered when the next appointment was – she'd have to check her diary. No doubt there'd be a clash with work. There always was. The counsellor didn't seem to get that police work wasn't always neat and tidy, nine till five with an hour for lunch.

In fact, the two-day break she'd managed to wangle over both Christmas Day and Boxing Day was a small

6

miracle. But given how yesterday had turned out – a high-strung mum, Christmas dinner, it was never likely to go well – she was wondering if it'd been worth the effort.

Today was going a bit better, though. At least she was with Matthew.

She turned away from the enclosure, let her gaze drift across the busy concourse. Kids everywhere. Little girl clutching a stuffed giraffe. Twins in a buggy slobbering over ice creams. Seriously – in December? A boy with an Elmo rucksack badgering his dad to take him to see the elephants. And a dark-haired girl in a blue duffle coat wandering away from her mum.

Cox felt her focus narrow reflexively, felt herself zero in on the kid. An instinct. Like a lifeguard at a busy swimming-pool. She found herself scanning the area for singles, dodgy-looking men, creeps, loners. This guy, smoking a cigarette under a dripping palm tree? Or this one, alone at a picnic table with a newspaper and a carrier bag?

She chided herself inwardly. Could just as well be someone's loving dad or granddad, she knew. But then, that was no guarantee. And it didn't have to be a man, of course. She'd read witness statements – from other countries admittedly – about women being used to tempt the victim to a snatch location.

Shook her head, told herself to get a bloody grip. She'd enough on her plate without worrying about other people's kids. She shuddered at the thought of what was waiting for her back at home: stacks of paperwork, briefings from the barrister, case notes – and she'd said she'd give Naysmith a call, too.

The woman who'd chided her earlier was glancing at her oddly. Kerry realized, in a moment of sardonic horror, that only one person looked dodgy around here.

Nearby a camera clicked, and she turned sharply, ready to unload a volley of abuse. She'd had more than her fill of paparazzi ... But, she saw, reddening at the realization, this wasn't a pap, wasn't some smirking sleazebag with an SLR and a moped. It was an old couple, arms about a grinning grandchild, making a pig's ear of taking a selfie by the chimpanzee compound.

One day, Kerry, she told herself, *you're going to have to stop expecting the worst.*

'Mum!'

She turned.

'Mm?'

'Look what the bear's doing.'

She lifted her chin to look over the rail.

'Oh, yes.'

'You didn't even see. It's not doing it now. Wait, look – it's doing it again.' The mother bear had picked up its cub in its jaws and was carrying it slowly up the slope. 'Why's it doing that, Mum?' Matthew wasn't happy. His face was pink, his voice winding up in pitch. 'Mum? Why is the bear eating its baby?'

'Oh, love. She's doing no such thing.' She moved to the rail, put a hand on Matthew's shoulder. 'She's just helping the baby bear out, you see? She doesn't want the baby bear to get hurt or fall in the water.'

Matthew nodded seriously. She could see him processing. Taking it in.

'A baby bear,' he said eventually, 'is really called a *cub*.'

Then he turned away from the enclosure and looked up at her, blinking in the milky winter sunlight.

'Where next?'

'Wherever you like, love.'

Matthew took her hand – the wool of his mitten was damp from the railing – and they moved off across the concourse.

As they walked, Cox had the oppressive feeling of being watched – no, not watched exactly, but looked at, *noticed*. Heads turned when they passed by. She saw uncertain flickers of recognition in people's faces, awkward grimaces as they looked away a moment too late. She wasn't imagining it. And why wouldn't they notice, if they read the papers.

She could do without this.

'Look!' Matthew stopped, pointing excitedly at a queue of young families outside the penguin pond. *Feeding time!* a sign said. A young woman in flip-flops and a zoo sweatshirt was chatting to the kids, a metal bucket hanging from her hand.

'Are they feeding the penguins?' Matthew asked, tugging at her hand. 'Can we go? Come on! It's dinner time for the penguins.'

Cox hesitated. Thought uneasily of sitting among a crowd of parents, all of them knowing who she was, what she did – thinking they knew her.

'Dinner time for mum, more like,' she said with false heartiness. 'Let's go get something to eat! I'll buy you a hotdog, how about that?'

To her relief, Matthew went for it.

'Okay,' he said. 'I want fish, though! Like a penguin.'

He waddled off ahead of her, ducking his head and waggling his elbows like flippers at his sides. Cox laughed – the sound of it surprised her, somehow.

They'd just picked up their trays in the zoo canteen when Cox felt her phone buzz in her jacket pocket. As she fished it out she watched Matthew make his way hungrily towards a display of fancy iced pastries. She could already see how the next few minutes were going to play out, when she saw the number. Her appetite vanished.

'Hello?'

'Kerry. Naysmith. Can you come in?'

The chief super. His manner as flat and blunt as his northern vowels.

'Guv, I've had today booked off for ages –'

'I know. But something's come up. A body.'

Christ, he knew how to play her. She could feel the buzz of excitement starting up somewhere in her chest; adrenaline beginning to pump.

'Go on.'

'I'll text you the address. See you there.'

Rang off.

She dropped the phone back into her pocket. Smiled ruefully as she watched Matthew struggling with the tongs to pick up a frosted muffin. Well, there'd be other days.

When she knelt beside him, curling an arm around his waist, it was like he already knew. His bottom lip poked out.

'Matthew, love . . .' she began.

'You're going, aren't you.' It wasn't a question. *Trust me to have the only psychic infant in London*, Cox thought.

'Yes, love, I'm afraid so. I'm sorry. But I've got to go and –'

'Save the world. I know.'

It was an old joke between them, a line they'd used for years, whenever she had to work nights, or was late home, or missed a birthday party or a school play . . .

But did he say it differently, this time? For the first time Cox thought she detected an edge of resentment in Matthew's voice.

'But I'll see you soon, love, okay? We'll come here again – I'll take you to see the penguins' feeding time.' She kissed his forehead. He was trying not to cry, she knew. She wondered where they got that from. Where did boys learn that tears were something to keep hidden, keep inside?

As they walked back through the zoo to the car park she dialled Aidan's number.

He answered sharply: 'Let me guess.'

'Look, Aidan, I wouldn't ask if –'

'If it wasn't urgent. Yes, I know the drill, Kerry.'

'Come on. It's not as if you're busy, is it?'

A deep, withering sigh down the phone line.

'You really think that's what this is about? Matthew really wanted to spend some time with you. It's Christmas, Kerry, for God's sake.'

'I know. I know.' How many times had they had this conversation? Cox felt herself engaging autopilot. 'I'll try harder in future. I promise I will. I'll have a word with my boss, try and sort out my work–life balance. But just –'

'Just this once.' Aidan's voice was heavy with cynicism. 'Sure. Bring him over. But you need to make it up to him, Kerry. You are his bloody mum, you know.'

'We'll be there in half an hour,' she said. Blipped open the car with the key-fob. 'Depending on traffic.'

The First Day of Christmas, 1986

'It's too dark, you berk. It won't work in the dark.'

He doesn't like me calling him a berk. He takes stuff to heart, does our Stan. Scrunches up his face.

'It flippin' does,' he said. 'Point it at the bottom of the door, you'll see.'

I call him a spaz, but I have a look anyway. Put my eye to the eye-thing and give it a turn. Patterns. Bit of colour.

Shrug, give him it back.

'I don't get it,' I say, because I don't.

'It's a kal-ide-oh-scope.'

'I know what it is. What's it meant to do?' Grab it back off him, turn it over in my hands. Feels gritty. Rub my fingers and thumb together. Oh, bloody hell. 'Here. Here, Stan, there's all stuff coming out of it.'

His eyes flick wide in the darkness. He snatches it from me.

'Careful, you'll get it everywhere –'

'Cause I can see bits of glitter coming out of the end of it.

'You broke it!' He's trying to cup his hand under the leak.

'I never. It was already like that.'

'It was fine when I was playing with it.'

'Give over, I bet it was already busted when they gave it you. Place like this, they're not going to give you something dead good, are they? Bet they bought it from Oxfam or something.'

Stan's holding his kaleidoscope like it's his favourite pet that's just died.

'Anyway,' I say, because I don't like seeing him look like that, 'you're too old for a toy like that. It's a kid's toy, that. You're nearly nine.'

He drops his face into his pillow. Mutters something — something about how Santa gave it to him, and Santa wouldn't give him something rubbish from Oxfam.

'You what? Speak up, mumbles.'

'I said' — he lifts his face up, and even in this gloom I can see he's got tears on his cheeks — 'it's off Santa, so it's not rubbish, Robbie, so shut up.'

I don't say anything. It was a second-hand toy, 'course it was, maybe third-hand, fourth-hand. Other kids' cast-offs, that's what bloody Santa brings at Hampton Hall. Same as the clothes, the comics. Stuff normal folk'd chuck away.

I look at Stan. He's got his blanket pulled over his chin and he's not crying any more, but his eyes are still open.

'Ro-ob,' he says, quietly.

'Wha-at.'

'There's a grate over the chimney.'

He's looking across the dorm, at the old fireplace in the far wall that hasn't ever had a fire in it as long as we've been here. It's just an alcove in the wall is all it is, but he's right, there is a metal grill-type thing over the hole that used to be a chimney.

'Yeah, so?'

'So how does Santa get down?' The worry in his voice, bloody hell, it's painful to hear.

I don't know when I realized Santa didn't exist, or why. Now I don't know how I ever believed in him. I must've been bloody daft.

I start to answer: 'Well, he's probably got a key, hasn't he, to the side-door, so he parks his reindeer in the car park and —'

A laugh from across the room cuts me off.

My fists clench.

Mark Duffy is sitting up in bed — I can see his outline. Recognize his snotty bloody laugh anyway.

'What's your problem, Duffy?'

'Your kid's a bit old to be believing in Santa, isn't he? He's such a little spaz.'

I know Stan's looking at me. I don't look at him.

'You shut your bloody stupid mouth.'

'Here, Stanley, how was Father Christmas when you saw him yesterday?'

Stan's voice is on the edge of breaking, right on the edge. 'I did see him, I did, he give me a present, a kaleidoscope, and —'

'I bet that's not all he gave you,' Duffy sniggers.

Stan doesn't say anything — doesn't understand. But I understand well enough. I don't know what Duffy's on about exactly but I know his tone, what it means. Something dirty.

Can't fight in here, not after lights-out, I'd get a proper bollocking. Only been in here a week, don't want to mark my card already. And they might take me away, to solitary or whatever — and Stan'd be left on his own.

'Why don't you fuck off, Duffy,' I say.

'Make me.'

'I'll see you in workshop tomorrow, then I'll bloody make you.'

He shuts up. Knows I could have him. That's a good feeling.

Then he says: 'I was only telling the truth. It's not Santa, it's only bloody Merton. Real Santa's not got bad breath and wandering hands. Real Santa might make you sit on his knee but that's all he does — not like Merton.' Duffy lies down, pulls his blanket over himself. 'Don't much mind whether you been naughty or nice, neither.'

What the bloody hell have we let ourselves in for here, Stan?, I think.

He's really sleeping now. Can tell by his breathing.

Wish he was awake. Wish we weren't here. Wish we were still in our old room.

What's it been now, nearly a year? Can't be a year yet 'cause we was at home last Christmas. Bloody Malky was already around then, though. Smackhead crackhead Malky. I'll never forgive him, that skinny, slimy, creepy bastard. For what he done to our mum. For what he done to me and Stan.

Not a fit parent, they reckoned. Not responsible. I told 'em, come on, she's never been a fit parent, our mum, it's me what's been cooking tea and looking after Stan, for years, like – she's lazy, our mum, and I don't think she ever wanted us – but she's our mum. We'll just carry on like we have been, I told 'em, whether Mum's on smack or whatever, it doesn't matter – we'll just carry on like always.

Didn't make no difference. Nothing we say ever makes any difference.

'Into Care.' It was like the bloody bogeyman when I was little, that. Mum used to threaten us with it when we was bad but I know she never meant it. If she'd meant it she wouldn't've been all crying and screaming when they took us away, would she?

I knew it was going to be bad. Stan didn't know, but I knew. That place, though – that place was worse than I'd ever thought.

We were lucky our dad's a bloody headcase. I mean, it wasn't lucky out in the real world because, well, he was a proper bloody headcase, but in there – he got us out of there. Found out where we was and properly kicked off. Started trying to get in, threatening, having a go at the staff, wound up in court –

I remember something Stan said: 'It's nice, isn't it, that Dad cares about us.'

Made me laugh, that. Anyway, they moved us on. And here we are.

Footsteps. Footsteps, out on the landing.

Stan wakes up sharply, frightened.

'Who's there? Robbie? What's that?'

From across the dorm, Mark Duffy tells him in a hiss to bloody well keep quiet. I lean over, touch his arm – tell him it's okay, I'm here, nothing's going to happen.

The footsteps come up to the door. I hold my breath. I think we all do. I can see the shadows of two feet through the crack between the door and the tiles.

Then the footsteps move on.

Bloody hell.

I reach under my mattress – if you can call it a bloody mattress, it's like an old sack full of coathangers – and pull out my picture. Can hardly see it in the dark but I just want to hold it. Mum, Stan, me, in the lounge of our house in Oldbury. Stan's only small. I'm about nine. All smiles, all saying 'cheese'. Happy bloody family.

'When will they let us go home?' Stan says suddenly, his voice wobbly, in the darkness.

Soon, I tell him. Dead soon.

I hear Mark Duffy make a noise under his blanket. Can't tell if he's laughing or crying.

2

The PC on the door knew who Cox was before she told him. Well, *of course* he did.

As she signed in, he gave her the details of the case. William Radley, sixty-eight. Ex-copper. Found dead that morning. The name rang a bell, but she wasn't sure why.

It was a big place, a Victorian townhouse in a leafy bit of Ealing. High ceilings, she noted as she made her way through the hall. Wood floors and a staircase you could drive a Routemaster up.

'This his place?' she called back.

'Yes, ma'am.'

'On a police pension? Must've made some sound investments.' A businesslike nod. 'Thanks, Constable.'

A white tent was being put up in the long back garden. Cox stood for a moment in the roomy kitchen (Belfast sink, marble worktops, a set of expensive and well-used cast-iron pans) and sized up the situation. Through a rose-trellis to the left she could see the neighbours – a constipated-looking middle-aged man and a woman with steel-grey hair wrapped in a fierce bun – gawping at the scene. A few uniform were standing around, looking bored. A female sergeant was talking to a man in a well-tailored dark suit who, with a cursory assessment of their body language (her talking more, nodding a lot; him brusque, authoritative, inquiring), she judged to be a superior officer. Didn't recognize him, though. Wasn't CID. *That* rang alarm bells. MI5? GCHQ? Trouble, anyway.

He turned and saw her as she stepped out through the French windows on to the lawn. Smiled fleetingly and extended a hand. His handshake was firm and brief.

'Sam Harrington,' he said. 'Ministry of Justice.'

'DI Cox.' She looked at him meaningfully. 'So, to what do we owe this honour?'

Harrington laughed lightly. *Not buying it*, Cox thought.

'Just a formality,' the MoJ man said, absently smoothing a lapel. 'Bill Radley was quite high up at the Yard. We have to make sure everything's done by the book.'

Thanks for the vote of confidence, she thought. 'Sure. So what's the story?'

'Hard to be sure at this stage, of course – but it looks a lot like suicide.'

'Suicide?' *Then what the hell am I doing here on my bloody day off?* she thought bitterly. Then the self-awareness kicked in. Come on, DI Cox, be honest – would you *really* rather be watching feeding time at the penguin pond right now?

She half-turned, looked up, taking in the layout of the house and garden. The back wall, thick with drab winter ivy, rose up three storeys to a shingled mansard roof. A balcony jutted from a second-floor room – a bedroom, she guessed. Must be a hell of a view from up there.

Turned back to Harrington. Something here didn't feel quite right; something about this set-up – something she couldn't put her finger on – was making her uneasy.

'What's the family situation? Next of kin?'

'No family that we know of. Radley never married.'

Confirmed bachelor, as the newspaper obituaries used to say, with a nod and a wink.

'Okay.' She nodded, gestured towards Radley's body – they'd put up the tent, and it lay under a sheet, parallel to the house, one arm flung out. There were dull burgundy blood-spots on the paving stone near the dead man's head. 'Shall we take a look at him?'

Harrington, thin-lipped, nodded grimly. Left it to Cox to bend down and draw back the concealing sheet.

William Radley – AC Radley, or DC Radley, or whatever he'd been at the Yard – was a slightly balding, grey-haired, middle-aged white man. No surprises there, Cox thought drily. His face, baggy and pale, was composed, perhaps slightly puzzled. Someone had closed his eyes, but hadn't bothered to cover his modesty where the navy-blue dressing-gown had flapped open. The dead didn't need dignity, thought Cox. Patches of purple lividity were already pooling in his buttocks and thighs. The back of his head was a pulpy, red mess, gummed to the spotted paving stone with viscous, part-congealed blood.

Looked about right for a head-first fall from three floors up, Cox thought grimly.

'Who found him?'

'Chap in the house opposite.' Harrington nodded towards the bottom of the garden. 'Heard a bang just after nine this morning, saw him lying here. Called the police.'

'Hmm.' Cox replaced the sheet, straightened up. Harrington, she noticed, was looking pretty green about the gills. 'I'm going to take a look inside.'

The MoJ man nodded mutely. As she turned away, she saw him press a handkerchief to his mouth.

It was warm in the house, but you couldn't call it cosy. She moved slowly through the kitchen and the hall, turning through the first door she came to into a dark-panelled dining room. The table and six chairs – oak, she thought – shone in the subdued lighting; the smell of furniture polish made her eyes sting.

For an older man living alone, Radley had kept the place immaculate. Every picture dust-free and straight on its hook; every book square on its shelf. The sitting room was the same. The TV and DVD remote controls might have been positioned on the coffee table with a set square. Well, he was a copper, Cox thought. Meticulous.

Back into the hall, up the wide staircase.

The first floor seemed a little more lived-in. Toothbrush and shaving things left by the bathroom basin (sink dry, she noted, shower screen too); shirts drying on a rack in the guest bedroom. A small study – computer, two filing cabinets, bookcase – was decorated with framed photographs of Radley dinner-jacketed or in full uniform, grinning beside various public figures. Home secretaries, lord chancellors, local MPs, anti-crime campaigners. In the pictures he looked engaged, genuine, his wide smile easy and unforced.

An old snap from a long-ago ACPO conference rang a bell in Cox's mind. She'd been there – Brighton, had it been? Bournemouth? – and, now that she came to think about it, she'd met William Radley there. The memory flared brightly from somewhere in her subconscious. Only briefly, long enough to exchange a few words of small talk, but she remembered the man's easy-going charm: 'Call me Bill,' he'd said, and never mind the badge of rank on his shoulder. That had been in the good years, what the papers later termed, with more than a hint of schadenfreude, her 'meteoric rise'.

The second floor of the house was divided into two big rooms, one either side of the steep staircase. On the right, facing south, was a bare-planked artist's studio, flooded with pale light from three tall windows. There were two large canvases set on wooden easels, one bare, the other a half-finished watercolour, a landscape – to Cox's eye, it looked pretty good.

Radley, she thought, had had nothing to fear from retirement. His books, his paintings, his love of food and friends – he'd built himself a life, a good life, on leaving the force. *Not like Dad*, Cox thought bleakly. DS Colin Cox had clung on to his going-nowhere career as long as he could, and been pensioned off at sixty-five. He'd found nothing to replace policing in his life – found, in fact, that policing *was* his life. Nothing she or Mum could say seemed to help. It wasn't that he wasn't kind, that he'd stopped loving them, caring about them, both of them, and Matthew, too – it was just that he seemed to have lost his way and could never seem to get back on the right track. He'd shrunk from the world outside; settled into his chair in front of the telly and waited for it all to be done with.

Was it really a year ago? Cox thought, moving from the studio out on to the landing. A year ago that the end finally came for DS Cox (retd). Mum'd been off visiting her sister in Kent. Cox had been roused from sleep by a phone-call at 3 a.m.: her parents' neighbours complaining about the TV blaring all through the night. Turned out he'd had a stroke; with no phone to hand – he couldn't be doing with new-fangled nonsense like mobiles – he'd grabbed for the TV remote and squeezed the volume button until his strength gave out.

Too little, too late. His body was cold when Cox found him.

She shook her head, tried to shake away the memory, to focus, as she pushed open Radley's bedroom door. The coldness in the room made her blink. The balcony door, of course: it was still open. The well-made maroon curtains stirred in the breeze. The duvet was thrown back, and Radley's size 13 slippers were on the floor by the bed. Nothing out of the ordinary.

So Bill Radley just woke up this morning, got out of bed, opened the curtains and jumped out of the window?

Cox circled the unmade bed and stepped gingerly out on to the little balcony. Took a breath and looked down. Only three storeys but Christ it looked like more, down to the garden, the trembling white square of the tent – and, beneath it, the bloodied body of Bill Radley. Her head spun; she'd never been good with heights.

As she stepped back into the room, the door from the landing opened, and Harrington stepped inside. He greeted her breezily: 'Find anything interesting?'

She replied with a non-committal shrug.

Harrington, one hand in his trouser-pocket, began poking desultorily around the room. Pulled open the drawer of the bedside table; peered into the empty tea-mug by the bed; picked up one of Radley's slippers and ran his thumb absently over the nap.

'You're disturbing a crime-scene, Mr Harrington,' Cox said sharply.

He looked up guiltily. Dropped the slipper as if it had suddenly turned white-hot.

'Sorry. Didn't realize it *was* a crime-scene.'

Cox eyed him sourly for a second.

Then she moved back to the double-glazed door that opened on to the balcony.

'Have you been out here?'

'Lord, no.' Harrington laughed urbanely. 'No head for heights, I'm afraid.'

Cox gritted her teeth.

'Have you ever attended at a suicide? A suicide by jumping?'

'Nope. Not really my field. I assume you have?'

'A few, yeah. And you know what they had in common?'

'A dead body?'

She let his facetiousness slide.

'Exactly. That's exactly the point. Jumpers, more than most other suicides, want to make sure. No second thoughts, no turning back. This' – she gestured to the little balcony – 'is what – maybe twenty feet? Hornsey Lane Bridge it isn't. It's not a sure thing, Mr Harrington. You're as likely to break both your legs as be killed. Or end up in a wheelchair being fed through a tube.'

'Could it be that, at the time of his suicide, poor Mr Radley was in no fit state mentally to carry out such calculations?'

Again Cox forced herself to ignore the faint note of mockery in Harrington's voice.

'It's possible,' she nodded. 'But look at this place. Nothing here suggests a man who's lost his grip on reality. Everything neat as a pin downstairs. The garden's been well cared for. And look at his painting.'

'Come on. Weren't all the great painters raving madmen?'

'This isn't the home of a man who's got nothing to live for,' Cox insisted.

Harrington followed her as she made her way back downstairs.

'I'm not jumping to any conclusions,' she said, over her shoulder. 'But I want to at least wait until we get the forensics report before I rule out anything suspicious.' She collared a passing constable. 'Are forensics here yet?'

The young PC looked at her in surprise.

'Ma'am?'

'Forensics. You know, the guys in facemasks and white jumpsuits. Have they arrived yet? They should be here by now.'

The PC opened and shut his mouth and glanced appealingly over Cox's shoulder. She heard Harrington clear his throat.

Oh, here we go . . .

'The thing is, inspector, we decided not to bring forensics in on this one.' Harrington, moving past her, patted the young copper on the shoulder. 'Thank you, constable. On you go.' Turned to Cox. His expression gave nothing away. *Either he's a hell of a poker player*, Cox thought, *or he's as clueless as I am.*

'It seems pretty open-and-shut,' he said calmly. 'William Radley killed himself. No need to waste scarce resources and call out overstretched personnel on a –'

'Whose decision was this?'

He shifted uncomfortably. 'I – this was my call.'

'I'd ask you what exactly you're trying to achieve here, Mr Harrington,' she said acidly. 'But it's clear to me that we've wasted enough time here already. I'm overruling you.' Turned away before he could answer. Called back the young PC – told him to bring in a full SOCO team, ASAP.

'And while you're at it,' she added, pulling out a business card and handing it to him, 'get in touch with this guy, Don DiMacedo at Quantum Data. Don't let him fob you off – I don't care if he says he's busy, tell him to call DI Cox as a matter of urgency.'

The PC hurried off. Cox lowered herself on to the bottom step. Ran a hand through her hair, blew out a breath.

'Well, that's me told,' muttered Harrington, a little coldly.

He moved away, sauntering hands in pockets through to the kitchen. She heard him call to someone to fetch him a cup of coffee.

Hell, maybe it *was* a suicide, she thought. Maybe Bill Radley had more going on than we know. Maybe he really did just wake up today and think: *That's it, I'm done.*

God knows, everyone had rough mornings – mornings when the world is just too much to handle.

Or is that just me?

She stood, smoothing her suit trousers. Whatever – she was a copper, after all. What kind of copper walks away from a dead body on the say-so of a pen-pusher from the MoJ?

And it wasn't as though she had nothing to go on. She made her way outside, into the garden. There was someone she needed to speak to.

The uniformed sergeant to whom Harrington had been speaking was sitting on a garden bench, reading through her notes. She looked up as Cox approached. Recognized her – stowed her notebook, got to her feet.

'Ma'am.'

'Sergeant – Adeola, right?'

'Yes, ma'am.'

'DI Cox, CID. You should know that SOCO are on their way, sergeant – let me know if our friend from Whitehall gives you any trouble. And for God's sake, get him a pair of latex gloves and some bags for his feet.'

'Will do, ma'am.'

'Harrington said it was a neighbour that called in the body?'

'That's right, ma'am.' Adeola snapped open her notebook. 'A Mr Jefferies. Number 54. Reportedly saw the body and dialled 999.'

'And asked for the police? Not an ambulance?'

'I thought that was funny myself, ma'am. But I guess Mr Radley being who he was, Mr Jefferies thought the police ought to know.' She shrugged. 'People make bad decisions in emergencies.'

'Okay. We'll come back to that. Now – has anyone talked to the cleaner.'

A blank look.

'What cleaner, ma'am?'

'There's not a speck of dust on that ground floor, sergeant. Kitchen surfaces gleaming, floors swept, wastebins emptied.'

'Maybe he just enjoyed housework. Some retired men do.'

'Yes, but it's a different story upstairs. Clean enough, I suppose – but not a professional job. Mug of tea by the bed, bathroom in need of a scrub.'

'But no one's mentioned a cleaner, ma'am.'

'I don't suppose anyone's asked. Who was first on the scene?'

'I responded to the 999 call. But Mr Harrington was already here when I arrived.'

Cox nodded thoughtfully.

'Okay. Look, I could be wrong – but have someone look through his papers, call the local agencies. I say there was someone here this morning – someone who only did half a job, because halfway through they came across Bill Radley lying in the back garden with his head caved in.'

'Then why didn't they phone it in? Why did they just leave?'

'That's what we're going to find out, sergeant.' She turned at the sound of footsteps: Harrington, striding towards them across the lawn. A bit pink-faced.

'Still here, inspector?'

'Very much so.' She gave him a hard smile. 'Just so you're in the loop, Mr Harrington: I'm about to order a door-to-door, three streets in each direction. Sergeant Adeola, I want full statements – and I mean full – from anyone who's seen or heard anything, anything at all, that might help us. Keep me posted. I'm going to have a talk with this Mr Jefferies.'

Harrington made an impatient grimace.

'I'm sure this officer has many more important things to be dealing with,' he said. 'Honestly, inspector, don't you think this is overkill for a straightforward suicide?'

'It would be, for a straightforward suicide,' Cox nodded. 'Now what I need you to do, Mr Harrington, if you can, is put a blackout on this. No press, no media of any kind, nothing on or off the record – total lockdown.'

'Look, inspector, if you're trying to make a point –'

'I'm not trying to make a point.' Cox cut him off bluntly. 'I'm telling you this isn't suicide, straightforward or otherwise. I'm telling you we're dealing with a murder.'

3

A hedged passageway between two houses a few doors down from the Radley place led through to a quiet, unmarked back-road. As she crossed the road towards number 54 – the address she'd been given for Mr Jefferies – she tried to figure out the sightlines. There was a high, solid-looking fence at the bottom of Radley's garden; a thick holly-bush rose behind the fence, further cutting off the view. As far as she could see, the only vantage-point from which this Mr Jefferies might be able to see into Radley's garden would be a small skylight in the roof. Even then, she thought, you'd have to crane your neck till you were practically out on the roof-tiles. And what could be happening in an old man's back garden to make any-one so desperate for a glimpse of it?

There was no car in the driveway of number 54. The curtains were pulled. No lights on that she could see. She paused at the bottom of the cracked concrete driveway, thinking through her strategy. All guns blazing? Or the diplomatic approach?

It'd depend, she knew, on who answered her knock – on what kind of man appeared at the door of number 54.

If anyone did.

She reached for the latch of the gate – but then pulled away sharply, jumping backwards in alarm as the dented front wing of a red Renault veered up the kerb with a juddering wheeze. The driver's door flew open – before she knew it, Cox was up on her toes, ready for a fight.

Then she clocked the guy's face.

'Hello, Kerry,' he said.

He banged the car door shut behind him.

'Oh, Christ.'

'Well, it's lovely to see you, too.'

Greg Wilson – or, as it said on his business cards, 'Award-winning investigative journalist Greg Wilson'. A mistake she'd made, a long time ago.

'What the hell are you doing here?'

He smiled awkwardly, leaned on the rust-pocked bonnet of the little car.

'Doing my job,' he shrugged.

'You're not helping, Greg.'

'Can you tell me what's going on? Off the record, if you like. I saw the SOCO van just arrive.'

'Short answer: no.'

'Help me out, Kerry. Seems like a big deal. SOCO, CID – a detective inspector, no less.'

'No comment. Let me spell that for you. En, oh, space, see, oh –'

'I've got a job to do too, Kerry.' He said it like it was an apology. Then he gave her a shrewd look. 'Doesn't Bill Radley live around here somewhere? The old Met chief – what was he, AC? Something to do with him? Cold case?'

She shook her head. There was no telling this guy. Tenacious, hard to shake off – she remembered that from their last encounter.

'What part of "no comment" don't you understand, Greg?'

'Whose house is this? You were just about to go and knock at the door, weren't you? Well, don't let me stop you.'

He leaned again on his car, crossed his ankles.

'You have to leave now.' She gave him a dry look. 'Don't make me run you in.'

'Aw, come on. For what? Asking questions?'

'This car, if that's what you're calling it, is illegally parked. And if that's all that's wrong with it I'm Dame Judi Dench. MOT all in order, Greg?' She booted a tyre thoughtfully. 'Brake-lights all working? Emissions under the legal limit?'

Wilson was already climbing back into the driver's seat, shaking his head with a rueful smile, as she added: 'I can have Traffic here in five minutes. Now get the hell out of my sight.'

The murky cloud of exhaust fumes that belched from the car as Wilson took off almost choked her. Over the crunch of gears she heard him call: 'Good luck at the inquiry, Kerry – look after yourself.'

Focus, DI Cox, she told herself. *Focus.*

It was too late. She knew that. But she called anyway.

'Hello?'

'Aidan – it's me.'

A sigh.

'It's gone nine. He's in bed.'

'I – I know. Of course, I knew he would be. I just – just wanted to say sorry to him. To you, as well.'

'I'm not waking him up.' Aidan's tone was unforgiving. 'I'm not waking him up just so's you can upset him with another half-arsed apology. Another promise you won't keep.'

'How was he?'

'You know him. Tries not to let it show.' A snort of bitter laughter. 'You've taught him well. But it hurts him, Kerry – you know it does.'

'I do know.'

'You should have called earlier.'

'I should, I know. I wanted to, I really did. But –'

'I know, I know. You were saving the bloody world, just like always. And now where are you? You're on your sofa in your poky flat in Shepherd's Bush, you're knackered and stressed, you've probably just poured yourself a half-pint of Pinot' – she glanced guiltily down at the glass in her hand – 'and you're feeling sorry for yourself. I don't blame you, Kerry. I'd be the same, if I were you.' Aidan paused, sighed. 'You should have called earlier,' he said again.

'I really couldn't. I was –'

'Busy, yes, I know.'

'This was important, Aidan.'

Instantly she knew she'd used the wrong word.

'Important?'

'I mean –'

'And Matthew's not important? Your son, your six-year-old fucking son? Jesus Christ, Kerry. I've never begrudged you your career, you know that, but – Jesus.'

'I don't do this job for the good of my bloody health, you know.'

'I know that. But there are people out there with good jobs, Kerry, good, well-paying, demanding jobs, who can get through a day at the zoo with their kids without having to run off halfway through to give a burglar an ASBO, or whatever it was this time. Who can sit through a whole school play. Who somehow, Kerry, manage to pick their toddlers up from nursery on time – instead of leaving them waiting in floods of tears for the best part of two bloody hours.'

'That was a long time ago, Aidan,' she said defensively. 'And it was a one-off.'

A soft, hard-edged laugh was his only answer.

Then he said: 'Did I tell you what Matthew told his teacher at school the other day?'

'Yes. You did.'

'Then I'm going to tell you again. Maybe eventually it'll sink in.'

'Aidan, you don't have to . . .'

'The teacher,' he went on remorselessly, 'was asking all the kids what their New Year Resolutions were. I expect they all said the usual stuff: to stop picking their noses, to play for Spurs, that sort of thing. Then, when it was Matthew's turn, and Miss Holloway asked him what his New Year Resolution was, he said: to see my mum every weekend.'

Aidan's voice was getting thick with emotion. Cox wondered if he'd been drinking. Would she blame him if he had?

'Aidan, I know –'

'As if it was his fault that you're not around. Do you see that? Does that register with you? *He thinks it's his fault.*'

She bit her lip.

When Aidan spoke again it was in a more normal tone of voice: still bitter, still pissed-off, but in control.

'Next weekend,' he said. 'Next Saturday. You're seeing

Matthew. Got that? Just before Twelfth Night. You know, when Christmas is over, and we all stop having such a wonderful, wonderful time.'

He hung up the phone.

DCI Pete Naysmith had definitely been drinking.

Cox had stayed on the sofa after talking with Aidan; finished her wine, watched some terrible TV, leafed through the newspaper. Most of all she'd turned over the afternoon's events in her mind: the pillock from the Department of Justice, the mysterious missing cleaner, Greg bloody Wilson and the lifeless, broken body of 'call-me-Bill' Radley.

It was a mess, but that was okay; every CID case was a mess, at least to begin with. Sometimes you made sense of it, sometimes you didn't – that was the job.

But this was different. Harrington made her uneasy; Wilson made her suspicious.

And now here was Naysmith, calling her up at 10.30 on Boxing Day night.

She switched off the television, tried to pay attention.

'– piecing together Radnor's last movements,' he was saying. There was an audible slur to his voice.

Naysmith being back on the booze wasn't going to help them at the inquiry, Cox thought darkly.

'It's Radley, guv. William Radley.'

'Yes, him. We're ... we're building up a picture, Cox. He didn't do very much, this Radley, or anyway not much that we know about. We do know from his appointment book that he went out for lunch on Christmas Day ...'

34

'Christmas Day.'

'Yes, exactly, Christmas Day, of course. Only we don't know who he went with, unless he went by himself, the sad old bastard, and we know he didn't exactly push the boat out because he only went to a shitty little Greek place on Ealing Broadway.'

'Olympus Grill. I know the one.'

'Well, you can look into that in the morning. We're piecing it together, Cox, piece by piece. D'you follow me? Piece by piece.'

'Yes, guv.'

A pause, a long pause. The noise of Naysmith taking a drink, a swallow – and then more silence.

'Guv? You okay?'

'Still here, Cox, still here.' He cleared his throat. 'Yes. Still here.'

She bit the bullet.

'Something on your mind, guv?'

A gurgling laugh, without any humour in it.

'You can read me like a fucking book, Cox, can't you?' True enough. The DCI had a lot of strengths, Cox knew – but subtlety wasn't one of them.

'What is it?'

'Harrington.'

Oh, hell.

'The MoJ guy?'

'So he says. He came to see me, Cox. This evening. He's very insistent, Cox, about this feller Radnor, Radley I mean – he's very keen, okay, on the idea that this *was* a suicide after all. And I know you have your own theories, Cox, and you know you have my full support, you know

35

that – but this Radnor, it turns out, Harrington says, had debts, massive debts – so there you are, there's your motive for him topping himself. What d'you say, Cox? Adds up a bit better now, doesn't it? What d'you say?'

Cox hesitated. Felt faintly sick.

'What did you say, guv, when he brought this up?'

'I stuck up for you! Of course I did. Not going to let some bloody wonk from Whitehall push *my* officer around. But –'

'He talked you round, right?'

She wouldn't have dared speak so bitterly if the DCI had been sober. But he was a long way from sober.

'He mentioned the inquiry,' Naysmith said heavily.

Her nausea spiked, an upsurge of bile burning the back of her throat. She swallowed hard.

'What did he say?'

'The *inquiry*, Cox. He knew all about it.'

She wanted to shake him by his shoulders, slap him across the face.

'What did he say, guv? What exactly?'

'He said he wasn't sure that getting bogged down in a wild goose chase over Radnor would show you in the best light, he said. With the inquiry and all that.'

'He *threatened* me?'

'Now, Cox, now come on, I didn't say that –'

'I've been threatened before, guv, and it sounded a lot like that. *Be a shame if you were to have a nasty accident. How unfortunate if someone were to leak this to the press.* Come on, guv, you've heard this heavy-mob stuff a thousand times.'

'This Harrington bloke didn't strike me as a leg-breaker.'

Cox could have screamed with exasperation.

'Guv, we don't know the first bloody thing about Sam Harrington.'

'All right, Cox. All right.' He took another drink – a long one. 'We'll – we'll talk about this tomorrow. We'll see where we are tomorrow, and we'll talk about it all once we know where we are.'

And once you've sobered up.

He was a good copper, Pete Naysmith, Cox knew. Good copper, good boss, good man. He'd been through a hard time, this last year or two. Maybe he'd handled it the wrong way, but hell, what was the right way?

Go easy, she told herself.

'All right, guv. I'll give you a call tomorrow, after I've been to the Olympus.'

'To the what? Yeah, okay. Call me tomorrow. Good-night, Cox.'

'Night, guv.'

'G'night. G'night.'

Cox switched off her phone and turned on the TV. Some old black-and-white film was on. It was late, and she had an early start in the morning – but that didn't matter, not now. She was on her own now, she knew that, today had told her that loud and clear – but maybe the TV, somehow, would make her feel less alone.

Did it work for you, Dad? she wondered. She watched the TV. Some wisecracking dame in dark lipstick was smoking a cigarette and flirting with a lugubrious detective in a trenchcoat. No doubt by the end he'd solve the case perfectly, tying up every loose end.

Real life wasn't like that, though. Cox had worked

enough cases to know that the dots never joined up perfectly – sometimes the picture was never clear. It didn't need to be. So what if Radley had some debts? So did loads of other people, up and down the country. Hell, the *country* was broke, but people weren't jumping out of windows left, right and centre. Naysmith was grabbing at straws if he thought that constituted case closed. He knew better than that.

Cox tucked her feet up on the sofa. Turned up the volume.

The Second Day of Christmas, 1986

A crust of snow on the grass, nothing really, no chance of doing a snowman or anything like that – but enough, at least, to smush a fistful into a slush-ball and catch Stan a proper stinger on the ear.

'Yes! Bang on target.'

It hurts, I can see, but Stan knows he had it coming – little sod put a handful of snow down the back of my neck earlier. His face and bare hands are bright red, glowing red. He sticks two fingers up at me, chucks a snowball. Falls apart in mid-air, and it was going miles wide anyway.

I'm already packing together a new one, hard, icy, size of an orange. Doing it with no gloves makes your hands hurt, but you can make better snowballs.

'Stan!'

He looks up just as I let fly. Goes like a rocket – belts him smack in the face.

'Argh!'

It's satisfying, for a second – until I see the blood.

Then I'm running over. He's crumpling to his knees, hands over his nose.

'Oh, Robert – I *did* tell you to be more careful.' This is Miss Halcombe, the biddy what supervises us. She gets to Stan before I do and starts making little 'coo' noises like a pigeon. She looks up at me. 'He's your brother, for goodness' sake. You're supposed to look after him.'

'Was only playing.'

'Funny idea of playing, if you ask me.'

But she's not really angry. Can see I only did it by accident. She's all right is Halcombe, I think.

Stan's properly crying, now he's seen the blood coming from his bust nose. Big heaving sobs.

'Come on, Stan,' I say. 'I didn't mean it.'

'Who's a brave boy,' Halcombe says, rubbing his back. 'Now, now.' She straightens up, brushes snow from her knees. 'Let me go get a hankie,' she says.

She goes off. I kneel by Stan and say I didn't mean it and stop being a sissy.

'You're a sissy,' he says, between sobs, and punches me in the arm.

We look up when a man comes out of the double doors further down the garden. He's got a tray of plastic mugs, all steaming.

'Hot cocoa!' he shouts. He's got a thin little voice.

It's Dr Merton. One of the blokes who comes round here sometimes, not like a warden or anything, just every now and then – some sort of specialist, probably.

Mark Duffy comes running past us, towards this Merton.

'Ho ho ho,' he sniggers.

We take no notice.

Most of the lads are gathering round Merton. A proper treat, cocoa. But Stan's still in a bit of a state, so we stay where we are.

Some of the older lads are hanging back too. Dunno why.

After a few minutes, though, he comes over anyway, this doctor. Grinning at us. He's got big grey teeth and sort of gingery hair. Going bald. I think he's pretty old, probably forty or something.

'Hello, lads,' he says.

We look up at him. There are a few mugs left on his tray.

'This cocoa won't drink itself,' he says. 'Help yourselves — it'll warm you right up.' He looks at Stan, makes a face. 'Oh dear — someone's been in the wars. Well, this'll help.'

Stan, his face still all blood and tears and snot, laughs and reaches for a mug. I take one too. I don't know why this doctor's bringing us cocoa, but in a place like this you take what you can get.

Merton squats down beside us. Tells us his name, that he's a doctor, a special doctor for children. He asks us our names, and we tell him.

'Why don't you work in a hospital?' I ask him. 'We're not ill.'

'Like I said, Robbie, I'm a special doctor. I work for the company that owns Hampton Hall, and a lot of other children's homes like it. It's my job to visit all the homes and make sure that everyone's okay.'

I shrug, nod. Not sure I like this doctor. Don't like being called Robbie by grown-ups.

Anyway, after a while Halcombe comes out with a hankie. While her and Merton are seeing to Stan — there's nothing wrong with him really, just a little nosebleed — I go off to where Mark Duffy's sitting on his own, drinking his cocoa.

He looks up.

'What d'you want?'

'Nothing. Just telling you to lay off our kid.'

'Lay off him? I never done nothing to him.'

Couple of Duffy's mates are wandering over. Duffy puts down his mug, stands up. Can't run away now. How would that look? Specially since I started it.

'Look, just don't keep getting at him, all right? He's only a little lad.'

'Aw, diddums.' He laughs, then scowls. A fighting face. 'I'll do what I bloody want.'

His mates are right behind him now. There's three of them. One of me.

Won't be the first good hiding I've had. I shove him in the chest, hard. 'Fuck off, Duffy.'

He stumbles backwards, into his mates. Comes back at me swinging. I move aside, he misses, but comes again, and I'm off-balance, can't get my hands up in time – here we go, I think, black eye, fat lip . . .

But one of his mates, the biggest one, Stevie I think he's called, grabs his shoulder, pulls him away.

'Careful, Marko,' he says in a hiss. 'You're gonna get copped. If you don't watch it they'll have you back in the cell.'

Duffy flinches. Steps back. Glares at me.

The cell? *Bloody hell, what's that?*

The other lad, dunno his name, black kid with a missing front tooth, nudges Duffy and nods over my shoulder. I look round: Halcombe's gone back inside, I see, and Merton's talking to our Stan.

I look back at Duffy and his mates.

'What?'

'Nothing.'

It feels like they should be laughing at me – the nudging and nodding, the fact they know something I don't. But they aren't laughing.

'What?'

They don't say anything. They turn their backs on me and walk *away. Stevie looks back once, over his shoulder – not at me, but at Stan.*

I go back to where they're sitting in the snow, Merton on his haunches, Stan on his knees, hands cupped around his cocoa mug.

I don't look at the doctor. I take the mug from Stan, upend it. There's only a dribble left really. It spatters the snow like a shitstain.

'Hey!'

Then I grab him by his elbow, hard enough that he can't pull away, and get him to his feet and lead him away, in spite of his 'ow' and 'oi'. I hear Merton say 'Bye, lads'. Ignore him.

'What did you do that for,' Stan says, once we're down the other end of the garden. He's rubbing his elbow and sticking out his bottom lip at me.

'I don't like that Merton.'

'Why? He's all right. That cocoa was dead nice.'

'Don't be a berk. That doesn't mean nothing. He's a bad man, Stan.'

'He's not. He's a doctor.'

I look over at Merton. He's standing hands on hips in the snow. Shiny blue bodywarmer, skinny little legs. Glasses glinting.

'He's a bad man and a doctor.'

'You don't even know.'

'Know more'n you.'

Stan's looking back at Merton too. Merton notices, gives us a wave. We both look away.

'Bad like Dad's a bad man?' Stan asks.

'No.' Shake my head. 'Different. A different sort of bad man.'

There's a cry, sharp, like a bird's cry. We look over. It's Merton – he's brushing snow angrily from his face, and looking our way. His left cheek's bright pink. Someone's copped him proper. Good.

'Ooh!' Miss Halcombe, from the doorway. 'Now who threw that? What a thing to do! Are you all right, Dr Merton?'

She hurries after him as he comes towards us. It was Duffy what threw it, I'm sure of that – him and his mates are sitting near us, and I heard their sniggering and whispering.

'Who was it?' Merton rasps, looming over us. Looks at me, looks at Duffy, looks at some of the other older lads. 'Come on. Which of you dirty little swines threw that snowball?'

I look at Duffy. Duffy looks at me.

'It was Robbie, Dr Merton,' he says. All innocent like. 'I saw.'

Stevie and the other lad nod along.

Merton looks at me, livid.

'You little shit,' he says.

Halcombe says: 'Oh, Robert. That just won't do, do you hear? There'll be no supper for you – and I thought you were such a nice lad.'

Her and Merton turn away. Merton mutters something to her as they walk back towards the building. I can't hear what.

You'd think in a place like this they'd know better than to believe whatever some stupid kid tells them, but they don't.

4

A still, silvery morning, glassy and cold. From the Tube station Cox walked quickly north, grateful for her coat and knitted scarf. The Broadway was choked with buses, black cabs, zippy cyclists and Chelsea tractors. The air was acid with exhaust fumes. Cox tugged her scarf up over her nose.

The Olympus Grill was a small place, crammed between a hipster burger joint and a phone repair shop, with a tanning salon upstairs. It'd been there years, as long as Cox could remember; one of those indestructible small businesses that somehow just hangs in there, knackered and grubby, getting by on hard work, long hours, low wages and know-how.

A heavy-set guy in fingerless gloves was hefting a crate of vegetables from a van when she arrived. She held the door for him – 'Thanks, darling' – and followed him inside.

The owner, a middle-aged guy whose hollow-cheeked face was half-familiar, was sitting at a table by the window with a coffee and a file of paperwork.

He looked up – made an apologetic face.

'Sorry, love. Not open for breakfast today. Lunch from twelve.'

Cox flashed her badge.

'Detective Inspector Cox, Hanger Lane CID. Can I have a word, Mr . . . ?'

'Andreou.' He rose, offered his hand. 'Of course – please, sit down.' Unruffled and polite. 'Can I get you a coffee?'

'An espresso would be great, thanks.' She set down her bag, unwound her scarf, breathed in the restaurant's fuggy atmosphere: charcoal, olive oil, garlic, just-baked bread.

She took a seat and looked out of the misted front window as Andreou clattered and banged at the vintage espresso machine. Watched the passers-by: a young dad with a bulging supermarket carrier-bag and two misbe-having kids in Santa hats; a teenager in outsized headphones, laughing on his hands-free; an old couple arguing over where best to cross the road. And then –

It was funny, how you could recognize a person, not by their face, not really by their walk or their height or their body-shape, but just by their *look*. Take this guy, across the street, maybe fifty yards away; he was in a long coat and a close-fitting woolly hat, and she couldn't see any-thing of him except his ears and his lower legs, there was nothing especially unusual about his height or the way he held himself – but Cox *knew* him. She was sure of it.

He was drifting along, moving slowly, looking in shop windows. Yes, something about him definitely rang a bell . . .

'One espresso.' Andreou smilingly set the little cup on the formica tabletop, and settled down in the seat oppos-ite her. 'Now, inspector – how can I help?'

Cox broke out her notebook.

'Were you working here at lunchtime on Christmas Day, Mr Andreou?'

He grinned. 'I've been here every lunchtime for the last six years,' he said.

Kerry returned the smile. When you spent every day dealing with difficult people, a straightforward one seemed like a miracle. 'Do you remember serving an older man, in his sixties, white, balding? He had a booking, I think, at one o'clock.'

Andreou pursed his lips.

'I think so. Wait one moment – let me check the book.' He stood, went to the counter, flipped quickly back through a dog-eared reservations book. Jabbed a finger in satisfaction at the page. 'Yes. A Mr – Rodley?' He frowned. 'Can't read my own handwriting. A reservation for two on Christmas Day.' He came back round the counter, returned to his seat. 'I remember, quite well actually, partly because it was just him and one other guy – and you know, with Christmas, it's usually families, couples. But mostly because they had this big row.'

'A row?'

'Uh-huh. On Christmas! Everyone else happy, laughing, singing songs – and here's these guys, at each other's throats. The older guy – Mr Rodley – stormed off without finishing his dinner, even. Left the other one to pay the bill.'

That could be helpful.

'How'd he pay?'

'Cash.'

Kerry scanned the walls – some pictures of Ancient Greek ruins, a statue of the Colossus of Rhodes. 'Any CCTV?'

Andreou grimaced and spread his hands. 'Sorry. But I could describe him for you.'

Cox jotted down the description – could've been

practically anybody, could've been Radley's twin to be honest (white, balding, middle-aged) – and gathered up her bag and scarf. Thanked Andreou for his coffee and his help; left him with a business card, in case he remembered anything else.

On her way out she saw the man again – still dawdling, still window-shopping, on the other side of the street. Still oddly familiar. And who the hell window-shops in weather like this? The numbing cold in her fingers and nose seemed to spread to her gut: a feeling, now, not just of cold but of dread.

She stepped off the kerb, making to cross the Broadway – but as she waited for a break in the traffic she saw the man hail a cab and duck swiftly into the back seat.

The chilling sense of dread subsided to a dull unease, low down in her chest.

Something was going on here. It felt big – bigger than an old man's suicide in suburban west London. Cox checked her watch, turned back towards the Tube station. Time to talk to Naysmith.

The DCI wasn't in yet – still sleeping off his hangover, Cox guessed. While she waited, she put a call through to Sergeant Adeola.

Good news, at last.

'You were right, ma'am,' the sergeant reported. 'There was a cleaner, and she was at Mr Radley's house yesterday morning. She wasn't keen on talking to us, but we, uh, leaned on her a bit – and she admitted she'd cleared off after seeing a body in the back garden.'

'Why didn't she call it in?'

'She's got a record. Nothing serious, and from twenty-odd years back – but you know how it is.'

'Sure. What else did she say? Did she notice anything odd? Apart from the corpse on the lawn, I mean.'

'There was a bit of a mess in the downstairs study, she said. Papers strewn all over the floor.'

'Was that unusual? We know how paperwork can be. Gets out of hand pretty quickly.'

'Sounds like it was a proper mess, ma'am. Radley was usually pretty tidy, she said – otherwise she'd have thought nothing of it.'

'Did she touch the papers?'

'She said she tidied them away, yes.'

'Okay. See if we can get prints from any papers that were out of place.'

'Yes, ma'am.'

'Oh, and I asked your young constable to get hold of Don DiMacedo for me. I haven't heard anything.'

'I believe he tried, ma'am. His secretary said he was in a meeting and couldn't be disturbed.'

Typical.

'Should I try him again, ma'am?'

'No – I'll call him myself. Good job, Sergeant Adeola. Thanks.'

Rang off. Brought up DiMacedo's mobile number, hit *call*. Voicemail. Double-typical.

'In an important meeting', 'Working off-site today', 'Speaking with a top-level client on the other line', 'Bang in the middle of a time-critical task' – she'd heard them all from Don DiMacedo down the years, and they all meant pretty much the same thing: Don DiMacedo is at a crucial stage in his video-game, probably halfway through a four-pack of beer and just wants to be left alone.

She'd first come across DiMacedo at the Met, when she was a DS and he was the FALCON unit's up-and-coming star in computer forensics. A former white-hat hacker with a Masters from Cambridge in Computer Science, he'd been tipped for great things. From what she'd heard, even back then Don was working on another level to the rest of his team; he was unpicking encryption systems the other guys hadn't even heard of and doing it without breaking sweat.

He got bored, in the end. Quit the Met to go and join the fraud squad at one of the big City finance firms. Now, Cox gathered, he pulled down a six-figure salary for three days' work a week.

The guys in the Met tech teams still talked about him like Arsenal fans talk about Dennis Bergkamp. The Master. They'd never see his like again . . .

Not bad for a fat guy from Walthamstow with hygiene issues and a sick sense of humour. Cox had always liked him. Now, she felt like she needed him, and not only because the guy was an IT genius. DiMacedo was an outsider now, a civilian; someone out of the reach of DCI Naysmith and Sam bloody Harrington.

When did you stop trusting your own damn police force? she asked herself, with a sense of disbelief.

DiMacedo's voicemail greeting came to the beep, and Cox left a brisk message: call me back, extremely urgent, extremely important, extremely interesting.

That last part was the hook, she knew.

Naysmith came in around twelve, in a foul mood and looking like hell. This, Cox knew, wasn't going to be any fun. She wondered how much of last night's conversation he'd remember.

'My office, Cox,' he called across the CID suite.

She sighed.

'Coming, guv.'

The DCI's office was scruffy and cramped and smelled thinly of last night's booze and instant coffee. Naysmith was slumped in his chair when Cox went in and closed the door; he glowered up at her, grey-faced and clearly unhappy.

'Sit down.'

The only other chair was threadbare, springless, showing its bones. The Bollocking Chair, they called it. Cox perched awkwardly on the edge.

'What's the latest, guv?'

'The latest? There isn't any latest, Cox.' He took a slurp of coffee from his stained souvenir Bradford Bulls mug. 'There isn't any latest because there isn't any case.'

'There's a dead body and no decent explanation is what there is, guv.'

'Don't get lippy with me, inspector. The MoJ is satisfied that Radley committed suicide – and if they're happy, I'm happy. The coroner's report will come to the same conclusion.'

'I'd like to know how you can be so sure of that. And what the hell has it got to do with the bloody Ministry anyway?'

'If they take an interest, what am I going to do, tell them to mind their own business? Get real, Cox, please. Radley was high up. Wouldn't be at all surprised if he'd done some work for them on the side.'

'You *tell* them,' Cox said, trying to keep a grip on the pitch of her voice, 'that your investigating officer is on the case. That she will conduct a full and thorough investigation into the circumstances of William Radley's death.'

'Only she won't, will she, Cox?' Naysmith said tiredly. 'Because I'm going to order her not to. I'm going to tell her she's wasted enough time on this already. I'm going to tell her she needs to leave it alone.'

The DCI's flat vowels lent a heavy emphasis to his final words.

'Harrington.'

The word escaped from her like steam from under a saucepan lid. Naysmith's eyes flashed.

'Mention that man's name to me again and I'll have you on fucking traffic duty,' he said.

Cox shook her head. *Keep it together, Kerry.*

But that was harder than it sounded. Sure, she'd had bad bosses before, bosses who were mean, or obstructive, or bullying, or even abusive – but this wasn't some over-promoted arsehole or a new guy trying to make a name for himself. This was Pete Naysmith. Christ, the things they'd been through together . . .

Cox didn't find trust easy, never had. But she'd trusted Naysmith.

Fuck it.

'You've changed, guv. Five years ago you'd have backed me up on this.'

He stared at her levelly.

'Yeah. And look where that got us.'

Cox acknowledged the point with a nod, gulping down an ache in her throat.

'I'm right about this, guv,' she said, after a moment. 'I know it. This wasn't a suicide. I followed up at the restaurant – Radley argued with someone the day before he died. Please –'

'Don't ask, Cox.'

'Just let me –'

'I said don't ask.' A dark look from under the heavy brows. A stifled sigh, a shake of the head. 'Keep it quiet,' he said. 'Not a peep do I want to hear about it – not a fucking peep. And if even a word, even a *whisper* that you're not leaving well alone gets through to the chief super, or to Har – to the MoJ – well, I won't be able to help you, Kerry.' He took up his coffee mug again. 'Now off you go. Not a word, remember.'

'Yes, guv. Thanks, guv.'

No reply. Naysmith had taken up a file from the desk and was pretending to be absorbed in it. Cox went out; closed the office door behind her.

One thing was clear, now: she was going to have to fight this every inch of the way.

5

All this, and her mother too . . . She'd tried to put off their
lunch meeting, explained that she was in the middle of a
big investigation, even dropped Radley's name (Margaret
Cox was sure to have known who Radley was: she tracked
the goings-on at the Met like other women her age followed the broadsheet Society pages). But it had done no
good. Her mother had insisted.

They'd arranged to meet at a café near the nick – five,
ten minutes' walk away.

Cox was about to turn off the main road, down the
side-street where the café was, when – once again on the
opposite pavement, once again concealed in a heavy coat
and hat – she saw him again. The man from Ealing
Broadway, the man she knew she knew . . .

He was hovering outside an upmarket florist's shop,
poking unconvincingly at the bouquets on display. Different get-up – a tweed cap and waxed riding coat, this
time – but, she was sure, the same guy.

She didn't turn down the side-road; instead she carried
on, a hundred yards beyond the junction, and slipped
down a passageway into a courtyard of swish independent
shops. No shoppers here, only an A-board advertising a
vintage clothes shop and a bicycle chained to an old-style
lamppost; the emptiness of the place made her feel

vulnerable. She kept moving, across the courtyard, out through another passageway into a half-full car park.

Here she waited, half-hidden behind a parked white transit. Caught her breath. Waited for the man in the long coat to appear.

She was going to be late for lunch. But her bloody mum could wait.

Five minutes. Ten minutes. She felt the lurch of anti-climax in her belly; he wasn't coming. Had she lost him?

Had he even been following her at all? Christ, it might not even have been the same guy.

She swore softly to herself.

Skirting the car park, she doubled back to the far end of the side-street. The café was halfway along, next to a butcher's shop; she walked normally, trying not to look furtive or afraid but nevertheless on high alert – expecting to see him, whoever the hell he was, at any second, appearing round a corner and stepping out of a shop doorway . . .

No sign. He'd gone.

The bell over the café door tinkled as she went in. It was a smart place, old-fashioned enough for chintzy table-cloths and hardback menus, with-it enough to offer frappuccinos and flat whites. Modern prints on the wall, tinkly jazz on the radio. A far cry from the Olympus Grill. For one thing, Cox knew, the coffee wasn't half as good.

Her mother was already in place, ensconced at a table in the corner (the better to keep tabs on the other customers – Cox had often thought that her mum would have made a good copper). She rose to give Cox a hug and a fleeting peck on the cheek.

'Sorry I'm late, Mum.'

'Oh, that's okay. I've only been waiting twenty minutes or so.' She sat back down, eyed her daughter anxiously. 'Are you all right, sweetheart? You look a bit pale.'

Cox forced a smile.

'I always look like that.' *And you always mention it.*

'No, but more so than usual.'

'Probably because I've been hurrying. Nothing a cuppa won't sort out.'

'Hm.' Her mother, looking unconvinced, shrugged, and caught a waitress's eye. 'I think we're finally ready to order now, dear,' she called.

Cox went for a jacket potato with tuna, her mother a green salad ('No onion, cucumber or tomato, thank you, dear'). They made awkward small talk until the food arrived.

Then, as Cox's fork was poised over her steaming potato, her mother said: 'I'm *so* sorry about Christmas, Kerry.'

The fork chimed loudly as Cox set it down on the side of her plate.

'Mum, it's all right,' she said.

'No, Kerry, it's not. I upset you on Christmas Day and I'm sorry for it. That's why I needed to see you today, even though I know how busy you must be. I wanted to clear the air.'

There'd be no cutting this short, Cox knew. No brushing it off. Margaret Cox had decided to make something of it, and now there was only one way this was going to end: with a long conversation and a clap-cold baked potato.

'Mum, you don't have to apologize. We both got a bit . . . worked up.'

'You don't have to try and put a brave face on things all the time, Kerry. I know, it's a part of who you are, I'm sure your job has something to do with it, your poor father was much the same – but the fact is, we ought to have had a lovely Christmas Day, and I spoilt it.'

Well, she wasn't wrong there.

It'd been their first Christmas without Dad; both a bit fragile, a bit weepy. Margaret was cooking dinner, at the old family home in Richmond. It was *so* odd, she said, as they sipped a glass of sherry apiece, not having a man about the place.

Cox had nodded along, murmuring agreement – dreading what was coming next.

Right on cue: 'It's such a pity you couldn't make things work with Aidan. It would be *so* nice to have Matthew here.'

And Cox had kept nodding, kept agreeing, yes it really was, yes it really would be . . .

And so it had gone on, the probing questions, the plaintive sighs, the moist, accusing stares. Christ, Kerry realized, she'd even put up a picture of Aidan and Kerry on the sideboard, from their wedding day. Talk about subtle . . .

The sherry hadn't helped. They drank the best part of half a bottle between them while they took turns checking on the turkey crown.

'Now that I'm on my own,' Margaret had said, 'I feel the absence of a grandchild more than ever.'

At that point Cox had cracked: 'Think how *I* feel,

Mum. Matthew's my son, for God's sake. It's killing me not having him here for Christmas.'

The look Margaret had given her said: *well then maybe you shouldn't have got divorced.*

'I wouldn't expect you to understand,' she'd said. 'It's different for grandmothers. One feels so helpless. After all, I didn't do anything wrong . . .'

From there, things had spiralled out of control pretty quickly.

Cox had asked her what, exactly, *she* was supposed to have done wrong; Margaret had said, well, they didn't give Aidan custody for nothing, now, did they? Cox had asked if she deserved to be punished forever for a single mistake, a mistake she made during the hardest week of her life – and Margaret had said she'd never have *made* that mistake if she hadn't always put her precious career ahead of the interests of her family.

Cox had driven home to Shepherd's Bush in tears. Christ, she'd missed her dad – missed his weary, patient presence, his 'Now, now', his 'What's all this fuss?', his 'Come on now, girls – it's not worth getting het up about'.

His hand on her shoulder. His long-suffering smile.

Now, she took up her fork again and said what she knew her mother was expecting her to say: 'We were both upset, Mum. I'm sorry too.'

Margaret nodded, chewing sadly on a pea-shoot.

She still hates the fact that I have a career, Cox thought. Still thinks the break-up was all my fault. Still blames me for not having Matthew around all the time.

But we can live with this. We'll get by.

Mothers and daughters, bloody hell, she thought. *No wonder Dad preferred the TV.*

'I thought,' Margaret said after a while, 'that it might be nice if we spent New Year's Eve together. Just us, Kerry.' She glanced up from her plate, briefly caught her daughter's eye. She wasn't playing games, Cox saw. She was lonely.

Cox knew the feeling.

'I – I'd like that,' Cox lied – already anticipating the awkwardness, the stilted silences, the pointed remarks . . .

Margaret nodded. Returned to her lettuce.

Cox was casting around for another topic of conversation when she saw an elderly couple, elegantly dressed and obviously well-off, enter the café. The woman, in conversation with her companion, had her back to the Coxes' corner table – but when she turned to address the waitress, disclosing a sharp profile and dark, intelligent eyes, Cox's stomach did a flip. Baroness Kent, chair of the parliamentary inquiry.

'Mum,' Cox hissed urgently. 'Mum, I've got to go.'

Margaret blinked at her.

'Go? What do you mean, go? You've barely touched your lunch.'

'It's – it's complicated, Mum.' She risked another look at the imposing baroness – and found the baroness looking back at her. She and her companion had been shown to a table near the door; the baroness, having sat down, had just taken the napkin from her wineglass. Now she let it fall to the tabletop.

She knew who Cox was. Cox knew who she was. And neither of them wanted to be seen in public within half a mile of the other, never mind in the same damn café. Not this week.

Cox stood abruptly.

'Mum, I've got to get back to work.' She fumbled in her bag for her purse – fished out a couple of crumpled banknotes. 'Mum? Here, this is for the bill – I've got to go, really . . .'

Margaret was staring up at her, her expression two parts confusion to one part hurt.

'But – but surely they must let you have lunch, dear? We've barely been here –'

'I know, Mum. I'm sorry. But really – it's very urgent.'

Her mum made a well-I'm-sure-you-know-best face. 'If you must, I suppose you must,' she said. 'But it does seem rather a shame . . .'

Cox didn't need another guilt trip on top of everything else. She left the banknotes on the tablecloth, muttered *sorry* a couple more times, turned quickly away and made for the door.

As she walked swiftly across the restaurant's plush carpet, she felt the blood rising in her cheeks. Hated herself for it. What was she, thirteen years old?

Kept her eyes firmly on the door as she passed Baroness Kent's table – only to be stopped by the baroness's hand on her sleeve.

'Detective Inspector Cox – I do hope you're not leaving on my account.'

She stopped, turned; the baroness was getting to her feet, a look of concern on her strong-boned face.

Cox's flustered first thought was: *how the hell are you meant to address a baroness?*

'I – just thought –' she stammered.

'You're very wise to be doing the diplomatic thing. It reflects well on you.' The baroness smiled, a smile not quite free of uncertainty or anxiety – but genuine, if Cox was any judge. 'But really. I don't think you ought to worry. If one can't enjoy a private lunch without being called to account by the Powers That Be – well, one might as well be in North Korea.'

In spite of herself, Cox laughed.

'I'm sure you're right. I wasn't really thinking about how it'd look to the authorities. I was more worried about the press.'

'I *meant* the press,' the baroness said, with a flicker of a sardonic eyebrow.

The gentleman seated opposite Baroness Kent had found his way to his feet; he was obviously pretty frail, but he was well-built and well-dressed; his thin silver hair was combed in firm waves over his ears. As Cox shook his hand – the knuckles thick with arthritis, but the grip solid, certain – the baroness introduced him as her husband, Sidney.

Cox mumbled something about being delighted to meet him.

She was thinking about her mother – who, she knew, was not ten yards behind her, who was quite certainly taking all this in, who would quite certainly have recognized the baroness, and who was now quite certainly wondering what sort of daughter leaves her widowed mother sitting all by herself to go off hobnobbing with peeresses of the realm . . .

She turned back to the baroness and mustered what was left of her resolve.

'I'm terribly sorry,' she said, 'but I really was leaving anyway. Duty calls. But it was lovely meeting you both.'

Then to the door – *don't look back, don't look back* – and out: out into the wintry sunlight, the grumbling traffic, the biting fresh air.

'Afternoon, Spook. Donnie Darko here.'

Cox sighed through a smile. For a genius, Don DiMacedo didn't half talk a lot of crap.

She'd called in at a grubby little pub on Leopold Road for a restorative drink, and to regather her thoughts, re-focus on the case, think again about where she stood – and who stood with her. She'd taken her glass of wine to a table in the deserted tap-room. When her phone had buzzed and DiMacedo's name had come up, she'd almost dropped the phone in her haste to answer.

'Don. Good to hear from you. Is your PS3 broken?'

'Yeah, right. Along with my Gameboy and my Sega MegaDrive. Keep up, Cox. I got hold of a prototype PS4, don't ask me how, but I'll tell you, once you've played one of these motherfuckers, you don't go back to boys' toys.'

'It's good that you're keeping busy.'

'Fucking snowed under,' DiMacedo sighed, without irony. 'Which brings us to the point. I gather you want to add to my exhausting workload.'

'I do, if you think you can handle it.'

'There's nothing you can throw at me that I can't han-dle,' he laughed.

Swiftly she filled him in on the Radley case, the unanswered questions, the gaps in the record. Didn't mention Harrington and the MoJ.

'And what do you want from me?' There was amusement in his voice.

She hesitated. She could practically see the smirk on his face.

'As you know, Don,' she said carefully, 'I'm . . . limited as to what I can ask you to do.'

'Tell me about it. I spend every day up to my bloody ears in injunctions and gagging clauses.' A short bark of a laugh. 'Guess how much good they do.'

'Don, I need to know more about William Radley.'

'And you're not fussy about how I come by the information.'

'I didn't say that.'

'Course you didn't, Spook. Give me half an hour.'

'You'll need longer than –' Cox began. But the line was dead.

She didn't rush her glass of vanilla-heavy pub red. A lot to think about. She wasn't worried about DiMacedo – he'd come up with the goods, one way or another, and she was damn sure he wouldn't leave fingerprints. Everyone else, though . . .

She'd had an email from Media Liaison, briefing her on the Radley press coverage so far. It hadn't made much of a splash in the mainstream press, thank Christ; the papers that had bothered covering the story had all run with the official line – tragic suicide of ex-Met chief – and none had given it more than a column or two. So Harrington had been good for something, after all.

Even better, he'd succeeded in keeping her name out of it – no mention of DI Cox, even in Greg Wilson's piece for one of the right-wing tabloids. *That* must have taken some doing, she thought. Again she felt a shiver of unease as she wondered exactly how 'persuasive' this Mr Harrington had been.

The embarrassing little scene with Baroness Kent hadn't helped her stress levels. She'd been doing her best not to think about the inquiry; told herself to focus, to do her damn job. But she was aware that, back at her flat, there was a fat briefing file that she hadn't even got round to looking at yet. Partly that was bloody-mindedness: what could a bundle of paperwork tell her that she didn't already know? Did they think she'd *forgotten*?

But mainly it was fear. Of going over it all again, facing down things she just wanted to put behind her; and of what might lie ahead. An inquiry like this, press all over it, the public demanding someone's head on a plate – it was every copper's nightmare.

You've been through worse, Cox reminded herself.

She was finishing off the last of her wine when her phone buzzed again. DiMacedo.

'Give me some good news, Don.'

'Define "good".' DiMacedo chuckled down the line. 'Death-threats in his email inbox? Suicide note in his drafts folder? No can do, Spook. Sorry.'

'Anything at all I can use?'

'Listen, this guy was almost offensively boring. I read through his emails and I can feel the life-force being drained out of me. He got newsletters from a hill-walking club. His search history is all art galleries and classical concerts. He recently ordered a guide-book for the Coast-to-Coast footpath.'

Cox sighed. She had a feeling she knew well, and hated:

the helpless feeling of a big case dying on her. Sources drying up, leads petering away to nothing. But at least it confirmed her previous suspicion. Radley wasn't suicidal. He didn't seem depressed. His life had been cut short.

'Anything financial?'

'Spook, I had, like, twenty minutes for this. You want me to hack his bank account, I'll need at least another five.' He laughed; Cox heard him take a slurp from a can. 'But listen, there was one thing.'

'What?'

'The day before he jumped –'

'Christmas Day.'

'Yes, that's right. Well, that day, he ordered some flowers, really pricey ones.'

'Christmas present?'

'Bit late for that. They were to be delivered to a funeral director's. A place up in Whitby, on the Yorkshire coast.'

'Can you send me the details?'

'Already did.'

Cox smiled as her phone hummed with a new-mail notification.

'Thanks, Don.'

'A pleasure. You need anything else, just shout. Oh, and hey – good luck at the inquiry, Spook.'

And he was gone – back to his video games.

The force had assigned her a six-strong legal team from one of the big London Chambers.

For a fortnight they'd been bombarding her with emails, calls, voicemails, asking her – no, ordering her – to fill out their forms, make time for meetings, re-examine statements, compile reams of personal information . . .

They didn't seem to like her much, but then they didn't seem to like anyone much. Anyway, the feeling was mutual.

'Inspector. Do you need me to call the IT team for you?'

Serena McAvoy QC was heading up the team. She had a manufactured RP accent and a glossy brunette up-do, a Cambridge Double First and a knack for pushing Cox's buttons.

Cox looked up from her computer. McAvoy was standing beside her desk, drumming her fingernails on the top of a box-file.

'Sorry? An IT team?'

'I just assumed that you must have a load of problems with your comms, as you don't seem to be getting the emails we've been sending. Or the voicemails we've been leaving you.' She smiled humourlessly.

'Oh. Right. Yes. Sorry.' Cox leaned back in her creaky office chair. 'I've been meaning to get back to you, I've just been, you know . . . busy.'

'We're all busy, inspector. In our case, we're busy working on *your* case. I know these requests can be tiresome, but this is for your own good.'

And you're doing it out of the goodness of your heart, right? Cox thought. She'd seen how much the force was paying for the legal team's services. Eye-watering. Money like that, she'd thought guiltily, could've kept a patrol of coppers on the beat for a decade.

Once this inquiry had buried her, they'd have to have another one into the wastage of tax-payers' funds on police advocacy, she thought wryly.

'I know,' she muttered. 'I'll try and –'

'Shall we say tomorrow?' McAvoy was already tapping an appointment into her tablet. 'Three o'clock. Unless you're – busy?'

'I – I don't think so. I'm not sure. Let's pencil it in and –'

'Three o'clock it is. If you could find time to look over the briefing file we compiled for you before then, we'd be ever so grateful.' She flashed her teeth again. 'See you tomorrow, inspector.'

Cox watched her walk away, the noise of her heels brisk on the carpet tiles.

Thirty seconds later, an appointment popped up on Cox's PC desktop. The woman was lethally efficient, she had to give her that.

She ignored it for the moment, went back to the file DiMacedo had sent over. It was an order confirmation from a high-end florist in the West End for a lavish bouquet of lilies to be sent to the Whitby address. Radley had specified that it should arrive on the twenty-eighth – the next day. That could be helpful, Cox thought.

Even better, he'd asked for a card to be delivered with the flowers – and he'd written the message himself.

Farewell, Verity, she read. *From your dear friend Bill x.*

Old flame, maybe? Or a friend from the hill-walking club, or an old colleague? Who knew? Whatever – it was a lead. She hadn't told Naysmith yet, for the simple reason that, on the face of it, the flowers weakened the likelihood of Radley's death being suspicious. No doubt Harrington would say Radley, grieving some former acquaintance, had topped himself.

She ran a quick search for the name of the Whitby funeral director, came up with a number. Dialled from her mobile.

'Cartwright & Sons Funeral Parlour,' a soft Yorkshire voice answered. Male.

'Ah – hello. I was wondering if you could tell me what time Verity's funeral is tomorrow? I had a card, but I seem to have mislaid it –'

'Of course, madam.' She heard a faint rustling of papers. 'Are you a relative of Miss Halcombe's?'

'No, just – a friend.'

'Well, the funeral is at ten. It's at St Andrew's, here in town – do you know it?'

She said she didn't, and took down the directions the man gave her.

'There'll be a big turn-out, I expect,' she hazarded. Worth a shot.

'Oh, I'm sure,' the man said. 'A lovely lady.'

Well, what else was he going to say? 'She was a right old bag, and to be honest I can't see anyone being bothered with it'? Cox thanked him and hung up.

It didn't feel great, taking advantage of a death like that, but in a case like this she knew she was going to get nothing for free; she had to squeeze every lead for all it was worth.

She closed her browser and opened the appointment notification from Serena McAvoy, QC. She ignored it, with an enjoyable thrill of guilt. She already knew she wasn't going to be at the meeting; she wasn't even going to be in London. She was going to be in Whitby, North Yorkshire, paying her respects to Verity Halcombe.

The Third Day of Christmas, 1986

Stan's pissed the bed.

'Those were clean on,' Miss Halcombe moans as she bundles up the damp sheets. 'I shouldn't have bothered, should I?'

He didn't do it on purpose, I want to say. But I don't want to get in trouble, not after yesterday. At least she's putting new sheets on. In that last place where we was, a lad wet the bed, and they made him sleep in it till the end of the week. Teach him a lesson, they said.

Some lesson.

Why did Stan do it? I dunno. He's not done it before, not since he was properly little.

He's not crying, at least. Just standing here, next to the bed. Face is pale, and there's blue shadows under his eyes. Nightmares, I s'pose. Hardly bloody surprising.

Halcombe's in a strop because she's already busy getting Hackett ready for his move. Gordon Hackett's off to Wolvesley. Some of the other lads know about Wolvesley, but we've not been there, me and Stan, we only know here and that other place. The other lads reckon Gordo's struck it proper lucky.

'It's first division, Wolvesley,' said Judd, one of the oldest kids, when they was talking about it. Judd's been around more'n most. 'Proper top class. You get puddings, every meal. And electric blankets.'

'If that's first division, what's this place?' Duffy, smirking, cracking his knuckles. 'Third division?'

'Vauxhall bloody Conference, you mean.'

Everyone laughed.

Then Judd said: 'Tell you what. There's girls at Wolvesley, too.'

That was something to think about. Girls. Bloody hell.

I asked them where it was, this Wolvesley place. Over in Shirley, they said. That's the other side of Birmingham – miles away.

Don't suppose we'll be seeing Gordo again. We all crowd around the dorm windows to see him off. He gives us a wave as he gets into the back of Dr Merton's car.

'He must've done something pretty bloody special to get moved to Wolvesley,' says Stevie.

6

Cox stirred a third spoonful of sugar into her tea and rubbed a hand across her eyes. It'd been a hell of a drive up to this fishing town on the Yorkshire coast; a six-hour slog of London traffic, light-smeared motorways, winding A-roads and sleet-swept moorland. She'd dropped into her B&B bed just before eleven; been woken at 4.30 by seagulls on the roof and fishermen passing under her window. She'd got up at six, brewed a cup of tea in the pitch dark to the sound of wind-stirred masts chiming in the harbour. Dressed herself in respectable funeral black.

Now, at nearly 9.30, she sat drinking yet another cuppa – this one so strong it made her shudder – in a greasy spoon on the north edge of town. She'd spent an hour – and chilled herself to the bone – checking out the layout of the district; St Andrew's, a squat late-Norman church, stood facing the sea on the hillside a half-mile away.

At about 9.45 she left her table and, parking her car at the café (she'd be less conspicuous, she figured, if she arrived on foot), headed up the sloping road towards the church.

There was a rust-pitted railing enclosing the church-yard. Stone gateposts, yellow with lichen, stood either side of a grit path to the church door. Cox hovered by the railing, the collar of her coat turned up and her dark wool beret pulled low over her brow. She pretended to be doing something with her phone as the mourners began to arrive; the main thing she noticed was that there weren't many of them. They were mainly pensioners, arriving by car in ones and twos. By 9.55, when the hearse pulled up with a low growl outside the gate, there were barely more than half a dozen cars parked up along the roadside.

She wasn't sure what she expected to find, but something about the whole scene struck her as odd. She knew people moved about, but this windswept corner seemed a million miles from Radley's urbane London life. It just didn't fit.

As the undertaker lifted the tailgate of the hearse and his staff bent awkwardly to manhandle the pale-pine coffin on to their shoulders, Cox made her way down the path and into the church. It was smaller, she found, than it had looked from the outside; the air was clammy, and there was a smell of damp and floor-wax. She slipped into a pew near the back. Pulled off her beret as, step by solemn step, the coffin was carried in.

No one, she noted, seemed especially upset. No stifled sobs, no tears; no one moved to put a comforting arm around a grieving widower, sister, daughter, son. The faces she could see were grim but composed. An old policing cliché rose up in Cox's mind: *follow the money.* Who, she wondered, had paid for this funeral?

The vicar, a blotchy middle-aged man with a wheeze in his voice, worked steadily through the usual platitudes; there was no mention of the dead woman's personality, family, values, how she'd lived, how she'd died – no sense that he'd even known Verity Halcombe. No one else spoke. A prayer was said, and then it was done. A popular classical piece played tinnily from a portable CD player as the mourners filed silently from their pews, out into the blustery churchyard.

Seagulls mewled overhead, bobbing on the updrafts. Tall stinging nettles nodded by the railing. The mourners, picking their way across the unkempt grass, gathered around the grave that was to be Verity's last resting place. There was no gravestone in place yet, of course; just a hole, and a heap of earth.

Cox was taking up a position towards the back of the meagre crowd when she felt her phone buzz in her pocket. Glanced at the screen: Naysmith. *Christ.* She thought about leaving it, but she knew there were some things he would *never* forgive.

The seaward gatepost gave her a bit of shelter from the bitter wind.

'Yes, guv?'

The DCI's mood hadn't improved.

'Where the bloody hell are you?'

'I'm –' Well, what was the point in lying? 'I'm in Whitby, guv.'

'*What?* What are you doing in fucking Whitby?'

'I'm following up a lead. Could be important.'

Naysmith sighed.

'I don't want to hear about this, do I?'

'Probably not.'

'And what the hell am I supposed to tell this McAvoy harpy? She's been chewing my ear off about your meeting this afternoon. She's expecting you to be there, with your homework all done and your hair in a braid.'

'She's going to be disappointed, guv. I'm sorry – but this is something that couldn't wait.'

There was a pause, and then another sigh, pissed-off and bone-deep weary.

'Okay,' he said. 'Do what you have to. But be back here as soon as you can, Cox, you hear me?'

'Yes, guv.'

'Bring me back a stick of fucking rock.'

Cox grinned as she rang off. Was Naysmith the most supportive boss in the world? Christ, no. But he backed her when it mattered. She appreciated that; sometimes, she thought it was more than she deserved.

She turned back to the grave, and the knot of black-clad mourners. The coffin had been carried from the church and was being lowered into the hole. Cox rejoined the group, standing a little way off to one side, beside an elderly couple. It didn't take long: the vicar again droned his way through the formalities, *ashes to ashes, dust to dust*, and with a murmured 'amen' the ceremony was concluded. Kerry remembered her dad's funeral – the pack of grizzled old coppers – a couple of ex-cons too – all offering their heartfelts to her mum, just waiting for the drinking to get started.

The crowd began to break up. Two burly lads who'd been sitting a discreet distance away, smoking fags in the lee of a stone angel, stood and took up their shovels.

Cox fell in with the old couple she'd been standing beside during the burial. The woman, her steel-grey hair cut in a neat bob, walked slowly, with a stick, holding on to her husband's arm with her free hand. She introduced herself as Barbara Hopson; her husband, a portly man in a black blazer and high-waisted charcoal slacks, was Eric.

'I'm Kerry,' said Cox. Tell as few lies as you can get away with – she'd learned that a long time ago.

It turned out that Barbara and Eric had been Verity's neighbours.

'She was there when we moved in, ooh, ten, eleven years ago,' Barbara remembered, stepping unsteadily around a neglected grave. 'Hers was the bungalow just across the road.' She pursed her lips and shook her head. 'It's terrible, what happened.'

'Awful,' Cox agreed.

'I mean, it could happen to any one of us, couldn't it? It could have been me or Eric, just as easily. And it could still. That's the frightening thing, isn't it?' She patted her husband's arm. 'At least we've got each other though.'

Cox said nothing, just nodded vaguely – waited for the silence to do its work.

Eventually Eric began: 'The funny thing was –'

'*I* wouldn't call it funny,' Barbara snapped.

'Well, no – peculiar, I suppose I mean. The peculiar thing was, Verity, towards the end, had the idea that someone was after her – following her, she reckoned. Poor thing.'

'It got to so she wouldn't go out, wouldn't even open her curtains,' put in Barbara. 'When she didn't put her Christmas lights up this year – and she usually put up such a lovely display, didn't she, Eric? – we thought that was why. Too scared.'

'But then –'

'Yes, *then* we found out the real reason why. She'd – she'd passed on.' Barbara sighed. 'Poor Verity.'

Cox probed gently: 'How do you mean "after her"? Like – a stalker? Someone she knew?'

'She talked about a feller in a donkey jacket,' Eric shrugged. 'Always on about him, seeing him here, there and everywhere. Told us to watch out for him, didn't she, love?'

'She did. A wrong 'un, she said.' Barbara looked at Cox; her eyes were fearful behind her thick spectacles. 'And who's to say she was wrong? That's the thing, Kerry.'

'They'd barely taken her poor body away,' Eric said sourly, 'and some toerag smashes in her back window, ransacks the place. Honestly. No respect, nowadays.'

'Drugs or, or, or something, I expect,' Barbara sniffed. 'Or just somebody else wanting something for nothing.'

Cox tried to keep them on track.

'But you think Verity might have had an idea that it was going to happen? Do you think it was this man who'd been following her that broke into her house?'

'Who knows?' Barbara shook her head miserably. 'People get confused, don't they. Older people. Perhaps she wasn't well. But I know this, Kerry.' She lifted her chin, gave a sharp nod. 'She was scared. Rightly or wrongly, I don't know. But Verity was scared out of her wits.'

They'd reached the Hopsons' car, a well-kept old green Ford, parked just outside the church gate. They were among the last to leave. As Eric helped Barbara into the passenger seat, he offered Cox a lift to the church hall; 'Tea urn, sausage-rolls, the usual,' he said with a sad smile, and the air of a man who'd spent too much time at funerals. She accepted gratefully. She'd already learned a lot from the Hopsons – but she had the feeling there was still a lot she didn't know.

It was a church hall much like any other: clean bare floorboards, posters and notices pinned to the walls, a cross-shaped east window. A table was laden with, as Eric had said, 'the usual': open sandwiches, cold quiche, hard-boiled eggs, sausage-rolls. As far as Cox could tell, everyone who'd been at the church had come along.

She couldn't drink another cup of tea, so helped herself to a glass of water, and wandered over to take a look at a flower display set out on a trestle table under the window. It was a nice arrangement, lilies and freesias and some green fern framing a set of photographs of a smiling, silver-haired lady with rounded cheeks and pale blue eyes – Verity Halcombe.

Or rather, Cox noted, bending to read a handwritten notice beneath the photographs, Verity Halcombe, OBE. There was a picture, in fact, of her proudly holding her OBE medal in the grounds of Buckingham Palace. It was the only one of the photographs in which Verity was by herself; in all of the others she was surrounded by kids, playing, laughing, pulling faces and showing off for the camera – or shy, and clinging to Verity's pleated skirt.

In one, Verity and the kids were joined by a group of smiling women in polo-shirts with logos. The caption read: *On Verity's retirement from Cromby House, Whitby*. It was dated a year earlier.

As Cox turned away, she noticed the lilies sent by William Radley. *From your dear friend Bill x*.

How had one of the most senior figures in London policing come to befriend a nursery worker from Whitby? Where was the connection?

She noticed another woman, smartly dressed in a black trouser-suit and around Verity's age, peering at the photographs.

'Lovely display, isn't it?' Cox said, moving alongside. 'I'm Kerry. An old friend of Verity's.'

The woman smiled, shook her hand.

'Helen. So you knew Verity back when she was in the Midlands, then?'

Think fast.

'Ah – no. Just since she moved up here.'

'Oh.' Helen looked disappointed. 'So not *that* old, then.'

'No.' She forced an embarrassed laugh. 'No, I suppose not, really, if you look at it like that.' Tried not to show that she was flustered; wondered how long ago Verity had lived in the Midlands – how long did you have to know someone to qualify as an 'old friend'? People Helen's age probably had different ideas about that sort of thing. Maybe you weren't *really* an old friend unless you'd swapped ration coupons or been through the Blitz together.

They made small-talk stiffly for a while, and then Cox made her excuses and headed outside.

The weather hadn't let up. If anything, the temperature had dropped, and the sea wind was gusting more strongly. It took her the best part of forty-five minutes to find the greasy-spoon café and her car parked outside; another half-hour – including a twenty-minute wait at the swing-bridge – to drive across town to Whitby police station.

'DCI Kerry Cox, Metropolitan Police.'

The constable on the front desk looked at her with a gormless mix of amusement and fear.

'From – from London, ma'am?'

'Yes, from London. You must have heard of it.' Cox's reserves of patience were at a low ebb. 'I'd like to speak with someone about the death of Verity Halcombe.'

The constable nodded awkwardly, as though his head were being jerked on a string.

'Y-yes, ma'am. I'll – I'll fetch the sergeant.'

He hurried away.

The sergeant, at least, seemed to be a man she could do business with. He was a thick-set, doughy-faced man with a receding hairline and a badger-grey moustache. He greeted her briskly, ushered her through the security door into an empty office suite.

'Now, how can I help, ma'am?'

Cox rubbed her face.

'A good cup of coffee would be a start,' she said. 'But I don't suppose there's any chance of that?'

The sergeant – Carrick, he'd said his name was – smiled bleakly.

'This is a police station, ma'am. It's brown stuff from the machine, or nowt.'

'Never mind, then.' She pushed her hair behind her ears, rolled her stiff shoulders – the after-effects of yesterday's long drive were starting to kick in. 'I'm investigating a suspicious death in London, sergeant. Trying to track the final movements of the victim. I'm here in Whitby because we think the victim might have some connection with Verity Halcombe. Miss Halcombe died recently.'

'That's right, ma'am.' The sergeant nodded. 'Although it'd be more accurate to say that we *found* her recently. Unfortunately, by that time, Miss Halcombe had been dead quite some time.' He grimaced; they both knew what that meant.

Sergeant Carrick went through the story in step-by-step police-ese. A postman had noticed a foul smell of decomposition wafting through the letterbox one morning, just before Christmas. He'd dialled 999, the police had attended the scene – and the body of Verity Halcombe, six weeks dead or thereabouts, had been found in bed.

No, he said, there were no suspicious circumstances; no, Miss Halcombe hadn't reported anything about a man following her.

He paused, then added: 'There *was* one funny thing, though, ma'am. Probably nothing, but –'

'Go on.'

'Her front door, ma'am. When we arrived, it was unlocked.'

'It'd been open all that time?'

'Hard to be sure, ma'am. We were told that Miss Halcombe was a very security-conscious lady – but would she have gone to bed without locking the door?' He twitched his moustache sceptically. 'That's why it struck me as funny, ma'am.'

Cox nodded.

'Thanks, sergeant.'

I wouldn't go to bed without locking the door, she thought. All right, Whitby's a far cry from Shepherd's

Bush, but still. Verity, by the sound of it, was borderline paranoid. Why would she leave the door open?

There are three options, she thought: someone else opened the door; Verity just forgot to lock the door before bed; or Verity knew someone was after her – and wanted them to find her.

7

The garden had been well looked after, once. Someone had cared for it. Now it was a rank strip of straggly off-yellow grasses, dead flowerheads, ragged hedges and leggy herbs. A hanging basket by the door held nothing but lankly drooping plant stems.

'She just lost interest, apparently, towards the end,' Sergeant Carrick said as he unlocked the front door. 'Never went out. Let the garden go to pot.' He cast a dull eye over the derelict lawn. 'Shame.'

He hadn't taken much persuading to let Cox see the place. Coppers were a cynical lot, but some words still worked a certain magic in any nick. 'Scotland Yard', for instance.

It was a small place, Verity's house, a 1920s redbrick on the end of a terrace of five; from the doorstep, you could see across a stretch of neat allotments to the far side of the bay and the dark, brooding ruin of the Abbey.

Something to do with Dracula, was it, the Abbey? It was written there, or set there, or something.

Well, we can probably rule out vampire attack in this case, Cox thought grimly as she entered the poky hallway. *But beyond that, who knows?* The coroner, she knew, had recorded a verdict of 'natural causes' – which seemed pretty vague, for a late-sixties woman in decent health. The state of decomposition had made things hard to determine with much certainty.

On the drive over from the station she'd asked Carrick about the burglary. He hadn't thought much of it. It was pretty common, he'd said, an opportunistic thing; word gets out that someone's passed on, and that means an empty house – it was a bloody shame, yes, but there you are.

Cox closed the door behind her, turned – and stopped. 'Jesus Christ.'

'Yep.' Carrick, hands in pockets, nodded. 'They really did a number on the place.'

'Did a number'? They'd practically taken it apart.

Cox moved carefully through the house, taking in the extent of the damage. In the sitting room, the sofa cushions had been slashed and the stuffing torn out; a roll-top bureau had been emptied of its contents, the bottoms of the drawers kicked through, stationery and bric-a-brac strewn across the carpet. In some places the skirting-boards had been levered away; in others, they'd rolled back the carpeting and jemmied up the floorboards.

It was the same in every room. The toilet cistern smashed. The stained mattress in the bedroom ripped open. Pictures pulled off the walls. Cupboards emptied, doors hanging off their hinges. Rags of torn loft insulation hung from the opening to the roofspace.

Whoever did this had been looking for something. There weren't many hiding places in a house this small – whatever they were after, surely to God they'd found it.

She headed back downstairs, to where Carrick was waiting. Cox felt like clicking her fingers in front of his face just to see if anyone was home. Did they seriously think this was just an opportunistic burglary? But it wouldn't do any good to antagonize the local force.

'Any idea what was taken?'

'Hard to tell, what with no family to say if there's owt missing. Telly's still here. Clock on the mantel, few bits of jewellery upstairs. She might've had an iPad, but I doubt it.'

'There's no one at all? Who inherits the house?'

'She didn't leave a will. Council'll sort all this when they come to auction it off. House-clearance company, I expect.'

His weariness was beginning to grate, so she picked her words carefully. 'Bit odd, isn't it?' She shoed cautiously through a heap of old bills on the floor. 'All this mess? Nothing apparently taken? Funny sort of burglary, if you ask me.'

Carrick shifted uncomfortably from foot to foot.

'Now you mention it, ma'am, it does seem a bit odd, as you say,' he conceded. 'But I thought – I mean, *we* thought – you know, old lady, natural causes, empty house, and, as I say, it does happen a lot, ma'am, and sometimes they're just junkies looking for cash . . .'

He tailed off. Cleared his throat.

'I understand, sergeant,' Cox said. Smiled thinly.

She knew the type. Anything for a quiet life. Didn't make him a bad copper – but didn't make him a good one, either.

Her eye was caught by a broken pane of glass on the floor by the window. It was the glass from a picture-frame, broken in three. Beneath it was a black-and-white photograph, creased but not otherwise damaged. She stooped, picked it up, shook away a few fragments of glass. It was of a young woman – looked a lot like Verity, at maybe twenty, twenty-five. She was grinning on the arm of a dapper-looking young man: high forehead, stiff collar, crooked half-smile.

She turned to Carrick.

'Verity never married, did she?'

'No, ma'am. She was never anything but Miss Halcombe, far as I know.'

Cox held up the picture.

'Any idea who this man is? Brother?'

'There's no brother anyone's heard of. Old boyfriend, p'raps?'

'Mm. Maybe.' She took out her phone, snapped a photograph of the old print. Behind her, she heard Carrick's radio crackle; he stepped out into the hallway to speak.

She moved around, pretending to be focused on taking snaps of the ransacked room. Carrick's voice was low, a strained mutter; she stood quite still, camera pointed at random, listening hard – couldn't make out the words.

When she glanced across she could see a section of Carrick's face through the gap between the door and the frame. The sergeant's brow was furrowed; something had cracked his unflappable, seen-it-all front.

When he stepped back into the shattered sitting room he had a hangdog, just-doing-my-job look.

'I'm sorry, ma'am. But we're going to have to go.'

'Go? Go where?'

'That was my CO. He's had a call from London, ma'am.'

Oh, here we go . . .

'And?'

'Word from – from your chief super.' He nodded to

emphasize the significance. 'He says – and this is just the message I was given, ma'am – that the Miss Halcombe business is to remain in the hands of North Yorkshire Police.'

'You're kidding.'

'This is just what I was told, ma'am. There's no connection between Miss Halcombe's death and your investigation in London.'

'Says who?'

'I don't know, ma'am. This is just what I've been told. He said I've to drive you back to your car, and that's that.' He spread his hands. 'So – shall we go, ma'am?'

Cox fixed him with a bitter look. Had to remind herself that it wasn't his fault; orders from on high, what was he supposed to do? He'd done her a favour bringing her here, anyway.

She thanked him – said she'd prefer to walk. Carrick did a bad job of hiding his relief.

Out in the street, she waited for the patrol car to pull away before she took her phone and – feeling a day's worth of frustration uncoil inside her – dialled Naysmith's number.

The phone rang for what seemed like for ever.

Don't you dare, she thought, pacing the pavement. *Don't you dare duck out of this.*

He answered on the seventh ring.

'Cox.'

She exploded: 'Guv, what the bloody hell is going on?'

'Now, Cox, I've been more than accommodating –'

'This is a serious lead, guv, a serious, valid lead on a major case. I'm not here for the good of my bloody health. Verity Halcombe –'

'Spare me the details of your wild goose chase, Cox. I said I'd give you twenty-four hours on this –'

'I don't remember that at all,' she said.

'– and your time's up. I've had enough.'

'You? Or the chief super?'

There was the slightest pause – that was answer enough.

'This has nothing to do with the chief super,' Naysmith said unconvincingly. 'This is my call.'

'Sure it is, guv.'

'Careful now, Cox.' An edge in his voice. 'You're *this* close to the line.'

'Guv, this is not a waste of time, this is not speculation, this is a *lead* –'

'Back here. Now. I want you on the road within the hour, and when you get to London the first thing you do is report directly to me. Do I make myself clear?'

Talking tough doesn't make you a leader, Cox thought. *And treating me like I'm a wayward teenager doesn't prove you're right.*

'This is a live investigation. The Halcombe death is –'

'It's an irrelevance, and a distraction, and you're going to walk away from it right now, Cox, because I'm ordering you to.' He paused, drew a breath. Then, in a wearier tone, he added: 'If you don't get your act together, we'll both have all the time in the world to relax at the seaside after this bloody inquiry rips us to pieces.'

'Guv, I'm not relaxing, I'm –'

There was a noise, a door opening, a man's urgent voice. 'Hang on,' Naysmith said to her sharply; muffled the phone with his hand.

When he came back on the line the brisk authority had returned to his voice.

86

'Stabbing in Battersea Park,' he said. 'Some proper bloody policework for you. Go there direct.'

You needn't sound so pleased about it, Cox thought.

'On my way, guv,' she said. She rang off.

When she got back to her car she changed out of her smart black funeral shoes into a pair of comfy trainers and climbed wearily into the driver's seat. Her back and shoulders were knotted with tension, her knees stiff, her eyes dry from sleeplessness. Six hours of driving and nothing to look forward to at the end of it but an inner-city stabbing. Still, it beat a face-to-face with Peter fucking Naysmith.

She turned the car deftly, drove uphill out of town on to a snaking moorland road. The ruined Abbey, a stark black outline against piled blue clouds, snagged in her peripheral vision as she drove; gave her the creeps, even from this distance. She let her gaze drift westwards along the horizon. The clouds grew darker, more forbidding, towards the south – high, bruised and full of storms. She shifted gear, pulled on to the A-road. She was heading into heavy weather.

The Fourth Day of Christmas, 1986

There's a copper here.

We're all on edge, really wound up — we've all of us here, except maybe our Stan, had our run-ins with the cops, out in the real world. All come off worse. They're a bunch of old bastards, and that's all there is to it.

This one's here because he's bringing in a new lad, a proper hard-knock by the sounds of it. The bastard's got his arm in a sling. Hope it hurt, whatever he done.

The kid's called Col.

'He was in here before,' Stevie told me. 'Got fostered. Dunno what he done to get brung back but he's a right nutcase, could've been anything.'

He don't look like much. I sit on my bed and watch as Halcombe leads him over to his corner of the dorm. Dark piggy eyes, frowning eyebrows. Bit of a porker.

First thing you always ask yourself when there's a new lad, is: could I have him? I reckon I could have him.

If he's mental, though, it's different. It's different when you don't know what they might do.

Everyone else steered well clear. He never smiled or said anything and anyroad everyone thought he was a nutter, word'd got round.

When we was all outside he just sat by himself. I went over and started talking to him. He's okay, really.

First thing was, I asked him why he got kicked out of his foster home. That was what I wanted to know, so I just asked him.

He looked at me, blinking like a mole.

'Stabbed my foster dad, didn't I.'

'Fuck off.'

'Straight up.' He almost smiled. 'Done him with a kitchen knife.'

'Killed him?'

'Nah. Just cut him.' He gave me another look. 'D'you see that pig what brought me here yesterday?'

'Yeah, I seen him.'

'That sling he had on his arm. That were me, too.'

'Fuck off.'

'He come for me and I knifed him in his arm. Dirty rasher bastard.'

He weren't what I expected, this lad.

Later in the day they took Col away. We saw him through the doorway being led downstairs.

'The cell,' Duffy muttered.

Our Stan looked scared. Bloody Duffy.

'What's the cell?' he said.

'It's bloody horrible,' said Stevie. He was all serious, like. Didn't look like he was on the wind-up – but still, I reckon he was only repeating what he'd heard. I know what these places are like.

'No heating,' said Duffy. 'No window. Bucket to shit in. You have to sleep on the floor and hope the rats aren't hungry.'

'Rats?' asked Stan.

Stan don't like rats. Who does?

'There was one lad I knew,' Duffy says, hamming it up something rotten, 'they put him in there and forgot all about him, and when they went back three days later to get him, there weren't nothing left but his bones and his belt-buckle.' Shook his head. 'The rats'd had the rest.'

Stan's about to shit himself, I can see. Put a hand on his shoulder.

'It's bollocks, Stan,' I tell him, giving Duffy the evil eye. 'There's no such thing as the cell.'

Duffy just shrugs.

Later on, when it's just us, I say to Stan: 'Listen. You saw Col when he was being took away, didn't you?'

He nods.

'To the cell.'

'To wherever they was taking him. Point is, Stan, he didn't look scared, did he?'

I'm not lying. Col really didn't look like he gave a shit. I've seen lads scared before, lads scared shitless and trying to hide it, trying to look hard. They don't fool me. But Col was different. He wasn't scared of Merton and all them, you could tell. He just hated them.

'No,' Stan says. 'Col looked – brave.'

'There you go, then. Col knows this place better than any of those other bastards. If there was anything to be scared of, he'd've been scared, wouldn't he?'

Stan's head wobbles uncertainly.

'Or maybe Col's just braver than other boys,' he says.

I've nothing to say to that.

Before lights out I go and find Miss Halcombe. Normally I'd stay out of her way, but there's something I want to ask her. I don't know if bloody Duffy and Stevie have put the wind up me or what but I don't want to stay here. I don't want Stan to stay here.

I find her having a brew with Dr Merton in the staffroom.

I want us to be moved, I tell. I say it all polite. I don't think this place is right for us, I say – I want us to be moved to Wolvesley.

I even say please.

Halcombe rolls her eyes and tuts at me, but Merton's giving me a look, sort of a thoughtful look. He nods, slowly. Maybe the creepy bastard's not as bad as I made out.

'We'll have to see what we can do,' he says.

Halcombe sighs, miserable old bag that she is.

'Whatever you say, Dr Merton,' she says.

I go back to bed feeling a bit better. Sort of hopeful.

8

She drove fast and made good time. When she hit the London traffic after Stevenage she broke out the blue light; the fast lane made way for her, and when she pulled up outside the gates of Battersea Park it was just gone six o'clock.

A ghostly white SOCO tent billowed and boomed in the wind. It wasn't as cold here as it had been in Whitby, but that wasn't saying much. She buttoned her coat as she made her way into the gloom of the park. Two teenagers with scooters were loitering under the trees, speculating gobbily on what had happened ('I *saw* it, bruv – there was bare blood, I swear down.'). As she approached the tent, a PC in uniform approached to cut her off: *Move along, miss, you're trespassing on a crime-scene* . . . Changed his tune sharpish when he got close enough to recognize her. Touched his cap; pointed her over to the far corner of the park, where two uniformed officers were speaking to a dark-haired man in a pale-grey suit.

For an irrational half-second she thought it was Sam Harrington, and her stomach lurched – but no, this was no MoJ fixer. It was Detective Inspector Robin Chalmers.

'Chalmers.'

The tall DI curtly dismissed the two uniforms; turned to her with a smile. Looked faintly pissed-off beneath it, though.

'Cox. Wasn't expecting you.'

'What's the story here?'

Chalmers looked over at the tent, ran both his hands through his thick hair, sighed.

'Pretty nasty,' he said. 'Old guy. Stabbed in the arm, bled out before anyone could help.'

'Where are we at?'

'The body's already been taken away. I've got uniform scouting for witnesses.' He looked at her. 'I've got it all under control, Cox. No need for you to hang around.'

She shrugged. She had no time for this kind of jockeying for position.

'Tell it to the DCI. He called me back from Yorkshire for this. No dinner and a five-hour drive says it's my case, Rob.'

Chalmers made a rueful face, held up his hands in surrender.

'All yours. Wasn't enjoying it much anyway.'

'So give me the detail.'

He flipped open his notebook.

'Reginald Allis, seventy-one. Found dead on the footpath just after noon. Preliminary examination indicates that he was stabbed in the arm, and the knife severed the brachial artery.'

'Unlucky.'

'Maybe, maybe not. He managed to crawl a few metres before he bled to death. Dog-walker found him, called it in. It's always bloody dog-walkers, isn't it? Poor fuckers.'

'Witnesses?'

'No one's come forward yet.'

'Do we have CCTV?'

Chalmers gave her a roll-eyed look.

'This is London. What do you think? I've sent to SecuriLab for the footage.'

Cox nodded. Mugging gone wrong, she supposed. Should've let Chalmers keep it. She was about to go inspect the murder scene – expecting not much more than a sad stretch of bloodstained footpath – when one of the scene-of-crime team came past, rustling in his disposable suit. Cox gave him a nod; noticed that he was carrying a wallet in a clear plastic bag.

She stopped him with an outstretched hand.

'Is that the victim's?'

The SOCO was a young guy, a Chinese-Londoner she'd encountered before.

'Yes, ma'am.'

'A wallet? It wasn't taken?'

'Maybe the mugger got spooked by the blood, made a run for it?' put in Chalmers.

She took the bagged wallet from the SOCO, turned it over in her hands. Looked at the guy.

'It's – Chang, isn't it? Mind if I take a look?'

'Be my guest,' Chang shrugged.

Cox pulled a pair of latex gloves from her coat pocket, broke open the sterile packaging, pulled them on with a practised snap. Opened the evidence bag.

It was a plain leather wallet, high street quality, nothing flash. Inside she found sixty quid in twenties, a cash card, credit card, driver's licence (she mentally noted the address in Pimlico), a loyalty card for a coffee-shop, a British Library pass, a diabetes card, with emergency contact listed (that would make things easier), a few receipts held together by a paperclip.

'Not much,' she muttered, half to herself. 'But more than enough to keep a smackhead happy.'

She thumbed absently through the thin wad of receipts: a petrol station in Acton, a tailor's in the West End, a computer-repair place . . .

No way . . .

The last receipt was for the Olympus Grill.

She smoothed it out with her thumb. Greek salad, kleftiko, moussaka. One litre of white wine. Dinner for two, surely. Dated 25 December.

She felt a jolt inside; was aware of a tremor in the hand that held the receipt. She slipped it back in the wallet, Chalmers gave no sign of having noticed her surprise: he was looking into the middle distance, smoothing a lapel. She took out the diabetes card and snapped shut the wallet. 'There's your next of kin,' she said.

She handed the wallet back to Chang, thanked him, turned back to DI Chalmers.

'So?' he said.

'So I want you to finish up here. Full statements from those kids with the bikes, okay?'

'Yeah, I know the drill. But what the hell, Cox? I thought you wanted this one. What was all that crap about driving all the way from Yorkshire?'

'Something's come up. Can't wait.' She smiled, gave him a nudge as she walked away. 'You're back on the case, Chalmers.'

9

The black concierge (Simon, his name badge said) looked too bored to care about anything.

'Do you know Reginald Allis? Old gentleman, white, balding with grey hair. He lived here.'

'Allis?' The concierge wearily consulted a wirebound folder. 'Yes, Allis, R. H. Allis. He lives here. Flat 59.'

'Do you know him? Personally, I mean?'

'Nah. Not really.'

'Could you let me into his flat?'

'Huh?'

Cox flashed her badge. It was either that or slap him across the face. It seemed to wake him up a little. He blinked.

'Mr Allis was found dead today,' Cox said. 'We're treating the death as suspicious. I'm DI Cox. I'm heading up the investigation.'

The concierge nodded.

'I – I see.'

'Just the key will do.'

Ten years ago, it would have worked nine times out of ten. Now people tended to be more cautious, and it was more like one in five. If he asked for a warrant, she was ready with the next level of excuses. *Do you really want me to get my chief out of bed? Better do this quietly, without upsetting any of the other residents, right?* After that it was the strong arm.

Can I see your work visa? Not got it with you? That's a shame . . .
Very occasionally, even that didn't work, especially if they really were hiding something.

'Can I see that badge again?'

'Sure.' She showed him, and he took a good long look. Cox tried to look relaxed.

If he insisted on a warrant, she'd have been screwed. A warrant would have meant going upstairs; and she was pretty sure someone upstairs didn't want her chasing up this kind of lead – didn't want her to join the dots.

But Simon was the one in five, thankfully.

'Just a second – I'll fetch the key.'

She waited while he fumbled through another folder. He produced a Yale and handed it to her.

'Here you go. Flat 59. Third floor.'

'You're not coming with me?'

'Do you need me to?'

'Um, no.'

'Then I'll stay here.' The concierge dropped into his seat, which wheezed. 'Just give me a yell if you need anything.'

'Thanks. You've been – really helpful.'

It wasn't even a lie; being left alone to do her job was exactly the kind of help Cox needed right now.

She took a lift to the third floor; stepped out into a gently lit carpeted corridor. This was a nice place: a block of retirement flats in Pimlico, south-west London, a stone's throw from the river. Cox guessed the rents way beyond pretty much anyone employed by the Met. Quite a change from Verity Halcombe's end-terrace. Bill Radley, it seemed, had maintained a pretty varied circle of friends.

If 'friends' was the right word.

She found Allis's flat, let herself in, closed the door quietly behind her. She put on another pair of gloves and flicked on the lights. Took a few seconds to scan the place. She was no design critic, God knew, but the way this flat had been kitted out struck her as wildly overdone. The furniture was ornate and heavy-looking, the carpet deep-piled, the drawn curtains dark and thick. Gaudy modern art prints decorated the walls. Cox found the overall effect suffocating.

The place smelled of expensive air-freshener. It was cold.

She slipped off her shoes and moved through the sitting room into a spacious study. Again, the writing table was a grand piece – eighteenth-century, maybe? – and highly polished. Above the table, in contrast to the modern prints in the other room, was a copy of a Victorian oil in deep reds and browns. A bookcase covered one wall. Cox scanned the titles: mostly pretty technical stuff, ranging across psychology, education, philosophy, sociology . . .

One shelf, she saw with interest, was given over to books by Allis himself. She picked one at random: *The Fundamentals of Child Psychology*. The back cover had a black-and-white photo of the author: Allis, in cord jacket and polo-neck, staring intelligently into the lens with a crooked, knowing smile. He looked about forty. She checked the publication date: 1984 – yep, that checked out.

She replaced it on the shelf. Nothing else here seemed out of the ordinary.

There was a laptop computer open on the writing table.

It had gone into standby mode. Who knew, Cox thought, what secrets that hard drive might hold? Who knew what she might uncover with a quick riffle through the Documents folder or a glance at Allis's search history? But she scotched the thought quickly. If she even touched the laptop, she knew, she'd be in way over her head. Oh, for the skills of a DiMacedo!

She was about to return to the sitting room when her phone rang. Its strident buzz startled her; it brought home to her how quiet the flat was.

Glanced at the screen – well, speak of the devil . . .

'Don. What have you got for me?'

'How do you know I'm not just calling for a chat?'

Cox smiled; took a seat in a wicker chair by the bookcase.

'Something must've piqued your interest to drag you away from GTA5,' she said.

'GTA5? What do you think this is, 2013? But you're right. I've been looking into the old girl your friend Radley sent flowers to.'

'For. Not to. She died.'

'Whatever. What do you know about her?'

'Not much. Worked with kids, from what I gather. They gave her an OBE for it.'

'Specifically, underprivileged kids. She worked at Hampton Hall, a big children's care home, very well thought of.'

'Is it in the Midlands?'

'Uh-huh. Good guess. Now, what's interesting about old Verity's career –'

'I knew there had to be something.'

'– is that, after years of diligent service at Hampton Hall, in 1987, she ups and quits. Just like that. Doesn't give a reason, just clears off. Leaves Hampton Hall and Walsall behind for ever.'

Walsall. That tripped something in her mind. Didn't Bill Radley start his career in the Walsall area? She'd have to check the file.

'Seems out of character.'

'Yes it does, Spook, well spotted.'

'Thanks, Don. Now, listen –'

'I'm going to have to stop you there. I sense you're about to ask me for another favour, but this is now officially well past knocking-off time.'

'Don. Come on. This is important.'

'You're forgetting I don't work for the police any more, Cox. No tidy overtime payments for me. Besides, I'm due at a cocktail reception in an hour, big client, three-line whip. And I'm not even dressed yet.'

'That's a mental image I could've lived without. But c'mon, Don – please? You can't let this drop now. You want to know why Verity Halcombe left Hampton as much as I do.'

A long pause.

A long sigh.

'Fu-u-u-u-ck. Cox, you owe me big-time.'

She grinned.

'I do. I know. I'll make it up to you.'

'I really do have to go schmooze at this thing, though. I'll cry off early and pull a late one on this – there'll be an email waiting for you in the morning.'

'Thanks, Don.'

'Now if we're all done with the emotional manipulation, I need to go put some trousers on. Later, Spook.'

She put away her phone. Took down another of Allis's books – after what DiMacedo had just told her, its title had new significance. *Outcomes for Children in Care.*

On a hunch, she flipped to the index. She wasn't sure what she was looking for. Radley wasn't there, of course. Nor was Verity Halcombe. But right there, beside where she would have been: 'Hampton Hall, Walsall, 152, 168'.

She opened the book. And there is was. A black-and-white picture of an austere Victorian mansion building. Cox snapped the book shut, laid it on the table. Sat for a moment, listening to her heart galloping.

What the fuck was going on? Bill Radley sent flowers for Verity Halcombe; Verity worked in a place that Reginald Allis wrote about; Reginald Allis had a falling-out over dinner with Bill Radley. The details were a mystery, still, but the outline was complete – and Cox didn't like the way it looked.

A suicide brought on by gambling debts. A death from natural causes, heart failure, maybe a stroke. A botched mugging in a London park.

Or three premeditated and connected murders?

Murder meant motive. The most important question in a murder investigation wasn't *who*; it was *why*.

Cox said it to herself, now, out loud in the stifling silence of Reginald Allis's study. Three people, respectable, middle-aged, pretty blameless as far as anyone knew, killed in cold blood, within a short space of time.

'Why?'

The Fifth Day of Christmas, 1986

Christ alive. There's something up today. They had us out of bed two hours early, for a start, to clean the dorm. Place stinks of carbolic, enough to make your eyes water.

Everywhere's swept and polished. Staff all in proper uniform, name badges, the lot. Merton's swanking about the place in a suit; looks like Halcombe's had her hair done special.

'Big day,' she keeps saying.

Eventually word comes down the grapevine: some specialists are coming to Hampton, to do a study, some sort of research. I don't know what sort of research you'd do here. Look at the bedbugs through a microscope, maybe. Test the food for bubonic bloody plague.

'Will they be specialists like Dr Merton?' Stan asks me.

'I dunno.' I shrug. 'I s'pose so.'

Stevie says he's seen Merton setting up a camera, a big video camera on a tripod, in one of the rooms — for interviews.

'Be like being back in the nick,' Judd grunts.

I don't like the look of it all. Dunno why. Merton's twanging like a wire. Tense. Halcombe's not right, neither; excited, frightened, don't know what. Whole bloody place feels on the brink of a nervous bloody breakdown.

Weather doesn't help. Gone ten now and we've still got the lights on. Dark, proper bloody dark. Clouds all the way across the sky, dark purple like bruises.

They arrive at eleven o'clock. Three cars pull up in the car park.

'This,' Dr Merton says, stepping into the rec room with a spindly bloke we've not seen before, 'is Dr Allis.'

We all look at him. Pinstriped suit, cane in his hand. Wire-rimmed glasses. He smiles without showing his teeth. Reminds me of Merton. There must be a bloody factory somewhere, turning out these skinny 'specialists'.

'Hello, boys,' this Allis says. His voice isn't like Merton's, it's deeper and rounder, like an actor's voice in a film.

Couple of the lads mutter, 'Hello.'

Merton tells us that Allis is going to be with us for a few days, conducting research for a 'very important study'. The pair of them seem very pally. Creeps of a feather. Sooner we get shifted to Wolvesley, the better.

I'm one of the first. There's no camera; just a table and chairs, Allis and Merton sitting opposite with mugs of tea and open notebooks. They don't offer me a cup of tea. Wouldn't have had one anyroad, but still.

They ask me a load of questions, stuff I've been asked a million times, by coppers, psychologists, social workers. Always the same bloody questions.

About my mum, my dad. About that bastard Malky.

'Did this Malky ever — touch you?' Allis asks.

Only to give me a smack in the mouth, I tell him.

They ask about how I am, whether I'm well, whether I'm happy. I tell them I'm all right. What else am I going to say? I am all right.

They ask me about Stan. I don't like them asking about Stan. I tell them he's eight, that he's clever for his age — which is true, he's a proper good reader — and I don't tell them anything else. I say he's all right.

'But you want to be moved to Wolvesley?' Merton says with a toothy smile.

I shrug.

'Yeah. It's s'posed to be nice.'

When they're done with me, after about half an hour, although it feels like loads longer, they tell me to send in Stan next.

I do, and I tell him not to be frightened, it's just a load of questions, same as always.

He says he's not frightened. What is there to be frightened of? he asks me.

I just tell him to hurry up, or else he'll be in bother.

He was always dead good at going to the doctor, was Stan. Even when he was little. He could get injected, even, and hardly even cry.

It was because he trusted them, I think. Knew they were there to look after him.

I'm twitchy till he comes out. Try to read a comic but I can't even concentrate on that. Desperate bloody Dan too much for me. Just lie on my bed instead. Stare at the cracks in the ceiling.

Then he comes out – and he's grinning and jiggling a paper bag of sweets in his hand.

'Jelly beans,' he says.

I didn't get any sweets.

'What're they for?'

'For being good.'

I give him a scowl.

'You don't want to be taking stuff off them,' I tell him. 'Next time, don't take nothing off them.'

He looks confused.

'Take what you can get, you always said, Rob.'

It's true. I used to say that.

'Well, this is different,' I say. 'It's different here.'

'Different how?'

I tell him to shut up. Shut up and eat his precious bloody jelly beans.

Then he says: 'I have to go back in, soon.'

I look at him. They didn't say anything to me about going back.

Why the bloody hell does Stan have to go back? He's eight years old. What is he going to tell them?

'What for?'

'Physical examination. Dr Allis's gone away but Dr Merton needs to give me a physical examination.'

Like at the doctor's, he thinks. Take your temperature, look down your throat, shine a little torch in your ear.

I'm not sure about this. I'm not bloody sure about this at all.

So when Miss Halcombe comes in and says that Dr Merton would like to see Stanley Trevayne again, I shove Stan down his bed – he spills a handful of jelly beans – and stand up instead.

'What's it for, Miss Halcombe? What does he want to see Stan for?'

She looks uncertain. Sometimes I think she's batty, Miss Halcombe.

'He just – he just wants to ask Stan some more questions, that's all.'

'Physical examination, he said. That's what Stan told me.'

She gulps. I can see her hand's shaking. Wonder if she's been on the gin or something.

'Well, he just – Dr Merton just needs to see that Stan's all right. That he's been looked after properly. A check-up.'

'He is all right. I told them that.'

Halcombe seems to get cross all of a sudden. Red in the face and stuff. Leans down – doesn't have to lean very far – to put her face right up close to mine.

'Dr Merton is a very important, very clever man,' she hisses. 'We are very lucky to have him here.' Straightens up. Tries to get a grip. He might impress you, missus, I think. He don't impress me.

'Well, Stan don't like being examined. He'll have a fit. Always used to make a proper big fuss when he had to go to the doctor's.'

She's looking at me uncertainly.

'Dr Merton specifically said –'

'I'll do it.' I make the decision just like that. Only it's not even a decision, I don't even have to think. The idea comes into my head and straight away I know it's the only thing I can do. 'I'll do it,' I say again. 'Whatever he wanted to ask our Stan – well, he can ask me instead.'

She doesn't like it much, I can see that. Says she'll have to check with Dr Merton – check that that's all right.

She goes tottering off, off to the office where Stevie says he saw the camera being set up. The blinds are drawn at the office windows.

After a minute she comes out again.

Very well, she says, you can take Stan's place on this occasion. I've spoken to the doctor, she says. The doctor says it's fine.

10

With regard to the Children's Aid and Rehabilitation Enter-
prise (CARE), participant care institutions — among which are
Hampton Hall for Underprivileged Children (HHUC), a care
institution which the present author serves as a member of the board
of trustees — were aligned in support of objectives targeted at
care-provision in child-welfare cases deemed particularly challenging
by a panel of early-years and education specialists . . .

It was dry stuff. Allis's writing style was pompous and
academic. But Cox read on: it *had* to be in here somewhere, the link, the key to this case; there had to be
something solid, something meaningful, that bound the
three deaths together. Something more than a bunch of
flowers and a disagreement over dinner.

She rubbed her eyes and turned the page to the next
chapter: *Changing Paradigms, Affecting Outcomes.* Sighed;
read on.

Then stopped.

A noise, in the next room. A window, she thought, being
eased open — by someone trying very hard not to be heard.

She set down the book carefully. Stood. There was a
cane, dark bamboo with a polished gold-and-glass top,
propped against the desk. She took it up, hefted it in her
hand. Its weightiness was reassuring.

But it wouldn't do her much good against a gun, a
machete, a taser —

Someone had killed Reginald Allis. Now someone –
someone moving softly, furtively, making no footsteps on
the thick carpet, but not able, not quite, to keep their
breathing unheard – was in Reginald Allis's flat.

Sounded like a man; something in the pitch or tone
of the faint, regular breathing. Cox waited. Strained to listen. There was a smell too – a familiar scent she couldn't
place.

Could she even hear him any more? Had he moved
away, into another room?

Or was he holding his breath and heading straight
for her?

She edged towards the study door. Couldn't see anyone
in the sitting room. She moved forwards, widening the
angle: still no one. But she could feel a cold draught from
the open window.

From here, she was pretty sure she could make it to the
door in, what, five paces? A matter of seconds. Get the
hell out of there; call in backup.

Backup. Backup meant questions, reports, a call-log.
Backup meant trouble.

And staying here? she asked herself sourly. *That's the safe,
sensible, no-worries option, is it?*

At least it meant she was in control. She was still in
charge.

In one movement she shouldered open the study door
and stepped out into the centre of the sitting room.

'Police. Show yourself.'

In her best copper's voice, all authority, not a hint of
wobble or weakness. She'd worked hard at that, down the
years.

She heard a sharp intake of breath from one of the adjoining rooms. Shifted her balance on to the balls of her feet. As the door moved cautiously open she raised the heavy bamboo cane.

'Kerry?'

Greg Wilson, a disbelieving half-grin on his face, stepped out from behind the door.

'Fucking *hell.*'

She was on him before he could move, forced his arms roughly behind his back, squeezed the cuffs on to his wrists. Wilson, pushed off-balance, stumbled, fell to his knees with a grunt.

Perfect. Cox took a breath; tried to compose herself, to ignore the rising nausea of the adrenaline drop.

The journalist looked up at her in bewilderment.

'What the hell are you doing here?' he said.

'That's my first question,' she said, settling herself on the edge of the sofa. 'And once you've answered that, I want you to tell me what you know about the murder of Reginald Allis.'

The blood drained from Wilson's face.

He didn't know anything about any murder. He'd never even met Reginald Allis. He'd had no idea the man was dead. The words spilled out of his mouth.

'Do you have any idea how many times I've heard that before?'

Wilson nodded, deadpan, weary-looking. She'd let him clamber up on to the easy-chair; he sat slumped, awkward, arms still cuffed behind his back.

'I know, Kerry. But in this case it's the truth.' He caught her eye. 'And yes, I know that's what they all say.'

'If you didn't know Allis was dead, why did you come here?'

'Same as you: following up a lead. Only I was hoping to ask the man himself a few questions.' He squinted thoughtfully at Cox. 'What were you hoping to find?'

'You're in no position to ask me questions. A lead? A lead on what?'

Wilson struggled to sit forwards.

'Listen, Kerry,' he said. 'You know William Radley didn't kill himself. It was a set-up, and not a very tidy one. I saw it a mile off. So I did some digging.'

She was surprised; if whoever was behind all this had the Ministry of Justice on their side, what were they doing letting Fleet Street off the leash?

'Does Mathieson know about this?'

Stan Mathieson, Wilson's editor, was a veteran news-paperman and a shrewd political operator.

'Mathieson? You *are* out of the loop.'

'How do you mean?'

'I'm freelance now.' Wilson looked uncomfortable.

'He fired you?'

'We – we had a parting of ways.'

She took that as a 'yes'.

'So you're here on your own initiative?' she pushed. '"Following up a lead"? What lead exactly?'

'A journalist never reveals –'

'You've got one minute, Wilson. One minute to give me a reason not to take you in.'

Wilson swallowed, sniffed.

'Okay,' he said. 'Okay. William Radley met Reginald Allis for dinner on Christmas Day. A place on Ealing Broadway.'

Cox nodded, kept her face carefully expressionless.

'I got a look at the CCTV files from the newsagent's across the road,' Wilson went on. 'Chased up the registration number of the guy's car. Mr Reginald Allis, resident at this address.' He shrugged. 'That was all. Not much to go on – but I had time on my hands.'

'So you thought, what the hell, let's go breaking and entering.' She shook her head. 'Christ, Wilson, you've landed yourself in a mess this time.'

'So are you going to take me in?'

She began to say 'no' then hesitated. If she said no, Wilson was going to want to know why – and how was she going to answer that? Just sit him down and explain that she was there without authorization, that she was going pretty drastically off-piste by sticking with this case, that she was on her last chance with her boss, that if anyone at the Yard found out she'd been there her neck would be on the line?

Or let him think that she was letting him go out of generosity or friendship – for old times' sake? That was a dangerous course, too, she knew, in its own way.

'I want to keep this simple.' She stood abruptly, leaned over and unfastened Wilson's cuffs. As she did, she leaned close to him and she caught another whiff of his aftershave and, despite herself, despite everything, it brought a tingle of carnality. *No, Kerry. Don't go there.* He gave a grunt of satisfaction, wrung his hands. 'Get out of here,' she said. Nodded towards the window. 'The way you came in. I'll forget you were ever here.'

Wilson was looking at her narrowly, rubbing his chafed wrists.

'And if I read this right, Kerry, you'd rather I did you the same courtesy?'

She returned his look.

'Like I say, I'd rather keep this simple.'

'I think it's a bit late for that.' He took a step towards her. 'Kerry. Come on. What the hell is going on here? First Radley, now Allis. What's the story?'

'That's all it ever is to you, isn't it? A story.'

'Come on. It's a turn of phrase. Something funny is going on here, we both know it. I'm not stupid enough to ask you to trust me.' He shrugged, self-deprecatingly. 'But remember, I can help you, if you need help.'

He almost sounded sincere, Cox thought. Almost.

'I don't need help.'

'Sure. But like I say – I'm here if you need it.'

He moved to the window; she watched him climb nimbly up on to the sill, clamber out on to the adjoining flat roof. She shut the window behind him. Locked it.

She woke in the night, alone in the dark. Heart hammering. Hair plastered to her brow with cold sweat.

Gulped down a breath. Let her eyes adjust to the blackness.

The same dream, always the same dream, though she hadn't had it for at least a fortnight. The man in the mask.

She'd seen worse things, far worse, back in her time with Operation Refuge. When she looked back on it now,

Christ . . . she wondered how she stood it. How she kept it together. Videos, photographs, transcripts.

You grew numb, she knew. You never quite got *used* to it, exactly – but over time you found you'd grown an extra skin, a layer to protect the raw parts, the parts of you that hurt too much to bear. And then, you found, the pictures and videos stopped being shocking; the things they showed were still nauseating, monstrous, vile – but you could look at them, watch them, without turning away.

What was the phrase she'd read somewhere? 'The banality of evil'. Yes, that was it.

You watched the videos, you made notes. You translated the horrors on the screen into pencil-marks on the page. *Oral rape; victim M, 5–7yrs; offender M, cauc, star tattoo lower midriff. Vaginal rape; victims F, 7–9yrs, 10–12yrs; offender M, cauc, no distinguishing features.*

People hurting people. That was all it was.

The man in the mask was different.

There was a victim – hell, there was always a victim – but you barely saw them, in the footage Refuge had. You saw an arm, thin, pale, a child's arm, striped dark-red with rope burns, bent at the elbow, blurry in the foreground; you heard a child's whimpering sobs.

But mainly you saw him.

It was old footage, low-res and flickering; probably it'd been transferred from videotape at some point. The camera was fixed, tilted slightly upwards from the horizontal.

He was tall, well built. He moved into shot purposefully, conscious, it was clear, of where the camera was, how to use the angles to dramatic advantage. He wore a white robe, toga-like, knotted over one shoulder.

And he wore a white mask.

Somehow, she hadn't been able to forget him like she'd forgotten so many other monsters, so many other horrors; somehow, he'd got under her skin. He wasn't like all the rest. What she'd seen on that flickering screen wasn't just abuse, wasn't just cruelty and pain; it was performance.

Cox threw back the covers, climbed from bed, shivering as the cold raised goosebumps on her bare arms and legs. Flicked on the bathroom light, blinked in the glare. Fumbled in the cabinet for a small, hard-plastic bottle.

One of these days, she thought, unscrewing the cap, *I'll give that bloody police counsellor a call.*

The pills were only ever a short-term answer, a stopgap measure to get her through a rough night or a long day. The force had been trying to bundle her into therapy for God knew how long; *they don't want to have any awkward questions to answer the day I finally snap and stick my head in the oven*, she cynically thought.

Gulped down a couple of the blue-and-green capsules. Yep, one of these days she'd go and get herself sorted, once and for all; but not now – how the hell could she find the time? And she needed to be sharp, together, to deal with this.

In the kitchen she flipped on the coffee machine and fired up her laptop. It was nearly seven. Dusty grey light filtered through the window-blind.

There was an email from DiMacedo – sent at 3 a.m. She poured coffee and sat down to read.

Morning, Spook. Bad news: nothing new on dear old Verity. Not yet, anyway. I'll keep digging. I admit it: you've hooked me.

Cox smiled, but it was a let-down: she had a feeling that

what happened at Hampton Hall was the key to all this – whatever the hell 'this' was.

Don, she knew, had taken the therapy option. *Christ*, Don DiMacedo – the sort of guy who'd been able to eat a spicy hot pizza while he'd sifted the megabytes of sick filth that came their way.

She read on.

I know you'll be crying into your coffee over this, so by way of a consolation prize, I dug out William Radley's full service record for you. It's attached. It all looks pretty standard to me, but maybe it'll help.

I blew off the cocktail reception, by the way. Hope they don't fire me. Love, DD.

She downloaded the file – a PDF, scanned from dog-eared typescript – and pinged it open.

Radley had begun his career in the Midlands, at Sutton Coldfield – what was that, maybe ten miles from Walsall? He'd had quite a reputation as a young PC, earning two commendations in his first eighteen months on the force; shifted to CID precociously early, made DS while still in his twenties; transferred to the Met, and kept on rising. In the early nineties he'd been seconded to the RUC in Northern Ireland, in an undisclosed capacity – the details had been redacted from the file. Then in around 2000 he came back to London and took up the well-paid Scotland Yard desk job that was every veteran copper's dream.

If anyone had ever deserved it, Cox reflected, Bill Radley had.

Her phone buzzed on the desktop – Greg Wilson. She ignored it, yawning, swilling the dregs of her coffee in the bottom of her cup. If she was going to stop this case spinning out of control, she had to keep Wilson at arm's length.

Should she call Naysmith? she wondered. No: she didn't have enough yet, didn't *know* enough yet. If she drip-fed him every new clue, every whisper and half-lead, he'd lose patience, pull her off the case for good. Before she went to the DCI, she needed a solid case, something that'd hit him hard between the eyes. Right now, that seemed a long way off.

Besides, calling Pete Naysmith at 7 a.m. – just as the hangover was getting to work – was never the smartest move.

Instead, she called up the number of the evidence room at Acton. As it was, based on what they knew for sure, the link between Radley and Allis was pretty weak – as thin and fragile as a creased restaurant receipt. There had to be more. Had Allis been found with a phone on him? An address book?

As she waited for someone in Evidence to pick up, she wondered who'd be on shift. Chang, she hoped. Maybe Chalmers would be passing through.

Just as long as it wasn't –

'Acton Evidence Room. DS Malory speaking.'

Cox suppressed a sigh. Gloria Malory. Not her best pal on the force.

'Gloria, it's Kerry Cox.'

'Good morning, inspector!' Her tone was glassy, bright and painfully false. 'How can I help?'

'The evidence from the Battersea Park stabbing, Reginald Allis – has it been logged yet?'

'Hmm. Let me see.' There was a pause, a rattle of a

keyboard. Then Gloria made a funny little noise, a bit surprised, a bit self-satisfied: '*Hmf.*'

'What?'

'Well, I'm sorry, ma'am, but it doesn't look as though you're the lead investigating officer on the Allis case.'

Keep your temper, Cox. You don't need any more enemies.

'No. No, I'm not, Chalmers is. But look, Gloria, I just need to know if we found a phone on Allis's body, and –'

'I'm *so* sorry, ma'am. I can't give out this sort of information without authorization from DI Chalmers or a senior officer.' A brittle laugh. 'You know how it is. "Computer says no"! I'm *so* sorry,' she said again.

'Look, Gloria, I know you've got the information I need right there in front of you. If you could just –'

Malory's tone turned faintly frosty, metallic.

'As per the latest data management regulations, ma'am, I am unable –'

'Yes, yes. I know all that.'

'DI Chalmers is due on shift at eleven this morning. If you'd like to come into the station in person, I'm sure he'd be happy to assist you with your inquiry. Was there anything else, ma'am?'

About as much warmth as a computerized answermachine, and about as helpful.

'If I keep pressing "9" will I get through to a human?'

'Pardon, ma'am?'

'Never mind. Goodbye, sergeant.'

It was a good thing you couldn't slam down a mobile phone, Cox thought, jabbing the red button to end the call. She'd get through ten phones a week.

She rattled out a quick email to Chalmers, asking him

to catch her up on the Allis case. She kept it short, avoided going into detail.

Poured herself another coffee. Stared into the middle distance. Felt lost.

Time to admit it: she needed help, real, on-the-ground help. And she was pretty much out of options. Pretty much – but not completely.

Naysmith would say she was off her head. Serena McAvoy and her legal team would take an even dimmer view.

No one has to know except me, Cox thought. *Problem is, even I think this is insane . . .*

She picked up her phone.

11

'Is this really necessary?'

He was bleary-eyed, shabby in a checked shirt and worn cords.

Cox popped open the passenger door.

'Just get in.'

The traffic was light – by London standards – out this way. Rain spotted the windscreen.

'So are you going to tell me where we're going?' asked Greg Wilson.

'North,' said Cox.

'I'd gathered that much,' Wilson muttered as they moved out on to the North Circular.

All she'd told him on the phone was that there was another lead, a lead he didn't know about, on the Radley case; that she was heading out to investigate, if he felt like tagging along; that she'd pick him up from his place in Kilburn in half an hour's time.

At first he'd been resistant: 'One minute you're clapping me in bloody handcuffs, the next you're bringing me along on an investigation?'

But his heart hadn't been in it. Just for show.

Now he said: 'I have a feeling I'm not the only one working freelance on this.'

Cox gave him nothing. Didn't take her eyes off the road.

'How d'you mean?'

'Come on. There's no way your chief super wants you working on Radley's death. There's pressure being brought to bear on this case, heavy stuff, from high up. I got a call from my old newsdesk last night, giving me a heads-up: there's a lot of legal noise being made in the background, Cox. Threats from the Radley family.'

'A man died, in inconclusive circumstances,' Cox said flatly. 'That merits a police investigation.'

'*I* know that. But I don't think Scotland Yard agrees.'

'I'm just doing my job,' she said. Pulled out on to the motorway roundabout; slowed as she saw a green light up ahead switch to amber. Wilson just shrugged; happy to drop the subject – at least for now.

Cox glanced in her rear-view.

'Can you tell me what we're looking for,' Wilson pressed, 'once we get to wherever we're going? I –'

He broke off as Cox slammed hard on the accelerator. The light was red when she roared through; a lorry lurching forwards from the left braked, rocked forward, sounded its horn gratingly. Cox checked her rear-view again; a grey Merc had come through the lights after her, slewing across two lanes to avoid an incoming motorcyclist.

She noticed Wilson's knuckles were white on the door-handle. Well, let him think she was just a madcap driver, for now. See what happens.

'We're after something solid,' she said. 'Something that makes *sense.*'

Swiftly she filled him in on Verity Halcombe, the flowers Radley sent, the info about Hampton Hall in Reginald Allis's book.

'That place is the common link here,' she said. 'That's my hunch, anyway.'

'You got me out of bed at eight o'clock on a hunch?'

'Don't pretend you had anything better to do.'

'So how do you read it? Some sort of geriatric love triangle?'

'With two deaths, maybe that'd be worth looking into. But three? Doesn't make a lot of sense.' She shook her head. 'I think it's something – something worse than that. Something that happened, that made Verity Halcombe leave so abruptly – something that Radley and Allis knew about.'

'They were killed to keep them quiet?' Wilson's tone was sceptical. 'Thirty-odd years later?'

'It's my best guess,' Cox shrugged. 'Let me know if you come up with anything better.'

The traffic got thicker, and the rain heavier, as she moved across the motorway to the filter lane for the M4 exit.

In a forced-sounding, casual, conversational voice, Wilson asked: 'How's things at home? How's it going with Matthew and – Aidan, is it?'

Cox felt an internal shutter go up. Happened automatically these days.

'Fine,' she said.

'You're still – separated?'

She moved quickly to stamp on *that* one.

'We're talking things through, working some stuff out,' she lied.

Wilson nodded understandingly.

'That's good. Listen, I never wanted – I never meant to

ruin things between the two of you. It was a mistake, and I'm sorry for it.'

This was a conversation she didn't want to have.

'That wasn't your mistake,' she said shortly. Moved out on to the spray-shrouded M4. 'It was mine.'

'My granddad died in a shit-hole like this,' Wilson said conversationally, sparking up a cigarette in the gravelled car park.

Cox took in the rain-darkened redbrick façade of what had once been Hampton Hall – now Evergreen Care Home ('Providing Safe and Secure Facilities in Later Life'). It looked like what it was: a run-down Victorian pile in a sprawl of suburbs near the Wolverhampton turn-off, repurposed, unloved.

Imagine having to live here, she thought. Imagine having to die here.

'Pretty bleak,' she said.

'Uh-uh.' Wilson nodded, trod out his fag. 'I've seen prisons look after their inmates better than some of these places.'

'Come on.' Cox started down the flagged path towards the front door. 'Let's see if anyone here remembers nice old Miss Halcombe.'

'Hope they've got long memories,' Wilson grunted.

A harassed-looking young healthcare assistant in a white tunic answered Cox's knock.

'We've no visitors booked in today,' she said.

Cox paused, badge in hand.

'None? No one in this whole place has any visitors today?'

The assistant shrugged, leaning on the half-open door.

'I'm very busy,' she said. 'We need to get the lunches ready. Who did you say you were here to see?'

Now she showed her badge. The assistant flinched, straightened up out of her slouch.

'Detective Inspector Cox, Metropolitan Police. We'd like to speak to the manager.'

'You mean Mr Latham? He's the owner, but he's not on site much. You might be able to talk to the matron, though. Mrs Hazlewood. I'll see if she's free. Hang on.'

She hurried off, leaving the door open. Cox exchanged an unimpressed look with Wilson; stepped inside.

The lobby carpet was threadbare, the walls magnolia-washed. Fine cobwebs drifted under the high white ceiling.

'Bloody hell, it was warmer outside,' Wilson said, zipping up his jacket.

There was a desk with a computer, a tray of files, a half-empty mug of tea. On the farthest wall, a dusty red fire-extinguisher was fixed beside a defibrillator. Three doors led off the lobby. One was marked 'Lounge & TV', another 'Staff Only'. The third was open and led into a corridor. A sign gave directions to the lifts and residential rooms.

It all had the feel, Cox thought, of a cheap hotel – the kind no one would stay at twice, given the choice.

The assistant reappeared out of the 'Staff Only' door, gestured impatiently at them to follow her and barged through into the 'Lounge & TV' room.

Cox caught the door before it closed, went through.

Paused to get her bearings. Heard Wilson behind her mutter, 'Christ.'

Seven grey faces were looking up at her from easy chairs ranged on both sides of a long rectangular room. Three striplights cast stark shadows; one, badly connected, flickered strobe-like every few seconds. It smelled as though the high windows had never been opened: a fug of disinfectant, drying linen, body odour, air-freshener and urine. There was, as promised, a TV, a big old cathode-ray set tuned to a gameshow re-run.

No one was watching it. They were all watching Cox.

'Good morning,' she nodded uncertainly, moving ahead – the assistant had already passed out through another door at the far end of the room.

An elderly woman, wearing a grubby T-shirt under a knitted cardigan, called out to her as she passed: 'I'm glad you've come, pet, Amanda's going to take us shopping . . .'

A man sat by the television worked his jaw silently, his lower lip hung with fine strands of drool. Cox heard a reedy male voice behind her call out to Wilson: 'It's our Trev! Over here, Trev. I'm over here, son!'

'Give me a one-way ticket to Switzerland over this, any day of the week,' Wilson said through gritted teeth, not bothering to keep his voice low. No one besides Cox seemed to hear.

The far door was marked 'Matron'. She knocked briskly, went in without waiting for a response; Wilson followed.

Mrs Hazlewood, the matron, was younger than she'd expected. She was seated at a desk, in conversation with the harassed assistant, when they entered; she broke off, looked up with a professional smile.

'Inspector. Good to meet you.' She stood, extended a hand. She was maybe thirty, thirty-five. Slim and long-faced, with dark hair knotted in a chignon.

She shook Wilson's hand, too. He didn't introduce himself; it was easiest, Cox supposed, for him to say nothing, to let people's easy assumptions take over. He was with a copper, who had a rank and a badge; he looked like a copper, as much as he looked like anything else; surely, then, he *was* a copper.

It was better than telling a lie. Lies, she knew, could trip you up.

As the assistant hurried away, disappearing through an unmarked door at the back of the office, they settled into the plastic chairs across the desk from Mrs Hazlewood.

'So, how can I help?' Again the professional smile: brisk, polite, faintly chilly.

'We're investigating a – a historic incident.' It sounded lame, she knew – she could almost *hear* Wilson's eye-roll – but what else could she say? 'To be honest, Mrs Hazlewood, we're just poking about at random in the hope that something will come up.'

'Historic?'

'How much do you know about Hampton Hall?'

'That was the name of this place before it became a retirement home,' Hazlewood said. She spoke slowly and carefully – the tone of someone in the habit of assuming that whoever they were talking to was half-senile at best.

Cox nodded.

'We know that. It was a children's home. Do you know anything about the place in those days?'

'No. Before my time, I'm afraid.' She showed her teeth briefly. 'But I believe Mr Latham was the owner back then. He might be able to help.'

She seemed keen to offload responsibility for answering their questions – or to get them out of her office. Fair enough, Cox thought. No one enjoys a visit from CID.

But they weren't done yet.

'What about records? Paperwork from back then? Aren't the Hampton Hall files kept here?'

Hazlewood poked out her bottom lip, shook her head.

'I wouldn't know about that,' she said. 'My responsibility is Evergreen Care. I'm sure Mr Latham will be able to give you the information you need. I can find his address for you. He lives out of the country now.'

Cox glanced across at Wilson, who shrugged. They weren't going to get much from Matron Hazlewood, that much was clear.

Cox stood, taking up her bag and coat. Hazlewood looked relieved.

'Well, inspector, it's been –'

'Could we take a look around?'

The matron looked momentarily thrown.

'Look around?' she echoed. 'Whatever for?'

Whatever's there.

'We'd just like to get a feel for the layout of the building,' Cox improvised. 'Put our investigation into context.'

Hazlewood still looked uncertain.

'We-ell – you won't be able to go into any of the

residents' rooms, of course. The personal dignity of our residents is very important to us.'

Cox ignored Wilson's snort of derision.

'Of course,' she said. 'There's no question of infringing anyone's privacy or security.'

'Very well.' Hazlewood, frowning slightly, sat back down. 'Feel free to visit any of the communal spaces. But please, try not to cause any disturbance.'

Once more she turned on the corporate smile. Then she took up a file of paperwork and studied the first page stagily. The message was clear: *interview terminated*.

They walked back through the grim 'lounge' – the old man who'd been confused about 'Trev' was crying, while the nurse stroked his hand; the TV blared out canned laughter – and into the lobby.

'I'll wait in the car,' said Wilson shortly, holding out his hand for the keys.

'Sure?'

'I need some fucking air.'

He was grimacing; looked as though he'd eaten something rancid.

'I won't be long,' she said.

'If you're more than a week I'll send out a search party.' He turned away, hit the button to unlock the front door.

When he was gone, Cox moved towards the open door that led into a long corridor of residential rooms. Ugly striped carpet. More unadorned strip-lighting.

A few of the doors that lined the corridor on both sides were open. Cox tried not to look inside as she passed; tried not to hear the things called out to her, not to think about the desperate loneliness of the people who would see out their days at Evergreen; tried to focus.

For her purposes, this wasn't Evergreen at all. This was Hampton Hall.

Halfway along, the corridor opened out into a square alcove. There was a knackered-looking lift, a cupboard full of cleaning things – and a door. She tried the handle; it wasn't locked.

She looked quickly back down the corridor – no one around – and opened the door. Steps, an unlit staircase sloping steeply down into a cellar. The light from the corridor made an off-white rectangle on the cellar floor. Looked like concrete.

Would Mrs Hazelwood consider this a 'communal area'? Almost certainly not. She stepped down into the gloom and pulled the door firmly shut behind her.

A single room, huge, cavernous. There was an old light-switch at the foot of the stairs, coming loose from the plaster – *thank Christ*. She flicked the switch; a bare 40-watt filament bulb came weakly alive.

Grubby walls, whitewashed but not recently. A dirt-streaked concrete floor. Nothing else; the room was empty. But there was a doorway, gloomy, leading through into another dark, derelict-looking space.

Cox took a pocket torch from her back pocket. Played its frail beam across the black doorway. She saw shadows, skeletal shadows.

That room was not empty. Cox moved carefully forwards. The dirty concrete was gritty underfoot.

Again the torch beam picked out the angular shadows. As she moved, they shifted and warped, shivering across the wall. Not bones, she saw – not human bones, anyway. These were skeletons of iron, rusted, brittle; they were the frames of children's beds. Perhaps three dozen, stacked haphazardly.

She moved closer. Reached out her free hand and touched the metal of the nearest frame. Cold as a grave, coarse with corrosion. Under the light pressure of her touch the stack of beds made a noise, a soft, high-pitched whisper of protest.

Something scurried on the floor. A rat, a mouse.

What, Cox wondered, would a rat find to eat in a basement filled with nothing but scrap iron?

She moved her torch beam across the beds. Dead brown springs, comfortless tubular frames. Then, in the corner – something different. Something solid.

She sniffed the air warily. Dust. Rust. Rat-shit. Moved towards the dark shape in the corner.

Bulky, straight-edged. The torchlight gleamed briefly on metal.

Cox breathed out. She felt a soft thrum of excitement in her chest.

A filing cabinet.

It, too, was encrusted with rust. Just two drawers. She tried the upper one; it stuck, the drawer-wheels jamming on the corroded runners – but it wasn't locked. The drawer was filled front-to-back with manila files.

There didn't seem to be any order. Cox thought about pulling on a glove, but they were in the car. No need. She riffled through the files. Drew one out at random: two sheets of A4 typing paper, a black-and-white photograph of a young boy's face, a few lines of personal details. Not much more: it was clear, now, what the rats had found to eat down here. The paper was filthy and gnawed away.

Still, though, it was something. She closed the file, slipped it back into the drawer. She was about to pull out another when she heard a noise behind her – became suddenly aware of a shift in the quality of the light in the cellar.

Slammed shut the drawer, turned. The door at the top of the stairs was open. A slender figure was outlined in the corridor light.

A thin but piercing voice called out: 'Are you ready, love? Amanda's taking us shopping! Chop-chop. Let's be having you.'

Cox moved fast, slapped off the light-switch with the flat of her hand, took the steps two at a time. The last thing she needed was this poor old thing bringing Mrs Hazlewood running.

The woman blinked at her, smiling uncertainly, as she emerged into the corridor.

'You'll need your woollies, duck,' she said. 'It's perishing out there.'

'I know, I know.' Cox forced a grin. She put an arm gently on the old woman's shoulder. 'There's no need to shout. I'm right here.'

'That's exactly what Amanda says. But then she turns the telly right up!' Cox winced as the woman's right hand closed tightly on her upper arm. 'Ages since I went shopping, isn't it, love? I haven't got the plastic thing, Amanda takes charge of that. Have you got the right money for the bus? It's robbery really.'

Cox tried to pull her arm out of the woman's grip, but the thick, hard fingers held on tight.

'I know, love,' she smiled desperately, scanning up and down the corridor. The woman's voice had a penetrating quality; someone was bound to hear them. 'It's a disgrace. Now come on – let go of my arm, and let's go to wait in the lounge.'

The woman's face creased in worry.

'Is Amanda here already? Only she's not meant to leave work till five, I don't want her to –'

'*Mrs Walker!*'

The old woman's hand fell away. You had to hand it to Matron Hazlewood, Cox thought, massaging her upper arm – she knew how to speak with authority.

'What's going on here?' She came bustling up the corridor, straight-backed, clipboard in hand and professional smile turned up full. 'Inspector?'

Cox thought fast.

'I was just waiting for the lift,' she said with a gesture. 'And Mrs Walker here stopped me for a chat.' She let a hint of asperity enter her tone; the faintest implication that Hazlewood's failure to properly manage her inmates was preventing her from carrying out important police work. She was damned if she was going to stand there and be ticked off like a misbehaving schoolgirl.

'I'm *terribly* sorry.' The matron bent at the waist to speak to Mrs Walker, adopting a sing-song tone. 'I'm afraid Amanda can't take you shopping today, dear. We're going to have to go back to the lounge.' She glanced up meaningfully at Cox. 'All of us.'

'Yes, I'm pretty much done here.' Couldn't resist adding: 'For now.'

Hazlewood nodded stiffly.

They trooped along the corridor, the matron leading, Mrs Walker shuffling along in the middle – and Cox lagging behind, mind racing, wondering what kind of information might be in the rat-eaten Hampton Hall files – and what other secrets this place might be hiding.

The young assistant came hurrying up when they reached the lobby. She took Mrs Walker by the elbow, but Hazlewood cut in briskly.

'I'll take care of Mrs Walker,' she said. 'You can show Inspector Cox here the way out.'

The way out was barely five yards from where they stood. The implication was clear: *make sure she leaves.*

Hazlewood shepherded Mrs Walker – who was still murmuring apologetically about Amanda and the shops – back into the dismal lounge. The young assistant hit the door-release button. As Cox was about to leave, the assistant touched her arm.

'My nan worked at Hampton Hall,' she whispered.

Her expression was furtive, excited and conspiratorial. Cox paused.

'Is that so?' Kept her voice neutral.

'That's why you're here, isn't it? One of *those* investigations. Like with Jimmy Savile and all that.' She looked over her shoulder, then back at Cox. 'I knew you'd come. It was only a matter of time.'

'Why's that?'

'The place closed down in the eighties, you know.'

'Yes, so I gather.'

'But you don't know why, do you? Social services "restructure", that was what they said. But my nan told me different. It got shut down because of' – her eyes widened momentarily – 'kiddie fiddlers. That's what she said. She meant, you know, paedos.'

Cox felt her stomach lurch, nausea rising in her throat; but at the same time, there was a kick, a buzz, the thrill – she couldn't deny it – of a case opening up, a cold lead coming alive.

She looked at the young woman gravely.

'That's a very serious allegation to be throwing around, Ms . . . ?'

'Matthews, Kirsty Matthews. It is, I know it is.' A defiant look. 'My nan wouldn't say it if it wasn't true, though. I'm not naming any names. But you'll see, if you look into it.' She nodded. 'You'll see.'

'Well – thank you, Kirsty.' Cox smiled briefly. 'You may be seeing us again.'

Wilson was leaning on the bonnet of the car, smoking the rest of his cigarette. He looked narrowly at her through a haze of smoke as she crunched across the gravel car park.

'Hope that was worth a two-hour drive through the pissing rain,' he said.

'It just might have been.' She pulled open the driver's door. 'Come on, get in.'

'Back to civilization?'

'Far from it.' Backed up the car, turned with a roar of gravel towards the exit. 'We're going to the police station.'

The Sixth Day of Christmas, 1986

They're staying clear of me. All the lads, they're not coming near me today. Don't blame them. Not in the mood for talking about bloody football or bloody BMXs or bloody Duffy's made-up bloody stories.

Even Stan's getting on my nerves today. He comes over.

'Do you want a jelly bean?' he says. 'I've got a few left. Saved 'em.'

'Fuck off with your jelly beans,' I say.

Upsets him, that. Didn't deserve it really but he'll get over it. I roll over in my bed, face to the wall. Want to sleep. Don't want to dream, though.

Late in the morning Miss Halcombe brings me a cup of tea. I've got nothing to say to her. I stay looking at the wall. She leaves the tea on the bedside table.

'Because your brother's not feeling too well,' I hear her say to Stan.

I fall asleep. You're not meant to sleep during the day, but they let me anyway.

When I wake up Stan's gone. There's no one in the dorm. I roll over; feel something sticky against my cheek.

He's left five fucking jelly beans on my pillow.

That's when I start crying. Can't help it. Just sit there on the edge of my bed with my hands over my face, bawling like a bloody baby.

With perfect timing, Duffy comes in. Try and stop crying but you can't just turn it off like a tap. Wipe my face, try to make it look like I just woke up.

Duffy's not buying it. Big smile on his stupid face.

'Is the little teacher's pet missing Dr Allis?' he says. 'Don't blub, Trevayne. I'm sure your new best friend will be back later to sit you on his knee and make everything all right.'

Other lads are drifting in behind him. Stevie, Judd, a few others. Stan, too.

I tell him to fuck off.

He can see I'm not mucking about. But he can't help himself, Mark Duffy.

'Knew it was only a matter of time before you got picked as the doctor's new favourite,' he says. 'Seen lads like you before. Acting tough as fuck – but all the time, underneath –'

I just snap. Something just goes bang.

I grab the mug of tea from the bedside table, chuck it as hard as I can – right in the bastard's face. He screams, a proper scream, like a girl. The mug bounces off his nose, hits the wall, breaks in half. Tea and blood all down Duffy's front.

'Have that, you prick.'

He's sobbing, clutching at his face. The tea had gone cold, worse luck. He'll have nothing worse than a broke nose. He can't say he wasn't asking for it.

Footsteps coming at a run down the corridor. I'm for it now, I know. But so what?

Before the orderlies get here to cart me away Stevie comes over and, leaning close, says: 'You did right, Robbie.'

Then I'm being grabbed, slammed into a restrain position, heavy hands on my neck, arms, wrists.

'Don't worry, Stan,' I shout, because I can hear him whimpering.

They take me away. As they're bundling me into solitary – the 'cooling-down room', they call it – I wonder what Stevie meant. Did he mean I did right just now, busting Duffy's nose for him, giving him the payback he's been asking for?

Or was he talking about yesterday?

*

They let me out after a few hours. It's Miss Halcombe who comes to turn me loose. She gives me the usual talking-to. I've heard it all before. Let yourself down, violence solves nothing, learn a bit of self-control, blah bloody blah. These fucking hypocrites.

Then, as I'm walking out the door of the cell, she says: 'If you don't get your act together, Robert, I think we may have to separate you and young Stanley. We simply can't have this sort of disruption.'

I turn and look at her. Try not to let anything show in my face, but she can see, all right. Fear, real fear – you can't hide it. It'll always show through.

Halcombe knows that, the evil old bitch.

The idea of being separated from Stan scares me right down to my bones.

'You can't do that,' I say.

'We don't want to, of course. But I'm afraid it may be the only course of action. I know Dr Merton has been considering it – if your conduct, Robert, doesn't improve.'

It'll improve, I tell her. I'll be good as gold, I tell her. She won't hear a peep out of me, I tell her, from now on – none of them will. I'll keep my head down and my nose clean. Just don't take Stan away from me.

I say 'please' about a hundred times. I practically fucking beg her.

Col comes to find me. It's getting dark, about half-four, and I'm in a corner of the garden. Just sitting, thinking. Snow's all gone. Crows are making a racket in the trees behind.

'It's all right,' he says.

I tell him no it's fucking not. He smiles, and says yeah, actually, you're right, it's not.

We both sit for a bit, not saying anything. My hands are cold, but I don't want to go back inside.

'We shouldn't let him get away with it,' Col says then.

'How d'you mean?'

I remember how Col knifed his foster-dad – and that copper, too. Realize that I never asked him why.

'I dunno.' He shrugs. 'We all know what he does, that bastard Merton. Him and his mates. We know it, and we just let it happen.'

Like I let it happen? I want to ask.

I hope Col knows I didn't have a choice.

12

'This tea,' Wilson said, 'is piss. Must be the soft water.'

Cox looked at him, bemused. 'I wouldn't have taken you for a connoisseur,' she said acidly.

Wilson shrugged. 'Given up the booze, haven't I? Three months and counting.'

'Give yourself a medal,' said Cox.

A young PC had just dropped a bulging cardboard box on to the table and stepped back, brushing the dust from his hands. That made four: four full crates of files.

The PC blew out a breath.

'That's the lot, ma'am,' he said.

'Thanks, constable.'

'Everything from back then is on paper.' He made an apologetic face. 'They've been talking about digitizing it, but we've just not got the manpower. Sorry, ma'am.'

She looked up at him wryly.

'That's all right, constable. Some of us, believe it or not, can remember a time before Microsoft and the iCloud.'

'We should be thankful it's not on floppy disk,' put in Wilson, setting down his plastic coffee cup, 'and we don't have to fire up the Amstrad.'

Cox smiled. The constable looked blank. He couldn't have been more than twenty-two. She thanked him again for his help and dismissed him.

She sat back, looked at the boxes. Didn't know quite what to expect. She'd asked for everything they had, every file on every case relating to domestic violence and the abuse of children, from Walsall, Wolverhampton, Sutton Coldfield, between 1980 and 1990 – and they'd brought her the lot.

It was an occupational hazard for a cold-case investigator, she knew. It was easy to get paranoid, to feel that the data-onslaught was strategic, that it was being done on purpose – that someone in a smoke-filled room somewhere was darkly muttering *bury her in paperwork* . . .

But the fact was, police work meant paperwork. What could you expect?

Wilson was looking grimly at the boxes, hands in pockets.

'This doesn't look like fun,' he said. 'Why don't we go down the council offices, speak to someone in social services? They'll be able to fill us in.'

'If you think you can find a council office that's open for business on a Saturday afternoon, be my guest.' Cox stood, prised open the nearest box. 'You're an investigative journalist, for Christ's sake, Greg. I thought digging through dusty archives was what you people lived for.'

Wilson muttered something offensive. Pulled off his jacket, rolled up his sleeves.

It was Cox that struck gold first. The files had been mixed up a lot down the years, it was clear – documents put back in the wrong places, alphabetical order lazily ignored – but the system hadn't broken down entirely; sure, the index cards were nothing more than vague hints, pointers in the right direction, but when Cox dug her way down to 'Ha–Ho', sure enough . . .

'Bingo.'

Hampton Hall, Sutton Coldfield. The folder was labelled '1985'.

Before Wilson – looking up from his own box – could say anything, the constable poked his head around the door.

'Another tea, guv?'

She shook her head.

'Not for me, thanks, constable. But I'm sure my colleague here would love another cup.'

The PC gave a brief thumbs-up, and disappeared.

'Thanks, *guv*,' Wilson said sourly. 'Come on, then. What've you found?'

Cox's heart was already sinking as she thumbed open the thin manila folder.

'Not,' she said, 'what I was hoping for.'

It was empty.

Alarm bells began ringing in her head.

Wilson reached over, took the folder from her. It was obvious that he, too, had the sense that this was no filing error.

'Nothing at all? That seriously doesn't add up.'

'But look.' She pointed. 'Look at the creases, here, in the cardboard.' Fine creases, running parallel to the folder's spine. 'This folder was *full*, bulging, at one point. So full the fucking folder got bent out of shape. And now nothing?'

Wilson was nodding.

'Someone's been here. Beaten us to it.'

'Jesus.' She snatched the folder back, slapped it down on the table.

'Plan B?'

'Radley.' She was already tearing open the second cardboard box. 'Anything on Radley. *Everything* on Radley.'

Wilson nodded grimly. He could play the part of the cynical hack as much as he liked, Cox thought; when it came down to it, Wilson cared about getting to the truth.

And he really, *really* hated being fucked with. They were as bad as each other.

After forty-five minutes they had a pile of papers a foot high. Wilson leaned wearily on the tabletop.

'Shall we see what we've got?'

Cox let the folder she was leafing through fall back into the box. Shrugged.

'Might as well.' This was a fishing expedition, she knew, and nothing more; a sweep through an armful of files pulled at random from a ten-year archive was unlikely to blow the case wide open.

But everything new they found out about William Radley let in a little more light.

'Crime report,' Wilson muttered, flipping through the top file in the pile. 'Domestic abuse, looks like. Signed off by one Sergeant Radley.'

'Same here. Child neglect, this one.' The file had been diligently filled out, neatly typed, thoroughly referenced; the work, as far as she could tell, of a conscientious young officer. But that wasn't news. They already knew Radley had been a good copper.

'Aaand another.' Wilson made a mock-yawn as he leafed through another folder. 'Stabbing. Ten-year-old boy, knifed his foster-dad! Christ. Must've been a little charmer, this young Colin Carter.'

Cox looked up sharply. Another link clicking into place? She didn't dare hope.

'Colin Carter?'

'Uh-huh. Name ring a bell?'

'Might do. Radley wrote up the case?'

'Yep. Attended at the scene, too – got a light knife-wound in the arm for his trouble. The kid was bad news, obviously.' Wilson turned the page. Stopped dead.

'What?'

Wilson gave her a look. Then he read from the report: 'The youth was subsequently transferred into the care of Hampton Hall for Underprivileged Children.' Shook his head. 'There it is. There's your link.'

He tossed the report to Cox. She grabbed at it, flipped back to the first page. A child's face, angular, dark-eyed, mistrustful, stared out at her in bleak grey and white.

A face she knew.

Colin Carter was a repeat sex-offender, pretty well known across the Met. Cox had interviewed him herself a year or two earlier – something to do with distributing child pornography, but they hadn't been able to make it stick. Last she'd heard he was on parole in south London somewhere.

The boy in the police report – it was him. Carter was almost bald now, marked by teenage acne, overweight, wore glasses, was missing a tooth in his upper jaw – but the flat cheekbones were the same, the bulbous lower lip was the same, the look in the dark eyes was the same.

Swiftly she scanned the text of the report. The

stabbing – non-fatal, though Radley reckoned the kid had been aiming to kill – took place at the foster parents' home in the suburbs of Walsall. A scuffle, a kitchen-knife to the neck. Then, when Sergeant Radley comes in the door, he gets the same treatment: a medical officer's photo in the file showed a curving wound up the inside of Radley's right biceps.

Then off to HHUC with the little swine.

But that wasn't the end of the report; there was an addendum, a typed statement appended to the file, presumably by Radley. It had been taken from a woman named Moira Yates – Colin Carter's foster mum.

Colin was a difficult boy, Mrs Yates admitted. There was no denying that. He was withdrawn – always *disappearing into himself*, she said. But with the right care, with love and a nurturing home, she was sure he could get better – she was sure, she said, that Colin was a good lad, underneath.

It was a moving statement, human and empathetic, given the circumstances.

Then Cox reached the final paragraph. It chilled her to the bone.

We want to look after Colin, Mrs Yates had written. *He is better off with us.*

The typed black-ink characters lent the statement a strange formality, but in this passage Cox could hear, loud and clear, the voice of a deeply concerned woman – no, not just a woman, but a mother.

It is not right to send him back. Please, Mrs Yates had written, *do not send him back to that place.*

*

142

On the drive home – a long haul south through damp gloom and holiday traffic – Wilson seemed to feel the need to make small-talk. His way of restoring normality, Cox guessed. Hampton Hall had spooked him. Spooked her, too.

'So – any plans for New Year's? You and Aidan doing anything nice?'

She laughed humourlessly. Too knackered, after the day she'd had, to keep up the pretence.

'We're not as close as I might have made out, me and him,' she said.

'How do you mean?'

'We're not really together, Greg. To be honest, I doubt we ever will be. Matthew lives with Aidan, except for every other weekend, when I get to be a mum again.' She looked across at Wilson with a self-deprecating smile. 'So New Year's? Half a bottle of cornershop plonk and an early night for me, I imagine.'

Wilson looked uncomfortable.

'Sorry,' he mumbled. 'I shouldn't have asked.'

'It's okay. It'll get better, one way or another.'

'I'm sorry if –' He broke off, sniffed awkwardly, fidgeted with a button on his jacket. 'I mean, I'm sorry, Kerry, if I, if we –'

She smiled. She had to smile.

'Let it go, Greg,' she said. 'What happened between us had nothing to do with it. Believe it or not, you're not *quite* the worst mistake I've ever made.'

'Flattery will get you nowhere,' Wilson grinned.

13

Twenty past three. She was late for her meeting with Serena McAvoy. Not on purpose, or not quite, anyway — somehow, she just hadn't felt able to prioritize a self-serving conference with a mob of Met lawyers.

She hurried across the station car park. Guy in a suit was coming the other way, out of the security-controlled staff doors. Not a copper she knew, from this distance. New CID recruit? She hadn't heard anything about that.

As he came closer, though, she saw that she *did* know him — and that he wasn't a copper.

'Mr Harrington?'

The MoJ man, who'd been peering at his smartphone as he walked, looked up in surprise.

'Mm?' He blinked at her. 'Ah, Inspector Cox.'

She looked at him curiously.

'Wouldn't expect to find you here, slumming it with us plods,' she said.

Harrington smiled. In his left hand, Cox noticed, he held a Mercedes key-fob.

'Just a flying visit,' he said breezily. 'Dropping off some paperwork in connection with the William Radley suicide. Making sure everything's nice and tidy.'

Nicely stitched up, you mean.

She nodded, forced a smile, said she'd better be getting on . . .

Cox being half an hour late hadn't done anything to improve McAvoy's personality. She found the QC in a third-floor meeting room, a dark-suited young associate lawyer at her side, stacks of files and ring-binders on the desk in front of her.

Cox apologized for being late, took a seat. McAvoy, as if she hadn't spoken, launched straight into her spiel.

'My job,' she said, fixing Cox with a look of lacquered professional indifference, 'is to make sure that you say nothing at the inquiry that might embarrass the police service.'

'Perish the thought.'

McAvoy didn't respond to the sarcasm. 'The inquiry will be looking to apportion blame, but they have no legal powers. We'd like to contain the scope of their conclusions.'

'And avoid any civil suits in future,' Cox added.

'We don't have long to prepare, inspector,' said McAvoy. 'I want you to pay close attention to what I'm about to tell you.'

Cox nodded.

'I'm listening.'

'One, be polite.'

Cox bit back a sarcastic reply: *why thank you, Serena, that would never have occurred to me.* The QC pressed on.

'Two, answer every question you're asked, but don't say anything more than you have to. Don't volunteer information. And three, don't lose your temper.' She paused. 'Inspector, I do think you should be writing these down.'

Cox snorted.

'I think I can remember three sentences, Ms McAvoy.'

McAvoy sighed. Crossed her arms on the desk.

'Inspector, you must be aware that your manner can at times – like now, for instance – be . . . abrasive. I suppose it comes with the job – but it will not come across well at the inquiry if you respond with aggression to hostile questioning.'

Cox was taken aback.

'How hostile will it be?'

'Expect the worst.' McAvoy lifted her eyebrows. 'Baroness Kent might look like a kindly old sort, someone you'd bump into in Fortnum's, but in the courtroom she's a shark. Underestimate her at your peril.'

'She does seem nice – as it happens, I ran into her the other day at lunch. I –'

McAvoy looked up sharply.

'You spoke to her? What did you say?'

'Nothing, nothing.' Cox moved quickly to reassure the QC. The woman already thought she was disrespectful and rude – she didn't want her thinking she was a bloody idiot, too. 'Just pleasantries. Nothing about the case.'

McAvoy nodded doubtfully.

'Okay.' Looked down, sifted through her papers. 'Now. Let's go over the case – what the inquiry know, and what they're going to ask you about.'

Cox nodded, ran a hand across her eyes. *I don't need to go over the case*, she wanted to say. *There's nothing about that case I don't remember.*

And nothing about it I wouldn't rather forget.

She only half-listened as McAvoy went through the key points.

DI Cox and DCI Naysmith had made the decision to

release Warren Boyd from custody after questioning in relation to the whereabouts of a missing eight-year-old boy, Tomasz Lerna; Tomasz was later found dead in a lockup used by Boyd.

'Now the Met's line,' McAvoy said, 'is that the force *did* follow due diligence in respect of Warren Boyd's release from custody.'

Cox nodded. 'Our intelligence was that Boyd didn't know where the child was. We had no good reason to doubt that.'

'Even though you turned out to be wrong?'

'We believed that Tomasz was in the hands of someone more – for want of a better word – senior than Boyd. Someone more deeply embedded in paedophile networks.'

'But he wasn't. Boyd had him.'

Cox hesitated.

'According to the official version, yes. But there was evidence that Tomasz didn't die in the lockup. According to the pathologist, there was a twelve-hour window – he could have died at any point within that period. What's more,' she pressed on, talking over McAvoy's attempt to interrupt, 'there's a fair chance that the DNA samples that tied Boyd to the killing were the result of contamination in the lab.'

McAvoy was looking at her levelly.

'So you don't accept that you were wrong?'

'I think there were – unexplained elements to the case. Boyd was a low-level abuser, an opportunist. He hadn't the connections or the means – mental, physical, financial – to keep a victim like Tomasz on the move, and under wraps.'

'So who did?'

The man in the mask. The image – the slitted eyes, the devil's horns – rose up again in her mind.

She grimaced.

'We don't know.'

'And Boyd disappeared, of course. Went on the run.'

'Or someone got rid of him.'

The QC sighed, shook her head.

'This sort of confrontational attitude will not wash with the inquiry panel,' she said.

'They won't want to hear the truth?'

'Your *version* of the truth, inspector, is not what the inquiry has been convened to hear.'

'You mean it's not what the Met wants me to tell them.'

'We need you to take *responsibility*.'

'Don't you *dare* talk to me about responsibility,' Cox snapped. Then she sighed, put her hand over her eyes. What had McAvoy said about her temper? 'Sorry,' she apologized shortly. 'Long week.'

'There's no conspiracy here, Inspector Cox,' McAvoy said. 'Please try and remember that.'

'So I've been told.' Impatient, exasperated, she made to stand. 'May I go now?'

'Just one more thing.' The QC made an officious sit-down gesture. Waited for Cox to make eye-contact. Then said: 'Greg Wilson.'

Oh, hell.

'What about him?'

McAvoy smiled knowingly.

'We'll do our best to prevent the inquiry from asking you about your personal life,' she said. 'It's not relevant, and we believe it would be overstepping the bounds of the inquiry's purview.'

'Good.'

'*However* . . . links between police and press are really under the microscope at the moment. That unpleasantness over phone-hacking, for instance, caused us a lot of awkwardness.' She gave Cox a frank look. 'So – is there anything we need to know? About you and Greg Wilson?'

Cox kept her poker-face in place. 'Such as?'

'For instance, are you in regular contact?'

Cox snorted. *Define 'regular' . . .*

'No, of course not.'

NONCE.

The letters had been scrawled in spray-paint across the white garage door. Someone had done a half-hearted job of covering it up with grey paint. Hadn't worked.

Two of the downstairs windows were boarded up with plywood. On the pebbledash wall by the barred front door there was a spatter of what looked like dogshit. The letterbox, too, was smeared with brown.

'Nice place,' murmured Wilson.

Cox had filled him in on the way. Colin Carter's background, in and out of care homes as a kid, in and out of prison as an adult. Numerous child-porn offences – always distributing, copying, storing. Never anything direct, she added. 'Does that make it okay?' asked Greg, as they climbed out of the car.

'No,' said Cox. 'But I don't subscribe to the view that he should be strung up and castrated.' She pointed to the picture someone had carved on his front door, showing a stick figure suffering just such a fate.

'You think he's behind Radley's death?'

'Who knows? But I doubt it.'

Wilson paused. 'Should we – are we going to need backup?'

'Nah. Carter's not that type.' She'd looked sidelong at him. 'Besides, if he turns nasty, I've got you to protect me.'

It stung, she saw. Wilson wasn't a small guy – he was maybe five-ten and decently built – he looked after himself, but she doubted he knew the first thing about self-defence. It was obvious to both of them that, if Colin Carter did kick off, it'd be Cox doing the protecting.

'I'm not going to take a bullet for you, inspector,' Wilson said. 'Not even for old times' sake.'

'Have you ever been in a fight in your life?'

'Kerry, I'm an investigative journalist. I don't have fights. I just get beaten up.'

Cox took the lead as they approached Carter's grim semi.

No answer to her knock.

'Think he's out?'

'He doesn't go out. Too risky. They know him round here.' She knocked again. 'He'll have seen us coming. Might've recognized me.' She made a bitter face. 'He'll be upstairs, deleting his hard drive.'

She kneeled, pulled her coat sleeve over her hand, and pushed open the letterbox.

'Mr Carter? Detective Inspector Cox, CID. We know you're in there.'

A smell from within of unwashed dishes and old

cigarette smoke. She could see nothing but a stretch of worn red carpet. No sound.

'Mr Carter, we need to speak to you.'

Still nothing.

'If you don't come to the door, Mr Carter, you'll be found to be in violation of the terms of your parole and –'

She broke off, had to put out a hand to keep from falling, as with a mutter of impatience Greg Wilson nudged her aside. She watched in surprise as he bent double and, cupping a hand to his mouth, yelled: 'What can you tell us about Hampton Hall, Colin?'

Then he straightened up, looked at her.

'*That's* how you doorstep someone.'

'Thanks.' She got to her feet, wiping her hand on the back of her coat. 'I prefer the textbook method, personally.'

Wilson shrugged.

'Different folks, different strokes.'

There was a sudden racket of bolts being slid from behind the door. Wilson gave her a deadpan wink.

The door opened; the iron bars stayed intact. Carter, Cox knew, wasn't paranoid; everyone really was out to get him.

Colin Carter wore tracksuit bottoms and a zipped-up black hoodie and had his sparse black-grey hair tied back in a ponytail. He'd been fat the last time she saw him and he was fatter now. His baggy jowls were pale grey with stubble.

'Hello, Mr Carter,' she said.

But Carter, eyes narrowed, lips pursed, was looking over her shoulder, at Wilson.

'Who the fuck are you?' Thin voice, drawling Black Country accent.

'This is my colleague, Greg Wilson,' Cox said. Carter didn't take his eyes off Wilson.

'I know who this one is,' said Carter, indicating her with a surly nod, 'worse fucking luck for me. But who the fuck are you? If you're a copper, she'd have said your rank.' He paused; his deep-set eyes shrank further into his face. Then he jabbed a stubby finger through the iron bars. 'You're a fucking journalist.'

Wilson sighed.

'Good guess, Obi Wan. I am.'

'Well, you can fucking –'

'How much? Thirty? Forty?' Cox looked round at Wilson in surprise. He was thumbing banknotes from an inch-thick roll. She sighed inwardly: *once a tabloid journalist* . . .

'Fifty,' said Carter. He said it quickly, keenly – he needed the money, it was clear.

'Fifty and you'll talk to us?'

'Fifty,' sneered Carter, 'and I'll tell you all there is to know about Hampton fucking Hall.'

The living room was predictably grim. Airless and dark, strewn with grease-smeared pizza boxes, used tissues, cigarette ends. There was a TV, a decades-old gas fire, a bookcase half-filled with loosely piled books and magazines. A metal garden chair and a sunken grey sofa.

An open door to the right led into a gloomy kitchen. A door ahead, in the back wall of the room, was closed – there was a lock on it, looked new.

Carter, Cox noted, steered them towards the other end of the room – kept himself between them and the locked door.

She gestured casually.

'What's through there?'

He looked at her insolently.

'Nothing.'

'Something you don't want us to know about?'

'Nothing that's any of your fucking business, unless you've got a warrant – and don't say you have, 'cause you haven't.' He dropped listlessly into the sofa.

Cox decided to let it go – for now. She sat down in the garden chair; Wilson, after a moment's hesitation, perched awkwardly on the sofa-arm.

There was a silence. Carter looked belligerently from one to the other.

'Well? What's going on?'

Tread carefully, Cox told herself.

'We're looking into certain . . . activities that took place at Hampton Hall in the 1980s,' she said, watching Carter carefully as she spoke.

The fat man snorted.

'Activities. That's one word for it. Jesus.'

'You went through quite a few care homes as a kid, is that right?' Wilson asked.

'You can call them care homes. I call them fucking concentration camps.'

'Did you,' Cox nudged, 'witness any abuse – physical, emotional, sexual – during your periods in care?'

'Are you fucking joking?'

'Is that a "yes"?'

Carter sniffed, wiped his nose on his sleeve.

'Hampton Hall wasn't the worst,' he shrugged. 'I been in worse. They left me alone there, most of 'em. I had a reputation.'

'What do you mean? How did you get a reputation?'

'Stabbing my foster dad was a good start.' He looked up at Cox. 'They knew I'd fight back, make a fuss. They don't like that, most of 'em.'

Wilson was looking nonplussed.

'So you're saying that this kind of abuse was wide-spread?'

Carter gave him a contemptuous look.

'"Abuse". That's another, what's the word, *euphemism*. Hear it all the time, don't you? No one's scared of saying it, newsreaders and that. "Allegations of historic abuse". Do you know what abuse is, really? Abuse is when you're ten years old and some old bloke comes to see you in the middle of the night. Wakes you up, pulls you out of bed. Puts you on your knees and shoves his cock down your throat. Jizzes in your mouth and forces you to swallow. That's what "abuse" is. Only they never put it that way on the *Six O'Clock News*.' He looked at Cox with a sneer. 'What were you doing when you were ten, inspector? Tea parties with your teddy-bears? Jolly-hockey-sticks at your posh school?'

Cox held his look. She was aware that between the two of them Greg Wilson was staring at her, white-faced and way out of his comfort zone. She knew what he was thinking. *How can you look him in the eye? How are you not shocked? How can you stand this?*

154

To which there was an easy answer. She'd heard it all before. Seen it with her own eyes.

'Tell me about William Radley,' she said.

'Who?'

'He was the officer who took you into custody after you stabbed Ken Yates. You stabbed him, too – wounded him in the arm.'

'Oh, yeah.' Carter allowed himself a twisted smile at the recollection. 'I remember him. Didn't know his name, though.'

'Did you see him again, after that day?'

'Oh yeah. He came to the Hall quite a few times. Not usually in uniform, though.'

Cox could feel a dark pit opening underneath her.

'Was he – one of your abusers?'

'Does it matter? He knew what went on there. They all fucking did.' He sniffed again, then frowned. 'Hang on. Radley. Was he the bloke that topped himself the other day? Heard it on the news. Fucking super-copper jumped off his balcony?'

Cox nodded.

'That's him. William Radley.'

Carter breathed out thoughtfully through his nose and scratched at his stubble.

'It don't make any difference to me now, of course,' he said. 'It's all the same to me. But still.' He looked at Cox. Something had changed, behind his lifeless dark eyes; there was less of a challenge there, now – more of a plea. 'But still,' he repeated, 'I won't be shedding any tears for your William fucking Radley.'

Wilson pulled out a pack of cigarettes; offered one to Carter, who took it without thanks.

'When did you last see Radley?' he asked as he flared his lighter.

Carter drew in smoke, shrugged.

'We didn't exactly keep in touch after I left,' he said. 'It'd be thirty-odd fucking years ago. Never saw him after I left Hampton and went into prison.'

Cox had never known Carter so talkative.

'You went straight into juvenile detention?'

'Yeah. Start of my glittering career.' He pulled again on his cigarette. 'I owe it all to Hampton fucking Hall.' Carter squinted at Wilson through the smoke. 'But listen. I've said enough. You want any more, boy, you're going to have to show me some of that fat bankroll of yours.'

Wilson smiled grimly.

'We haven't had our fifty quid's worth yet.'

'It's a seller's market, pal.'

'Don't push your fucking luck.'

Carter scowled, started up from his seat, bunching a white fist. Wilson stood, raised his hands. But Cox moved faster than both – she was between the two of them in a half-second, palms upraised, forcing Carter to meet her eye.

'Easy, now,' she said, her voice firm, calm. 'Easy. Sit back down. We don't need to make this difficult.'

Carter, flashing a last look at Wilson, swore and subsided on to the sofa. Sucked on his cigarette and said: 'Tell that cunt not to talk to me about luck.'

'Here we go,' Wilson muttered.

'Pricks like you have let me down all my life,' Carter

spat, 'and now you talk about fucking luck? Lucky, was I, that my dad was in Wandsworth, my mum was a smack-head, my nan didn't give a fuck, let her alky boyfriend stub out his fags on my arm? Lucky to get stuck in home after home, where I was nothing but fresh meat for rapists and perverts?'

'Perverts?' Wilson butted in. 'That's a bit fucking rich, coming from you.'

Cox gave him a sharp warning look. For a second it looked as though Carter was going to swing for him again – but instead he shrugged one shoulder, made a grimace.

'You wouldn't understand,' he muttered. 'Cunts like you never do. Anyway,' he added, with a resentful glance in Cox's direction, 'I've served my time.'

'No one's saying you haven't,' Cox said. Trying to settle the mood; trying to stop this situation lurching out of hand. They were here to do a job. 'I've just got one more question, Mr Carter. Then we'll be on our way.'

Carter sighed. He looked exhausted, broken.

'Go on then.'

She took out her phone, brought up the snapshot she'd taken at Verity Halcombe's house; the black and white picture of Verity as a young woman, with a half-smiling young man on her arm. It was a long shot, but they needed a break.

She turned the screen of the phone towards Carter.

'Do you recognize this man?'

Carter leaned forward, peered at the image.

His jaw fell slack. His face paled to paper-white. A flicker of fear passed across his eyes.

'I think we can take that as a yes, too,' Wilson murmured.

'Doctor Midnight,' said Carter. He blinked, gulped, turned to Wilson. 'Can I have another fag?'

'Sure.'

They waited while, with quivering hands, he lit the cigarette, drew in a deep lungful. Coughed, wiped his cuff across his eyes.

'Fucking hell,' he said. He looked at Cox. 'It's a long fucking time,' he said, as though apologizing, 'since I saw that fucking face.'

'It's okay,' Cox reassured him. 'It's all right.'

'Dr Midnight, you said?' Wilson prompted.

'Yeah, that was what we called him. Used to come pay the boys a visit after lights-out. Liked to touch. Creepy fucking bastard.'

'Do you remember his real name?'

'They weren't big on formal introductions. I think they called him Dr Merton, Dr Martin, something like that.' He looked away, blinking. 'Didn't think I'd ever see that cunt's face again. Christ.'

Wilson reached out and took the phone from Cox's hand. Frowned at the screen.

Then he looked at Cox.

'We need to talk,' he said softly. 'Outside.'

The Seventh Day of Christmas, 1986

'Here's to Hampton fucking Hall,' says Stevie. Upends the bottle of vodka over his mouth. Drinks till it spills over his spotty chin. Laughs like a madman.

I asked him, before, where he got the vodka. Says he got it in a trade with one of the gardeners. What'd you trade for it, I asked him. Doesn't matter, does it, he said. Broke the seal on the bottle and took a big drink.

They're having a party down the hall, in the staff quarters, we can hear the music and laughing, so we thought we may as well have a party of our own, here in the dorm. Not much of a party — twenty unwanted kids and a bottle of supermarket vodka — but better than nothing. It's New Year's Eve after all.

We all pass the bottle round. Even the young ones have a slurp — Stan, too. He gags on it and then says it was nice. We all laugh at him. Everyone's telling jokes, telling stories, talking rubbish. It's nice, almost.

'Off for a wee,' Stan says, getting up. He walks wobbly, pretending like he's drunk. Daft lad.

Col scoots over to sit next to me. We've both had more'n our share of Stevie's vodka. He starts asking me about my family. It's not something I talk about much — but I don't mind, with Col.

I tell him about our mum, how she had it hard growing up and maybe wasn't much of a mum but was all right before Malky and his drugs come along.

'How about your dad?'

'He's a nutter. Never really knew him. Wasn't around, except to cause trouble for us.'

Col nods, says he knows what that's like.

I start talking a bit about our dad, and about him going mental and getting us moved on from that last place we was in – and then I look round and think, our Stan's been a bloody long time having a piss.

I tell Col I'm going to go look for him. Col just nods. He's more pissed than I am, I reckon. Not that I'm sober, not by a long bloody way. Bump into the doorframe on my way out.

Music's still thumping down the hall. Gone midnight, I think. Happy new year, eh.

Push open the door of the boys' toilet.

Merton's in there.

Stan's standing by the urinals, looking a bit awkward but okay, I think, and Merton's leaning on one of the sinks. He sees me come in and smiles.

'Ah, Robbie,' he says. 'Stanley and I were just having a nice little chat.'

He's off his tits. I can see that at a glance – got used to seeing it, with our mum. He can hardly stand up straight, that's why he's leaning on the sink.

'A chat about what?' I say. I'm proper mad. He shouldn't be in here. They shouldn't be in here.

Stan looks from me to Merton and back to me. Chews his little finger anxiously.

'Doctor's questions,' the bloke says.

And that's it, that does it, just like before, with Duffy and the mug of tea. Merton might be bigger'n me but he looks like he's made out of pipe cleaners, and I bet he's never had a fight in his life. I'll give him a fucking fight.

I lunge at him, not even throwing a proper punch but just chucking my body forward, hoping something connects, fist, elbow, forehead, knee, not bothered which — just want to hurt the dirty old prick.

Merton stumbles to one side. I don't really see what happens. The tiles are a bit wet, splashed tapwater, splashed piss. His feet go from under him.

I grab Stan by his elbow, yank him out of the way.

Merton goes over, falling full-length, too off his head to even put his arms out. His head goes clonk on the edge of a urinal, and he hits the floor hard.

'What did you do that for?' Stan wails.

Oh, Christ, I think. There'll be trouble now.

14

They'd left Carter slouched on his grotty sofa, with the rest of Wilson's cigarettes and DI Cox's business card, plus another twenty. *Call me if you want to talk some more*, she'd said. Fat chance of that.

Now they walked quickly through a fine drizzle back to where they'd parked the car, near to where the main road through the estate met the A-road.

Wilson came swiftly to the point.

'Where did you get that picture?'

'The woman was Verity Halcombe. The photo was in a frame in her house up in Whitby.'

'And you don't know who the man is?'

'Uh-uh.' She looked at him. 'I'm guessing you do.'

'Dr Euan Merritt.'

Cox frowned. Didn't ring a bell — but it wasn't far off Carter's guess of *Merton*.

'You say it like I should know the name.'

'You obviously don't watch as much shitty TV as I do. *Tame Your Toddler? Kid Conflict?*'

'He's on TV?' Cox blinked. 'Jesus.'

'He's a big name, Cox. He's the guy they always call when they need an expert on, you know, *nightmare toddlers* or whatever. Smooth manner, perma-tan, lots of letters after his name. The whole package. Look.' He took out his phone, shielding the screen from the rain with his free hand, and brought up a gallery of images. 'Imagine him forty-odd years younger.'

Cox took the phone from him.

Yes – it was the same guy, no question. He wore heavy-framed glasses now, and a dodgy dark-grey hairpiece. His smile twisted to the left, just like in Verity Halcombe's photo.

'He separated from his wife last year,' Wilson supplied. 'Footnote in the tabloids.'

Cox handed back the phone. Sighed.

'What's up? This is a big lead.'

'No, it's a big *story*. It's a scoop for you, Greg, but it's a fucking headache for me. A senior policeman, a beloved children's worker, and now a bloody TV star . . .'

'It *is* a great story,' Wilson conceded.

'But imagine trying to get it past the CPS. In fact, imagine trying to get it past my chief super. And on what grounds? A few educated guesses, the word of a convicted paedophile. A nightmare.'

They walked on for a minute in silence.

Eventually Wilson ventured: 'So –'

'We can't arrest Merritt. We just can't. We'd be laughed out of town.'

'You'd like to, though.'

'Bloody right I would. You saw Carter's face. He's a sly bastard but he wasn't faking that.'

'Do you think Merritt's tied up in the killings?'

She made a face.

'Doesn't add up, does it? But if there was abuse at Hampton Hall –'

'*If?*'

'– then he was involved. I'd put money on it. And with Radley dead, Halcombe dead, Allis dead . . .'

'He's at risk.'

Cox nodded. 'Exactly. Question is, what the hell do we do about it?'

They'd reached the car.

'Anonymous note?' Wilson suggested as they climbed in.

'Very *you*,' said Cox drily, switching on the ignition, 'but not really my style. I'd rather do this face-to-face. Is there a number?'

Wilson glanced at his phone.

'There's a number for his agent – or anyway, his agent's agency.'

'Let's give them a call,' Cox said thoughtfully. 'I want to meet this Dr Midnight.'

They pulled up in the car park of a McDonald's on the edge of Battersea for Cox to make the call.

'I'm bloody starving,' Wilson grumbled. 'You speak to this agent – I'll go and grab some hamburgers and coffee, okay?'

Cox, already tapping in the agency's number, nodded distractedly; she watched Wilson jog across the wet car park, pulling his jacket up over his head to keep off the rain.

'Good afternoon, Jeremy Ronson Associates.'

A woman's voice, clipped, well spoken.

'I'd like to speak to whoever represents Dr Euan Merritt, please.'

The receptionist didn't even pause before issuing the

164

smooth rebuff: 'I'm afraid Mr Cornwallis is in a client meeting. Perhaps I could take a message?'

'Perhaps you could tell him that this is Detective Inspector Cox, with the Metropolitan Police CID. And yes, it is urgent.'

The line went quiet; there were a few seconds of light-classical 'hold' music, and then the phone was snatched up, and a man's voice, tight with anxiety, said: 'Yes?'

Cox smiled to herself. Sometimes, the power a police rank could give you frightened her, made her uncomfortable; at other times – like now – it was a blessing.

She explained to Mr Cornwallis that she wasn't after him; she was simply keen to speak to Dr Merritt in connection with an ongoing police investigation.

'I see.' Oily professionalism replaced anxiety in the agent's tone. 'Is there a fee?'

Christ.

'No.'

'Ah, well. I'm afraid Dr Merritt is currently exceedingly busy with television work – in fact, he's filming a new series of *Conflict* at the prestigious Portland Studios as we speak. I *do* feel that unless a fee is available he won't really be able to consider your proposal, though of course I'm sure he's grateful for your interest. Is it for *Crimewatch*?'

Cox bit her lip. Forced herself to remember: *this is serious.*

'I'm afraid you've misunderstood me, Mr Cornwallis.

This won't be a public appearance. We have reason to believe that your client may be able to help us with our inquiries.'

A pause, as the agent shifted mental gears.

'*Do* you indeed?'

'We do, yes, sir. Perhaps you could ask him to give me a call?'

'Inspector, unless you have a *very* good reason –'

'I do, believe me.'

'I, we . . .' Cornwallis faltered. 'I think you would do better to contact Dr Merritt's solicitor. I really don't feel that it is appropriate for you to pursue Dr Merrit through my agency in this connection.'

Cox grinned, so that Cornwallis could hear the grin in her voice.

'That's no problem,' she said brightly. 'We'll contact him direct. You've been very helpful. Good afternoon to you, Mr Cornwallis.'

She was still chuckling to herself when Wilson reappeared with a rain-spotted paper bag and two cardboard cups of coffee.

'What's tickled you?' he grunted as he climbed in. His jacket was dark with wet, and his hair was plastered across his forehead. Passed her a cup. 'Here. It'll be foul, but you're a copper, you're used to it.'

'Thanks.'

He wiped a hand across his eyes, blinking away rainwater. 'This *weather*. It's getting worse. How'd it go?'

'You might want to do something with your hair,' Cox said. 'We're going to call on a celebrity.'

*

166

Prestigious, Cornwallis had said. It sure as hell didn't look it. Portland Studios was a big place, sure, a stretch of warehouse-like redbricks set into the tunnels of the overground line a little way north-west of Baker Street. But its grand sign, decked out in white lightbulbs, was missing two letters (PO TLAND S UDIOS), and the façade had a run-down, out-of-date feel.

They'd googled it on the way over. It was a busy operation, run-down or not. Quiz shows, cookery shows, shopping channel broadcasts, they all came here to shoot; everyone who worked here, Cox gathered, was on their way up, or on their way down.

'This is the national capital,' Wilson said as they crossed the road towards the showily canopied entrance, 'of shit TV.'

Glass swing-doors led through to a spacious atrium with a tiled floor and an L-shaped sofa. A coffee table was covered with fashionable magazines, carefully arranged; clocks on the wall showed the time in London, New York and Los Angeles.

A bored-looking young man in a badly knotted tie was reading the *Metro* at the reception desk.

'Good afternoon,' he said as they approached, hefting a visitors' book on to the counter. 'Who are you here to see?'

'Dr Euan Merritt,' said Wilson confidently. 'He's with *Kid Conflict*.'

'Oh-kay. That's Studio 2.' The receptionist was already filling out security passes. 'If you could just pop your names and where you're from in the book. Thanks.'

Cox scribbled two names in the relevant column,

making them carefully illegible. The receptionist took back the book without looking, tossed a pair of laminated passes on green lanyards on to the counter.

'Know where you're going?'

'Oh, sure,' smiled Wilson.

They moved off purposefully towards a set of double-doors marked 'Two'. No one gave them even a passing glance.

'Not exactly Fort Knox, is it?' Cox muttered as the doors swung closed behind them.

Wilson gave her a look that took in the unpainted walls, the cracked floor-tiles, the loose wiring in the ceiling and suggested that maybe Portland Studios didn't have anything of any value to protect.

The corridors ran on for what felt like miles. Staff in branded black T-shirts passed back and forth, yammering urgently into their headsets.

Wilson stopped one, a young guy with a clipboard and an afro, couldn't have been more than eighteen.

'*Kid Conflict* green room,' he said sharply. 'Which way?'

'Down there, on the left.' The guy jerked a thumb over his shoulder. 'Not sure they're out of studio yet, though. Who do you need?'

'Dr Merritt – we need to go through some script changes for the next run.'

'Uh-huh.' The guy nodded. 'Well, if he's not out yet you can wait.'

As he moved off, and they walked on in the direction he'd indicated, Cox looked at Wilson thoughtfully. It was useful, she thought, Wilson being such an accomplished liar – but it worried her, too.

The green room wasn't exactly movie-star standard. They had to squeeze by a trolley of mops and buckets to get down the corridor; a hand-scrawled sign – 'Kid Conflict' – was Sellotaped to the door. They went inside, Cox leading the way.

A trestle-table of curly-edged sandwiches and foil-wrapped biscuits. Jugs of juice and iced water. An instant-coffee machine. There were posters on the wall, dull promo-prints of gameshow hosts from decades past.

Two sofas faced each other from opposite sides of the room. On one, a stringy-looking woman in a vest-top and trainers was trying to keep control of three young kids – a boy, maybe six or seven, noticeably overweight, and a pair of yelling toddlers who were surely twins.

On the other sofa, legs crossed rather daintily, was Dr Euan Merritt. He was holding a plastic cup of coffee, reading a paperback book and trying to pretend that the unruly family opposite didn't exist. He was a small man, with a thin neck and boyish hands; his suit, in bold blue, contrasted with his white shirt and the terracotta tone of his skin.

'Dr Merritt. I wondered if I might have a word?'

He looked up. Unzipped a bright TV grin. The whiteness of his teeth made Cox blink.

'Of course, my dear.' He set down his book, stood, extending his hand. 'What can I do for you?'

'I'm Detective Inspector Cox. I was hoping to speak to you in private.'

The smile shrank into a crinkled grimace. 'And how did you get in?'

'Through the front door,' Wilson put in.

'I'm a very busy man, inspectors,' Merritt said. 'I don't have time for –'

'It's in connection with the death of William Radley,' said Cox.

Merritt opened and shut his mouth. Frowned.

'Should I know the name?'

'I couldn't say, Doctor. All I know is that he's dead, and we want to know why.'

'Well, that's very sad, I'm sure, but I don't see –'

'Do you know the name Reginald Allis?'

This time there was a reaction, minimal, well-contained, but it was there: a flicker in Merritt's expression, a pinkening of the tan skin over his delicate cheekbones.

'Allis? The child psychology fellow?' A note of bluster had entered his tone. 'Goodness me, I worked with him donkey's years ago.'

Wilson – in his best copper's monotone – put in: 'At Hampton Hall for Underprivileged Children. And at the Children's Aid and Rehabilitation Enterprise.'

Merritt looked at him, obviously taken aback. Another direct hit.

'Well, possibly, possibly . . . But, as I said, inspector, I really am very busy here, and . . .'

'If you preferred,' Cox said, raising her voice a little, 'we could do this down at the local police station.'

In the corner of her eye she saw the woman on the other sofa look up interestedly. Merritt saw her too. He swallowed awkwardly.

Then he turned, guiltily, as the door opened. A young woman in a headset poked her head around the doorframe.

'Guys? We're going to call it a day, okay?' She smiled wearily at the woman with the children. 'You get off back to your hotel, Mrs Flanshaw. We'll see if these little monkeys are any more cooperative after a good night's sleep,' she said.

One of the twins was hitting the other one repeatedly over the head with a plastic Disney princess. The older boy was singing a pop song loudly to himself as he pulled the stuffing out piece by piece from a rip in the sofa.

Their mother shrugged listlessly.

'Can't make any promises,' she said.

The young woman turned to Merritt.

'Thanks for today, Doctor. Some great takes. We'll see you tomorrow.'

She vanished; the door banged shut.

Into the uncomfortable silence that followed, Cox said: 'So maybe you can just give us five minutes of your time, then, Doctor?'

They waited till Mrs Flanshaw and her children had left – trailing wet-wipes and drinks cartons – and then they sat, Merritt and Wilson at angles on the sofa, Cox on a metal chair she'd pulled from under the sandwich table.

Merritt reached into his jacket, took out a slim silver flask. Unscrewed the cap and poured a large measure of whisky into his emptied coffee cup.

Took a long drink. Grimaced. Topped up the cup.

'Tell us about your relationship with Reginald Allis,' Cox said.

Merritt spread his hands.

'I'm not sure what to tell you,' he said.

The truth would be nice, Cox thought.

Wilson: 'You worked with him.'

'*Years* ago. Back in the eighties. I was a consultant paediatrician, he was a child psychologist. We crossed paths, naturally.'

'Heard from him lately?'

'No.' Merritt eyed Cox suspiciously. 'Has he been talking about me? What's he been saying?'

'Not a lot,' Cox said flatly. 'He's dead.'

Merritt gulped.

'Dead?'

'Murdered. It was made to look like a botched mugging, but we have good reason to believe it was personal.'

Merritt knocked back the rest of his whisky. That was fine by Cox: a suspect who'd had a drink was liable to get brave, and brave meant stupid. *Keep drinking, doctor. And keep talking.*

'You've got a bloody nerve suggesting I had anything to do with this,' Merritt said belligerently.

'Nobody's suggesting that. We're just hoping you could fill us in on some of the background to the case.'

'Helping you with your inquiries, eh? Oh, I know what *that* means. And so will everyone else,' he added bitterly, 'when they read it in tomorrow's tabloids.'

Greg, Kerry noted, didn't even flinch.

'Hopefully it won't come to that, Dr Merritt. But going back to Reginald Allis –'

'I told you, I haven't seen hide or hair of Reggie Allis in *decades*. Now, I don't know what nasty lies Butcher has been spreading about me, but I can tell you it's absolute bullshit.' He glared at them. 'Bullshit,' he repeated, venomously.

Butcher? Cox kept her expression impassive, but made a mental note of the name.

'Do you remember a young boy named Colin Carter?' Wilson asked.

He wanted to keep up the pressure, Cox guessed; wanted to keep Merritt from getting comfortable. But bringing up Carter was a big move. Too big? Too much? She watched the doctor closely.

'No,' he said.

'Because he remembers you.'

Merritt gave him a look of fierce dislike and squinted at the name-tag.

'I'm sorry,' he said, 'I saw this lady's badge, but who the hell are you?'

'Name's Wilson,' said Greg with false easiness.

'Constable Wilson? Inspector Wilson? Wing-commander Wilson? Where's your ID?'

'You're in no position, Dr Merritt, to be demanding –'

'Oh, I beg to differ, *Mr* Wilson.' He looked sideways at Cox. 'There's something funny going on here,' he said.

'Three people are dead,' Cox said, getting to her feet. 'I wouldn't call it funny.'

Merritt was pink-faced and goggle-eyed.

'Get out,' he snapped. 'Get out, both of you, now, or I'll call security.'

'Is that the gormless kid with the afro?' said Wilson.

'Okay,' said Kerry, soothingly. 'We're going.' She pulled a business card from her pocket, and dropped it on the sandwich table. 'This has my private mobile number and my email on it. Please do get in touch, Dr Merritt, if you remember anything that you think might be helpful to us.'

Merritt wasn't looking at her. He was refilling his plastic coffee cup with whisky from his flask.

'Fuck off out of my sight,' he said.

15

Cox drove Wilson back to his place in Kilburn. Pulled up by the kerb – the car sounding as knackered and cranky as she felt – on the road adjoining his.

'I'll tell you what,' Wilson said, unbuckling his seatbelt and stretching in his seat, 'I feel like I need a hot shower after the people we've been mixing with today. Or at least a big drink.' He looked across at Cox. 'Fancy a quick one?'

Cox shook her head shortly.

'I don't think that's a good idea.'

'I meant a drink, you know. Not a shower.'

She managed a smile.

'Same applies.' She pinched the bridge of her nose. 'I need to get hold of Allis's phone records. I'll get on to Chalmers in the morning.'

'I reckon it's that greasy bastard Carter you want to be checking up on,' Wilson said seriously. 'I don't think he was lying, but he was holding out on us.'

Cox nodded. He had been chatty. And that in itself was suspicious. She knew how it worked sometimes. They talked and talked, and gave you every bit of information bar the one they were keeping hidden.

'We got something for nothing there,' she said. 'That stuff about Merritt, he coughed it right up.'

'Wanted to get rid of us. The guy's hiding something.'

Kerry nodded. 'Well, look at his record. That pretty much goes without saying.'

'So can't you, I dunno, seize his computer, search his house?'

She shook her head.

'Carter is low-level,' she said. 'He's not a priority in this case.'

She'd said it without thinking. But she looked up when she realized that Wilson was staring at her.

'Low-level?' he said, incredulous. 'Jesus, I thought *I* was hard-nosed.'

That stung. She went on the defensive.

'It's not my job to –'

'For God's sake, Kerry.' Wilson shook his head. He didn't seem angry, exactly; more bewildered, blindsided. 'You're a mum,' he said. 'How can you think that way?'

She turned the question over in her head, over and over, looking at it from every angle, on the dark, rainy drive back to Acton and the nick. It was a good question.

First port of call was Robin Chalmers. He had his feet up on his desk and was chewing his pen over a broadsheet crossword puzzle. Hadn't made much progress, Cox noted.

He swung his feet down and tossed aside his paper when he saw her approaching.

'Ah, Cox. Been expecting to hear from you. Gloria said you'd been sniffing around, wanting a piece of the high-octane action on the Allis case.' His tone was heavy with irony.

'Been all go, has it?'

'Oh, God, yes. If poring over hours of CCTV footage is your idea of heady action, anyway.'

'Anything?'

'Something.' He sighed, stood up. 'I'll show you. What are you after, anyway?' It was a making-conversation question; nothing more behind it than the mildest curiosity.

'Bit of background on another case,' she said evasively. Chalmers let her leave it at that.

They walked over to the CCTV unit. Chalmers cued up a fragment of footage.

'This is from the off-licence near the park where we found Allis,' he explained. 'Not a lot to go on. Anything catch your eye?'

She grabbed a seat, watched the grainy footage spool by. The timestamp read 19.45. Chalmers pointed out Allis, a spare figure with a rapid, short-paced walk. He wore a knee-length mac and a tweed cap.

'Now watch.' Chalmers jabbed a finger at the screen. 'This feller. This is the guy we need to talk to.'

He passed the camera perhaps two minutes after Allis: a man of heavy build, big-shouldered, muscular, maybe six-one, six-two, in a short, dark coat over a pulled-up hoodie. Jeans, trainers, hands in pockets. Rucksack over one shoulder. Nothing to single him out. Nothing to go on.

He wasn't Colin Carter, anyway. But beyond that –

'Could be anyone, right?' Chalmers said moodily.

She nodded. Chalmers would've already put out a call, posters in the area, a slot on the local news, but it was hard to see it doing a lot of good.

Her phone buzzed.

Aidan's number.

She glanced apologetically at Chalmers.

'I need to take this.'

'No worries.' Chalmers stood up, stretched. 'I'm going to go grab a coffee, anyway.'

She waited till he'd sauntered out of earshot, then hit the green button.

'Hello. Everything okay?'

'Hiya, Mum.' It was Matthew. He sounded, Cox thought, a little anxious, as if he were ringing a stranger.

'What's up, love? I'm at work.'

Matthew started talking breathlessly about a party: about how it was going to be *brilliant*, because there'd be loads of people coming, and games and food like Christmas only better because there wouldn't be any sprouts — and because she'd be there.

She realized he was talking about New Year. Kerry smiled wistfully. So that's what her mum was up to. Orchestrating a family get-together, being the matchmaker. Thinking she could glue them back together with some cold cuts and a sing-song as the clock struck twelve. It would be touching, if it weren't so transparent.

'You are coming, aren't you, Mum?' Again the tinge of anxiety in his reedy voice.

'Mm? Yeah. 'Course I am love.'

While she spoke the CCTV footage ran on.

'Dad says I can stay up late. Maybe all the way to midnight, he says, if I'm very good.'

'Well, you'll have to be very good then, won't you?'

No one passed by the camera as the timestamp crawled

178

upwards. A lonely place: a good place for a mugging – or a murder.

'I'll be good if you're there, Mum.'

'Don't you worry, love. I'll –'

Timestamp 19.54. A man, six-one, six-two. Built like a brick shithouse. Blue down jacket, baseball cap, tracksuit bottoms. Walking back in the other direction. And over his shoulder . . .

She grabbed for the mouse, froze the image.

'Mum?'

'Sorry love, just a sec.'

Different clothes. Same rucksack. Same guy. She was sure of it.

'*Mu-um.*' On the brink of tears, she could tell.

'Matthew, love, I'm sorry, Mum's really busy just now.'

'But will you come to the party? Do you promise you'll come?'

'I'll be there. I promise.' She bent close to the screen – as if just by squinting she'd be able to drill down through the grainy pixels, make out a face, an identity . . . 'Matthew, love, I've really got to go. But I'll see you at the party, okay? Love you, sweetheart. Bye.'

'But, Mu-u-um . . .'

She rang off. The sharp bite of guilt died quickly; she was on to something here . . .

Chalmers returned, shambling in with a cup of muddy-looking faux-cappuccino. He clocked Cox's expression; sat down with a slow grin on his face.

'Go on then,' he said. 'Impress me.'

'It's really not much.' She said it to convince herself as

179

much as Chalmers. 'But this guy, the big guy – did you notice him?'

'Of course I noticed him. I sat through nine bloody hours of CCTV footage. I noticed everyone. What about him?'

'Notice the rucksack? It's the same as your suspect's.'

'You mean it's a 20-litre Berghaus 'Venture' daysack, the best-selling rucksack in Greater London?' Chalmers crossed his ankles, smiled tiredly. 'Coincidence, Cox. Sorry.'

Cox shook her head firmly.

'No. No way. Forget the detail, just *look* at the guy.' She wound the tape back, set it running again. 'Trust your instincts. Look at the way he walks, the way he holds himself. The size of him. Ignore the clothes, clothes can be changed. This is the same guy.'

Chalmers cocked his head. Looked unconvinced.

'There are a lot of people who look like that in Battersea. I dunno, Cox. I mean, if he had a wooden leg, or an extra head or something, okay, yeah, it wouldn't be coincidence. But as it is . . .'

'He went after Allis,' Cox insisted. 'He followed him into Battersea Park. He killed him. Then he changed his clothes, stuffed them in his rucksack and walked away.' Sat back, shaking her head. 'It was no mugging. Muggings are opportunistic. This was premeditated. This was murder.'

Chalmers made a face.

'Nope,' he said, after a while. 'Don't buy it.'

Cox bit her lip; thought fast, changed tack.

'Phone records,' she said. 'Do you have them? Have you been over them?'

'We've got his phone,' Chalmers nodded. 'But the tech team haven't scraped the data yet. They're short-staffed down there just now. Christmas, flu, you know how it is.'

Cox thought of the laptop on Allis's writing desk.

'What about his computer? Have you been through that?'

He squinted at her.

'His computer? You mean his home computer? The guy was stabbed by a mugger. What's his computer got to do with it?'

She'd gone too far. Again.

'I – I just think it might be a good idea to go through his computer. See what shows up.'

Chalmers was looking at her levelly.

'Steady on there, Judge Dredd,' he said. 'A, this is my case. I might not be bubbling over with excitement about it, but it's a fact. My. Case. And B, this was a mugging that went wrong. I'm not going to strip down the guy's hard drive. Nor do I propose to waterboard his known associates.' He swigged from his coffee. 'You need to take it down a notch, Cox, if you don't mind me saying. Book a day off, for Christ's sake.'

Cox was about to reply when she heard her name called from across the office suite. She turned.

It was Coombes, a young DC from Naysmith's team.

'The DCI wants to see you, ma'am,' he said. 'Urgently, he says.'

Cox's heart sank. She'd been making progress, not quickly, nothing earth-shaking, but she'd been getting somewhere. Now she'd bet a pound to a penny Naysmith had found a way to chuck another spanner in the works.

She stood, headed over to Naysmith's office.

Coombes was hovering uncertainly by the door.

'I don't want to speak out of turn, ma'am,' he said, uncomfortably, 'but you ought to know – he ain't at all happy, ma'am.'

Cox forced a confident smile.

'He never is. Thanks, constable.'

Coombes nodded, hurried off.

Before she went in, Cox straightened the sit of her jacket, smoothed her hair, brushed a smear of grit off the toe of her shoe. Wouldn't matter a damn to Naysmith, of course – but it made her feel better. Slightly.

She knocked, waited for the hoarse *get in here*, pushed open the door. Naysmith wasn't alone. The man sitting opposite him was middle-aged, grey-suited, bespectacled and smoothly intelligent-looking. And there was another man, a man she half-knew, by sight anyway – one of the force's in-house lawyers.

No preamble, not even a 'hello'.

'This here,' barked Naysmith, 'is John Harris from Garraway, Blunt and Harris.'

That didn't sound good.

'I'm a solicitor,' the grey-suited man said in a soft Scottish accent, smiling faintly, 'acting for Dr Euan Merritt.'

Oh, shit.

'Pull up a seat, Cox,' said Naysmith.

*

Harris had the full story – the visit to Portland, the interview, the veiled threat of arrest – and now so did Naysmith.

'Go ahead,' the DCI said gruffly, folding his hands across his thick stomach. 'Explain yourself.'

Justifying an off-the-record visit to a high-profile suspect on the evidence of a tip-off from a convicted paedophile in front of two high-powered lawyers and your bad-tempered commanding officer . . . this was the stuff of a CID copper's nightmares.

Take it slow, Kerry. Step by step.

'I had reason to believe,' she said carefully, 'that Dr Merritt may have been in danger.'

Harris smiled thinly, checked his notes.

Addressing Naysmith, he said: 'This, DCI Naysmith, is a very far cry indeed from the impression my client received during his encounter – I would not call it an "interview" – with DI Cox and her associate. There was no mention, direct or implicit, of any danger to my client's person. On the contrary, my client was given the distinct impression that, far from being the object of DI Cox's compassionate concern, he was in fact a suspect in a murder inquiry.'

'A misunderstanding,' Cox tried.

'DI Cox isn't currently involved in a murder inquiry,' Naysmith said abruptly, carefully avoiding Cox's eye. 'Your client must have misunderstood.'

'My client,' Harris said smoothly, 'has two PhDs and is a noted expert in human behaviour. I think we can agree it is more likely that any *misunderstanding*' – he stressed the word sarcastically – 'was a result of DI Cox's failure to communicate the context of her conversation with my client.' He crossed his legs, coughed delicately. 'DCI Naysmith, my client is not a vindictive man.'

Naysmith nodded; looked thrown by the shift in tone.

'Glad to hear it,' he said.

'May I speak freely?' asked Harris. 'Off the record?'

Naysmith glanced sideways at the police lawyer, who gave the slightest of nods.

'The man from Del Monte says yes,' Naysmith said. 'So please, go ahead.'

'Thank you. I believe it will be best if I lay my cards on the table, so to speak.' Another delicate clearing of the throat. 'Some years ago,' Harris said, his voice soft but clear, 'my client was the victim of a very serious smear campaign. A number of outrageous and utterly unfounded allegations were made against him. It goes without saying that the subsequent investigations by police and other regulatory authorities into the allegations in question resulted in the complete exoneration of my client – and, I might add, more than one successful prosecution for defamation, libel and harassment. Nevertheless, as you can well imagine, this was an extremely challenging period for my client. He had not at that time attained his present level of academic prestige and media profile, but the allegations caused him acute personal embarrassment and considerable professional difficulty. As a consequence, my client took the difficult decision to change his name by deed-poll – to the name by which he is now known – and to relocate to a different part of the country.'

The lawyer paused for breath.

What were the allegations? Cox wanted to ask – knowing

full well what the answer was likely to be. But this was no time for stirring up trouble.

'Speaking in the very strictest confidence,' Harris said, 'I can tell you that prior to 1995 my client went by his birth-name, which was –'

Let me guess: Martin? Merton?

'– Ian Merton. I tell you this,' Harris added, turning for the first time to look directly at Cox, 'because I wish to assure you that if *any* attempt is made, at any time, by any officer or associate of any officer, to publicly repeat, revisit or reinvestigate the unfounded allegations made against Ian Merton, this will be met with a highly robust legal response.' Harris nodded and tapped his notepad on his knee. 'Highly robust,' he repeated.

Cox had crossed swords with enough top-end criminal lawyers to know what that meant. 'Robust' meant war. 'Highly robust' was the nuclear option.

She nodded.

'Understood,' she said. The police lawyer chimed in: they were all agreed, they had all voiced agreement, agreement had been reached by all parties, the usual boilerplate legal crap – and the force unreservedly apologized to Dr Merritt for any inconvenience or embarrassment caused by the actions of DI Cox.

They all stood.

Cox took one more chance.

'Would you be able to tell me, Mr Harris,' she asked politely, 'who Mr Butcher is?'

Harris turned. His blue-grey eyes were severe behind his rimless spectacles.

'I'm afraid, inspector,' he said, 'that the name is not

familiar to me.' Turned away, shook hands stiffly with Naysmith.

'I'll show you out,' offered the police lawyer.

Then it was just the two of them. Naysmith, sinking again into his seat, breathed out, a long, steamy, exasperated sigh through his nose.

'What *is* it with you, Cox?' he said at last. 'You and this constant need to keep pushing your luck. Is it the excitement? Are you one of those risk addicts you read about? Have you not been getting laid recently, is that it? Is this your way of getting your kicks?' He slammed his hand on the table, swore foully. Looked back up at Cox. 'I can't keep giving you second chances,' he said.

Cox met his gaze. He was right – she couldn't ask for anything more from him, not without giving him something in return. It was time to front up.

She told him about Colin Carter.

'The nonce?'

'That's him.'

Told him about the details of the abuse, the rape and torture. About the visitors to HHUC. About the man who used to come to the children – young kids, nine, ten, eleven years old – after dark; about Dr Merton.

'They called him Dr Midnight,' she said. 'You can guess why.'

Naysmith's face was impassive. He didn't speak for a minute.

'Go on,' he said thickly.

She took a breath – and told him everything. The connections between Verity Halcombe and Bill Radley, and the allegations that linked them both to years – hell, maybe decades – of child abuse at Hampton Hall; Reginald Allis's ties with the institution as a member of the board of trustees; Verity's long-standing relationship with Dr Ian Merton, or whatever he called himself nowadays.

The only thing she left out was Greg Wilson's part in the investigation. It was already complicated enough.

'It's all there, guv,' she finished. 'It all adds up.'

Naysmith gave her a calculating look.

'Or,' he said, 'Verity Halcombe dies of natural causes, which is just enough to push her dear old pal Bill Radley over the edge, and he takes his own life. In an unrelated incident, a wealthy old man goes for an unwise walk in Battersea Park, gets mugged, fights back and is fatally stabbed.'

Cox shook her head in frustration.

'How about Radley's lunch with Allis? We've got evidence for that.'

But Naysmith just shrugged.

'Two old farts with nowhere better to go on Christmas Day. Big deal.' He shifted in his seat. 'Look, Cox, use your head. This isn't about what's *true*; it's about what we can prove, and prove conclusively. Stuff like this, you don't go in half-cocked.'

Cox opened her mouth to answer, but Naysmith, raising a finger, cut her off.

'Don't come to me with Colin Carter,' he said. 'If your case relies on putting Carter on the stand, forget about it right now. We're not here to give the CPS a laugh.' He sighed, ran a hand through his scrubby hair. 'Look. Leave it with me, Cox. I've let you make your case, okay? Now leave it with me.'

Cox nodded. Felt suddenly exhausted. Drained.

'One other thing.'

Lifted her chin.

'Yes, guv?'

'If you're going to insist on taking Greg fucking Wilson with you on these fishing expeditions, keep it low-key.'

'Guv?'

'You're too smart to play dumb, Cox. That smooth bastard Harris gave me a very detailed description. I didn't let on – thank me for that later. Managed to keep him out of it; it was you he was really after, anyway. I s'pose he figures that you'll pass on the message.'

Cox nodded.

'Yes, guv.'

'Now, like I said: leave it with me.' He said it slowly, heavily, dropping each word like a stone. 'Take tomorrow off. You need some family time.'

'But –'

'That is a direct order, inspector.' He looked up at her from under his creased eyelids. 'I do not want to see your face in here till 2015, is that clear?' Tilted back in his seat, he stretched his arms wearily behind his head. 'Happy fucking New Year, Cox.'

Time was, a day off – hell, even an evening off – was something to get excited about. When things were good between her and Aidan; when Matthew was around. Now it was just time wasted, opportunities missed, the trail going cold, the truth drifting away –

Family time? Fat chance of that.

The TV was playing a repeat of an American sitcom she'd seen a dozen times before. She stood, walked to the kitchen, opened the fridge. There was a bottle of half-decent Chablis in the door-shelf.

Well, what the hell. She'd earned it. Opened the nearest wall-cupboard, reached up for a wine glass.

Over on the coffee table, her phone buzzed stridently.

She lowered her hand. Sighed; rested her forehead momentarily against the cool fridge door. Christ, she was tired.

The phone buzzed on and on. It'd be work, of course. Naysmith, or Wilson; the copper up in Whitby, maybe, or the nurse at Hampton Hall – or Colin Carter, ready to talk some more, or Euan Merritt, drunk and wanting to tell his side of the story . . .

An evening without work was an evening with – what? With nothing but herself. She didn't have the strength for that. Not now. She crossed the room. Picked up the phone.

It was Wilson.

'Listen, Kerry, don't be mad –'

Not a good start.

'– but I've been, uh, staking out Colin Carter's place.'

'For fuck's sake, Greg . . .'

'Look, he might be small fry to you, but I say the guy's up to something – and who knows, it could be something big.'

'I thought you were supposed to be helping *me* with *my* investigation,' Cox said irritably. 'Is this your idea of helping? Going rogue and playing at detectives?'

'I know what I'm doing, Kerry.'

'Do you? Greg, guys like Carter are nasty and they're smart. And they don't like being watched.'

'I'm touched by your concern.'

'Don't be. Do you have any idea how much trouble I'd be in if you got yourself hurt?'

'There's nothing to tie me to you.'

She snorted.

'You sure about that?'

She filled him in on that afternoon's painful interview with Naysmith and the lawyers; explained how Naysmith had managed to keep Wilson's name off the record.

There was a pause. Then Wilson said: 'Sounds like I owe your boss a drink.'

'That's the last thing he needs. My advice would be to stay as far away from him as possible for the foreseeable future. And keep the hell away from Colin Carter while you're at it.'

'If that's your position,' Wilson said, a little frostily, 'I don't suppose you'll want to know what I found out.'

Cox sighed.

'Don't be a child, Greg. Go on. What did you find?'

'Carter's got a houseguest.'

'How do you know?'

'You were wrong about Carter. He does go out, after dark. Thing is, a light went on when he was out. Saw someone pull down a blind. Someone was there.'

'And?'

'And what?'

She wanted to scream with exasperation.

'It sounds crazy, I know, but maybe Colin Carter's

made a friend,' she said, forcing herself to keep her temper in check. 'Stranger things have happened. Maybe he's got a lodger, maybe he's got family visiting. None of those things are illegal, Greg.'

'No, but –'

'Greg, this is *not a lead*. This is not helping. If you do want to help, you can do some digging: press, social services, anything on CARE, anything on HHUC. A list of employees would be a great start.'

'Kerry, I –'

'Or just take the night off, for God's sake. Go home and open a bottle of wine. Just please, stop playing at being Philip Marlowe and jeopardizing my investigation.'

'But –'

'Goodnight, Greg.'

She rang off. Set down the phone. Ran a hand across her eyes. She felt wrung-out, tense, knotted-up. She knew what she needed – and it wasn't a bottle of Chablis.

The cold night wind felt good, slipping through the vents in her helmet, blowing the hair back from her face. Her muscles – legs, back, core – felt strong; her pedals rose and fell in brisk, regular cadence. And it was good to feel her heart beating fast in her chest, not through stress or fear or worry but because she was *using* it . . .

Night-time was the best time for cycling, Cox thought. Not as much noisy, nerve-shattering traffic; not as much smog and smoke. It was just you, chasing a beam of lamplight, a white line down a black road. Gave you time to think. And time to *not* think, too, which was just as important.

She'd crossed Putney Heath and was heading further out of town, up the hill towards Richmond Park. You got a good view of the city lights from up there.

Best way to see London, she thought wryly to herself. *From a safe distance.*

It took her back, this. Riding her bike through the dark, up to Richmond or out into the quiet, wealthy suburbs, had been her go-to stressbuster, at one time; even in a hard week, she'd found time for three, four rides a week.

There'd been a lot of hard weeks, back then.

Climbing steadily, body and bike locked into a smooth side-to-side rhythm, Cox found herself thinking back to those days. Would they ever find Warren Boyd, she wondered? She could still picture his face, clear as day. A face she'd come to know all too well. That look, that childish pout, had been his only answer to every question she'd hit him with. Stonewalled everything, right up until the end.

Afterwards, the papers said he was 'tough'; a 'hard-as-nails villain', one of them called him. She'd laughed at that, not because it was funny – nothing much had been funny, back then – but because she hadn't known what else to do. How else to feel.

She'd seen the look in Boyd's piggy eyes, and seen it up close. It wasn't defiance, wasn't contempt, however the press – and Boyd himself, come to that – tried to dress it up. It was fear. Plain and simple.

After they'd let him go – and there were plenty on the force, back then, who'd have rather seen Boyd have an 'accidental' fall on the nick's back steps than walk away a free man – Cox, on a hunch, had followed him.

He'd gone no further than the nearest pub. Went in there around lunchtime and stayed there. He was drinking, the landlord told her later, like a man on borrowed time; drinking like there was no tomorrow.

He wasn't wrong.

West of the park, the road fell into a long, steady downhill. Cox heard a car coming up the road behind her. Its lights painted a long shadow across the asphalt ahead. She kept tight to the verge; for some drivers, she knew, lights, reflectors and a high-vis vest weren't enough. The car slowed, matching her speed maybe five yards behind her rear wheel. She waved an arm, signalling for it to come past. It was safe to overtake; the road ahead was black and empty.

At last, the car revved. But it didn't overtake.

Her back wheel went from under her. She felt her right pedal come loose as the bike's rear mech crumpled, as the car's offside wing lunged across her line of momentum —

She yanked her leg free of the toe-clip, tried to go down, to pull the bike into a slide, maybe roll away — but she was going too fast, and her centre of gravity had lurched forward. The handlebars spun, and jammed; she was thrown, the bike racketing away into the hedge; the world, for a long half-second, was a blur of white light — and then she met the ground, elbow-first, her body cartwheeling, howling pain jolting up her arm. Her head struck the kerb. The edge of her helmet broke apart; her forehead was driven into the gritty road.

She tasted blood, felt vomit rise in her throat. The car, she thought, was driving on — she heard its engine go quiet, the glare of its lights grow dim.

It'd either driven on – or it'd stopped.

Her vision blurred; grew dark. The world fell silent. The pain in her arm and shoulder faded to nothing. Everything faded to nothing.

The Eighth Day of Christmas, 1986

Not seen Merton yet. All we've had today is Miss bloody Halcombe.

'Someone in this dorm is responsible for bringing this into Hampton Hall.' She waggles the empty vodka bottle, holding it like it's the most disgusting thing she's ever seen in her life. Who's she trying to kid? 'This is a very serious breach of our rules – what's more, it's completely against everything we stand for as a caring, responsible organization.'

And so on. Same old line we've been hearing all our lives: someone owns up, or the whole class gets detention after school . . .

I look over at Stevie. He's on his bed, knees tucked up to his chest, not meeting anyone's eye. Looks like shit. He must've shifted half that bottle himself.

I don't feel too bad. What happened in the bogs must've sobered me up.

'Do you all want to be punished?' Halcombe yells. 'Is that it? You all want to be punished?'

I look at her fat pink face, the empty bottle shining in the grey light from the window, the skinny kids sitting around on their bony beds. How weak they all look. How bloody hopeless.

Screw it, I think. Screw Hampton Hall.

I put up my hand.

'It was me,' I say. 'It's my vodka, my fault. It was me.'

Halcombe lowers the vodka bottle and looks at me, quivering, furious. Everyone else is looking at me, too. I feel like the big man. It's not a bad feeling – but I can't enjoy it, not really, not now.

'Well,' Halcombe says. 'Well.'

I look back at her. She says I'm in big trouble now – that after yet another infraction she has no choice but to revoke all my privileges and put me in the cell for the night.

I hear Stan's sharp intake of breath. Give him a wink. Don't want him worrying.

I'm not worried, anyroad. The cell? Being left to yourself for a few hours? Sounds like a bloody holiday to me – given the alternative.

'Come with me,' Halcombe says. 'We'll see what Dr Allis has to say about this.'

Fine by me, I think. We'll see what he has to say about this. Then we'll see what he has to say when I tell him what Dr Merton does to the little boys in his care.

It's just me and him, in the office. Allis is wearing a cravat thing instead of a tie, and a waistcoat. Fancy bastard.

He's all right, though. Better than I thought. That's the thing with people – the bastards always surprise you. Works both ways, though. Good and bad.

We talk a bit about the vodka; he gives me a little lecture on the dangers of alcohol abuse, on the importance of following the rules, respecting the values of the institution – but it don't seem like his heart's really in it.

So when there's a pause I just come out with it. I say it as plain as I can, dirty words and everything. He hardly blinks, Dr Allis. But he leans forward seriously and lowers his glasses.

'That, Robert,' he says, 'is very worrying. Very worrying indeed.'

You're telling me, doc, I think.

'It's true.'

'I don't doubt that you're telling me what you think is the truth,' he nods. I don't know what that's meant to mean. 'I'm going to act on this immediately,' he says. 'I'm glad you came to see me – this is

a very serious allegation, and I'm going to make sure it's properly investigated.' Looks at me over his wire rims. 'Now that, Robert, may require us to involve the police. It's simply the only way to address such a grave allegation. Do you understand?'

I nod. I do. Even the pigs have their uses sometimes.

He nods, sits back. Even though he's skinny there's a baggy flap of skin under his chin that wobbles when he moves.

'What happens now?' I say.

'Leave this with me, Robert,' he says. 'Just you leave this with me.'

Col says I shouldn't have bothered – that I was wasting my breath.

'They're all in it together,' he says. 'It won't do no good.'

Shrugs, looks away.

How can he be so bloody hopeless? He was the one talking about doing something – stopping that bastard Merton. It makes me so mad I could hit him.

But then he might be right, I know that. Christ I hope he isn't.

It's nearly lights out. Before I go down to the cell I ask Col to keep an eye on Stan for me – he don't like sleeping when I'm not there, and I don't want him pissing the bed again. Col says he will.

The cell's a cell. Bed, walls, piss-bucket. Half-window covered with a grille, up at the top of the wall. Christ, it's cold, though. They push me in, lock the door noisily behind me.

I sit on the bed. The mattress is no better than the ones in the dorm but it's no worse, either. No rats – fuck you, Duffy.

I lie down under the thin blanket. Smells of puke. Not much to do but lie there and shiver. So bloody cold I can see my breath – until, without warning, they turn off the lights.

16

Kerry couldn't have said which hit her first: the pain or the nausea. She came awake, saw glaring white light, breathed in the cloying smell of asepsis, felt her stomach cramp and at the same time groaned as a riptide of fierce pain swept the left side of her body.

Couldn't keep it in. With a choked cry she bent over the side of the bed – *what the hell was she doing in bed?* – and threw up on the tiled floor.

Footsteps.

'Oh, dear.' A gentle hand on her shoulder, helping her back into the bed as she fought to catch her breath. 'It's okay. You're okay.'

It was a woman, young, her hair tied back in a ponytail, wearing a uniform. Copper? No. Cox thought hard. A nurse. That was it.

'How are you feeling?' the nurse asked. 'Arm hurt?'

' . . . Yes.'

'You came off your bike, out in Richmond. You have a compound fracture of the forearm but it's nothing we can't fix. I'll get you some painkillers. How's your head?'

My head? Is something wrong with my head?

She tried to lift a hand, to feel her head, her hair, her skull, but the hand was clumsily entangled in the bedclothes.

'It – it throbs,' she said. Felt close to tears.

'Hey. Don't try to move.' The nurse reached out a hand to brush a strand of hair away from Cox's eyes. 'You had a bang to the head when you fell, but you're going to be fine, you hear me?' She perched on the edge of Cox's bed. 'Can you tell me your name?'

'Kerry. Kerry Cox.'

She knew that, at least – the certainty felt good.

'Okay, Kerry. A doctor's going to come and see you soon, run some checks. You took quite a tumble.' She smiled. 'But you'll be back on your feet in no time. Is there anyone you'd like us to call? Family, a partner?'

She said the first name that came into her head.

'Naysmith. Peter Naysmith.' She reeled off the DCI's mobile number.

'No problem.' The nurse noted down the details. 'We'll give him a call. And I'll get you those painkillers.'

She smiled; went away.

Cox closed her eyes, settled her head back into the cool pillow. Bit her lip as again the bone-deep ache gripped her body, as again her gut boiled up in revolt. She could feel the cold sweat on her face, brow, forearms.

She remembered. The bike, the road, the night, the car, the crash . . .

An accident?

No. She remembered that, too.

By the time the nurse returned with pills and water, it was as though a fog had descended in Cox's mind; the pain from her arm, the throbbing in her head, the nausea, the unreality of it all . . . She fumbled the painkillers into her mouth, gulped them down, drank as much of the water as she dared – any more, and she'd puke again.

Then she must have fallen asleep, or passed out, blacked out.

When she awoke, Naysmith was sitting by her bed. He smiled. Looked stressed and baggy-eyed.

'Happy New Year,' he said.

Cox blinked. Hadn't occurred to her to wonder what time it was, what day it was – Christ, even what year it was.

'It's the new year?' She struggled to sit up. 'God, I said I'd be at Matthew's party . . .'

'You don't need to worry about that.' He lifted his eyebrows. 'You were out for more than thirty hours, Cox. Bleed on the brain – I gather it's stabilized now.'

'Who – who found me?'

'Passing motorist, around one in the morning. You were unconscious. He called an ambulance, they brought you here. Hammersmith, if you were wondering.'

'And Matthew . . .'

'I told you, you don't need to worry about that. When you didn't show up, your mum phoned the station.' He smiled drily. 'Assumed you were at work. We told her you were on leave.' Nodded towards the bed. 'When I told you to go away and put your feet up, by the way, this isn't what I had in mind.'

'Do they know I'm here now?'

'Uh-huh. I rang them myself on my way over. They'll be here soon.'

'With Matthew? I don't want him to see –'

'No, just Aidan and your mum. You do look a bit X-rated in that bloody bandage.' He chuckled, shook his head. 'They showed me your bike helmet. Split open like a nutshell.' The chuckle faded. 'You were lucky, Kerry. You could've died.'

'I could've been killed.'

'That's what I said.'

She closed her eyes; pinched the bridge of her nose between finger and thumb.

'Guv,' she said.

'They said your bike was practically bent into a figure-eight.'

'*Guv.*'

'What?'

She remembered the roar of the revved engine.

'It wasn't an accident.'

He smiled uneasily.

'Funny thing to do on purpose. I'd already given you the day off.'

'Guv, you know what I'm saying. It wasn't just a hit and run. The driver did it on purpose.'

Naysmith shifted awkwardly in his seat.

'Kerry, you've made some enemies in your time, we all have – but do you really think anyone'd go that far, just for a bit of payback?' Scratched his nose, shook his head. 'Nah. I know, it can be hard to believe, the way some people drive – some prick in an A3 doing seventy on an unlit road, you can't credit it, can you? But –'

'It wasn't payback.'

'Well, then –'

'It was to shut me up.'

Naysmith stared at her.

The double-doors at the end of the ward opened. Aidan dashed in, with Mrs Cox following behind.

Kerry saw Aidan's face, in the seconds before he realized that she was awake and talking, that she was going to be okay. His hair was uncombed, his jaw unshaven. He looked shocked, shaken – he looked terrified.

He smiled, a broad grin of relief, when he saw her looking at him.

Then he came closer, and the grin warped into a grimace of horror.

'Jesus Christ, Kerry, what have you done to yourself?' He approached the bed. 'You've made a proper mess of yourself.'

'Lovely to see you too, Ade,' Cox muttered.

Aidan smiled.

'Sorry. Christ, I'm glad you're okay. I mean – *are* you okay? You must have taken a hell of a whack. You look like hell.'

'Could we leave the personal remarks for now?' Cox retorted. 'I'll be okay – so I'm told.' She paused. Grimaced. 'Am I really that bad?'

Her mum, half-hidden behind an armful of expensive-looking flowers, said: 'You *have* looked more presentable, darling – but oh, *goodness* I'm happy to see you.' She handed the flowers to Naysmith without looking at him and pushed past Aidan to embrace her daughter.

'Careful, Mum,' Cox murmured, as Mrs Cox's elbow brushed her splinted right arm – but it felt good to be hugged, good to be loved.

Naysmith carefully laid the flowers on the floor and stood.

'I'll be off, then,' he said, a little stiffly – not good with families, Naysmith.

'Thanks for coming, guv,' said Cox, as her mum reluctantly released her from her embrace. 'But listen – could you do something for me before you go?'

'Sure. What?'

'Get me a mirror?'

'No problem. I'll grab a nurse.' He moved off purposefully.

At Cox's side, her mother let out a long, whimpering sigh.

'Is that *wise*, darling?' she said, bending forward to touch Cox's forearm anxiously. 'Do you really want to see yourself in this state? You'll look *much* better in a day or two, once you've had a chance to put a bit of makeup on and do something with your hair –'

'Ah, come on, Maggie,' Aidan butted in, dropping into the chair Naysmith had vacated. 'She's a copper, she's seen worse – though not much worse. No harm in her seeing the truth.'

Cox nodded.

'He's right, Mum.' She fumbled for her mum's hand, gave it a squeeze. 'I want to know how bad it is. I'll be fine, I promise – I just want to know.'

Margaret Cox nodded, uncertain. Cox looked at Aidan; he winked at her. Christ, that took her back.

Her head was pounding again.

Naysmith returned, a nurse in tow. The nurse was carrying a small hand-mirror.

'Bear in mind, it looks a lot worse than it is,' she said as she handed it over. 'Nothing that won't heal. Probably won't even leave a mark.'

Cox nodded, lifted the mirror to her face.

In a way, it was good to know that she looked as bad as she felt.

A bandage covered her forehead from the eyebrows up. No blood, except on the tips of a few strands of hair that'd worked loose from the dressing. Her right eye was dramatically bloodshot, the socket around it blue-black, the skin of her temple a mottled yellow-brown. A layer of skin had been scraped from her nose. Bruising covered the whole right side of her face, down to her jaw. There was an ugly scab on the right side of her chin, and the left side of her lower lip was puffy and red.

'I look like I've been twelve rounds with Joe Calzaghe,' she muttered.

'Beauty is only skin deep,' supplied Aidan jovially.

The nurse leaned in to take the mirror back.

'You should probably get some rest now,' she said, with an apologetic sidelong look at Naysmith, Aidan and Mrs Cox. 'Your body'll do a great job of healing itself, you'll see – but it needs sleep, and it needs quiet.'

'Don't we all,' Naysmith mumbled.

Cox smiled.

'Okay – clear off, all of you.' She pulled her mum in for another hug. 'Take care. Ade, don't tell Matthew how bad I look.'

'Do you think I want to give him nightmares? He was asking for you.'

'What will you tell him?'

'That your bike broke down, and that was why you couldn't come to the party.'

Cox nodded. That'd do.

'Thanks,' she said. Felt helpless.

As they turned to leave, she called Naysmith back: *work stuff*, she explained in response to the others' questioning looks.

They waited while the nurse picked up the flowers Mrs Cox had brought – said how lovely they were, and said it was a shame they'd have to be kept out in the corridor, not on the ward: *regulations*.

Then it was just the two of them.

Naysmith shrugged; looked anxious.

'So?'

'I need to get out of here,' Cox said.

'What's your hurry? I'm pretty sure they want to keep you in at least another day or two.'

She gritted her teeth.

'Someone,' she said, 'tried to kill me. They followed me, ran me off the road. They tried to kill me.'

'Who?'

'I don't know, and I'm not going to find out sitting in here.'

'Okay then – why?'

She looked at him until he met her gaze. Then: 'You know why.'

Naysmith looked older and more weary than ever; hunted, run down.

'This Radley thing?'

'You know I'm on to something here, guv, and you're not the only one. There's some seriously dark stuff out there. If I keep digging, I'm going to find out where the bodies are buried. And then –'

'Then there'll be hell to pay,' Naysmith finished. He rubbed his chin, looked at her pensively. 'Look,' he said.

'*If* you're right, you needn't be in such a hurry to get back out there. You're pretty safe in here.'

'This isn't about me being *safe*. It's about three suspicious deaths – and God knows how many more.' A thought occurred, in step with the *thump* of her headache; a memory she'd been skating over. She lifted her chin. 'Here, guv – what do you know about Sam Harrington?'

Naysmith looked surprised.

'Harrington? That gonk from the MoJ? What's he got to do with anything?'

'That's the question, isn't it? He was first on the scene at Radley's death.'

'Come on. The guy's a civil servant, just another Oxbridge desk-jockey. Only in it for the fat salary and the pension pot.' He paused. 'Isn't he?'

Cox shrugged – winced at the pain in her arm.

'I can't prove otherwise,' she said.

'Well, then. And while we're on that subject.' He looked at her seriously, drumming his fingers on his knee. 'I looked over the evidence from the Allis murder. The wallet.'

'The restaurant receipt?'

'Well, that's the thing. The wallet was there, contents logged in the file: credit cards, a few receipts, for petrol, stuff like that – but nothing from any Olympus Grill.'

Cox turned cold inside.

'What?'

'Nothing from Christmas Day at all.'

'But guv, I saw it, I'm telling you – I had it in my hand. Chalmers was there, and the guy from SOCO, Chang –'

'Did you show it to them?'

'I – no.' She remembered: how uncertain she'd felt, there in the park – how uneasy. Mistrustful.

Now she felt like she had a lead weight in her gut. 'I didn't know then what I know now,' she muttered.

'Look, Cox. Is it possible you got – carried away?'

She fixed him with a look.

'Guv. After all we've been through. For Christ's sake.'

'Don't get defensive. You're under a lot of stress, I know that. Stress makes people do funny things.'

'Like make up evidence?'

'I'm not saying that.'

'It's exactly what you're saying. Or do you think I hallucinated that bloody receipt?'

Naysmith frowned.

'Watch your tone, Cox,' he rumbled with little conviction.

Cox was about to reply – about to snap back with something angry and unwise – when she noticed the nurse hovering uncertainly behind Naysmith.

'I'm sorry to interrupt,' she said, with a nervous smile. 'But really – you do need to get some rest, Kerry. Perhaps the work issue could wait till tomorrow?'

Cox hated herself for her first thought: *how much did she hear?*

Naysmith was already rising to his feet, reaching for his coat.

'She's right, Cox,' he said. 'This can wait. You try and relax. Get yourself better. We'll talk again soon.'

She swallowed down her exasperation. What else could she do?

'Sure. Okay.'

'You look after yourself.' He nodded emphatically. Stomped out.

Cox asked if she'd had her phone with her when she was found. *Found.* The word tasted bitter on her tongue – she hated the passivity, the helplessness of it. Yes, the nurse said – tucked in her leggings pocket, and fine except for a bit of scuffing.

'Better than me, then.' Cox smiled. 'Could I have it? Then,' she added quickly, 'I promise I'll go to sleep.'

It was in the drawer of her bedside table. The nurse, with a bit of tutting and if-you-really-must frowning, passed it to her.

'I just need to send a text,' Cox said.

She texted Wilson; funny, she thought, how quickly she'd got into the habit of turning to Greg bloody Wilson when she needed help. She asked him to come to the hospital the next day, and bring her some clothes from her flat.

A reply buzzed back quickly: *What are you doing in hospital?*

Cox – head thumping, bones aching, mind spinning – barely had strength to reply, *Tell you later*, before she sank into sleep.

17

She was, with some difficulty, buttoning up her shirt when the nurse pulled back the curtain.

'Kerry? What are you doing?'

'I can't stay here.' She pulled on a grey jumper, sat down to put on her shoes.

'Are you sure this is wise?'

No.

'I haven't got a choice.' She swore as a pulse of pain throbbed in her arm. 'There are things I have to do.'

The nurse sat beside her on the bed.

'I think your boss – Mr Nesbit? – was right,' she said. 'You really do need time to –'

'To *let my body heal*, yes, I know.' Cox sighed, straightened up. 'I'm sorry. I didn't mean to snap. I appreciate that you're looking out for me.' Turned – painfully – to face the nurse. 'Listen, I'm a police officer. There are times when I just can't afford to take it easy. You can understand that.'

'When duty calls.' The nurse smiled ruefully. 'Yes, I can. But still –'

'It's just pain, isn't it?' Cox stood, straightened her clothes. 'I mean, my arm's going to hurt, my head's going to hurt, but that's all, isn't it? I'm not going to drop dead from a delayed reaction or anything?'

The nurse shrugged.

'I wish I could say for sure,' she said. 'That's why we want to keep you in, for observation – to make sure there are no nasty surprises waiting for us. Head injuries aren't to be taken lightly.'

Neither is murder, Cox thought. *Neither is child abuse. Neither is conspiracy.*

She barely listened as the nurse talked her through her after-care: how to take care of the cast on her arm, to wear a sling as often as possible, how to change the dressing on her head, what sort of after-effects to look out for. Wilson was waiting in the car park, and they had work to do.

She thanked the nurse, who shook her head.

'You don't have to thank me. But I do wish you'd stay – at least until tomorrow.'

For a half-second, Cox hesitated. Her hip and leg hurt more than she'd expected, now that she was standing up. Her headache made it hard to think straight – and if things turned nasty, how much use would she be with her right arm out of action? She couldn't even drive, for Christ's sake.

But Wilson had said he had new information – a lead. Things were moving fast. Playing safe was no longer an option.

'Please take care,' the nurse pleaded as Cox stuffed her phone and a bottle of painkillers into her bag.

'I will,' Cox promised.

The nurse grinned.

'Why don't I believe you?'

'You've got to believe me. I'm a police officer.' She shouldered her bag, trying to ignore the protests of her joints, her muscles; left the ward.

Wilson had agreed to drive her home. He was waiting at the wheel of his beaten-up old Renault; couldn't wait to tell her what he'd dug up. After a pretty cursory inquiry about her health, he started in as they were pulling out of the hospital car park.

'I've been looking into CARE – this Children's Rehabilitation whatever-the-hell-it-is,' he said, as they motored throatily along Kingston Hill. 'It was a charity, but it had a big wad of private backing – set up and financed from Jersey, by a guy called Gandry, John Gandry.'

'I feel like I know the name.'

'You might. Wasn't averse to getting his name in the papers. Multi-millionaire, naturally. Generally described as a "philanthropist".'

'There's a word that rings alarm bells.'

'Ha, doesn't it just? Such cynicism. Anyway, Gandry died years back, so there's not much to work with there – but he was a Midlands boy, born in Dudley.'

'Hence the Walsall connection.'

'Yup. Now, CARE was officially wound up in the early nineties. It only put out one research paper. By –'

'Reginald Allis?'

'Co-authored with a Dr Ian Merton.'

'Uh-huh: Merton is Merritt. We had a visit from his agent the other day. Changed his name to escape some unsavoury allegations.' She gave Wilson a warning look. 'Tread carefully there, though. He's got his lawyers on Defcon One.'

'You know me, soul of discretion.' They swung on to the A306. Traffic was starting to bunch; Wilson geared down, went on with his briefing. 'The paper was published, but in a journal that's long since closed down, *Sociology Today*, *New Adventures in Sociology*, something like that. It's not online but I'll look it up at the British Library tomorrow.'

'How about Hampton Hall? Did you get a chance to look for a list of former inmates?'

'I did. Moved hell and high water to get a response from West Mids child services during the holidays, but no dice. No such records exist in their files.'

'That doesn't mean they don't exist somewhere else.'

'Give me a break, Kerry, I only had two days. I'm working on it.' The traffic had ground to a halt on the approach to Hammersmith Bridge. Cox's headache was getting worse; felt like her brain was beating in her skull like a heart. 'So you're going after the revenge angle?' Wilson asked. 'Someone who was abused as a kid, getting his own back now?'

Cox shrugged uncertainly.

'Who knows? But I don't think so. Thirty years is a long time – why wait so long? Five years, ten years, I could buy, not thirty.'

'So what's your theory?'

'I've got a few, but I'm not keen on any of them. Blackmail? Someone who was in on the abuse – an orderly at HHUC, a copper who covered Radley's back – gets an anonymous letter, or a phone-call, threatening to go public with what happened back then, unless they hand over fifty grand or whatever. But instead of paying up –'

'They set about silencing everyone who might have known anything?' Wilson blew out a breath. 'Whew. That'd be a big job.'

'I said I didn't like it much. But I haven't got a lot else.'

They speculated, trading potential motives, possible suspects, mocked-up backstories, as the little Renault crawled through Hammersmith. Cox knew all along it was still nothing but a guessing game; she hoped Wilson did, too.

They still needed a way in, a real lead. They were still waiting for a break.

Hammersmith gave way slowly to Shepherd's Bush: grey-brown, cloud-covered, unlovely. Cox directed Wilson to the end of her street.

He stopped the car with a jerk.

'So what now?' he asked, turning to Cox, propping an elbow on his seat-back.

'I'm going to take some drugs and go to sleep.'

Wilson rolled his eyes.

'I meant for the investigation. What's our next step?'

'I know you did, and there isn't one.'

'We do nothing? Come on.'

She nodded.

'We do nothing.' Gave him a look. 'Nothing, till after the inquiry.'

Wilson slowly lifted his eyebrows.

'Aaah. Right.'

'Some of us,' said Cox drily as she unlatched the car door, 'haven't forgotten about that.'

Back in her flat, she filled a tumbler of water and downed a few of the painkillers she'd taken from the hospital: her headache was almost unbearable now, an unrelenting thunder behind her eyes. Her arm, too, had grown painfully stiff in its sling. The skin of her face felt raw, peeled.

She was physically exhausted – but mentally wired. Time for the *other* medicine . . .

Took down the hard-plastic bottle from the bathroom cabinet, shook out a handful of capsules. No sense in half measures. She had to feel better; right now, she just couldn't afford to be weak.

Gulped down the pills. Sat down on the bed. Closed her eyes for a second.

Was she being paranoid? In the early days, it was an occupational hazard in her business: when you worked in the shadows, you soon started to see bogeymen everywhere. But as you worked on more cases, some successful and some not so, you realized it was dangerous. Sometimes you could join the dots, be sure you had a picture, but you were kidding yourself. Life, society, it was full of coincidences and random connections that really were just that. Some things didn't make sense – some motives were flimsy and some crimes were chaotic, because that's what people's lives were like.

So someone had run her off her bike, sure, but Naysmith had a point – there were a lot of crazy drivers out there. Yeah, they hadn't stopped – so maybe they were uninsured, or over the limit, or just a selfish arsehole? If the studies were to be believed, there were a lot of sociopathic people out there. Maybe the driver had run her down deliberately, on a whim, just because – well – he could.

But think about the timing. Just after they'd zoned in on Euan Merritt. She didn't think it was Merritt who'd tried to kill her, but someone else – who? – might have got word that the net was closing, that she was getting too close for comfort, and decided to take drastic action.

More guessing games, she thought, blearily. More speculation.

She stood – felt unsteady. Well, her body had taken a hell of a battering, of course she was unsteady. She'd get used to it.

Moved through to the kitchen. Realized that she had pretty much no idea what time it was; since the bike ride, the fall, her hours and days had been all out of whack. Blinked at the microwave clock. Couldn't quite make out the numbers.

Seemed darker, gloomier, than it should have.

She was sick of guessing. Sick of being lied to, being strung along. She needed answers. *So*, she thought, *let's go and get some* . . .

There was an inch of cold coffee in the pot. She poured a cup, slurped it down. It was bitter and viscous – but it had a kick, and that was what she needed.

She tugged clumsily at the knot of her sling; her fingers didn't feel right, felt numb, but the knot gave way eventually. The sling fell loose. She shook it away, flexed her arm experimentally. The cast covered her arm from elbow to wrist. The bone ached, but it was nothing she couldn't handle.

Walking carefully – the bang to her hip must've really screwed with her balance, she thought – Cox went to the door. Took her car keys from the hook. Went out.

Merritt's home address was on file, from a minor traffic infringement a few years before. A call to the DVLA had confirmed he was still at the same address. A posh sub-urb, outside Tunbridge Wells. It took Cox a minute to figure out the route – when she tried to visualize the roads (M25? A20-something?), they somehow slithered from her grasp – but she hit the road anyway.

Felt dizzy. Her inner ear wouldn't settle down.

You shouldn't be driving, a part of her nagged.

Yeah, well. There were a lot of things she shouldn't be doing.

Crossed the river at Hammersmith. Didn't seem to be much traffic. Just as well. The car wasn't handling well.

What was she going to say to him? Well, she'd figure that out when the time came. It was what he was going to say to her that mattered. He knew more than he was let-ting on. He was keeping something back from her, the slippery bastard. Holding out on her.

Just like everyone.

She carried on driving, beyond London, and eventually arrived at the outskirts of Tunbridge Wells. Being a TV quack-for-hire must pay all right, she thought, muddily. House prices in these parts were insane. Every driveway she passed had a sports car or a 4x4 – many had both.

Slowed, scanning the street signs, after she crossed London Road. Somewhere round here . . .

Took her the best part of half an hour to find it. A lot of wrong turnings and clumsy three-point turns. There was definitely something wrong with the steering, the lit-tle car was handling like a bloody Sherman tank . . .

Carleton Avenue. This was the one. Parked up; made a pig's ear of it, but what the hell.

It was cold, clear. The sky a deep indigo.

'The Hollies': this was Merritt's place. Nothing so common as a house number for the good doctor. The long driveway was stone-flagged, lined with rose bushes.

Cox eased open the iron gate. Approached the house. Two-storey, detached, Georgian design but probably 1940s, the red brick picturesquely worn, the new uPVC windows out of place.

The front door was open.

A sharp edge of fear cut through Cox's disorientation.

'Hello?' Her tongue felt thick in her mouth. 'Dr Merritt?'

Eased the door open with her foot. A high-ceilinged hall, sparsely decorated: grandfather clock, a tall hat-stand, two sepia landscape prints on the wall.

Stepped inside. The nausea had come back, but now it had nothing to do with the crash, her injury, the drugs . . .

Her copper's instincts were screaming at her. *This is bad. This is trouble.*

She could smell blood. Looked down.

Fat red spots on the off-white carpet. A dark patch of spilled water – a vase, she saw, had been knocked from a side table.

Okay, Kerry, she told herself firmly. *This isn't something you want to do alone.*

Fished out her phone. Dialled. 996. *No. Christ.* Damn fingers wouldn't do as they were told. 99#. 989. 999. *There.* Hit 'call'.

'There's been an accident,' she told the operator. 'The Hollies, Carleton Avenue, Tunbridge Wells. There's been – there's been some sort of accident.'

The operator asked her to repeat the details, said that a patrol car was on its way.

'Thank you,' said Cox.

There was a short pause on the line.

Hesitantly, the operator asked: 'Have you been drinking, madam?'

Cox rang off. *I wish*, she thought darkly.

She thought about going back to her car, waiting for uniform to show up. She didn't know this place, its layout, didn't know who might be here, what might have happened. Christ, she wasn't even meant to *be* here. That police lawyer would have a bloody seizure if he knew.

But those copper's instincts had you both ways. She knew something bad had happened here. And she knew she wasn't leaving till she found out what it was. It wasn't even a choice.

She moved forwards stealthily, trying to keep her shoes from making a noise on the polished hall floorboards.

The hall, she saw, led on, down a step and through open glass-panelled wooden doors, to a cavernous kitchen.

She stopped in the doorway. The kitchen smelled like a butcher's shop.

Maybe Merritt joints his own Sunday roasts, Cox thought wildly, stepping down into the room. *Maybe he likes his black pudding home-made* . . .

The jack-hammer pain in her head had returned.

There was blood on the floor, a broad, dark smear across the pale boards, between the left-hand worktop and a central island.

The kitchen was L-shaped. At the far end, French windows looked out on to a sweep of lawn. There was a pine table with five chairs around it, but room for six. The right wall of the kitchen was hung with copper pans beside a chalk-painted Welsh dresser and a wide black Aga. The trail of blood, Cox saw, approaching warily, led around the right-angled corner, to the left.

It occurred to her, belatedly, that she should have told the operator to send an ambulance as well as a patrol car.

Then she turned the corner and saw that an ambulance wouldn't be necessary.

Euan Merritt's body, stripped naked, was propped in a kitchen chair. Blood had pooled thickly on the floor beneath him and was creeping up the grain of the chair-legs.

Cox covered her mouth with her hand. The world was lurching; she blinked, fought for focus.

The man had been stabbed to death – hell, he'd practically been ripped apart. There were what looked like knife-wounds in his chest, arms, thighs and throat, the blood around them darkening as it dried. His face was a mask of red, only the TV-white teeth showing.

On his chest . . .

Time seemed to swim. What year was it? Where *was* she? Because this, Cox knew, choking back rising bile, was an image from a recurring dream. And she dreamed it because she'd seen it – a long time ago.

The outline of a head, a simple oval with slits for eyes – and horns, like a devil's horns, projecting from the temples. It had been carved in blood over Euan Merritt's heart.

The Ninth Day of Christmas, 1986

Come out blinking, sleepless, cramped from the cold and the hard bed. There weren't any rats, but I couldn't sleep for fear of someone worse than rats coming knocking on the door. Nowhere to run down there – nowhere to hide.

It was Allis what come and got me in the morning.

'Sleep well, Robert?'

You're having a bloody laugh. Muttered a 'Not really.'

'Yes, well, I'm sorry you had to go through that.' He sighed, lifted his eyebrows. 'We prefer not to have to use solitary confinement as a punishment, but, well, rules are rules. Discipline must be maintained.' He nudged me – that gave me a start. 'You can't go round smashing crockery in people's faces, Robert,' he said. 'Even if the little tyke deserves it.'

Little tyke. That's one word for that arsehole Duffy.

Now I follow Allis up the stairs, back into the familiar corridors. The smell of carbolic and polish has faded; back to BO and boiled veg, stale piss and damp walls. Still – and I know how bloody daft it sounds – I'm glad to be back up here.

I turn right, back towards the dorm – I want to see Stan – but Allis, with a hand on my shoulder, steers me left instead. Down the corridor, into an office.

There's a man in there, sitting at a desk.

The blinds are drawn.

My stomach shrivels up in a cramp.

'This,' says Allis, 'is Inspector Radley. A policeman,' he adds, like I'm stupid. I look at the bloke. No uniform. CID, then. Maybe they're taking me seriously.

He's frowning at me, this copper.

'Hello, Robert,' he says.

Allis shuts the door and leaves us to it.

Well, I go into it all again. I don't like talking about it. It's not as bad as it actually happening but it's not that much bloody better. Anyroad, I know I have to, so I do. Talk and talk. The sound of my own voice starts to make me feel sick.

When I stop, this Radley's just staring at me.

'Your sort,' he says, 'aren't usually this talkative in police interviews.'

I don't need to know what he means by 'your sort'. I've had it all my life.

'Yeah, well. This is important.'

He looks down at his notes.

'These are extremely serious allegations,' he says. Folds his meaty hands together, puts them on the table. 'Extremely serious.'

'I know they are.'

'Lying about this kind of thing, Robert, can get you into a lot of trouble. A lot,' he repeats, 'of trouble.'

Sounds like a threat. Gets my temper right up, that. Places like this, you get threatened a lot – you soon learn how to deal with it. You call them out, or you take your medicine. Either way, you don't back down.

Not going to start now.

'Yeah, well. I'm not lying, am I?'

'Aren't you?'

I'm not going to answer that.

We sit in silence for a minute, and then he reads my statement back to me, and it nearly makes me gag, and then I sign it, and he stands up to go.

'That it?' I say.

'No,' he says. 'You've not heard the last of this.'

Like I say, in a place like this, you soon learn to recognize a threat when you hear one. Starting to wonder if Col was right.

Me and Stan sit together on my bed. Raining outside. Most of the lads are down in the rec, playing ping-pong or whatever. I'm not in the mood.

'So were there rats?'

He wants to know all about the cell. No harm in telling him.

'No. I did have to wee in a bucket though.'

'Did *you*?'

'Yeah. And I did a poo. A massive one. So big it nearly filled the bucket.'

He laughs.

'So it wasn't that scary?'

'Nah. It was nothing really. I was fine.'

'Good.' There's a pause while Stan picks his nose. Then he says: 'I didn't like you not being here.'

'Wasn't really my fault, y'know.'

'I know. But I still didn't like it.'

'Well, I'm back now. And I'm not going anywhere.'

'Good,' he says again. Then he starts snivelling a bit. I nudge him, ask him what's up. He says it's nothing, but it's not nothing. So I ask him again, and he says he misses Mum.

I know he's only eight. I know he's only a little lad and he can't help it, but still – that winds me right up.

'It's me that looks after you, Stan,' I say. Try not to shout but I think I am shouting a bit. 'Always has been, ever since you were little. Not Mum. Wherever Mum is,' I say, 'is the least of our bloody worries now.'

He's trying not to cry. He's a good lad, really.

'She looked after you, when you were little, she must have done,' he says.

True enough. I look away. Can't be seen crying twice in two days, not even by Stan. He'll think I've gone weak, and I can't be weak.

'We might not see Mum for ages and ages,' I say. Cruel to be kind and all that. Try not to look at his face. 'I dunno, Stan. Thing is, mate, we might not see our mum ever again.'

He must be crying. He's not making any noise, and I can't look at him. But I can feel his hand creep into mine. Squeeze hard.

'Robert. A word.'

I'm popular these days. It's Halcombe, this time, calling for me across the rec room. I follow her out into the corridor, into an office. Merton and Allis are both in there. Merton's got a whopper of a bump on his balding head, big as a golf-ball, purple and angry-looking — cheers me right up to see it.

Then I wonder what all this lot are doing in here together. Does Merton know what I've been saying about him?

I hang back, staying near the door.

'Sit down, Robert,' says Allis. 'There's nothing to worry about. We have some news for you.'

I sit down, feeling a bit sick. There's only one sort of news you get in these places: someone's died. Has to be our mum, or our dad. We haven't got anyone else.

'What is it?' I say.

I keep up a front. I'm fucked if I'm going to cry in front of this bastard Merton.

But it's not what I think. No one's died.

'We've been speaking to our colleagues at Wolvesley,' says Allis. Wolvesley. Division One.

'They're very busy,' puts in Merton, 'as we all are. Too many broken families – too few resources.'

'But,' Allis smiles, 'they have a vacancy.'

The hope that was rising in my chest deflates like a balloon when the knot busts.

'A vacancy? Just one?'

Allis nods.

Christ.

'Give it to Stan,' I say.

There's a bit of a pause, and then Merton – of all fucking people – says: 'It really is very admirable how you always put your brother first.'

I could smack him. But I sit still instead and stare at the tabletop.

While we pack up his stuff, me and Stan talk about what they'll have at Wolvesley.

'Sweet shop, I bet.'

'Swimming pool, with a slide.'

'A zoo!'

'Dodgem cars. Waltzers.'

'No, I don't like waltzers. A big wheel.'

'Okay. Illuminations, like at Blackpool.'

Not that we've ever been to bloody Blackpool.

'A plastic football pitch, like QPR have got.' He grins at me. 'You can play on it even when it's raining. I'll go in goal, and you can shoot.'

Been feeling sick all day, ever since they told me about Wolvesley. Now I have to turn away, choke back a big lump. The acid of it burns my throat.

Christ.

I've not told him. How can I tell him? I fold his pyjamas, stick a *few comics in the bottom of his case (they're not really his, but no one's going to miss 'em).*

'When are you packing, Robbie?'

'Later. I'm – I'm going on a different bus than you, Stan.'

'Oh.' He sounds put out.

'Don't worry, mate.' I punch him lightly on the shoulder. 'Once you're there, it'll all be right as rain.'

He nods.

'Hope we get a room together,' he says.

I hold it together. Fuck knows how, but I do.

Fucking Merton. That fucking bastard.

We're in the car park, and Miss Halcombe's big old car's there, engine running, ready to go. Halcombe puts Stan's case in the boot, dusts her hands together.

'All set,' she says.

Stan's nervous, I can see, who wouldn't be, but he's doing okay, and I haven't lost it yet, though God knows how long that'll last after this car drives away –

Merton, who's come down to see Stan off, says: 'Give your brother a big hug, Stanley.'

And me and Stan hug like the soft sods we are, and I tell him not to worry, everything's going to be all right, there's some comics in his case if he gets bored waiting for me, and I'll be there really soon, as soon as I can. He's crying a bit, but that's okay.

Then just as he's climbing into the back of the car Merton says: 'I'm sure we can arrange for Robert to come and visit you, Stanley. Once you've settled in at Wolvesley Grange.'

He slams the car door behind my brother.

Stan's only eight but he's not daft. He twigs right away.

Hammering on the window. Screaming my name.

225

I want to kill Dr Merton.

I want to smash open the car door and drag our Stan out of there.

I want to cry.

I can't, I can't. I can't do anything. What I do is, I turn and run. Back to the building. Back to Hampton Hall. I can still hear Stan screaming. I hear the car pull away, out of the car park. It's soon gone. But in my head I can still hear Stan screaming my name.

18

Cox sat on the low back step outside the French windows of the Merritt place, head in hands. Felt like her skull was on the brink of breaking apart.

Naysmith wasn't happy. What else was new?

Inside the kitchen, SOCO lamps glared, and the crime-scene photographers stalked back and forth, snatching every angle – every wound, every drop of blood. Cox had attended plenty of murder scenes, some pretty gory, but nothing like this. It wasn't the severity of the injuries that made it stand out, she realized, it was the fact she'd spoken to the victim, seen him a living, breathing, walking person, just a couple of days earlier. Normally they were just corpses, and she didn't even have to imagine what they were like before someone took their lives.

More than anything, Dr Euan Merritt looked like slaughtered meat.

Naysmith stood with Chalmers on the lawn. They'd been there maybe ten minutes, and the DCI hadn't said a word to her.

In the silence her pain – head, bones, skin – seemed to expand, to fill the world. Couldn't think about anything else. She wished Naysmith would just say *something* – even if it was only to give her a bollocking.

Eventually, he stepped away from Chalmers. Cleared his throat.

'So, DI Cox,' he said. 'Would you like to tell me what you were doing here?'

His tone was conversational, almost casual. She'd known Pete Naysmith long enough to know that that meant trouble was coming.

She didn't look up. Couldn't. Couldn't bear to lift her pounding head.

'It was,' she muttered, 'a legitimate line of inquiry.'

'Legitimate?' Naysmith laughed, lightly, facetiously. 'After you were very specifically warned, in the presence of two lawyers, to keep away from Euan Merritt at all costs? That's a very interesting definition of "legitimate", Cox. Very bloody interesting.'

A flicker of temper in his tone.

'I was following up –' Cox began.

'You shouldn't have been following fucking anything,' Naysmith exploded. He swore, kicked in exasperation at a loose tree-root in the flowerbed. 'A few hours ago you were in a fucking hospital bed with a bleed on your brain. Now you're prowling around looking for trouble?' Shook his head with a bitter sigh. 'I worry about you, Cox. You're going off the fucking deep end.'

Cox took a breath, looked up at the fuming DCI.

'I told you Merritt was in danger, didn't I?' she said, struggling to keep her voice level. Jerked her head towards the kitchen annex where the psychologist's body still sat propped in the bloody chair. 'Looks like I was right. Or are you going to tell me that was suicide, too?'

She heard Chalmers, off to her left, stifle a snigger.

Naysmith's skin-tone darkened from pink to puce.

'This is getting way out of fucking hand,' he said. 'I've

already had to pull rank on the local force. They wanted the case; I had to call in the fucking MoJ to square it with them.'

Cox's heart sank.

'Harrington?'

The look Naysmith gave her was challenging, defiant.

'Him, or his people,' he nodded.

'Great, guv. Fucking great.'

Naysmith was about to reply when Chalmers called him over. He had Annie Stevenson, the chief SOCO, with him. Naysmith grunted something about continuing the conversation later on; went over to join them.

Cox, with an effort, dragged herself to her feet. This was a briefing she couldn't afford to miss. It was odds on Naysmith would deny her access to the case files afterwards.

She limped across the lawn, took up a discreet position behind Chalmers's shoulder, out of Naysmith's eyeline.

' . . . never seen anything like it,' Stevenson was saying. She looked – not shaken, because you just couldn't shake a senior SOCO of twenty-odd years' experience – but definitely stirred up.

'Give us the run-down,' Naysmith said. 'What's the cause of death?'

'We're pretty sure he bled to death.'

'From the throat?'

'No.' There was a flicker of a bone-dry smile on Stevenson's angular face as she addressed the two men. 'He was castrated. Bled out.'

'Fu-u-cking hell,' Chalmers murmured in a low voice.

Naysmith just nodded.

'Nasty. What else?'

'He was – well, he was put through hell, guv.' Stevenson shook her head. 'Multiple knife wounds, deep, more like surgical incisions than stabbings. Skin removed from his arms and face. Multiple cigarette burns on his thighs, back, hands, face. One on his right eyeball.'

'Christ. Do we have a weapon?'

'Butcher's knife. Merritt's own, looks like, from a block in the kitchen. The killer washed it and left it in the sink.' She grimaced. 'We'll do what we can, but I doubt we'll get anything from it.'

'And what about that business on his chest – the face?'

'Cut into the skin with the same knife, I think. But that was definitely post-mortem.'

Naysmith nodded thoughtfully, dismissed the SOCO. Turned to Cox.

'Anything to add to that, Cox?' he asked gruffly. 'Seeing as you were on the spot.'

She thought back. Christ, even *thinking* hurt.

'The door was open,' she said.

'Forced?'

'I – I'm not sure. But it was open – not just unlocked, open – when I arrived.' She lifted her chin. 'You can't keep downplaying this, guv. Radley, Halcombe, Allis – now this. All linked, one way or another, to Hampton Hall.'

'You came to me with a load of –'

'I came to you with a *theory*. And here –' She pointed through the French windows – 'here's the proof. All the proof you need.' Shook her head. 'It's no coincidence, guv. You and the chief super and the MoJ and God knows who else can't keep pretending it is.'

'What's your read, Cox?' Chalmers asked her seriously. 'On this guy. Why the torture? Some kind of payback? Wanted to see him suffer?'

'That's one possibility,' she nodded. 'The other is that Merritt knew something – and the guy who did this wanted very badly to find out what.'

'Either way,' Naysmith said firmly, 'we keep this in-house. Is that clear? If I read anything, *anything*, about what happened here in the papers, I'm going to hold you two responsible. This is strictly confidential.' He looked at Cox. 'I don't take kindly to having my orders disobeyed, inspector. You'd do well to remember that.'

Fair point, Cox thought.

A memory sparked.

'Butcher,' she said aloud, without meaning to.

The two men looked at her.

'Huh?'

Quickly she gathered her thoughts.

'We need to speak to John Harris, Merritt's solicitor,' she said. 'When we – when *I* spoke to Merritt, he said something about someone called Butcher who he thought had been spreading rumours about him. Then when I mentioned the name to Harris – remember, guv? – I got a death-stare. There's something there, I'm sure of it.'

Naysmith nodded.

'Okay. It's a start. Chalmers, get on it, would you?'

'Yes, guv.'

As the DI hurried off, Naysmith, hands on hips, turned to look in through the French windows. His expression was distant.

'If whoever did this is called "Butcher",' he said, 'the fucking headlines will write themselves.'

SOCO had packed up and gone. The remains of Dr Euan Merritt had been shipped off to the morgue. Naysmith was at the table in the kitchen, sorting through his notes before heading back to the nick.

Cox sat down opposite him. Waited for him to look up. Eventually he set down his pen.

'There's no need to apologize,' he said, leaning back in his chair. 'It's done with now.'

'I'm not here to apologize, guv.'

'Oh?' He blinked. 'Well, you fucking should be. What you did today was a fucking disgrace.' He wiped a hand across his eyes. 'So what did you want?'

Cox hesitated. She'd thought long and hard, since she found Merritt's body, about bringing this to the DCI – about mentioning it to anybody, come to that. *You're going off the deep end*, he'd told her. What if he was right? The pressure, the fall, the drugs.

The nightmares.

'The – the face, guv.'

'Face? What face?'

'The face cut into Merritt's chest.'

'Oh, yeah. Nice touch, that. Some fucking people, eh?'

Cox swallowed. Took a breath. The mental image was already forming in her head – the image that haunted her . . .

'I've seen it before, guv.'

'What? Where?'

'Not on a body, nothing like that. It was a mask. I saw

a man wearing a mask, exactly the same, the slit eyes, the horns.'

'What man? What are you talking about?'

'It was in a video.' Cox stared at the tabletop as she spoke. Looked up. Naysmith was frowning at her. 'Guv, I think this thing goes further than Hampton Hall.' Speaking fast, trying to say what she had to say before she thought better of it. 'It's not just about care homes. I think there's a link to trafficking, child trafficking.' She met Naysmith's stare. 'I think there's a link to Tomasz Lerna.'

Naysmith rocked back in his chair. She couldn't read his expression.

'Guv? Did you hear me?'

He sighed. Looked away.

'Jesus Christ,' he murmured.

He looked sick; the solid, thick-built DCI looked like he'd aged five years in a minute.

'Guv, are you okay?'

He looked at her. Nodded, slowly.

'I'm fine, Kerry,' he said. 'Are you?'

Smith's knuckles were white on the grip of his gun.

'Ma'am, we really can't guarantee your safety.'

'So you said.' Cox jerked the fastenings tight on her protective vest. 'I'm coming with you anyway, sergeant.'

Smith nodded tersely, muttered a word into his mic. The side-door of the van was pulled open; the Armed Response Unit spilled out into the darkness, Cox stumbling along behind.

It was just after eleven o'clock. They were at a block of

flats in the arse-end of Hackney to bring in Steven Kenneth Dudley Butcher.

Chalmers must have gone in hard on Harris the lawyer; he'd coughed up the details double-quick. Stevie Butcher was another care home kid; another disturbed youth with a twisted grievance, Harris said. He'd started targeting Merritt a year or so earlier, after seeing him on TV. Low-level stuff, really – threatening letters, defamatory blogposts – but obviously, Harris had said, he was working his way up to something bigger: murder.

The ARU officers moved in fluid synchronicity across the car park, falling into well-practised formation at the foot of the main staircase.

As she ran to catch up, Cox glanced upwards. Any chance of this being a surprise raid, she saw, was long gone: a bunch of local kids, BMX handlebars gleaming in the streetlights, were gathered at the railing of the walkway above. Smartphone cameras winked in the gloom.

'Smile, bitch,' a high-pitched voice shouted.

She limped into the darkness of the stairwell.

Stank of piss. The ARU officers' powerful torch beams raked the graffiti-scrawled concrete walls. She could hear Sergeant Smith's voice only as a murmur, soft but authoritative.

She didn't hear him say 'go' – but suddenly they were off, running up the scuffed, littered steps, and she was running with them, arm bouncing painfully in the sling.

Second floor, flat 24, that was the last address they'd dug out for Butcher. He was on parole: drugs, theft. Butcher's record was pretty much par for the course in this part of town.

The officers surged from the stairwell on to the walk-way. Cox saw a couple of young lads at the far end turn startled white faces towards them; dropped their plastic bottle of booze, ran for it.

Flat 24 was halfway along. Again the officers fell easily into formation, surrounding the gated door. Cox, out of breath and limping, moved to the front. Positioned her-self to one side of the door; wasn't unknown for a copper knocking on a suspect's door to get a gunshot in reply.

Reached across, hammered with her fist on the wood.

'Police,' she shouted. 'Open up.'

She heard a yell, a squeal of a car taking off down in the car park – a dealer, spooked by the 'p' word. Nothing from inside. Cox counted one, two, three – gave Smith the nod.

An officer stepped forward, and in a spray of sparks and splinters the door went through, iron gate and all.

Cox pressed her back to the clammy wall as the ARU unit poured past her into the flat. Smith's voice rose over the noise of their bootsteps: *armed police, show yourself, armed police, come out with your hands up.* After a second, she heard screaming, a woman's screaming, and then a man's voice. She smelt dope smoke, rich and strong.

Less than a minute later two officers emerged through the shattered doorframe, dragging between them a wire-thin man in tracksuit bottoms and a basketball vest. Badly done tattoos covered his arms; his head was shaved except for a lank, dark mohawk. He was beaky, hollow-cheeked. Looked about forty.

Wasn't steady on his feet. From the doorway of the flat, as the rest of the unit filed out, a woman in a terrycloth bathrobe was screaming: 'He ain't done nothing! He ain't done nothing wrong!'

The man eyed Cox emotionlessly as she approached.

'Steven Butcher?'

'Yeah.'

'Mr Butcher, I'm arresting you on suspicion of the murder of Euan Merritt. You do not have to say anything. However, it may harm your defence if you do not mention when questioned something which you later rely on in court. Anything you do say may be given in evidence.'

Butcher looked vacant while he digested this information.

Slowly, his face broke into a smile. There wasn't a tooth in his mouth.

'So someone finally done the cunt, then?' he said. 'Good. *Good.*'

19

No alibi. That was something. But Butcher was giving them nothing else.

'I didn't have fuck-all to do with it.'

'So you've said, Mr Butcher.' Cox had insisted on getting first crack at the guy. Her case. Her suspect. Chalmers was in on the interview, slouched wearily in his chair, but she'd made it clear to him that she was taking the lead.

She took a sip of bottled water, looked at Butcher steadily. 'So you weren't in Tunbridge Wells earlier today?'

'I don't know where that is. I ain't been out since yesterday, except only down the road once, to Chicken Cottage.'

'Have you *ever* been to Tunbridge Wells?'

'I'm not sure that's relevant,' put in the duty brief, a worn-looking man called Hosking.

'Yeah. And I ain't, anyway. I don't even know where it is.'

Cox sighed.

Since they'd pulled Butcher in she'd been waiting for a phone to buzz, for a PC to put his head round the door, tell her they'd found something, anything, in Butcher's flat, to tie him to Merritt. Nothing.

'Could you tell me about your relationship with Dr Merritt?'

Butcher glanced sideways at his brief; kept his mouth shut.

She leaned back in her chair.

'Mr Butcher, we're under no illusions about what kind of a man Dr Merritt was. We know you were in contact with him. You might as well tell us how –'

A knock on the door interrupted her.

Thank Christ.

'Quick word, ma'am?'

She excused herself, stepped out into the corridor. A young constable, with news from Hackney. A bag of weed in Butcher's flat. No great surprise.

'How much?'

'Enough to get him on intent to supply, ma'am.'

'He's in breach of his parole either way. Thanks, constable.'

Back in the interview room, she went straight for the jugular.

'Looks like you're going back to Pentonville, Stevie.'

Told Butcher about the drugs, the parole breach. He gaped at her.

'It – it's my girlfriend's.'

'Funny – she says the exact opposite,' Cox lied.

'Bitch would.'

'I guess you can argue it out in front of the magistrate.' She gave him a hard smile. 'Look, Stevie, we need your cooperation here. If you didn't kill Merritt, why not help us figure out who did? We may be able to have a word with the Parole Board. Get them to overlook what they found in your flat.'

'Help you?' he said dully. 'Help you how? I don't know who killed him.'

Took a shot in the dark: 'Tell me what you had on Merritt. We know you were blackmailing him. What with? What do you know about him?'

Hosking, eyeing Cox with weary hostility, put a warning hand on Butcher's elbow.

Butcher shrugged him off. Showed his pink-grey gums in a slack-lipped laugh.

'I know fucking everything about him!' he smiled. 'But I weren't blackmailing him, I didn't want nothing from him. I told the truth, happy to tell the truth, do that for free. Tell the world what he done.'

Cox folded her hands on the table, leaned forward.

'What did he do?'

And they were off.

Butcher mentioned Hampton Hall without prompting; he'd been in care there for three or four years as a pre-teen. Dr Merton used to come by pretty often, he said; give the boys 'medicals'.

'Medicals? What did that involve?'

Butcher sneered unpleasantly.

'D'you need me to draw you a picture?'

'Let's be clear. Are we talking about abuse?'

'Yer.'

'Sexual abuse?'

'Yer.' Butcher sniffed wetly. 'It depended, though. He had his little system, like.'

'How d'you mean?'

'Rewards. Bribery. Like you, here, offering me favours

if I cough up the goods.' He smiled unpleasantly. 'Only I know you're only doing your job. With him, it was, you know, a trip to the arcades in town, a fucking takeaway pizza. Don't sound like much now,' he added, defensively, 'but believe me, in there, you take what you can get.'

'And in return?'

'I never did it myself.' He said it quickly, firmly. 'I could see the price weren't worth paying. But other kids – twisted little bastards, they must've been – well, they were fucking queueing up to take part in Dr Merton's "studies".'

'And what happened to them?'

Butcher shrugged.

'Got fucked in half, prob'ly,' he said emotionlessly. 'I dunno. You'd have to ask them.'

Cox ignored the gust of nausea that ran through her.

'Mr Butcher, could you please state for the record that you believe Dr Merritt – then known as Dr Merton – engaged in the systematic sexual abuse of children in care at Hampton Hall?'

'Yer, that sounds about right.'

'And how long did this go on for, to your knowledge?'

'Dunno. Long as I was there, I know that.'

'What about the other staff?'

Butcher opened his mouth to reply but was interrupted by an exasperated sigh from Hosking, his brief.

'I struggle to see how all this relates to the accusations in hand,' the solicitor complained. 'Do you intend to charge my client? If not –'

'Nah, nah.' Butcher waved away his protests. 'I don't mind. We're just talking, ain't we? People need to know about all this. Nice to have someone listening for a change.'

The solicitor shrugged his narrow shoulders.

'Very well,' he said, flashing a disapproving look at Cox. 'As you wish.'

Most of the other staff, Butcher said, knew what Merton was up to – they just did nothing about it.

'Why do you think that was?'

'Dunno. Maybe they got "special privileges" too.' He rubbed his thumb and forefinger together meaningfully.

'But Dr Merton never abused you, personally?'

Butcher shook his head slowly – even, it seemed, proudly.

'Nah. Never. Maybe I weren't his type. Or maybe he knew I weren't going to play along. I weren't going to bend over and bite the pillow like a good little boy. Nah, fuck that.' He picked his nose thoughtfully. 'I reckon they know, nonces, who they can mess with and who they can't. I reckon they've got like an instinct for it.'

Cox frowned. This could be a problem. If Butcher had no direct experience of abuse by Merritt, was any of this more than hearsay and guesswork?

But then, there were any number of reasons why the guy might not want to tell them if Merritt *did* abuse him at Hampton Hall. Maybe he just didn't want to talk about it; he might've even blanked out the memory – it wasn't an uncommon response among victims of abuse.

Then there was the fact that Butcher seemed to take a dim view of the boys who, in his words, *played along* with Merritt. There'd be a lot bundled up there, Cox guessed: guilt, shame, self-hatred, disgust. This kind of abuse, she knew, left more than physical scars.

And there was another possibility: Butcher had twigged

that having been abused by Merritt gave him a motive for killing him. He was just trying to stay out of trouble.

'How do you know for sure,' Cox said carefully, 'that Merritt – or rather Merton – was committing abuse?'

Butcher glowered at her indignantly.

'Ain't you been listening?'

'I have, Mr Butcher, yes. But I want to know, if you weren't yourself a victim, exactly how you can be so sure what went on. Did someone tell you?'

A nod.

'Yeah.'

'Who?'

'All right. All right, here's a story for you.' Butcher leaned forward across the table, arms folded tight under his ribs. 'I had a mate in Hampton, a lad a year or so younger'n me. Robbie. Little fucking trouble-maker he was.' Butcher grinned faintly at the memory – but the grin quickly faded. 'The stupid little cunt let himself be bought off by Merton.'

'You mean he was abused?'

'Yer, that's what I mean. Got all the fucking pizza he could eat, though. For him and his little brother. Parents were skagheads, or something like that, so both brothers ended up at Hampton.' Another toothless grin. This one was utterly mirthless. 'He used to tell me what went on. Horrible fucking stuff, it was. Robbie just took it, though.'

'And do you remember Robbie's surname?'

He shook his head, grimacing bitterly. 'Didn't have much fucking luck, that kid.'

'Why do you say that?'

'His brother got moved, to another place. Died in a

fire. Robbie went fucking crazy after that. Christmas, too. Not that we exactly had merry fucking Christmases in that place, but still . . .'

Cox snapped to attention.

'A boy died?'

Butcher clicked his fingers. 'Wolvesley, it was called. Wolvesley Grange. Had a reputation for being a bit of a softer digs. Y'know, better food and all that.'

'Do you know what the boy's name was?'

Butcher poked out his lower lip, shook his head.

'Nah, man, too long ago. He was just Robbie's brother. But Robbie, fucking hell – he was just never the same after that. Know what I mean? After that Christmas, he was a different fucking person.'

Cox nodded, mentally filing away the details. She'd given up on the idea that Butcher was responsible for Merritt's death – hell, had she ever really believed it? – but still, he might be able to give them the lead they needed.

'Let's go back to Dr Merritt,' she said. 'You didn't answer before when I asked if you'd ever been to Merritt's house. But that's okay, because we know from our records that you were apprehended trespassing on the property just over a year ago.'

Butcher sighed. Let his head drop.

'Yeah,' he said.

'You had it in for Dr Merritt.'

'I – I dunno. I saw him on the telly and – and summink snapped.'

The brief butted in again: 'Mr Butcher, I'd advise you not to answer any more questions.'

But Cox kept up the pressure. Took out a manila folder, opened it. It contained six glossy colour photographs.

'These are images from the crime scene,' she said. Held up one. A close-up of Merritt's face: the red mask, the jutting white teeth.

She glanced at Hosking: the solicitor had paled and was holding both hands over his mouth. Butcher, though, only blinked, once, slowly, and said: 'Weren't me.'

Another photo, this one showing the deep wounds to Merritt's legs and genitals; from Butcher, the same impassive response.

The third photo was the kicker in the three-card trick.

A full-frame close-up of the face cut into Merritt's chest.

'I thought this one might be familiar,' she said.

She watched Butcher closely. Saw his eyes widen, just for a second; saw him bite his lower lip. Then saw him shake his head.

'Nah.'

'You're sure? Look closely.'

Butcher gulped.

'Nah.'

'Mr Butcher, you're telling me you've never seen this image before?' *Careful, Kerry, careful – don't push it.* 'Take a long look. Think hard.'

Butcher peered at the image for a drawn-out moment – then he looked sharply away and slapped at the picture angrily with his hand.

'Stop waving these fucking pictures at me, man,' he protested. 'It's sick.'

'No, Stevie, what's *sick* is what Euan Merritt did to you

and a lot of other boys. I know what they called him – Dr Midnight, wasn't it?'

'You don't know nothing about it.'

'Then *tell* me, for God's sake.' Shook the photo of the face-shaped wound. 'You know what this is, don't you? Dammit, Stevie, I *know* you do.' She brought the flat of her hand down hard on the table. Her bottle of water jumped.

Straight away she knew she'd gone too far.

Butcher's jaw was clenched; a vein beat rapidly in his shaved temple. Cox heard Chalmers let out a breath.

Into the silence the solicitor said: 'I don't think my client will be answering any more questions today, inspector. Do you and your silent partner here' – he indicated Chalmers with a dismissive waft of his hand – 'intend to charge Mr Butcher? Do you, indeed, have any evidence to link him to this crime?' He had taken out a handkerchief and was fastidiously wiping his hands. 'Or should you, in fact, admit that this was nothing but a fishing expedition and release my client from custody?'

Cox felt her own heartbeat slowly return to normal; brought her breathing steadily under control.

'I don't think so,' she said firmly. 'Mr Butcher still has an awful lot of questions to answer.'

The Tenth Day of Christmas, 1986

'Maybe he's been banged up,' says Stevie.

'Dream on,' grunts Col.

We've not seen Merton today, and Stevie's heard from one of the orderlies that he's not going to be back here for a while. Good bloody riddance, I thought. At first.

Then I remembered what he told us, that day in the garden before Mark Duffy beaned him with a snowball: his job is to go round all these places, not just Hampton Hall, but all the others in the area. 'Make sure everyone's okay.'

Does that include Wolvesley Grange?

Duffy comes in. Still got a cast on his face from the broken nose I give him. He realizes we're talking about Merton and comes strutting over.

'I hear he's staying with a young friend over in Shirley somewhere,' he says. Grinning.

Everyone looks at me.

Last time felt like something snapping inside. This isn't like that. This is like someone else is taking me over. Someone who doesn't care about anything – who just wants this bastard Duffy to suffer, to hurt – who'll hurt him, and keep hurting him, and won't stop – can't stop.

That's not who I am. I'm not that person. But that's who I turn into when Duffy says that.

In two seconds I've got him by the throat, on his back, on the floor.

It's not clear what's happening. It's a blur – of blood, shouting, screaming.

I know I'm hurting him. I know I'm not going to stop unless someone makes me.

And when my focus comes back and I look down all I can see of Mark Duffy is his stupid spiky haircut and his stupid fake Villa shirt and a glossy pool of red where his face should be.

A mouth opens in the blood. Says, 'Help.'

And then I'm on the floor myself, eyes scalded with mace, an orderly's heavy knee in the small of my back.

'I want Stan back here.'

I've had four hours in the cooling-off room. I've washed the blood off my knuckles, off my forehead. Couldn't get it out of my T-shirt.

Miss Halcombe is looking at me like I'm the scum of the earth. Maybe I am.

'You've changed your tune,' she says. 'Remember, it was you who asked us to arrange the transfer.'

'But —'

'And I know Stanley's departure was very upsetting for you — it was for us all — but it in no way excuses your assault on Mark Duffy today.' Shakes her head. 'We can't just let this go, Robert.'

I shrug.

'He wound me up — about our Stan. I lost the plot. How is he?'

'Duffy? He'll live.' Didn't sound like she gave much of a shit about it. 'But you could have killed him. If we hadn't restrained you, you might well have.'

Can't say anything to that. She's right, and there's no 'might' about it. I bloody would have.

'Bring him back,' I say.

'You're in no position to be giving out orders.'

'Then send me there.'

'You're going nowhere, young man.' She taps her pencil on the desk. 'You're staying right here *until Dr Merton and I decide otherwise.'*

247

I turn sharply away, knowing I need to hit out, to kick out at something, anything, or else I'll go for this fat bag Halcombe, and there's no one here to stop me . . .

The glass in the door is wire-reinforced. I swing my right fist, hard as I can. Feel the glass break against my bone. Feel my skin rip open. Feel my ligaments tear.

There's a sharp shout, a rumble of heavy bodies coming near. I scrunch my face up in case they mace me again — brace myself to be thrown to the floor, knotted up, sat on . . .

But there's only a hard, painful grip on my left wrist, a tearing noise, and a jab, an injection in the soft flesh of my arm.

I think of Stan, how good he always was at the doctor's.

I wake up in the cell.

I'm groggy but I'm steady enough to lift up the bed-frame, on to its end, and prop it against the wall. Climb up till I can nearly touch the ceiling.

I'm weak but I've got the strength to heave at the grille that covers the half-window. They don't maintain nothing properly in this shithole: damp's got into the stonework over winter, and I can see the rusty screws working loose.

This is how Santa gets in, Stan.

It comes away in a shower of crumbled concrete.

I smash the green-stained glass with the narrow end of the oblong grille. Hell of a noise, but they won't hear me way down here. Brush away the glass.

I'll cut myself to bloody ribbons climbing out of here, I can see. Windowframe's still studded with little triangles of dirty glass.

And if I don't *climb out of here?*

I pull myself up — it's hard, one-handed, and it fucking

hurts — and stick my head out. Cold, dingy, wet. Looks like the window's at the bottom of a ditch or a vent or something.

All I've got to do is climb and keep on climbing.

Then all I've got to do is find our Stan.

20

Two hours later. Cox sat in the CID suite, swirling the dregs of another tasteless coffee in her cup. She felt deadened, stale. Butcher was still downstairs, sweating it out in his cell. Not for long, though: his girlfriend had confirmed his alibi, such as it was, and their neighbours in the tower-block hadn't given them any decent reason to doubt it.

'Face it, Cox, we've got fuck-all,' Naysmith had grunted. 'Turn him loose.'

He was on his way home. First day of the inquiry tomorrow, he reminded Cox, as if she needed reminding; he had homework to do. He was going to be asked to lay out the background of the Tomasz Lerna case.

Cox gulped down the last of the coffee. Screw it; she was calling it a day, too. The DCI was right, they didn't have anything like enough evidence to charge Butcher with murder. Time to kick the poor bastard out. She headed downstairs.

In the car park she passed Dan Chalmers. He was leaning on a bollard, smoking a cigarette. Must've worked his way through a pack at least, today. He didn't show a lot on the surface, Chalmers – but the Merritt murder had rattled him. It'd rattled everybody.

'You off?' he called.

She nodded. Chalmers dragged on his cigarette, discarded the butt.

'He's telling the truth, isn't he?' he said, looking uncomfortable. 'I know the background, the abuse, harassment, it all points to Butcher – but Cox, I don't think he did it.'

Cox rubbed her stiff neck, made a face.

'I don't think so either,' she said. 'The guy's got a grievance, a serious one, too, who can blame him, but what was done to Merritt – Christ, it's in another league.'

Chalmers jerked his head back towards the nick.

'Want me to have one last crack at him?'

'Nah. Let him go. I think we've got all we're going to get from Stevie Butcher. Sort out the recommendation to the Parole Board, would you? Breach of conditions to be overlooked in recognition of exceptionally helpful blah blah blah. You know the drill.'

Chalmers nodded; flipped her a lazy wave by way of goodnight.

In her car, as she buckled her seatbelt, she wondered if she should've said something to Chalmers about what'd happened in that interview room – why she'd lost the run of herself over a crude sketch of a face. Chalmers was a decent guy, not fazed by much. But how could he ever understand, really understand, what it meant?

No. This was something she'd have to deal with alone.

She called Greg Wilson before she drove off. She'd been keeping him posted – by text, and very much on the quiet – as the day had worn on: the murder of Merritt, the raid on Butcher, the mention of a child's death at Wolvesley Grange.

He'd been busy.

'There was a fire at Wolvesley, early 1987,' he said. 'That's on the record: press coverage as well as local authority reports. And there was a death: a young girl, Jessica Arnott, seven years old. Fire service reckoned she'd started the fire herself, playing with matches.'

'And the boy? This Robbie's brother?'

'No record of a boy being killed.'

Cox sighed.

'Shit. I was hoping we might actually be on to something here.'

Wilson made a tutting noise.

'Cox, Cox, Cox,' he said. Hearing the smile in his voice, she could see it in her mind's eye: cynical, excited, wolfish. 'Have you learned nothing? I said there's no record of it. But that doesn't mean it didn't happen.'

The buzz of her phone woke her. She blinked, pushed her hair out of her face. The room was steeped in muted silver-grey. Light already? Squinted at the clock: just gone eight. She'd climbed into bed a little before eleven. When was the last time she'd slept for nine hours straight? Must be good stuff in those painkillers . . .

She took up her humming phone from the bedside table. Clocked the number; swore softly.

'Serena. Good morning.'

The barrister sounded cross – more so than usual.

'DI Cox, are you with DCI Naysmith?'

'Naysmith?' She rubbed her bleary eyes. 'No. I've just woken up. Are you at the inquiry?'

'*I* am,' McAvoy snapped back. 'But your chief inspector is nowhere to be seen. He's due to be called in two hours' time, and we've barely begun briefing. He's not answering his phone, either.'

It's not my fault, Cox wanted to reply. But being petulant would get her nowhere. Besides, it was a worry – what the hell was Naysmith playing at?

He didn't always cope well with stress, she knew.

'We sent a car to his home,' McAvoy went on, 'but apparently there was no one there. No one in any fit state to answer the door, anyway.'

Cox sighed. So the QC knew about Naysmith's boozing. *Good job she's on our side*, she thought, before correcting herself: McAvoy wasn't on their side, she was on the side of the Metropolitan Police Service.

A few years ago, it'd never have occurred to her to make that distinction.

'I'll go round there now,' she said. 'Take a look. I'll let you know as soon as I know anything.'

'Please do,' McAvoy huffed. The line went dead.

Naysmith lived in a three-bed new-build up in Ladbroke Grove, near the Westway. His car – a blue Focus, nothing flashy – was in the driveway. Curtains pulled. No sign of any trouble – yet. She parked two doors down, approached the house warily.

A square-edged privet restricted her view of the house-front. The estate employed a gardener who kept everything tidy, tasteful and lifeless. It was a place for overworked professionals, mostly single, no kids, people who wanted a decent place to live – and could afford one – but hadn't the time or energy to think about cleaning or upkeep.

She walked up the bricked path. Nothing out of order. Reached up to take the spare key from where Naysmith kept it tucked in the matting of a hanging basket. She'd given him some ribbing over that, first time he'd told her about it: *we've got PCs going round telling people how to secure their homes, and here's a DCI keeping his door key where any mug could find it . . .*

She was glad of it now. Wiped the dirt off the key, eased open the door. The chain snapped tight.

'Guv? You here?'

No reply. She called again.

When, after a few seconds, there wasn't a sound, she put her good shoulder and all her weight into the door. The chain gave way easily.

She stepped cautiously into the hall. Her foot chinked against broken glass. Looked down; red liquid was seeping into the fabric of her shoe.

Oh Christ . . .

But the surge of panic quickly subsided. The stink of alcohol was overpowering. Not blood, but cheap wine – Naysmith must've dropped a bottle when he was bringing in supplies.

She kicked the shards aside angrily, wiped the wine from her shoe and marched through the hall into the living room.

TV on, tuned to a late-night soft-porn channel. Three empty bottles of red lined up on the coffee table. Foil carton greasy with takeaway leftovers. Half-pint bottle of supermarket whisky on its side on the carpet – that, too, was empty.

Naysmith was asleep on the sofa in yesterday's clothes. Tie loosened, one sock on, one sock off. A shirt-button had given way, exposing three inches of bloated gut. He had his mouth open, and his tongue lolled against his lower lip.

'For fuck's sake,' Cox sighed.

She dug a toe-end into Naysmith's side. The DCI grunted, turned over heavily. Cox chewed her lip irritably; she wasn't in the mood for this. The man was meant to be her boss, for Christ's sake. She didn't feel in the slightest guilty about busting the chain.

'Guv,' she shouted. 'Wake up.'

Gave him another kick.

Naysmith opened his eyes.

'Inquiry day,' said Cox.

Naysmith's cheeks bulged.

'I'm gonna be sick,' he said.

Cox turned away, biting down hard on her anger and disgust. Tried to ignore the noise of Naysmith vomiting painfully on to the carpet; stepped out into the hall, dialled Serena McAvoy's number.

No preamble.

'Have you found him?'

'Yes. He's – indisposed.'

McAvoy snorted.

'I'll assume you mean dead drunk. Well, I can't say it's an enormous surprise. I've already sounded out the inquiry – discreetly, of course. They're prepared to adjourn for the morning. It was made quite clear to me, however, that the inquiry will be in session this afternoon. That means either that DCI Naysmith will have to be *feeling better* by then – or that you, inspector, will have to give evidence in his place.'

Cox's insides froze up. Behind her, in the living room,

Naysmith was on his feet – she could hear him talking loudly to himself. *Gonna give this so-called inquiry hell . . . Proud to work with you, Cox, bloody proud . . . Poking their noses into police business . . .*

That man was not going to appear before an inquiry today.

'I – I haven't been briefed, or, or –' Cox protested.

'Then perhaps you should have turned up to one of our briefing meetings,' McAvoy said crisply. 'Have you any idea how much the state pays to convene these things? We'll see you at the inquiry at two o'clock sharp.'

Cox felt like she'd been led out to face a firing squad. Would've been easier if they'd blindfolded her. Then she wouldn't have had to see this lot . . .

A lot of dark suits, a lot of designer glasses. A couple of the faces she knew by sight; she'd never been one for following politics. There were five of them, MPs from all the main parties. They were ranged along a semi-circular desk; Baroness Kent, smart in a petrol-blue jacket, sat in the centre.

Cox had Serena McAvoy on one side of her, two other middle-aged guys from the Met legal team on the other – but God, she felt alone.

Plenty of press there, too. They couldn't take photos, there in the Westminster committee room, but the television cameras were rolling.

'Tread carefully,' McAvoy had told her, concluding a woefully inadequate half-hour briefing session in a side-room. 'Most of them will just be after the truth, and that's fine – but some of them want to tear you apart. At least your appearance will lend you some sympathy. How is the arm by the way?'

'Getting better, thank you.' Didn't think McAvoy really gave two shits.

She poured herself a glass of water, trying to keep a steady hand.

Baroness Kent thanked her for appearing, especially in light of her recent accident; asked her to state her name, rank and connection with the case – she managed that without a stumble, thank God – and then suggested that, by way of introduction, she should tell them exactly who Tomasz Lerna was.

You can do this, Kerry. She scanned the MPs' faces: every one of them, it seemed, zoned keenly in on her, hawk-like, predatory. *You've been through way worse. You've got this.*

She took a deep breath, leaned in to the microphone and told them exactly who Tomasz Lerna was.

'Tomasz was an eight-year-old boy, a Latvian boy,' she said. 'Lived with his parents in a suburb of Riga. His mother reported Tomasz missing in January last year. The report was followed up by the local police but wasn't logged with Interpol or any other transnational agency – there was no reason to suspect Tomasz had left the country.

'However, we believe that in April – or possibly as early as March – Tomasz was smuggled into the UK, probably through Calais in a lorry or a car, but we can't be sure of that.'

Baroness Kent looked up from her notes and slid her reading-glasses a little way down her nose.

'Could you describe the circumstances of Tomasz's

death? They're not pleasant, I know – but please go into as much detail as possible.'

'He starved to death,' Cox said flatly. 'He was found in a lockup, already dead.'

One of the MPs, a man – a Conservative back-bencher, Cox thought – interjected: 'Where was this lockup?'

'Near Bishop's Stortford. The lockup,' she added, 'belonged to a local man – a Mr Boyd.'

'We'll get to that later,' Baroness Kent said, making a note. 'You say Tomasz was "found" in the lockup. Was he imprisoned there?'

'Yes.'

'For how long, do you think?'

'Five weeks, more or less.'

'That seems a very precise figure. How did you come by it?'

Cox hesitated. Well, they wanted the truth . . .

'It was an estimate,' she said, 'based on the quantity of faeces surrounding Tomasz's body when we found him. By factoring in the extent of his starvation, we were able to arrive at what we think is a pretty accurate estimate.'

She looked again from face to face to face. They all looked sickened. So they should, Cox thought. She could hear someone weeping in the public gallery.

A young MP, a blonde woman with a neat bob who was, Cox gathered, a rising star on the Opposition front benches, asked about the boy's body. Had he been abused, mistreated?

'Yes, he had,' Cox confirmed. 'Extensively, and systematically.'

A few people walked out of the public gallery over the

course of the next five minutes – one or two reporters, too. The MPs' faces grew steadily paler, sicker; mostly, they looked like they regretted volunteering to sit on the inquiry panel.

Cox spoke calmly and authoritatively about the physical damage inflicted on the boy: the broken bones that had never healed, the severe harm to his anal cavity and rectum resulting from repeated penetration, the infected lesions caused by the repeated application of tight binding – cable-ties, it was thought – to his wrists, ankles and other body parts, the untreated sexually transmitted infections from which he was found to have been suffering.

'In short,' Cox finished, 'Tomasz was subjected to sexual and physical abuse on a scale that, as far as we know, was unprecedented in UK criminal history.'

She stopped. Took a sip of water. None of the MPs seemed to have much stomach for further questions.

Baroness Kent, however, was nowhere near done. She was a smart woman, Cox knew – sure, she was well liked, could be affable and empathetic, but before moving into politics she'd been a partner in the Criminal division at one of the big City law firms: that meant forensic intelligence, tactical nous, technical knowhow and no small amount of courage. She'd been tipped for elevation to the High Court Bench before she'd surprised everyone by taking up local politics. Within two years she was heading up the Tory council in Harringey. A seat in the Lords followed soon after.

Cox remembered McAvoy's words of warning: *tread carefully.*

'Do you think,' the baroness asked, tapping a pen thoughtfully on her notepad, 'that anything could have been done to prevent Tomasz's death?'

Cox could feel Serena McAvoy's eyes boring into her. She nodded.

'Yes, I do.'

'Could you please elaborate.'

Another sip of water.

'One, Tomasz's disappearance wasn't registered with any transnational agency. In retrospect, that would have been helpful.'

The MPs were all taking notes, she saw. If she made a misstep here, there'd be no wriggling out of it.

'But that wouldn't have been standard practice?' Kent prompted.

'No. The Latvian police had no reason to suppose Tomasz would be transported out of the country. You asked me what *could* have been done, considering the case in retrospect. That's very different to saying what *should* have been done.'

She paused. It seemed to her like a key point, and she thought she'd made it well – but no one on the panel was writing it down.

'Very well,' said Kent. 'Please go on.'

'Two, Tomasz was brought into the country illegally, by organized traffickers. Obviously, that suggests an operational failing on the part of the Border Force. Beyond that, I'm not qualified to comment. Three, it's likely that after his arrival in the UK Tomasz passed through the hands of a number of known paedophiles and sex offenders, of whom Mr Boyd was just one. This suggests a major failure –'

'*I* should say so,' harrumphed the Tory back-bencher.

'– not only operationally – in terms of the surveillance and management of known offenders – but strategically, in terms of the failure of a number of police authorities to coordinate their efforts and to share information in respect of paedophile networks operating across the jurisdictions of various authorities.'

There was some murmuring in the public gallery. She heard the faint hum of a television camera zooming in.

The back-bencher steepled his fingers.

'You seem very accomplished,' he said, 'at pointing out other people's shortcomings.'

There seemed to be nothing Cox could say to that – so she said nothing. Poured herself more water.

The young female MP spoke up again.

'Could I try and narrow this down, inspector? Do you think there's anything that *your department in particular* could have done to prevent Tomasz's death?'

Kent put in: 'For instance, didn't you take Warren Boyd into custody quite early on in the investigation – while Tomasz was still alive?'

Cox swallowed. Her throat felt bone-dry. She glanced across to the press benches; she could tell from their faces that they were on high alert. She had the uncomfortable feeling that she was about to write the next day's headlines.

'At the time, we were stretched extremely thin in terms both of staff and resources –' she began.

'Excuses, excuses . . .' the back-bencher droned.

'We brought in Warren Boyd, yes. But he was one of a large number of known sex offenders who we interviewed as part of our investigation. He had been an exemplary parolee, he had been attending his mandatory therapy sessions, and we had absolutely no reason to link him with Tomasz Lerna. As you say, it was at a very early stage. At that point we were still looking for leads.'

'And,' put in an MP who hadn't spoken before – a dark-haired man, around forty, telegenic and suited in smart blue-grey, 'you let him slip right through your fingers.'

Here we go, Cox thought. *They can smell blood.*

'That would be a dramatic way of putting it,' she said, trying not to sound too defensive.

'If you'd banged Boyd up there and then, Tomasz Lerna would still be alive, isn't that true?'

'No. We still wouldn't have known where Tomasz was being kept.'

'Come on,' the man scoffed. 'Boyd would have told you, if he thought he was facing a hard time. Everyone knows, for better or worse, what happens to his kind inside.'

He was testing Cox's temper. She was almost glad it was her and not Naysmith who was getting this treatment. The DCI would have blown his top by now, especially if he had a hangover.

'I don't know what you think we should have done,' Cox said evenly. 'We simply didn't have the evidence to charge Boyd.'

'You should have *done your job*, inspector,' the backbencher crowed, rheumy eyes glittering. There was a spatter of applause in the public gallery.

Cox felt bewildered. All at once, she was under siege.

'We – we did everything we could,' she said.

'But it wasn't enough.'

'Look, the team's record on tackling people-trafficking—'

'We are not talking about the team's record,' the dark-haired man put in sternly. 'We are talking about poor little Tomasz Lerna, starving to death in an abandoned lockup while, as far as we can gather, the Met's finest do nothing but chase their own tails.'

More applause. This was getting way out of hand. Cox glanced across at Serena McAvoy – but McAvoy was studying her notes; wouldn't meet her eye.

On your own again, DI Cox . . .

Baroness Kent restored a degree of calm.

'Perhaps,' she said, offering Cox a hint of an encouraging smile, 'you *could* give us a little bit of context with regard to the team's operations. I think that would help us to understand how the investigation into Tomasz's disappearance came about.'

Cox nodded gratefully. This was firmer ground. Facts.

'The taskforce I was assigned to had a great deal of success in tackling trafficking gangs that were smuggling women into the UK – mainly from eastern Europe and the Baltic states – for purposes of prostitution. That was the taskforce's principal remit. We rescued, for want of a better word, more than a hundred women from traffickers and made numerous arrests, most of which led to successful prosecutions. The vast majority of the women being trafficked,' she added, 'were over eighteen. The practice of trafficking children for purposes of abuse wasn't really on our radar.'

'And when did it, so to speak, appear on your radar?'

'When we spoke to the trafficked women. They told us stories about children as well as women being smuggled from Latvia, Estonia, Belarus. Even then, it wasn't much more than rumour – but it put us on the alert.'

'Do you think you should have been on the alert before then?'

'A force can only act on the information it has. Going by guesswork isn't an option.'

'So you wouldn't say the taskforce was negligent?'

'I wouldn't.'

The back-bencher snorted.

'Turning loose a predator like Warren Boyd sounds pretty negligent to me, inspector.'

He pronounced *inspector* as though the word had inverted commas round it. Cox looked at him sharply.

'We deploy our resources as we see fit,' she retorted. 'There was more to this case than Warren Boyd.'

The press pack snapped to attention.

On the edge of her vision, she could see McAvoy staring at her and writing something urgently on her notepad. It was her turn to look away.

Baroness Kent tilted her head and looked at Cox curiously.

'That seems an extraordinary thing to say, inspector,' she said, 'given that the boy was detained and died on Mr Boyd's property.'

Cox held her eye.

'That's true,' she said. 'But it's my belief that Mr Boyd wasn't aware of Tomasz's presence on his property.'

The silence that gripped the room felt taut, tensioned. *They wanted the truth*, Cox thought truculently. *Well, they're getting it.*

'Could you explain that statement?'

'It's my belief that Tomasz was planted in Warren Boyd's lockup in order to implicate Boyd and protect the people who were really responsible.'

Kent took off her glasses and looked at Cox along the line of her strong nose. Now her half-smile seemed superior, mocking; now she looked like a QC. It wasn't often that Cox felt a lot of sympathy for criminals, but Christ, she was glad she never had to face this woman from the dock.

'That,' Kent said, 'is what I think is called a conspiracy theory.'

'The framing of Warren Boyd,' Cox replied, 'was what I think is called a conspiracy.'

At least one of the press pack was already on his phone, texting. So much for a Twitter blackout, thought Cox. The number of camera lenses trained on her seemed somehow to have multiplied; the public gallery was buzzing with conversation.

To her surprise, Baroness Kent smiled.

'You said, I think, inspector, that a police force cannot rely on guesswork.' She slipped her glasses back on. 'I think we should all try and remember that the same principle applies to this inquiry.'

By five o'clock, things had turned personal. Cox had been expecting it; that didn't make it any easier to handle.

'You were a liability on this case, isn't that true?' The Tory back-bencher, slouched low in his seat, blinking at her malevolently, was leading the inquisition. 'Physically, mentally – you were simply not up to the job.'

There was no point in getting mad. Apart from anything else, the guy had a point.

'The stressful nature of my work on the taskforce meant that for a time I had trouble sleeping,' she said. 'At times I was extremely tired. But I'd put it to you that many people are tired when they have difficult jobs and work long hours. Perhaps it's the case for MPs?'

A couple of people laughed, and though Cox felt a moment's respite, the faces of the panel hardened.

'This isn't a time for jokes,' said Baroness Kent.

Cox nodded, chastened. 'What I mean is that, although I was tired, I could still do my job.'

'How would you describe the support you received from your superiors during this period?' Kent put in.

'Outstanding. DCI Naysmith had my back.'

'But medically, psychologically?'

'We were all under the supervision of an excellent specialist medical team,' she said – a line McAvoy had fed her in the briefing. 'They monitored us throughout the investigation.'

Or at least, they did if you turned up to the sessions.

The back-bencher – Cox had gathered that his name was Ridley – returned to the attack.

'You mention this fellow DCI Naysmith.' He peered theatrically at his notes. 'I understand he was scheduled to appear before us today, but was unfortunately, ah, taken ill?'

Cox pasted on a poker-face.

'That's right.'

'And he was your commanding officer during the time we're talking about?'

'Yes, he was.'

He took off his glasses, tapped one of the plastic temples against his teeth in a show of contemplation.

'I'm wondering if there were any disagreements within the taskforce with regard to the investigation,' he said. 'I mean to say, a complex operation, high levels of stress, a lot of strong characters, no doubt . . .'

'Of course there were,' Cox nodded. 'There were disagreements over strategy – that's inevitable. But I wouldn't call them personality clashes – we're professionals. There are chains of command in the police service, and we respected that.'

'You don't recall any serious disagreements?'

Where was this going?

'No,' she said. 'I don't.'

Baroness Kent shook out a folded sheet of A4 paper.

'I'm going to read something to you now, inspector. Afterwards I'll ask you to comment on it.' She cleared her throat. '*A source close to the investigation revealed that notorious predator Warren Boyd was put under surveillance by Scotland Yard as part of the probe into the disappearance of little Tomasz Lerna, 8 – but that the bungling cops let the convicted paedophile get clean away.*' She set the paper down, looked up. 'You'll excuse the tabloidese, but I don't believe the factual content of the piece has been challenged. Do you recognize that report, inspector?'

She'd recognized it within two seconds.

'Yes, I do. It was a news report by Greg Wilson in one of the tabloids.'

'And what's your opinion on Mr Wilson's version of events?'

'Heavily biased. Highly selective. Utterly sensational-ized.' She shrugged. 'Exactly what you'd expect from a tabloid news story.'

'But the events Mr Wilson describes – did they in fact take place?'

'No. We placed Boyd under surveillance after his release from custody, that much is true – but we didn't lose him. We took the decision to call in the surveillance team.'

Another harrumph from Ridley.

'That's even worse!'

Cox stonewalled.

'It was a strategic decision.'

'A strategic decision to let Boyd get away scot-free.'

'To focus our resources elsewhere.'

'I have some simple questions,' Baroness Kent said. 'I'd be grateful if you could try to answer them simply.' She folded her hands delicately on the desktop. 'Who ordered that Mr Boyd be put under surveillance?'

'I did.'

'Why?'

'We wanted to see where he might lead us.'

'More guesswork,' Ridley heckled.

'An informed strategic decision. We called the team off, as I said, after a couple of days.'

Kent affected a puzzled frown.

'But you had some suspicions about Mr Boyd, then? Even after you released him?'

'I didn't think he was responsible for Tomasz's dis-appearance, if that's what you mean.'

'In view of subsequent developments, it seems that your judgement was flawed.'

'Not in my view. I still don't believe that Boyd knew where the boy was.'

Kent paused – then asked, with a barrister's steel-edged precision: 'Whose decision was it to call the surveillance team in?'

Cox shifted in her seat.

'It was DCI Naysmith's.'

'Did you support his decision?'

'Of course. He was my commanding officer.'

'Then let me rephrase my question. Did you *agree* with his decision?'

'I – I understood it.'

'But you wanted to see where Mr Boyd would lead you. An informed strategic decision, you said. Did you argue with DCI Naysmith over his order to withdraw?'

We fought like cats in a sack.

'We talked it over. It was a resource issue. As I say – I understood the decision.'

Baroness Kent nodded, reached for her glass of water. Cox let out a sigh. She'd fought on through another round; no one had landed a knockout blow on her yet. But there was a lot more scrapping to come.

She scanned the room with tired eyes. The press benches were fuller now, she thought, than they had been a few hours before; word must've got out that DI Cox was good box office.

Then, at the farthest end of the front bench, she saw a familiar face. Couldn't place it for a second – was he one of the crime reporters on the regular west London beat?

Then it clicked, and her stomach lurched.

Harrington.

What the hell was he doing here?

When the answer struck her, like a slap to the face, she couldn't believe she'd been so damn stupid. With this inquiry approaching, Harrington had been tasked with keeping tabs on *her*; he hadn't been at the Radley scene because of who Radley was – he'd been there because of who *she* was.

She felt a yawn coming, covered her mouth. Saw Baroness Kent watching her wryly. With a thin smile, the baroness covered her microphone with her hand, and mouthed: *nearly done*.

Then the questioning began again.

'Let's return to an earlier point – your exhaustion during the investigation.'

'Not exhaustion.' Firmly, emphatically. 'I was tired.'

'Tired, exhausted. I feel we're quibbling. Did your superiors ever suggest to you that you should take time off as a consequence of your tiredness?'

Cox hesitated. She saw where this was going.

'I – I was given the option of taking leave on medical grounds. I didn't take it.' She shifted in her seat, forced herself to look the baroness in the eye. 'And I'd be interested to know what prompted you to ask me that.'

Kent ignored her last remark.

'Why did you reject the recommendation that you take sick leave, inspector?'

'It wasn't a recommendation, it was an option.'

'You wanted to see the case through to its conclusion, I suppose?'

'Yes. Yes, of course I did. I wanted to see the case solved – and I believed that I was the person most likely to do so.'

Kent nodded, made a face that seemed to Cox condescending, even pitying. She took off her glasses and set them carefully on the desk.

'I think we're arriving at the crux of the problem,' she said to the room at large, with a faint sigh in her voice. 'Investigating officers pursuing their own agendas; critical, relevant intelligence not being properly disseminated; due diligence not being undertaken. A catalogue not, perhaps, of errors, but of fundamental, systemic operational shortcomings.'

Cox felt herself colouring. *How to Rile a Police Officer #1: talk as though you know how to do their job better than they do.* She knew that McAvoy, on her right, was giving her a warning look.

She ignored it.

'If the baroness knows of a better way to conduct a police investigation, I'd be glad to consider her suggestions,' she said.

The look Kent gave her was iron-hard.

'The question of how the investigation might have been better conducted is what we are all here to address,' she said softly. 'I know it has been a long afternoon for us all, inspector – but there is no need to raise your voice.'

That was an old trick: no quicker or easier way to undermine someone than to suggest that they'd lost their temper. She'd done it herself in the interview room. Suddenly, you were unstable, or panicked, or hot-headed, or worse . . .

She heard a noise, from up above, from the public gallery; shouting, and the sounds of a scuffle. The MPs all looked up sharply. Cox spun in her seat. Something struck her hard in the chest, on the left-hand side.

'Unnhh –'

Her jacket, her desk, her notes were splattered with red. She put a hand to her breast – the red liquid was cold and thin.

Not blood – not even wine.

She saw that the rubbery rag of a burst water-balloon had fallen at her feet.

Looked up into the public gallery. Two uniformed stewards were tussling with a young woman, long raincoat, cropped chestnut hair, who was leaning far out over the balcony edge and staring with wide, dark eyes directly at her.

Cox recognized her. Oh, Christ.

'Child killer!' the woman screamed hoarsely as she was hauled away. 'Murderer! Child killer!'

The room erupted; cameras flashed, chairs tipped over, TV lenses wheeled to capture the moment.

The woman's name, Cox knew, was Kaisa. She was Tomasz Lerna's mother.

21

'We can request an adjournment,' McAvoy said. 'I'm sure the panel would be sympathetic.'

That'd make a nice change.

Cox was buttoning up a clean blouse she'd borrowed from McAvoy ('Always keep a spare outfit in my car – presentation is everything'). Her arm ached badly.

'It's fine,' she said. 'We've come this far, we might as well see it out.'

The barrister nodded, smiled briefly, moved away to speak to one of her colleagues on the legal team. Cox made use of the break to check her phone; wondered if there was any news from Wilson or Chalmers.

One missed call – and a voicemail. She didn't recognize the London number.

'You lying fucking cow.'

I'm popular today, she thought sourly.

It took her a second to place the voice: Stevie Butcher.

'Have a word with the fucking Parole Board, you said. Now here I am back in-fucking-side and all the cunts in here think I'm a fucking nonce. What the fuck have you been saying?' Must've been calling from a Pentonville payphone, she surmised. What the hell? 'Listen, I want out. I'll tell you what you want to know, all of it. Merritt was fucking *nothing*, you get me? The fucking mask. I'll tell you, and only you, all right. If you can fucking get me out of here, I'll tell you it all. I'll –'

The voicemail service cut him off. Cox hit 7 to save the message, quickly dialled up Chalmers. Butcher was supposed to be cut loose, not banged up again. Must've been a breakdown in communication somewhere.

'Cox. What's up?'

She sketched out the message she'd just received; asked what the hell Butcher was doing in Pentonville. Had Chalmers forgotten to send over the recommendation to the Board?

'Not me,' Chalmers said. 'I sent it over, *i*s crossed and *t*s dotted. The Board were all set to let him off, till word came through that Butcher's breach was under no circumstances to be overlooked. Orders from on high, I gather.'

Cox had a sinking feeling.

'How high?'

'Couldn't say for sure, but from what my contact on the Board said I'd guess AC, maybe commissioner level.'

'Christ.'

'I know. How does a scrote like Stevie Butcher make enemies in such high places?'

From across the lobby, Serena McAvoy was signalling to Cox to cut short her call – the inquiry was due to reconvene. She thanked Chalmers quickly, rang off. Switched off the phone. All that could wait till later, she told herself. It'd *have* to wait. She'd need all of her focus to get through the rest of this session; she couldn't afford to be distracted.

Still felt shaken, though, as she took her seat. The MPs

were already in place. Baroness Kent smiled at her as she reopened the session – but Cox wasn't buying the ex-QC's act this time. She was getting a bit sick of being manipulated.

Kent asked if she felt all right to continue; she replied breezily that yes, of course she did – the implication being, she hoped, that a Met DCI wasn't thrown off her stride as easily as they might think.

'Very well,' nodded Kent. Folded her hands in a down-to-business manner. 'Is it difficult, inspector,' she asked, 'maintaining a police career and a family life?'

Here McAvoy cut in.

'Is this line of questioning really pertinent to the matter at hand?' she objected. 'We aren't here to scrutinize Inspector Cox's personal life. And,' she added bitingly, 'I rather doubt that a male officer of Inspector Cox's rank and experience would be asked such a question if he were in her place.'

Nicely done, Cox thought.

'I was merely trying to clarify the inspector's state of mind during the period in question,' Kent said. 'We were given to understand that the Tomasz Lerna case dominated her life. I was curious as to the extent of her preoccupation. But very well – your point is noted, Ms McAvoy.' She veered sideways – came in on an unexpected tangent. 'Inspector, is leaking information to the press a regular feature of your job, would you say?'

It caught her cold.

'*What?* I mean, no – no, of course not.' She sounded flustered, she knew. A flat, one-word denial would've done.

'It's not something you'd consider central to your duties as a police officer?'

'It's not,' Cox said, 'a practice I'm familiar with.'

Baroness Kent raised an eyebrow. That meant trouble; she had something up her sleeve, and Cox, her head beginning to ache, could guess what it was.

Kent let Ridley, the Tory back-bencher, take a turn.

'It seems jolly odd to me,' he said, 'that all this stuff – the surveillance decision and suchlike – should find its way into the papers so readily. In fact, I seem to remember there being some criticism of this fact at the time.'

Cox nodded. So did she. But she'd no intention of helping the panel out here; Christ, they were more than capable of gutting and filleting her without her assistance.

'Do you have a question?' she stonewalled.

Baroness Kent sensed her moment.

'I have here,' she said, drawing a sheet of paper from her file, 'a copy of a newspaper article published on the morning before Tomasz Lerna's body was found. It includes several pieces of information that – one would imagine – would be known only to an individual with privileged access to the investigation. The piece was written by Mr Greg Wilson – the same journalist who covered the alleged escape of Warren Boyd from police surveillance.' She looked at Cox beadily. 'Do you have any idea, inspector, how Mr Wilson might have come by the privileged information in question?'

'He's a professional journalist,' Cox said. 'Those people have their sources.'

'But in this case specifically – who do you think might have given Mr Wilson this information?'

'There were dozens of officers involved in the investigation, without even taking into consideration the huge numbers of police support staff. In theory it could have been any one of them.'

Kent smiled coldly.

'In theory, perhaps. But in practice?'

'I couldn't say.'

She could almost *see* Baroness Kent's well-honed courtroom instincts kicking in, could sense her readying to strike – closing in for the kill. The glasses were high on the nose and gleamed white under the chamber lights.

'Do you know Mr Wilson, inspector?'

'A little.'

'Elaborate, please.'

'He took a considerable interest in this case, and several others. We crossed paths many times in a professional capacity.'

'Always professional?'

Cox swallowed. Where the hell had they got this from?

'I'm – I'm not sure what you mean.'

'Sorry; I'll clarify. Your relationship with Mr Wilson – was the relationship ever anything more than might normally be expected between a DCI and a crime reporter?'

She tried to stall, knowing how much good it'd do: '"Anything more"? What does that mean?'

The dark-haired MP interjected.

'Baroness Kent means "more intimate", inspector.' He smiled nastily. 'To put it more frankly still: did you have a sexual relationship with Greg Wilson?'

There was a noticeable stir in the press benches. Here it was, Cox thought. Tomorrow's front page.

McAvoy – more out of duty, it seemed, than conviction – protested, argued that again the panel was seeking to pry into Cox's private life, that the line of questioning was prurient and verged on the offensive, that Inspector Cox's sex life had no bearing whatever on the death of Tomasz Lerna.

This time, Baroness Kent batted her aside like a fly.

'It is thoroughly pertinent,' she said calmly. 'And I'd be grateful if Inspector Cox would furnish us with an answer.'

'Inspector Cox is not obliged to –'

'She is obliged to tell the truth.' Kent's voice was like a jagged edge of ice. 'Inspector, I am losing patience. Please answer "yes" or "no": did you have a sexual relationship with Greg Wilson?'

Cox paused. Every police officer knew it was a mistake to go into a hazardous situation without knowing where the exits were – without an escape plan. But right now, no matter where she looked, she couldn't see a way out.

She took a sip of water. Set down the glass carefully.

'Yes,' she said.

Uproar.

Baroness Kent was a still point at the centre of the chaos, sedately pouring herself water as MPs called to one another across the semi-circular desk array, as the press pack broke apart, dashing off to find wi-fi signals, file their urgent copy, as stewards fought to maintain order in the public gallery. Cox could hear someone up there yelling *shame, shame*, over and over again.

She turned to McAvoy, who was sliding her notes back into her file.

'I'm sorry,' she said.

Without looking at her, the barrister shrugged, shook her head quickly. It might've meant: *no problem, don't worry about it*, but Cox guessed otherwise. It meant, she thought: *this isn't our problem any more – it's yours.*

Baroness Kent's voice rang out sharply over the hub-bub. They were adjourning for the day, she declared; the inquiry would sit again in the morning.

Cox stood. She was half-aware of her legal team filing out in stony silence behind her, of Baroness Kent watching her carefully, of the back-bencher Ridley rocking back in his chair and chuckling to himself – but her real focus was on Sam Harrington, who had left the press benches and, walking quickly, had slipped out of a fire exit at the back of the chamber.

Scotland Yard had sent a car; it was waiting, engine running, outside a rear exit of the warren-like Westminster complex. The inquiry stewards had told her that this was the best way to avoid the scrum of photographers and journalists – but still, there were maybe a dozen waiting for her in the London drizzle as she hurried down the steps, jerking up a grey umbrella, keeping her eyes on the ground.

She'd thought this kind of thing was behind her, that the media had long ago had its fill of DCI Kerry Cox, the copper who let an eight-year-old boy starve to death.

Well, she'd just piqued their appetite again.

She pushed her way past the snapping cameras, the

shouted, provocative questions (aimed at getting a reaction, not an answer), dived into the welcoming dark of the back of the car, banged the door shut. She knew the driver slightly: Dipesh, his name was. He gave her a sympathetic half-smile over his shoulder and hit the gas. Westminster, a muted grey through the windows' blackout glass, dissolved away into the rain.

Cox closed her eyes. Sighed. God, she could use some sleep – but there were things that couldn't wait. Stevie Butcher, for one thing, was suffering Christ-knew-what in a Pentonville prison cell.

She took out her phone and called DCI Naysmith.

'Cox. Fucking hell, I'm sorry.'

He sounded wretched; his voice was weak, ragged. She knew he'd have been giving himself hell ever since he sobered up, sometime in mid-afternoon – it was no more than the stupid bastard deserved, she thought, but she couldn't see any point in twisting the knife.

'What's done is done, guv.'

'I know what that means. It means you'll pretend to forget all about it, until such a time as you need to use it against me in future. Something to look forward to.' He cleared his throat noisily. 'I fucked up, Cox. Badly. And I'm sorry. End of. Now – how'd the inquiry go?'

'You'll be able to read all about it in the papers tomorrow.'

'That doesn't sound good.'

'No. No, it wasn't good. But guv, that's not what I'm calling about.'

'Oh?' He sounded wary.

'Yesterday, guv. Steven Butcher, the guy we pulled in

for the Allis murder. We struck a deal with him – he gave us some useful info, we promised the Parole Board would overlook the bag of weed we found at his flat. But he just called me – from Pentonville Prison.'

'Tough break.'

'Did you know about this?'

'We didn't need him any more, did we?' Naysmith's tone was querulous, defensive. 'I thought he'd told us everything he knew.'

Cox wanted to scream at him. She forced down the lid on her anger.

'Well, maybe, maybe not, but that's not the point, is it? I made the guy a promise.'

'Then you should consider this a lesson,' Naysmith said, 'in not making promises you can't keep.'

The line went dead.

Christ. When Naysmith was drunk, he was an irresponsible mess; when he had a hangover, he could be a nasty piece of work.

This seemed worse than usual, though. It wasn't like Naysmith to be heartless – when the subject of Butcher had come up, he sounded downright callous. That, Cox guessed, was a defence mechanism; the DCI's default response to having his hand forced, to being made to act against his own inclinations.

Naysmith was backed into a corner. Cox didn't know how, or who by – but she needed him to come out fighting.

She leaned forward, tapped the driver on the shoulder.

'Change of plan, Dipesh,' she said. 'We're not going back to the station.'

'No problem, ma'am,' he said without looking round. 'Where to, then?'

'Pentonville Prison.'

'Lovely.'

Spray hissed up around the car as he pulled off the main road, swung deftly through a double-junction, merged into the traffic heading north.

Stony faces on the black-clad guards at the main gate. A heavy, louring atmosphere in the entrance lobby. Cox showed her ID at the desk, said that she was there to see Steven Butcher; the officer on duty, a heavy-set woman with a West Indian accent, told her to take a seat and wait. Cox sensed a faint hostility in the woman's tone; thought back, with a quiver of unease, to what Butcher had said on the phone: *they think I'm a fucking nonce . . .*

Screws were no keener on sex offenders than prisoners were.

She took a seat on a plastic chair marked with a black cigarette burn. There was no one else in the waiting area. Idly, she scanned the notices pinned to the walls: info about drugs, booze, mental health, sexual health, rehab programmes, support groups, back-to-work schemes for ex-cons . . .

Life inside was bloody tough, Cox reflected – but once you'd done your time, making things work on the outside was no picnic, either. Stevie Butcher didn't have a lot to fall back on; sooner or later, she thought, he'd have slipped up again and wound up back here anyway.

It was no comfort. Fact was, Butcher was in here, right now, because of her; because she hadn't kept her promise.

'DI Cox?'

She turned. She was expecting a prison guard – black uniform, bunch of silver keys – to take her to Butcher; standing in front of her, hand extended, was a middle-aged man in a suit, with neatly parted grey hair and silver-framed glasses.

'I'm Richard Dovey,' he said. His handshake was dry and firm. 'I'm the governor here. I gather you're here to see Steven Butcher?'

'That's right. It's about the judgement of the Parole Board.'

'I see.' He folded his hands together. 'I wondered,' he said, 'if I might have a word with you in private.' Gestured to a side-door. 'Just through here.'

Cox, puzzled, stood and followed the urbane governor through to a corridor and to an empty office furnished sparely with a desk and two chairs.

It was here, speaking slowly and with an expression of profound sadness, that the governor informed her of the unfortunate death of Steven Butcher. He had fashioned a blade from part of an iron bed-frame, the governor said, and opened his wrists in the shower that morning.

The Eleventh Day of Christmas, 1986

Used to knock around in Walsall a bit when I was a kid. Had a mate there. That sounds like it was a fucking hundred years ago – feels like it, too. What was I, nine, ten?

Bus driver let me on for free. I'm piss-wet, covered in grime and blood – said I'd had an accident, had lost my bus-money. Showed him my broken hand – Christ, it's a right sight.

'I can call your mum and dad if you want, son,' the bus-driver said. I told him no, it'd only worry them.

Interfering old sod. But it was good of him to let me on his bus.

Got off in the city somewhere, south-east side. Found a bus-shelter. No one about; must be pretty late.

Felt mad, falling asleep in a Birmingham bus-shelter. But I huddled up in the corner and tucked my arms inside my T-shirt and in hardly any time I felt my eyes starting to close. Maybe it was the effects of that fucking sedative. Or maybe, once you've learned to fall asleep in Hampton Hall, you can fall asleep bloody anywhere.

Proper crick in my neck now.

Still drizzling. Still dark, too. God knows what time it is. There's a few people around, a few cars. It's morning, anyway. Time I moved on. No one calls the cops on a teenager sleeping in a bus shelter – and that's a bit mad, if you think about it – but I don't want to risk it.

Shirley's out west somewhere – but what am I going to do, wander around west Birmingham till I find it by magic?

A bit down the road there's a WH Smith's. It's open – so it's not that early, maybe half six, seven o'clock. Go in. There's an old feller standing there looking at a porno mag, right in the middle of the shop. Dirty bastard.

I keep behind him, proper shoplifter-shifty. I get to the shelf where they keep the A–Zs without the lad at the till seeing me. What's he going to do, anyway? Looks about ten.

Snatch a Birmingham street map and make a run for it, back out into the rain. Keep running; don't look back. I know it's only a 50p A–Z, they're not going to send the Flying Squad after me – but running feels good, anyroad.

*

This is Shirley, I reckon. Nice houses. Street after street of nice houses. The rain's made a bloody mess of my A–Z, can't make out the street names – but I'm not far off, I know that.

In one front room I can see a family watching breakfast telly, eating breakfast.

We were never like that. We weren't a proper happy family, like off an advert. But we were a family. And any sort of family, I reckon, has to be better than no family.

I'm hungry. If I keep walking I don't feel it as bad, but every time I stop my belly thumps, and I think I might puke.

Doesn't help that every time I hear a police siren in the distance I nearly shit my pants.

There's a feller coming the other way, wheeling a racing bike. Middle-aged bloke in a cap. Nothing else for it.

''Scuse me, mister – I'm a bit lost. Where's Wolvesley? Y'know, the children's home?'

He looks at me, does a stupid grin.

'Runaway, are you?' he says. Laughs. Yeah, very funny, mate.

'D'you know where it is?'

'I do.' He points back the way I've come. 'About two mile that way, son. Was a farmhouse when I was a lad.'

So I turn around and I carry on walking.

It's up a lane, an unlit lane, part gravel, mostly mud. It's just starting to get light; I can see the building from the road, a bloody big place, not a farmhouse any more, new brick extensions every which way.

There's a wooden sign: Wolvesley Grange Children's Home.

I trudge up the path. Should be trying to sneak up, trying to duck and dive, but I'm too tired. It's not like they'll be expecting me – bet those bastards at Hampton haven't even noticed I'm gone.

Christ, I'm knackered.

There are some flash cars out the front, proper nice, a big Rover, a classic Jag – and one I know. A bottle-green Ford. We watched Gordo being driven off in that, never to be seen again. Merton's car.

I go round the back. There's a door, but it's locked. No glass in it, solid wood, so I can't bust my way in. A window'll have to do.

The far end of the back wall is in the shadow of an overgrown hedge. That's the best bet. There's a window there. There are shutters over it, wood shutters like on a house you'd see in a bloody picture-book – been here since it was a farmhouse, I s'pose.

The staff here are no better at maintenance than those lazy bastards back at Hampton. The screws holding the shutter-hinges in the wall are fucked. I force my good hand into the gap, levering it wider. And from here I can see the glass of the window – and what's behind the window.

There's a light on, a sort of lamp-light. And there's someone there. A woman in a dressing-gown, I think. No, it's not a dressing-gown – it's a robe, and I think it's a bloke what's wearing it. A monk or some bloody thing, I don't know.

Feel properly sick. And then the bloke turns round and I nearly wet myself.

This is some fucking place, I think.

The bloke's wearing a mask, a mad mask with horns on. And I can only see him from the waist up but I can see he's got nothing on under his robe.

I duck, trying not to breathe, trying not to make a sound.

He can't have seen me, not with the light on in there and it being so gloomy out here. He can't have.

But what if he has?

There was a phone-box back on the main road, I remember. And you don't even need 10p to call 999. Even if I have to go back to

Hampton, even if they pack me off to juvenile detention or prison or whatever – I can't leave our Stan in there, can I?

*And the coppers might be bastards but once they know what's going on in there, what sort of mad stuff I just seen, they'll have to do some*thing, won't they? They can't just ig*nore* me . . .

I find the phone-box. It stinks of piss inside, like they all do. Pull the door shut behind me.

Grab the receiver, hammer the button like mad.

I hear a voice answer, hello, emergency serv –

And then I feel a cold gust, right up my back, and I turn round, and the door of the phone-box is open, and there's a man there –

He grabs the receiver from me, bangs it back on its hook.

'*You're a long way from home, Robert,*' *he says.*

It's Radley. The copper.

22

She stared at him.

'*What?*'

'Our on-site medical team did their best,' Dovey sighed, 'but I'm afraid it was too late. He had already lost too much blood.'

Cox wondered if a Met DI outranked a prison governor; if she was allowed to give this guy – yet another grey middle-aged man, pulling strings, arranging the world to suit himself – a real piece of her mind.

'How on earth could this have happened? He'd barely been here a day!'

The governor pressed his hands together, palm to palm, as if in prayer.

'Prison,' he said, still talking like a vicar at a funeral, 'can be a very stressful environment. Certain individuals find it simply impossible to cope – Steven Butcher, it seems, was one such individual.'

'Wasn't he supervised? How does a man just slit his wrists and bleed to death with no one noticing?'

'I'm sure you're aware of the staffing pressures we face in the prison service,' Dovey said. 'We simply don't have the resources to watch everybody, all the time – and we had no reason to believe that Butcher was a suicide risk.'

Cox glowered. That, at least, was a fair point – she hadn't seen this coming. Butcher just didn't seem the type.

Cutting your wrists wasn't always fatal, Cox knew. It was gruesome, dramatic, but bleeding out that way could take a long time. Only if the incisions were very deep – deep enough to fully sever the blood vessels – was death a guarantee.

To put it another way, to die like that, you had to really mean it.

'Besides,' Dovey added, 'Mr Butcher was only with us temporarily; he was due to be transferred to a Category C institution – much lower security – in a few days.'

A few days could be a hell of a long time in Pentonville. Especially if you'd made enemies . . .

'He told me that some people in here had the idea that he was a sex offender,' Cox said. 'Do you know anything about that?'

The governor shook his head.

'No. But you know how these places are. A rumour – even a misplaced one – doesn't take long to become established fact.'

Cox felt sick with exasperation. She stood up.

The governor looked relieved. He rose too, and extended his hand.

'Well, as I say, inspector, we're all very sorry about this – if I can be of any help in future –'

'I want to see the shower-room,' Cox said flatly.

Dovey lowered his hand. Frowned.

'The shower-room?'

'Where Steven Butcher died. I'd like to take a look at the scene.'

The request seemed to fluster the governor.

'That would be rather irregular,' he stuttered, fidgeting

with a button on his suit-jacket. 'Besides, there isn't a lot to see, I don't know what you –'

'I'd like to see it,' Cox repeated.

The governor opened and shut his mouth. She looked at him contemptuously: saw another 'powerful' man backed into a corner, another authority figure finding out how little their 'power' really meant.

Two grainy, dark-pink spots at eye-level, missed by the cleaner's sponge. All that was left of Steven Butcher.

Dovey – his formal wear incongruous against the white tiles and stark steel showerheads – spread his hands.

'I told you,' he said, 'there was very little to see. We cleared the scene hours ago.'

'Did you take pictures?'

'Why would we?' A small, condescending smile. 'Suicide is an unfortunate but common part of prison life, inspector. We cannot afford to treat every incidence as a major crime.'

'So you just cart off the carcass, wipe down the tiles, get on with your lives?'

Dovey winced.

'That's a rather crude way of putting it,' he said. 'But, in effect – yes. What happened here this morning was a tragedy. I acknowledge that. But this is a prison, Inspector Cox. We are well accustomed to tragedy.'

'So no forensics.' She looked around the bleak shower-room, hands on hips. 'No blood-spatter analysis, no dusting for prints . . .'

'There'll be an autopsy, of course,' Dovey shrugged, 'but I can already tell you what it will conclude. Steven Butcher took his own life.'

His tone suggested that his patience was coming to an end.

But Cox wasn't done with him yet.

'I want to speak with witnesses.'

'I told you, there weren't any.'

'The last people to see him. The people who knew him, shared his cell. The person who found him.'

'Really, inspector, this seems a gross overreaction . . .' He caught Cox's eye, clocked that she was in no mood for debate. He swallowed, straightened the sit of his jacket. 'It'll take time to arrange,' he said. 'At least a day or two. I can't disrupt the routines of a high-security prison simply to satisfy your curiosity.'

Cox felt the blood rising to her throat and cheeks.

'What if I told you I was treating Butcher's death as a murder inquiry?'

To her surprise, the governor laughed.

'How absurd.'

'I don't think this is funny, Mr Dovey.'

He straightened his face.

'Of course – but really, inspector, you are getting carried away. A few spots of blood and you're ready to call out the murder squad. *We* see this kind of thing every week.'

'Has it ever occurred to you to do something about it?'

Dovey's face darkened.

'I don't like your tone, inspector.'

'I don't give a damn what you like and don't like,' Cox snapped. 'A man died here – and I think he was murdered. Steven Butcher was about to give us some very significant information. Ample reason for someone to kill him – and frame it as a suicide.'

Dovey shook his head irritably.

'This is sheer fantasy, inspector.'

'Leaving Steven Butcher unprotected was a serious oversight, Mr Dovey. In fact, I could make a case that it was damn near negligent.'

'We take the welfare of our prisoners very seriously.' Dovey jutted his jaw. 'But we take the welfare of our staff seriously, too. I simply cannot – will not – make the lives of my staff more difficult than they already are by sending them on fool's errands.'

'Like saving a man's life?'

'You think we should fly into a panic over one police officer's ill-informed hunch?'

'I think you should do your fucking jobs.'

The words echoed hollowly in the tiled room.

Dovey went from pink to pale.

'I'll be speaking to your superiors, Inspector Cox,' he said.

'How nice for them.' What the hell – she didn't feel like she had a lot to lose. 'I'll be out of your way momentarily, Mr Dovey – and you can get back to "managing" your prison. I want to see Butcher's cell before I go.'

The governor was thin-lipped with fury.

'Very well,' he said. 'Very well.'

Stepped out into the corridor; called over a guard, an overweight man in his thirties with two-day stubble and an unhurried manner.

'Yes, sir?'

'This is Detective Inspector Cox,' he said shortly, with a gesture. 'I want you to show her to Steven Butcher's cell. Let her take a look around – and then escort her to the exit.'

'Yessir.' The officer eyed Cox lazily. 'This way, please, ma'am.'

As she was led down the corridor, deeper into the prison-block, she called over her shoulder: 'Thank you for your assistance, Mr Dovey. You've been very helpful.'

But Dovey was already far away, hurrying back to his top-floor office, the soles of his polished shoes click-clacking rapidly on the hard prison floor.

It was a jail cell, and that was all it was. No sign that Steven Butcher had ever been here.

Butcher's cell-mate, a fat black youth who the guard had called Marley, was waiting outside on the landing, smoking an e-cigarette. The guard stood at the door, hands behind his back, staring into the middle distance.

Cox's frustration grew as she searched the tiny cell. Nothing under the mattresses or in the stiff, grubby pillows, nothing on the sparse shelves, nothing in the drawer of the scuffed writing-desk – nothing anywhere, save a chipped coffee mug and a stack of dog-eared lads' magazines.

'Finished, ma'am?' the guard said casually, after ten minutes' futile searching.

Too furious to speak, head pounding, Cox just nodded – let him conduct her wordlessly back to the main gate.

She hit eighty on the A-road back through the city. She was too mad to drive safely; she felt helpless, besieged, as though everything – and everyone – was against her.

But at the same time, the desperate urge to get at the truth, to see this thing through, consumed her like fire.

Naysmith was waiting for her back at her desk in HQ.

'Cox.' He nodded at her. Still looked like shit.

'Guv.'

For a short moment they looked at one another; she, in her mind's eye, was still seeing the pitiful, fat-bellied drunk passed out on the sofa – while he, she guessed, was seeing the joke of a copper who'd royally fucked up at the inquiry.

But that was all irrelevant, for now. The case was what mattered.

'I've just been to Pentonville,' she began, pulling up a chair, reaching for her notes. 'Steven Butcher is dead – they reckon he killed himself.'

Naysmith's face registered little emotion.

'That's a bad break,' he said, but he seemed detached, distracted.

'The place is a joke,' Cox pressed on. 'Not even the most basic forensics. I want to go back there, speak to the other prisoners on the block, the guards –'

Naysmith cut her off with a heavy, gut-deep sigh. She looked at him questioningly.

'Guv?'

'We need to talk, Kerry.' He didn't look at her as he spoke. 'Let's do this in my office.'

Heaved himself to his feet. Plodded heavily across the CID suite. *This is a man under too much pressure*, Cox thought, following him; *this is a man ready to break*.

In the office, he invited her to take a seat; she declined. She preferred to take her bollockings standing up – and she was pretty sure that was what she had coming.

'Please yourself.' The DCI scratched his jawline, looking up at her anxiously. Or was it fear? Guilt? 'Cox,' he said, 'you landed yourself in a lot of bother at the inquiry. A *lot*,' he added, with emphasis, 'of bother.'

'I know that, guv.'

'Then maybe you'll know what's coming.' Another deep sigh. Gave her a hunted look. 'I'm going to have to suspend you from duty, Kerry. As of now.'

She'd guessed it might come to this – still, it hit her like a speeding bus.

'Guv, I –'

'There's no point arguing, Inspector Cox.'

She clenched her jaw. Couldn't tell what she was feeling – anger, despair, fear, grief.

In another half-second, though, anger had taken the upper hand.

'I *protected* you,' she said. 'Christ, I was only there because you were too pissed to be seen in public – and I did nothing in there, guv, but cover your arse.'

'I know. More than I deserved.' Naysmith's tone was utterly flat. 'Point is, this is for your own good. I can't protect you out there.'

She paused, wrong-footed.

'Protect me? I can protect myself, you know that.'

'I used to,' the DCI nodded. 'Not sure any more.' He shook his head sharply, as if to snap himself out of a daze. 'Chalmers'll take over the Merritt investigation. He's a good copper. You know that.'

'Sure, given a fair chance. But this is a big case, guv. Being parachuted in like this, he won't know where to start.'

Again Naysmith avoided her eye; pretended to sort some loose papers on his desk.

'I think he'll have a pretty good idea of where to start *and* where to finish,' he said without looking up. 'Butcher looks a safe bet to me. Should be open-and-shut.'

Cox's jaw fell open. Couldn't believe what she was hearing. Was this really DCI Pete Naysmith sitting in front of her, peddling a bullshit line like that and then ducking her gaze like a guilty schoolboy?

Well, that was the point, she realized grimly: sure, Naysmith's lips were moving – it was his flat Yorkshire grumble she was hearing – but were they really Naysmith's words?

She asked him straight out, struggling to keep her voice level: 'This your decision, guv?'

He hesitated. That was all the confirmation she needed.

She turned for the door. Heard Naysmith say softly: 'I'm sorry.'

Turned back sharply, leaned over Naysmith's desk, hands flat on the desktop.

'This stinks, guv,' she said. 'This whole thing. It stinks like the Tomasz Lerna case stank – and we all know how *that* turned out.'

Straightened up; left the office without a backward look.

Dark, now, outside; no rain, but a Baltic wind scoured the station car park. Cox called up her voicemail service as she hurried to her car.

She'd clocked the number of the missed call, was expecting to hear Aidan's voice, checking if she was well enough to take Matthew at the weekend, or chasing up a missing toy or pair of socks . . .

Matthew's voice caught her cold. She stopped dead in the car park, frozen in the act of taking out her keys. Swallowed down a painful lump in her throat.

'Mum, it's me – Matthew.' *Christ, I know that, you stupid, wonderful boy.* 'I hope you're not poorly any more. I know you were at the hospital so I wanted to ring you up, and Dad said it was all right. I'm ringing you up to say I hope you're feeling better, Mum, and I love you. Bye, Mum.'

Then the cold, impersonal voice of the voicemail service, telling her to press 2 or 7 or whatever the hell it was. She put the phone away, climbed in the car, started the engine. She couldn't wait till the weekend; couldn't wait another hour. She needed to see her son.

Aidan's place – how long since it'd been *their* place? – was way down in Dorking, a good hour's drive south of the city. The miles went by in a blur; all Cox could think of was seeing Matthew – of how surprised and happy he'd be to see her. Yeah, it was a little way past his bedtime, but she was sure Aidan would be reasonable about that. They'd got on okay when she'd been in the hospital, after all.

She drove carefully through the too-familiar roads of the residential estate where Aidan and Matthew lived. There were warm yellow lights on in practically all of the houses she passed – young families, mostly, she knew; parents spending time at home with their kids, watching TV, helping with homework . . .

The job had always got in the way of that, for her. And most of the time, that'd been okay – she liked her job, felt it was important, worth making sacrifices for, even if Matthew and Aidan hadn't always understood that.

The problem was when work went badly – or, like now, gave way under her like a rotten bridge – well, what did you do? What was left? What else *was* there to keep you going, make your life worthwhile?

She pulled up outside the house. Hadn't been here for a while; when it was her turn for time with Matthew, Aidan normally dropped him off in the city.

Aidan had let the garden get a bit scruffy, she noticed, but there was a bright new pot-plant by the front door. The living-room curtains were closed, but the lights were on.

She parked up and hurried to the front door; rang the bell.

She heard movement inside, Aidan's voice, the chain being slipped off the door –

A woman stood there. Thirty, thirty-two, slim and dark-haired, barefoot in jeans and a loose-fitting T-shirt. She was holding a glass of wine. Smiled at Cox politely.

'Hi?' she said.

Not this, Cox thought wildly. *Not now. Not after the day I've had.*

'Who are you?' It came out more abrupt, more hostile than she'd meant it to.

The woman's smile became puzzled.

'I – I'm Bev.' She blinked, peered at Cox – then her eyes widened. 'Oh! You must be Matthew's mum.'

Behind her, Cox saw Aidan step out into the hallway; he was in a white T-shirt and checked pyjama bottoms – he had a glass of wine, too.

He saw Cox; moved quickly to the woman's side. He looked alarmed.

'Kerry? What's wrong? What are you doing here?'

Cox felt off-balance, caught between alienation and the desperate need to see her son.

'I – I was hoping to see Matthew,' she said, trying to keep her tone light, conciliatory. 'He left me a message. I – I wanted him to see that I'm still in one piece.'

Forcing a smile felt like an act of heroism.

But suspicion was replacing alarm in Aidan's expression.

'He's in bed,' he said sternly. 'We have a schedule for a reason, Kerry. You should have called me.'

'Could you maybe wake him?' She knew she was sounding desperate – but hell, she *was* desperate.

'He's knackered, Kerry – needs his sleep. He had a long day.'

Not compared to mine, Kerry thought bitterly.

She saw the woman – 'Bev' – nudge Aidan gently in the ribs. Aidan looked at her, frowned, blinked, finally caught on – reluctantly made introductions: Bev – Kerry, Kerry – Bev.

They shook hands awkwardly, said insincerely that they were pleased to meet each other . . .

The wine glass in Bev's hand caught Cox's eye. It was a nice one, with a long stem and a subtle, delicate pattern circling the rim. She knew it well; she'd bought it herself, picked it up at a street market in Urbino, when she'd been there on holiday with Aidan.

She hasn't done anything wrong, she told herself, feeling a depth-charge of emotion going off in her gut. *It's not her fault.*

She turned a challenging stare on Aidan.

'I thought we were starting Relate sessions again in February,' she said.

He looked at her like she was mad. Maybe he wasn't far wrong.

'We are – but that's about Matthew, Kerry. About bringing a bit of stability into our relationship, for his sake. You know that. It's not –' He looked awkwardly from Cox to Bev and back again. 'It's not about *us*.'

Kerry swallowed. She felt cold, bruised, alone.

'I want to see Matthew,' she said – it came out almost as a sob, much louder than she'd intended.

Aidan looked lost for words.

With an anxious half-smile, Bev suggested that, if they weren't careful, they were going to wake the poor kid up . . .

Then, from upstairs, thin, sleepy, bewildered: *'Mum?'*

Right on cue.

It was as though someone was pulling her by a rope. She pushed aside Aidan – he said something ineffectual, 'Oi!' or 'Hey!' – and went into the hall. The hallway light was a bleary smear; she wiped a wrist across her eyes, started up the stairs.

He was already there, on the top step, in his *Toy Story* pyjamas.

'Mum?'

She smiled up at him – and he shrank back. Fear in his eyes. What the hell . . . ?

Then she remembered the mess the bike-crash had made of her face. The fat lip had subsided, but the scrapes on her nose and chin were only half-healed and from her temple to her jaw was a contused chaos of blues and browns. Enough to frighten anyone.

She touched a hand to her cheek, and grinned.

'I fell off my bike, didn't I,' she said. 'Ouch! But I'm still me, love – I'm still your mum . . .'

Aidan had come up the stairs after her.

'You can't do this, Kerry,' he said, his voice quiet but tense with anger. 'It's not right.' He put a hand on her upper arm.

She shrugged him off, flailing her arm backwards in annoyance. She was *sick* of being told what she could and couldn't do . . .

Aidan stepped back, lost balance. Grabbed for the bannister but missed. As he tripped awkwardly down the bottom three steps, his left hand flew out – a half-glass of red wine slopped down the front of Bev's T-shirt. Looked like she'd been shot.

She gasped; Aidan swore, flashed Kerry a vicious look.

Didn't hang about to be told to leave – told to leave her own son, told to leave the house she'd paid half the deposit on, half the mortgage, that she and Aidan had searched high and low for, and put all their savings into, never mind all their hopes, all their dreams . . .

She told Matthew she loved him. Told Aidan she'd see him on Saturday. Told Bev not to make a fuss – the wine'd come out in the wash.

Then she was off, out into the dark and cold.

23

Cox tried to stay off hard spirits – unless she'd had a *really* tough day.

This, she thought, half-filling a tumbler with vodka from the freezer, definitely qualified.

She took her drink to the sofa, pulled a cushion over her knees, took a sip – jarring, ghastly-cold, enlivening – and ran through the case in her head. A lot of victims, now. Not so many suspects. Radley, Halcombe, Allis, Merritt – and the kids whose lives they blighted, Colin Carter and Stevie Butcher among them.

She found herself dwelling on Carter and Butcher, a pervert and a petty criminal. Victims, once – innocent victims of the sick regime at Hampton Hall. What were they now? Few people looked on them as victims; no one argued their innocence. At some point – when? – society had turned on these men, deemed them unworthy of pity, condemned them to a life on the margins. Did they deserve it? Ah, Christ, who knew? Cox took another slurp of vodka.

When she was a kid, back in Guildford, there'd been a vicar who'd come to the school every now and then, to speak in assembly. Sometimes he'd talk about criminals, or drug users, or people who were in prison or living on the streets. *There but for the grace of God go I*, he used to say. It could just as easily be you or I in that jail cell, he meant; all it took was an unlucky break, a single wrong turn.

The phrase had stuck with Cox. You seldom heard it nowadays, she reflected.

She was becoming more and more certain that Hampton Hall was at the root of the killings, at the centre of the web. Abuse like the kids at that place had suffered . . . hell, you couldn't imagine what it could do to you, the scars it could leave, the damage it could cause.

She thought about Matthew and the damage they were doing to him. It wasn't even intentional, but who was to say how it would affect her son when he came out the other side? When he started playing up at school, when he made a bad decision and stayed out too late with a bad crowd? God, it made her want to weep when she thought he might *suffer* for the mistakes of his parents, for *her* mistakes, her crimes.

She necked the rest of the tumbler and reached for the bottle. An involuntary wince as she thought of the press cameras flashing in her face. The pack scenting blood. Their collective hunger. The country loved this sort of thing – the chance to condemn a villain, their chance to mourn a victim. *Poor* Tomasz Lerna, dying in the dark while evil Kerry Cox indulged her carnal desires. Black and white. They didn't stop for one second to wonder what Tomasz would have been like if they'd got there in time. What he would look like in twenty, thirty years. Happily adjusted to society? *I think not* . . . No, then they'd be baying for him too.

They didn't understand what time, and pain, could do to a person. Time and pain.

But why now?

Why thirty years later?

Perhaps the Hampton Hall theory was wrong. Maybe she was in danger of imagining the dots connecting, when really they didn't at all. If this did go all the way back to Hampton Hall, the killer had waited a hell of a long time. What, nearly thirty years? That made no sense. If he'd wanted to hurt Radley and Allis and all the rest, surely he could have done it decades ago, when the pain was fresh. The people who'd caused all that hurt at HHUC had gone on to live successful, happy lives – and God only knew how many others they'd harmed along the way. Why had he stood by and watched, all this time?

The simple answer was, he hadn't. Because she was wrong.

She took another drink, feeling lost. The harsh flavour of the vodka didn't shock her any more. Soon, she knew, she'd barely taste it at all. Not long after that, all being well, she wouldn't feel anything at all.

I'll drink to that, she thought. Lifted the glass again, but this time she paused with the glass on her lips; on the edge of the angry fog a thought of clarity.

Unless he hadn't had a choice.

She took a slow, thoughtful gulp.

She'd been fixating on the idea that the killer had *deliberately* waited three decades to take his revenge on the people who tormented him. But what if he'd only waited because he *had* to wait – because there was nothing else he could do.

Cox set down her glass. Her mind was racing. Suffering abuse as a kid could screw you up, she knew, but throw in thirty-plus years in prison, and . . . Christ. What would the world look like to you, when you came out?

How would you feel, about yourself, about your life?

And how would you feel about the people you held responsible?

She took up her phone; dialled Don DiMacedo. It was late, but she wasn't going to let go of this. Naysmith and his bosses might think she was off the case. Let them. She knew, deep down, she'd never walk away from this one – not till it was done with.

DiMacedo answered sleepily.

'Don. It's Kerry Cox.'

'Bloody hell. It's – it's gone one o'clock, Spook. Are you drunk?'

'A bit. But that's beside the point. Don, I need some data.'

'Data? What sort of data do you need at this time of night?'

'The law never sleeps, Don, you know that. I need to know who got released from prison in November.'

'Oh, is that all?'

'Only long stretches, say twenty years or more. It's to do with the murder of Euan Merritt – and Christ knows what else.'

There was only dull silence in reply. He wasn't biting.

'Don?'

He sighed.

'This isn't my business, Cox. I don't mind helping you out when I can – but this, this is a million miles away from my world now. It's not what I do.'

In the background she heard a murmur, a man's voice, not DiMacedo's. DiMacedo muffled the handset; she heard him say, 'Nothing – you go back to sleep.'

Came back on the line with a crackle.

'Sorry, Spook. I'm out.'

'Don, you don't understand. You can't back out now. Everything we worked on, back then – everything we went through –'

'Don't get sentimental on me now, Spook.'

'– it's *all tied in* with this. You can't just forget about it, pretend it didn't happen.'

There was a pause. Then DiMacedo said quietly: 'I think you'll find I can. I think you'll find I have.'

'Don, I –'

'I heard a whisper,' he interrupted her. 'I hear a lot of whispers, whispers are my job, but this one had the ring of truth to it. I heard you'd been suspended. Is that right?'

She hesitated. What did it matter, really? All her work with DiMacedo was off the books, anyway.

'Yep,' she said.

'Good. It could be the best thing that's happened to you in years.'

'Come on, Don.'

'I'm serious, Kerry. The shit you do takes a lot out of you – trust me, I know this. When was the last time you had a break, I mean a real break? I bet you can't even remember.'

Fair point. But the idea of taking a break now . . .

'Don,' she said. 'It's the guy in the mask. He's back.'

A silence. Got him. Don had seen the footage too, during Lerna. He was the one who brought it to her attention. Perhaps ten seconds went past. She heard Don moving about, and when he spoke again his voice had a different quality. Sounded like he was outside.

'Tell me what you need.'

Swiftly she sketched out the parameters of the search: the man – it had to be a man – would be maybe forty to fifty years of age; he'd have served a long sentence ('Let's say anything more than ten, to be sure'), somewhere – anywhere – in the UK; he'd have been released at some point prior to Christmas last year ('Go back as far as October if you need to').

'Can you do it, Don?'

'It'll take a while. Is it worth it? Sounds like a long shot to me, Spook.'

'It is. I'm sure of it.' She rubbed her eyes. God, it was good to have DiMacedo on board. It wasn't much – but it was a glimmer of light. 'I need you with me on this, Don. Naysmith's bottled it. Dan Chalmers is a decent guy, but he won't rock the boat. There's evidence going missing, there's strings being pulled higher up the chain, who knows how high . . .' Paused to let out a breath. 'Your help means a lot,' she said. 'I mean that.'

Another pause. DiMacedo's voice, when he replied, was studiously stripped of emotion.

'No problem,' he said. 'I'll do what I can.'

'G'night, Don.'

'Nighty-night, Spook. Now go to fucking bed.'

He rang off.

Cox smiled. Sat back. Picked up her drink.

She woke up to a mild, muddy hangover and the noise of someone thumping on the door. Slid blearily from bed, pulling the duvet with her; peered carefully through the blinds. A smart-looking young man in a knotted grey scarf stood on the doorstep, flanked by a bald guy with a boom microphone and a woman wearing a waterproof coat and toting a camera on her shoulder.

Cox sighed, turned away from the window. *Not today, thank you . . .*

She sat down on the bed, still holding the duvet round her body, and checked her phone. Sure enough: voicemails, missed calls, texts from crime reporters, feature writers, TV news researchers . . . and a message from her mum. The bloody press had been after her, too. She quickly texted back: *Sorry, Mum. I messed up. Don't tell them anything, will you? Love K. x*

She glanced at the clock: 9.15. Jumped in the shower.

When she came out, wrapped in a towel and – in spite of the vodka – feeling sharper than she had in days, there was an email waiting from Don DiMacedo. She prepped a pot of coffee, got quickly dressed while it brewed. Poured herself a cup and sat down at the table.

'*Good news and bad news,*' DiMacedo's email began. He'd spent the early morning trawling the databases ('*you don't want to know exactly* which *databases*'), and come up with only two results.

Kerry's heart sank a little. On the positive side, it was a narrow field; a thousand 'maybes' would have been a nightmare to check out, but two was easily doable. On the other hand, well, there were only two of them – what were the odds either of them had been at Hampton Hall?

She opened the files DiMacedo had attached. No picture; just a stark data sheet. Lawrence 'Larry' Eggers – career thief, looked like. Mid-fifties. Did time all over the place in the seventies, for burglary mostly, then made the step up to armed robbery in the early eighties. Got sent down for life after shooting a bank clerk in High Wycombe. Clerk survived. Released 8 December.

Seemed an unlikely match for the Merritt killing. Cox took a mouthful of coffee and opened the other zip folder titled 'R. Trevayne'. There were several files in various formats.

Robert Trevayne.

The hair on Kerry's neck bristled, and she felt a little light in the chest. Hadn't the childhood friend Butcher had talked about been called Robbie?

She sat back, conscious that her heart was pounding. The first file was actually a jpeg – a scan of a newspaper front page. Christ knew how DiMacedo had located it. '"Twisted" Drifter Jailed For Halesowen Slaying'. *Express & Star*, 12 February 1991.

Hadn't she seen a sign on their way into Birmingham for Halesowen?

The police mugshot of Robert Trevayne filled fully half of the newspaper's front page. He was thick-necked, shaven-headed; the file indicated that he would've been thirty-five at the time, but he looked older. He was staring into the camera with dark, dead-looking eyes. Cox could see why the *Express* editor had run the picture so prominently on the cover – it was a hell of an image.

The accompanying text was light on biographical detail; skimming the two-page spread, Cox learned only that Trevayne had been notorious in the west Birmingham area as a loner, a hard drinker and a man you didn't want to cross. It alluded to his history of violent crime and incarceration and characterized the brutal killing of the newsagent – a Mr O'Brien – as just another random act of violence in a life strewn with similar incidents.

She moved to the other files.

Trevayne's parole reports. Psychologist reports. Briefing notes – some typed, others informal and handwritten – passed from prison to prison whenever Trevayne was transferred.

This was the full works. People had written biographies with less.

She fixed more coffee, spread a knifeful of cream cheese on an out-of-date bagel and sat down to study.

By lunchtime, she felt she knew the guy inside-out.

As the *Express* journo had suggested, Trevayne's early life in and around Birmingham was marked by violence and extreme anger issues. From his first spell inside, the people who worked with Trevayne noted his hair-trigger temper and frightening physical strength (in the margin of one of the official transfer briefings, someone – a prison guard, Cox supposed – had scribbled a brief heads-up: *Watch yourselves, lads*).

It was the same over the millennium. The initial tariff served, subsequent infractions and dangerous behaviour kept him inside. But after 2007, the tone of the reports changed. The subject of his fearsome aggression came up less and less often; psychologists and guidance counsellors wrote instead of a new side to Trevayne, thoughtful, introspective, even philosophical. They traced the alteration in his character to a period he spent at HMP Leeds in early 2009; it was there he'd grown close to a Christian prison chaplain, a Reverend Macaulay. By 2012 the reports were all in agreement: suddenly and sincerely, Robert Trevayne had found God.

He'd been released from HMP Northumberland in late October last year. Cox drained her coffee, suddenly buzzing with excitement. *Born-again or not*, she thought, *this is our man.*

She thought briefly about calling the Yard, putting out an urgent APB, but guessed Naysmith would have something to say about that. Instead she reopened Trevayne's release form, signed by the newly ex-con in a surprisingly tidy hand. He'd also filled in a forwarding address: Cox grabbed a pen and started to jot it down – then stopped.

19 Azincourt Walk, Calais Buildings, Walworth.

No fucking way. Didn't she know that address?

She pictured a grotty, graffitied pebbledash semi – dogshit smeared across a letterbox – an unwholesome smell of dirt, smoke and neglect.

It was Colin Carter's address.

24

An overweight man and a blonde woman in a branded Range Rover. A paparazzo leaning on his moped, smoking a cigarette. Two guys looking bored at a window-seat in the café over the road. Maybe the news agenda had moved on; anyway, it wasn't quite the slavering press-pack she'd feared.

She'd dug out her fold-up Brompton, a handy backup for journeys across town. She figured she could lose the handful of journos without too much effort; with any luck, she wasn't even a big enough story to be worth chasing.

If she couldn't lose them, well, then she'd have a problem: she'd arranged for Greg Wilson to pick her up three streets away. But then, the damage had already been done in that respect – how much worse could the coverage get?

She zipped up her black down gilet, pulled up her hood, swung her backpack – stuffed with the hastily printed-off Trevayne files – across her shoulders. Readied the bike by the door. A fast start was the key here.

Yanked open the door, hit the leading pedal hard, let the door swing shut and click locked behind her.

Kicked forward down the street. The pap with the moped shouted something after her; she heard a car start up – the Range Rover, she guessed. But by then she'd reached a turn-off, access restricted by bollards, and zipped through into a half-developed strip of brownfield. A path cut to the right between apartment blocks; after that, she just had to make a turn through two lanes of traffic to where she'd agreed to meet Wilson.

She stopped at the kerb, pulled back her hood, breathless and exhilarated.

And here came Wilson's clapped-out car, bumping noisily into a layby. He popped the boot; she folded up her bike, stowed it carefully.

When she opened the passenger door she saw Wilson quickly reach across to snatch a newspaper, one of London's evening tabloids, from the seat. But she had had time to read the headline – *DISGRACED OFFICER ADMITS AFFAIR* – and seen the front-page picture of her being splattered with red dye at the inquiry.

She sighed as she sat down.

'Looks like I'm a celebrity again.'

'You're not the only one,' Wilson muttered, veering out into the lane of eastbound traffic. 'They're calling me to the inquiry, too.' He gave her a sidelong look. 'Thanks a bunch.'

'Didn't you actually used to write for that one?' she said.

'Touché.'

As they crawled towards the river, Cox filled him in on Trevayne's background: the violence, the murder, the supposed transformation after finding God in prison.

'You don't buy the "reformed character" shtick?'

'Not as a rule.'

Wilson laughed at her cynicism.

'With an attitude like that,' he said, 'you'd fit right in on Fleet Street.'

They drove in silence for a few minutes; felt to Cox like Wilson was thinking something through.

Eventually he said: 'Do we have any, uh, you know – backup?'

Cox smiled inwardly. But she couldn't blame him for getting cold feet. She'd been doubting the wisdom of this plan ever since she'd sussed that Trevayne was at Carter's place.

She lifted her chin in a show of bravado – for her own sake as much as Wilson's.

'Nope,' she said.

'Oh-kay.' He swallowed nervously. 'No problem. Fine. I eat murderous prison-hardened psychopaths for breakfast, me.' Then he made a gesture towards the car's glove compartment. 'Bit of light reading for you in there, by the way. If you don't fancy the newspaper.'

Cox looked at him questioningly, clicked open the compartment door. Found a sheaf of A4 paper fastened with a paperclip.

'What's this?' She took it out, scanned the cover page. '"Pathways to Positive Outcomes: Intelligence and Internalization in Children Raised in Care". Fascinating stuff, right up my street.'

'It's Allis and Merritt's paper, written for CARE,' Wilson explained. They were crossing the river now. Vauxhall Bridge was fogged with traffic fumes, and a low, dirty mist clung to the surface of the Thames.

Cox flipped through the paper. It was dry, academic stuff; seemed to be mostly concerned with IQ trends among care home kids. The pages were crowded with complex charts and statistical analyses in fine print.

'Too early in the day for that,' she concluded at last, dropping the paper into the footwell.

The mood in the car grew tense as they moved through Kennington, grew nearer to Carter's run-down neighbourhood. Wilson whistled anxiously between his teeth as he drove. Cox felt a nervous ache in her stomach – felt empty, hollowed out.

It's always like this before a raid, she told herself.

But on a raid you have stab-vests, batons, radio links, backup, put in a doubtful inner voice. *This isn't a raid – it's a kamikaze mission.*

They left the car on the edge of the estate. It was maybe half a mile to Carter's place. The air here was damp, the light hazy and grey. Someone on the estate was having a fire: there was a drifting smell of burning rubber. They passed two kids kicking a twanging plastic football against a wall; an old guy asleep on a bench with a half-jug of corner-shop cider at his feet.

Carter's house looked much the same as before. Still run-down and dirty; still a place you'd cross the street to avoid passing by.

They approached the door, Cox leading the way. They'd had to play games with Carter, last time, to get him to cooperate.

There'd be no games this time. Cox hammered on the door with her good hand.

'Police,' she yelled. 'Open up.'

Hammered again – kept on hammering until she heard shuffling footsteps and the clatter of locks being unfastened.

'Bloody hell,' hissed Carter, pulling open the door,

unlatching the iron gate. He was wearing a frayed beanie hat, stained white T-shirt and tracksuit bottoms; his right eye-socket looked darkly bruised. 'Keep it down, can't you? Do you need everyone on the fucking estate to hear you? I get enough grief as it is.'

'You're due a good deal more,' said Cox.

Carter looked meanly at her, pale-faced and piggy-eyed.

'What do you want?'

'I want you to know that you're going back to prison, Colin.'

He frowned, unfazed.

'Fuck off.'

'Where's Robert Trevayne?'

An artfully puzzled look.

'Who?'

'Nice try.' She moved forward, shoulder-first; Carter had no choice but to squirm aside as she barged past him into the fetid hall. Wilson followed quickly, banged the door behind him.

'Trevayne,' said Cox, backing the fat man up against the wall. 'Where is he? Talk, or I'll have you back inside like *that*.' Snapped her fingers.

'For what?'

'For whatever I damn well like.' She smiled nastily. 'You know what us CID lot are like. We've a funny knack for finding just the right "evidence" we need, whenever we need it.' Let the smile fade. 'Trevayne.'

She had him rattled, though he made a good fist of hiding it.

'All right, bad cop. Easy now. I ain't seen him – ain't seen him in years.'

316

'You did time together. At Wakefield.'

'Yeah. Like I say – years ago. Ain't seen him since.'

Wilson weighed in: 'Bullshit. Trevayne was in this house just last week.'

Carter looked at him, dead-eyed. Seemed hesitant, at first – then a defiant smirk wormed its way on to his face.

'Maybe he was,' he shrugged. 'So?'

'So you've just obstructed a police investigation,' Cox said. 'We'll put that top of the list of parole violations, but I'm sure I can come up with plenty more.'

She turned away from him, began to look desultorily around the hallway, up the stairwell; poked her head into the gloomy living room. Just to plant an idea, give Carter the impression that they could search the joint if they wanted – make him have a good hard think about what they'd find if they did.

Carter swallowed.

'He was here,' he said, 'but I dunno where he is now. That's straight-up. We hardly said a word to each other when he was here, and now he's fucked off fuck-knows-where.'

'How did he contact you? You must have his number.'

The fat man gulped again. Trevayne must've scared him, Cox thought. She could see him weighing up his options, such as they were: on the one hand, this nutjob Trevayne, on the other, twelve more months getting the shit kicked out of him inside.

He didn't say anything, but his eyes flickered to the kitchenette at the end of the hall.

Cox moved fast, darting down the hallway.

The kitchenette was dark and rank, the blinds drawn,

the surfaces filthy with fag-ends, pizza-crusts, smears of spilled food.

There was a phone. An old Nokia mobile. She snatched it up.

'That's *mine*,' Carter bellowed, lumbering up behind her. 'That's private property, that. You can't just walk in here and –'

Wilson stepped between him and Cox.

'Shut the fuck up,' he growled – a halfway-convincing impression of a tough guy.

Cox was already scrolling through the call register. Not a lot of calls lately – not a popular guy, Colin Carter. But there was one number, an outgoing call – from just after their last visit to the house.

She hovered her finger over the 'call' button – turned to Carter inquiringly.

His bolshie front fell away.

'Please,' he said. His lower lip was trembling.

Cox masked her surprise. She'd never seen him so afraid – Christ, had she ever seen *anyone* so afraid? She gave Wilson a quick glance; he gave her a 'what-the-fuck?' shrug.

'What would happen if I called Robert Trevayne right now?' she asked Carter softly.

'He'd fucking bury me.' Carter sniffed, wiped his nose. 'Seriously. He'd fucking kill me without thinking twice.'

'Where is he?'

'Do you think I'm fucking joking with you?' Getting panicky. 'Look.' He jabbed a finger towards his black eye. 'Look.' Hauled up his T-shirt: above his fat white belly, a raw red wound, marbled with bruising, scored upwards across his ribs. Let the T-shirt drop. '*He* done that, and that weren't nothing to him. And you ask me where he is. You can't fucking imagine what he'd do to me.'

She looked at him seriously.

'We can protect you,' she said. 'If you help us, we can protect you.'

'Yeah?' Carter's sneer was bitterly sceptical. 'Like you protected Stevie Butcher?'

Christ. How did he know about that?

'That happened inside. We can keep you out of there, move you somewhere safe.' She made a sympathetic grimace – if he hadn't fallen to bits, Carter would have scoffed at her sharp shift to good cop. 'Face it, Colin,' she said. 'What options have you got?'

Carter wiped his brow. Asked for a fag, which Greg dutifully supplied. Then, sitting on a Formica kitchen chair, he began talking, fast, fearful.

'This guy, he's something else. I'm fucking telling you. He come here out of the blue – like I said, I ain't seen him since I been in Wakefield, what, ten years since? He was a big cunt then but fucking hell he's massive now. Must be on steroids or something but they ain't any good for him because the fucker's off his head – I mean proper mental. You lot want to watch yourselves – he's tooled up and all, fucking guns, knives, I don't know what else. He's a fucking monster.'

He stopped, breathed deep, each breath long, juddering, on the brink of a sob.

Cox pushed further.

'Where's he been since he came out of Northumberland?'

Carter said nothing. Shook his head, trembling.

'He's been killing people, Colin.' Watched him closely as she spoke. 'People from Hampton Hall. He's out of control – we need to stop him.' Let a hard edge creep into her tone. 'You have no choice, Colin. You're out of options. Either you tell me where he is, where he's headed, or I put you away – and I'm talking the hardest time you ever did.'

He stared at her. Nothing but animal fear in his deep-set dark eyes.

'I dunno.'

'Colin –'

'I swear I don't know! Oh, Christ.' He wiped a forearm across his eyes. 'He's looking for someone. That's all I know, I fucking swear on my life. He's looking for someone – I dunno his name. Some bloke what had something to do with his brother dying, way back when – some bloke with a mask.'

Cox's heart was thumping hard in her chest.

'What do you know about the brother?'

'You don't wanna know.'

'Was it Dr Merton? Dr Allis?'

Carter sniggered, a laugh on the verge of mania. He sucked down the end of the fag until his lips were touching his yellowing fingertips.

'I *told* you,' he said. There was a glimmer of his old defiance in the look he gave her. 'Why don't you cunts ever listen? This goes so much higher than those fucking perverts. Merton, Allis, they're nothing, they're fucking *nothing*.' Then the fear returned; the baggy face grew pale, the light died in the eyes. 'But if I told you –'

'*Tell* us,' Cox urged. 'We'll protect you. With your help, we'll nail Trevayne – and with him inside, you'll have nothing to fear.'

Again the laugh, nerve-jangling, chilling.

'It wouldn't be Trevayne I'd be worrying about,' Carter said. His voice was high-pitched.

'Then who?'

'Oh, Christ. You don't even know. You don't have a fucking idea. It's the ones who killed Robbie's brother. The ones who killed fuck-knows how many others, too.'

'Tell us *who*, for Christ's sake. Help us find them – stop them.'

Carter was sobbing now, his unshaven cheeks smeared with tears. He blinked at her helplessly.

'They don't give a fuck about the police,' he said. 'It don't matter what I tell you. They ain't scared of you. You can't do nothing.'

She turned away, boiling with frustration. So many secrets, so many lies, so much *fear* . . .

Behind her, Wilson was muttering to Carter; she heard a lighter scrape. Carter's breathing started to return to normal; she heard him sniff, spit, swear to himself under his breath.

Waited another few seconds for him to pull himself back together – then turned, and looked him in the eye.

'Call Trevayne,' she said.

'You're having a fucking laugh.'

'Call him, and get him back here.'

Carter shook his head, jowls wobbling.

'Robbie's a nutter, but he ain't a fucking idiot. Proper

paranoid, and all – he ain't going to walk into a trap for you.'

Cox scowled, changed tack.

'How long was he here, before?'

'That's the thing, he came and went, never more'n two or three days at a time. Moving target, like. Barely saw him after you lot come knocking last time. Like I say – he's proper paranoid. He's muttering all the time about fucking God. And paying for sins. All that shit. He's got this ink on his chest – Jesus, on the cross, but the face is a fucking skull. I mean, it looks like prison work, but what sort of fucker wants that? Shit, looks like he did it himself with a rusty fucking nail.'

Cox nodded. Fixed Carter with a steely look.

'You've got my number,' she said. 'If you see him, hear from him, get a bloody postcard from him – you call me, straight away. Understand?' She put her face close to his. 'Remember, Mr Carter. You're all out of options. And I'm the nearest thing to a friend you've got.'

The Twelfth Day of Christmas, 1986

They've made a proper job of it, this time. Good workmanship.

There's fuck-all else for me to do except lie here on this bloody bed and stare at it: a heavy, narrow-meshed steel grille, the bolts sunk deep into the new concrete.

No way out now.

Staring at the grille means not thinking about what I seen at Wolvesley. Or anyroad that's the idea. Mostly I can't help thinking about it – whatever the bloody hell it was.

It wasn't right, I know that.

I know Stan's in there, in that bloody place.

I stare at the grille. I try and think about nothing at all.

The clunk of the lock wakes me up. Don't know what time it is, but it must be daytime: the lights are on. I sit up, wiping my eyes.

'Robert?'

It's Halcombe. First time I've seen her since I got back. It was the orderlies – fucking *just-following-orders Nazis* that they are – what bundled me off down here after Radley dropped me off.

I'm expecting a bollocking off of Halcombe, but it doesn't come. Instead she looks worried – scared, even.

'Robert, could you come with me, please?'

'Please'. There's a word I've got used to not hearing. I shrug, stand up.

'What do you want?'

'We just want a word.' She swallows, gives me a weird look. Her eyes are pink around the edges. Has the old bat been crying?

Then she says it – the phrase that makes my heart drop into my guts.

'We've got some news,' she says.

They've shipped in some woman from the council, child services or something, to help break the news. She looks like a social worker. I've spoke to enough of them – and anyroad, I've nothing to say now.

'Do you understand what we're telling you?' Miss Halcombe says.

I nod. Of course I fucking do. But what's the point in saying anything?

The council woman says: 'I know how you must be feeling, Robbie.'

'Do you fuck,' I say.

Can't help myself. She sits back. Looks hurt.

A fire, they said. A fire, in the night, at Wolvesley Grange, caused by an electrical fault. They've found one body – Stan's still missing, they said. We're dreadfully sorry, they said.

I stopped listening after that. There was nothing they could say that I might want to hear – nothing that'd make any difference. Nothing that'd mean anything.

Now I just sit here. I think they're still talking at me.

I could ask: did Dr Merton make it out okay? What about his mate Mr Radley the copper? They did? Well, isn't that lucky.

I could ask: what about the owners of those flash cars I saw parked out front?

I could ask: what about the feller in the robe, and the mask – what happened to him?

But I don't. Maybe there'll be time to ask those questions later. Maybe there'll even be answers. But not now – now I just feel the world fall away around me, like the outside of a candle falls away around the flame.

They talk on and on.

I see the slit eyes and mad grin of the man in the mask.

I hear Stan's voice screaming my name.

I won't cry, not here, not now, not in front of them. I bite the knuckle of my ruined right hand. I taste blood.

25

She wasn't much in the mood for talking on the drive back west; she felt exhausted by the confrontation with Carter and sick at the prospect of revisiting her memory of the man in the mask. But she couldn't keep Wilson in the dark. He asked about it as soon as they got past the Elephant and Castle roundabout.

She talked slowly, thoughtfully, at her own pace, as Wilson drove.

'I must've watched it a hundred times. It was — haunting. Horrible, in a way all the other stuff I saw — *way* worse stuff, on the face of it — somehow wasn't. It was the feeling of performance, of — well, of *showing off*. Sounds crazy, I know. He had a mask on, for Christ's sake. But still, somehow, it felt shameless; this guy, he could inflict all the pain, terror, suffering he liked, and we couldn't stop him, didn't know who he was, where he was — and God, didn't he just know it. He got off on the pain he caused, I'm sure, like they all did, the sick bastards — but there was more to it, for him. You could tell.' She sighed, shook her head ruefully. 'It's crazy, like I say. All this from thirty seconds of old videotape.'

'It's not crazy.' Wilson's expression was grave. 'It sounds — well, it sounds fucking creepy. I wouldn't question your reading of it. But I would say it sounds a bit far-fetched — the link with Merritt, I mean. The thing on his chest – it was a scrawl, circle, slits for eyes, ears, or horns if you like. Not exactly a registered trademark. Do you see what I'm saying?'

Cox nodded.

'I do. It's a leap, I know.'

'I'm not writing it off. And Trevayne looking for this masked geezer helps your case. But yeah, it's a leap, and a big one – just as long as you know that.'

She did. It was a hunch, sheer instinct. Wilson was right: she had to keep that in mind.

'I was thinking about Merritt,' she said. 'About Trevayne looking for this guy who killed his brother. I think we know now why he did what he did to Euan Merritt. It wasn't revenge.'

Wilson nodded.

'He wanted information. Thought Merritt knew where this guy was.'

'Or *who* he was.' She chewed her lip thoughtfully, frowned. 'Wish we knew whether Merritt told him.'

'If he knew, he told him,' Wilson said with certainty. 'Christ, Trevayne cut the guy's balls off. I don't care how scared you are of the consequences – if a guy holds a kitchen-knife to your scrotum and asks you a question, you fucking well answer.'

He winced, shook his head.

Cox called Naysmith from the A4. He'd be all right with her pursuing the case off the record, she guessed; she wasn't coming to him with hunches and conspiracy theories any more – this was a solid lead, a name, a face, even a last known address. They had to get an APB out on Trevayne, and fast. Either he'd found out who killed his brother and was gunning for them or he knew someone who might know something and intended to make them talk.

'Hello?'

Cox hesitated. Wasn't Naysmith's voice.

'Chalmers?'

'Ah, Cox. How's tricks? Yeah, the DCI got signed off sick earlier today – something to do with the medical he had recently? His calls are redirecting to me.' There was the noise of Chalmers slurping from a cup of tea; he smacked his lips, made a satisfied 'ah', then said: 'So – anything I can do for you?'

This had caught her off guard. She stammered a 'no', ended the call. When she looked across at Wilson, he must've read the anxiety in her face – he slowed the car, swung into a layby.

'What's wrong?'

She told him, quickly.

'This feels all wrong,' she said. 'Head north, when you can – we need to get to Ladbroke Grove.'

'Huh?'

'Naysmith's place.'

Wilson drove fast and well. As they rattled up the A3220 to the Westway, Cox – her mind racing – took another look through the Merritt/Allis paper on children in care. She hadn't, she realized, given much thought to Allis's death – to Allis's stabbing in Battersea Park.

She lowered the paper, looked at Wilson.

'Why didn't he torture Allis?'

'What?'

'Allis was in on it too – the abuse at Hampton Hall.

327

Surely he was just as likely as Merritt to know something about the death at Wolvesley Grange. Why would Trevayne torture Merritt, and not Allis?'

'I don't know. Maybe he didn't get the opportunity. It's not something you can easily do without people noticing. No evidence he tortured Verity either – perhaps they didn't have the info he wanted. Not found any indication Allis or Verity were abusers.'

'Or maybe Allis was softer than Merritt – gave up the goods right away. Pointed Trevayne in the direction of his old colleague.'

'Merritt? Could be.'

Once you injected a dose of fear, of panic, into that HHUC network, Cox realized, it transformed the dynamic. Did Radley's death spook Allis into throwing Merritt to the wolves? And how about Radley himself? He might've known the truth about Verity Halcombe's death – if he suspected that he was next on the list, maybe he *did* top himself after all.

'What a fucking mess,' she sighed.

She riffled exasperatedly through the pages of the paper – stopped at the final page, the authors' acknowledgements. *Names.* Names were useful – names were leads. Besides, it was the only part of this bloody paper she'd be able to get her head round. She quickly scanned the page – it was short, just two paragraphs.

'The authors thank the trustees of CARE for their support and assistance; in particular, they wish to acknowledge the contributions of trustees John Gandry and Sidney Thomas.'

She let the paper fall to her lap.

She'd heard the name, she knew she had. *Sidney Thomas*.

Fished out her phone, ran the name through a search engine. A picture of a silver-haired man popped up, along with a paragraph of Wikipedia text. So that was why she knew the name: Sidney Thomas was the solicitor general, one rung down from attorney general; his name cropped up now and then in news stories, legal briefings, that kind of thing.

What surprised her was that she knew the face, too. But from where?

She closed her eyes.

'You okay?' Wilson said, sounding concerned.

'I'm fine. Just – just shush.'

She let her brain do the work – follow the threads, trace the connections. It was in there somewhere, she knew. That face, that wavy silvery hair, those broad shoulders, that stolid, dignified expression –

Sidney.

A memory, a barely-there memory, not old but overlooked, creeping to the surface –

This is my husband, Sidney . . .

Cox opened her eyes.

'Stop the car. Stop the car *now*.'

Wilson hauled on the wheel, slewed the car leftwards, up on to the kerb; the exhaust rig clunked on the concrete; the car jolted to a grinding halt. Two overtaking cars, swerving across lanes, sounded their horns angrily.

He stared at her wide-eyed.

'What? What is it?'

'Sidney Thomas.' She jabbed the page with her finger.

'Sidney Thomas is Baroness Kent's husband. I've *met* him – at a café, just the other day.'

Wilson rolled his eyes, let his head loll back against the headrest.

'Jesus Christ,' he said. 'I thought at least you were having an aneurysm or something. What the hell . . . ?'

A wave of dizziness hit Kerry; couldn't breathe. The nerve endings across her body seemed to be firing all at once.

'Kerry?'

She took a deep breath; tried to slow down her thoughts, but they were rushing headlong.

'Look, it's the MoJ that's been trying to shut us down – trying to kill off this whole investigation, right from the start. Thomas is the solicitor general. To all intents and purposes, he *is* the MoJ. Now it turns out he's not only married to the woman who tried to bury me at the inquiry, he's got documented links with Allis and Merritt, too.'

Wilson was frowning.

'I'm losing track. Can you draw me a diagram or something?'

But Cox didn't answer. She was looking at the picture of Sidney Thomas. A clammy feeling had started to take hold of her. Thomas was getting on a bit now – in his seventies, at a guess. So in the 1980s he would have been in his forties . . .

Surely not. *Surely.*

She closed her eyes, and the image of the man in the mask rose up behind her eyelids.

'So?' prompted Wilson impatiently. 'What now? Onwards to Ladbroke Grove?'

'No.' She was rooting in her bag – she knew she had Sam Harrington's business card in there somewhere. Found it, drew it out; turned it over between her fingers. Read out the address.

Wilson looked nervous.

'Whitehall?' he said. 'Christ, that's worse than Walworth.'

Cox nodded firmly.

'If we want answers,' she said, 'we're going to have to take this to the top.'

26

'We should take it to the press.'

They'd parked in a small pay-and-display near Petty France, central London. Cox was unbuckling her seatbelt. She looked at him disbelievingly.

'The press? Are you kidding? The way they've treated me?'

'Look, I understand the press. You – with all due respect, Kerry – aren't a big story. *This* is a big story. If we break this, you'll be off the front pages for good.' He checked his watch. 'I could get something in the evening papers, if we're quick.'

Cox scowled at him.

'Just another scoop for you, isn't it?'

He sighed.

'No. No, Kerry, it's not. You've got to understand, it's a two-way street. Sure, they'll use you to sell papers. But you can use them, too.'

'How do you mean?'

'Think about it. We've got the information, we've got the story. What's the one thing they've got that we need?'

'I don't know. The moral outlook of Jack the Ripper?'

'Think straight, Kerry. *Power*. Look what we're going up against! The fucking MoJ. The two of us, against *that*?' He gestured in the direction of the looming Whitehall office blocks. 'The press has power, a terrifying amount of power. I say we give them the story; get them to do our heavy lifting for us.'

Cox hesitated with her hand on the door-latch. It was tempting; it would be good to have some serious weight behind them. But even now, she knew they didn't have enough. Links, horror stories, but nothing tangible. If she went public with this, it would look like sour grapes – just an attempt to discredit the inquiry.

'No,' she said flatly.

'Christ.'

'I take your point, Greg. But I've got to do this the right way – and besides, I prefer to fight my own battles.'

Harrington's building was a brutalist concrete tower, a sixties monolith squatting grey and rain-washed in the heart of Petty France. It was busy: men in suits – they *were* mostly men, Cox noted – came and went at a brisk, businesslike pace.

She didn't much fancy presenting her credentials at the security-heavy front desk – let alone Wilson's.

Instead, she dialled Harrington's number.

He answered promptly.

'Inspector Cox.' She sensed an uneasiness in his voice. 'Good to hear from you.'

She told him that she needed to speak to him – urgently, and in person.

There was a long pause. Cogs turning, she guessed.

'I'm awfully sorry,' the MoJ man said at last, 'but I'm in the office and I'm *really* snowed under, so –'

She saw her opening.

'That's quite all right. I'm just downstairs, in the lobby

of your building. I only need two minutes of your time.'
Threw in the kicker: 'I want to talk about Sidney Thomas.'
Rang off.

She took up a position by the door; waited. Wilson lingered outside, smoking a cigarette.

It took Harrington less than five minutes to clear a gap in his schedule. He came through the security doors looking harassed, walking quickly, his suave smile less self-assured than usual.

'Inspector.'

'Mr Harrington.'

They shook hands, each eyeing the other calculatingly.

'I'm surprised to see you, I must say,' Harrington said. 'I thought you'd be keeping a low profile – considering your suspension. I take it you're not here in an official capacity?'

Cox kept it vague: 'I'd like to talk off the record.'

Harrington smiled.

'I don't doubt that you would,' he said. He glanced up, over Cox's shoulder – his smile stiffened. Shit – he'd seen Wilson. Cox kept her face neutral, polite, engaged.

'I see you've brought a friend,' Harrington said.

'An associate.'

'That's an odd word for it.' No smile now; his pale eyes were glazed and hostile. 'I think,' he said, 'you had better have a *very* good reason for being here.'

'I have.' Kept her chin up, her voice level, her eyes on his. 'Should we talk in private?'

Harrington folded his arms.

'I think not. Here is fine.'

'Okay.' She shrugged. 'Can you tell me on whose orders you've been trying to compromise our investigation?'

He smirked.

'What a preposterous idea.'

'If it's so preposterous, why did you come running down here like a well-trained puppy when I dropped the name of your boss?'

Harrington's face was taut.

'I came to see,' he said, 'if it was necessary for me to have security escort you from the premises. I see now that it is.'

He turned to signal to the nearest blue-uniformed officer.

Cox swallowed. This had escalated more rapidly than she'd expected. Nothing else for it – she only had one card left to play.

'Fine,' she said. 'But don't be surprised when Sidney Thomas turns up dead.'

Harrington looked at her sharply. He laughed – an unconvincing, mirthless gurgle – but he called off the security officer, waving him away with an open hand.

'That's quite a thing to say, inspector.' He tucked his hands in his pockets, rocked back on his heels. Looked at her narrowly for a moment. 'Are you serious?'

Cox ticked the names off one by one on her fingers.

'William Radley. Verity Halcombe. Reginald Allis. Euan Merritt. All dead. All murdered.' Let her hand drop. 'I have good reason to believe that Mr Thomas is the next name on that list.'

Harrington tilted his head thoughtfully.

'Why?'

He must be a hell of a poker player, Cox thought.

'You tell me,' she said.

He looked at her for a half-minute more – than he smiled, shook his head.

Dammit, thought Cox. She thought, for a second, she'd had him; now, she saw – in his smile, in his half-turn back towards the security desk – that her last chance had gone.

And who knew, maybe Sidney Thomas's last chance, too.

'As it happens,' Harrington said, 'Mr Thomas isn't even here today – he called in sick; some sort of gastric trouble I understand. Had to cancel quite a few meetings. He's at home, safe and sound. So no need to worry yourself, inspector.'

Worth a shot.

'Home? Where's that?'

Harrington's smile was contemptuous.

'Now if you'll excuse me –'

He turned away decisively.

Something in Cox – some part of her that was sick of being turned away, being denied, lied to, ignored, talked down to and forced to compromise – surged up uncontrollably. Before Harrington had reached the security doors that led to the sanctum of the upper floors, she shouted after him: 'Euan Merritt's killer is still on the loose, Mr Harrington. He thinks your boss is a sex offender, he thinks your boss killed his brother, and he's –'

Harrington had turned in alarm at her first words; now, red-faced, he raced back across the lobby, waving his arms furiously in a 'cut' gesture.

Well, that seemed to do the trick, Cox thought. She didn't bother to finish the sentence. Folded her arms.

'Keep your bloody voice down,' Harrington hissed.

'Do you know, you're the second liar to say that to me today.'

'You obviously make a habit of slander.' Harrington looked about him, a little wildly. Buttoned his jacket. Gave her a glare. 'I'd hate to see you up on trial for defamation, inspector, as well as unemployed.'

'I didn't say those things were true. I wouldn't know either way. I said that's what Merritt's killer thinks.' She watched Harrington's expression grow thoughtful. 'Just give me his address – I'll have a patrol sent over.'

Harrington shook his head dismissively.

'I can't do that.'

'But –'

'We'll keep this in-house. Last thing we need is a vanful of uniformed plods rolling up at the solicitor general's home, sirens blaring.'

'Well, quite,' Cox said sarcastically. 'What *would* people say?'

Harrington looked at her with clear dislike.

'We'll go there now. You and me. We'll keep this *strictly* on the QT, inspector. Do you have a car?'

'Mr Wilson does.'

The man didn't bother to try and hide his disdain.

'How cosy,' he said.

As Wilson piloted the cramped car through the choked roads of the city, heading south-west, Harrington, in the back seat, tried to get through to Thomas's home phone on his mobile.

'No answer,' he muttered. 'That *is* unusual – he ought to be contactable, even if he is off sick.'

'Tried his mobile?' Wilson suggested.

'Mr Thomas doesn't use one. He's a rather traditional man.'

Cox twisted in her seat to address Harrington.

'What's the set-up at Thomas's house? Is it just him and his wife?'

'Him and Baroness Kent, yes.' Harrington – seated sideways, his knees squeezed in behind Wilson's seat – frowned and brushed some lint from his tailored trousers. 'It's a large-ish place, south of Esher, detached, several acres.'

'No neighbours, then?'

'None within a hundred yards.'

Cox pursed her lips. Didn't like the sound of it.

Harrington directed them via a route that took them some way off the main road. Cox suspected he was doing his best to delay them, so tortuous was the route he was taking.

After multiple turns through a series of picturesque villages, they wound up at a sprawling stone-built pile, thick with yellowing ivy, screened from the road by dense, dark-green holly bushes. The driveway, paved with pricey-looking pale stone, had the dimensions of a decent-sized car park; a bottle-green classic Jaguar was parked there, alongside a silver two-seater.

'Nice his 'n' hers,' Wilson murmured, crawling to a halt at the roadside.

Cox climbed out, opened the back door.

'Mr Thomas is a classic-car enthusiast,' Harrington said, unfolding himself from the back seat. 'He has several more in his garage.'

'Nice for some.'

It was growing dark. A bird was making a racket in a nearby tree. There were a few cars parked along the road; Cox jotted down their numbers ('You never know,' she said to Harrington).

She felt tense, uneasy. As the three of them crossed the driveway she was checking out the layout of the place with a copper's eye. Doors front and back, of course – probably a third, a kitchen door, at the side, too. The windows in the upper floor were whitewashed wood with leaded glass; here at the front they opened on to a sort of terrace – from there it'd be an easy scramble down to the ground.

Ops in old places were a nightmare, she knew. Too many ins, too many damn outs.

They reached the doorstep; Harrington rapped confidently on the door.

'I'm sure this is all quite unnecessary,' he said airily. 'I'm sure Mr Thomas is perfectly all right.'

Cox said nothing. *Who are you trying to convince?* she thought.

No one came to the door.

Harrington looked at her, his expression caught between impatience and concern.

'I do feel it's somewhat out of order to bother a sick man at his home,' he said.

Cox, hand cupped against the glass, was peering through one of the front windows. She could see the outlines of wooden chair-backs, a bowl of flowers on a table, photograph frames on a sideboard under the sill. No movement.

'Try again,' she said. 'It's a big place – maybe he didn't hear you.'

Harrington sighed, rapped again on the wood.

This time there was a noise from inside – an interior door opening, Cox thought. A key was turned in the front-door lock.

Sidney Thomas opened the door.

Cox left the window, moved back to stand at Harrington's shoulder. Her first impression of the solicitor general was of a very poorly man: maybe, she thought guiltily, they shouldn't have bothered him after all. He was recognizable as the fragile but well-built old gent she'd met in the café – same silver hair, same arthritis-swollen hands, same regular, forgettable facial features. But that man had been well-dressed and urbane, had carried himself – for all his evident physical frailty – with a certain amount of enduring dignity.

Now, in a dressing-gown, rumpled pyjamas and slippers, he looked weak, bowed-down, broken. His skin was greyish and mottled with sweat. His broad shoulders were bent. In the café he'd looked maybe six-two, six-three if he stood at his full height; now he slouched and seemed barely taller than Cox herself.

He didn't look surprised to see Harrington – that was odd, Cox thought.

'Ah. Mr Harrington. Ah,' he croaked.

'Good evening, sir,' Harrington said respectfully, with a formal bow of his head. Cox thought back to her own encounter with DCI Naysmith the previous day – dead drunk, passed out on the sofa. So *this* is what it's like to have a boss you really respect, she thought sardonically. It showed the kind of deference for rank you only learned at the better public schools.

'I *do* apologize for the unwarranted intrusion,' Harrington went on, 'and I very much hope you're feeling rather better, but if it isn't too much trouble –'

We don't have time for this. Cox took over.

'Mr Thomas,' she interrupted, ignoring a daggers look from the MoJ man, 'I'm Detective Inspector Cox from the Metropolitan Police.'

The old man looked at her sharply.

'Police?' What was that quiver in his voice? Fear?

'That's right. We need to speak with you in connection with an ongoing –'

'Unthinkable.' Thomas cut her off. His voice wavered, and his eyes gleamed unhealthily. 'You oughtn't have come here. Didn't I tell you I was ill? Terrible head cold.'

Cox squinted at him.

'Gastric trouble, I think you said, sir.'

He waved a liver-spotted hand: 'Bit of everything, bit of everything. Ghastly business – and the last thing I need is you people keeping me from my rest.'

Still that odd quiver in the man's voice.

Harrington launched into a smooth, wordy apology. Greg Wilson, meanwhile, caught Cox's eye; looked like he was signalling to her, behind Harrington's back, doing his clumsy best to be discreet.

She frowned at him.

He was nodding his head downward – at the front step? At the hallway carpet?

She followed his gaze, trying not to be obvious.

Nothing on the step that she could see; nothing on the carpet.

But there was a coin-sized spot of blood on the toe of Thomas's left slipper.

Cox moved fast.

'We need to come in, sir,' she said, speaking over Harrington. 'It really can't wait.'

'Out of the question.' The old man hadn't opened the door fully; the gap between door and frame was only a foot or so. Now he clung to the door two-handed, as if he were drowning and it was all that was keeping him afloat. 'You have to go. You really do have to go now.'

Cox took a step forward, placed the flat of her hand on the door.

Thomas's voice wound up in pitch.

'No!' He sounded like an old woman. 'No – please. No.'

She'd had enough of this.

She shoved at the door, pushing off from her back foot, putting the heft of her body behind the move. Thomas let out a sort of squeal. The door opened inwards, maybe another eight inches, then stopped with a bump – Cox heard a pained, angry grunt.

Sam Harrington had to take a step backwards as Thomas, whimpering, tumbled out of the door, down the step – practically flung himself into Harrington's arms.

'I've got you, sir, I've got you,' she heard Harrington say – but now her focus was elsewhere. A man had lurched from behind the door, blood from his nose smearing his upper lip. He held a gun, a heavy revolver, in his right hand.

Tall, broad, muscular, murderous. Trevayne.

Carter hadn't been kidding; the guy was a monster. His biceps, each ridged with a bulging vein, stretched the fabric of his blood-spotted T-shirt; his neck was bullishly thick, his torso a slab of muscle. His red-rimmed eyes focused on Cox – it felt like being caught in the crosshairs of a bomber plane.

She pivoted, bringing her right foot round in a fast half-circle; her boot connected cleanly with the inside of Trevayne's wrist; the gun went skittering across the pale stone flags.

The big man spun, lunged back in through the door. He tried to slam the door behind him; Cox, leaping forward, managed at a stretch to jam her foot against the frame – the heavy wood crashed into her ankle.

She swore, yelled for someone to call 999 – pelted into the house after Trevayne. He was headed, she guessed, for the back of the house.

Too many damn outs.

A dining room, dark but bright with polish, flashed by, then a kitchen, country-ish and airy – she saw Trevayne, bald head slick with sweat, hauling open a door in the French windows.

'Stop, police!' she bawled – knowing how much good it'd do.

Trevayne was out the door and moving fast across the broad, up-sloping lawn. Beyond the end of the garden, by the look of it, was nothing much but stubble farmland; there were trees and a church steeple on the horizon.

As she followed Trevayne through the open door she saw him cut right, towards some outbuildings: a long,

343

flat-roofed shed, a moss-stained greenhouse, a clutter of compost heaps, water butts and tall bamboo canes.

Saw him vanish into the shadows there, as she was crossing the lawn.

She moved forwards with caution, fighting painfully for breath. Maybe, she thought, he'd gone past the shed and carried on going, through the bordering hedgerows and the smallholding beyond – maybe she'd lost him.

A part of her hoped she had.

But Robert Trevayne, she knew, wasn't a man who shrank from violence; wasn't a man who'd turn and run if there was anything to be gained by standing and fighting.

She approached the nearest corner of the shed. There was a smell of mouldered wood, wet bark. The grass had been allowed to grow longer here; she could feel cold dampness seeping through the fabric of her trousers.

No sound, save the repetitive beat of water dripping on to a plastic dustbin-lid from a flaw in the shed's guttering. No sign of Trevayne.

She moved close to the planked wall of the shed, edged warily along to her left. Felt conscious of her ragged breathing. He must've seen her coming after him – must know where she was –

Queasy with anxiety, she glanced back towards the house. She'd never ducked out of a chase, not once. DI Cox was a good copper to have on a manhunt, everyone knew that: fast, strong, tenacious as hell . . .

But then she'd never gone after Robert Trevayne before.

She held her breath – edged another inch towards the corner of the shed.

A blur of movement, a moment of shuddering impact. Her first, startled thought was: *how the hell did a man that size move that fast?* Then the pain kicked in.

She was dimly aware of Trevayne crashing away through the wet trees to the right – of Wilson yelling something, and running footsteps pounding up the lawn. But it was all nothing beside the burning in her lungs as she gasped, gagging, weeping, for air, and the jagged-edged pain ripping through her from her lower ribs.

The half-rotten log he'd hit her with lay in the wet grass beside where she lay, clutching her midriff, jaw working helplessly.

'You're okay, Kerry.' Wilson, kneeling beside her, rubbed her heaving shoulders. 'You'll be okay. He's gone.'

I lost him, she thought, rolling on to her knees, burying her face in the wet grass.

From the road near the house, she heard the furious roar and squeal of a car taking off at speed.

Sidney Thomas was shaking so hard he could barely hold the glass of water Harrington had brought him. He held it gripped in both hands, suspended between his knees, as he sat on the drawing-room sofa, a blanket around his shoulders, staring at nothing.

'Thank you,' he kept saying, tremulously, over and over again. 'Thank you, thank you.'

Cox, standing facing him in the centre of the room, had stopped listening a long time ago.

Her mouth was dry; her ribs ached, but she'd stopped caring about that, too. She didn't know what to say – barely knew what to think.

Ranged along the wall in front of her, above Thomas's bowed head, were five masks of polished leather. Each had a different expression, of joy, of horror, of surprise, of confusion – and, on the last one, a grin of wicked mischief, horizontal slits for eyes, and devil's horns curling upwards from the temples.

She looked across at Wilson; he was leaning in the doorway, watching her, his expression grave and troubled. Then she looked down at Sidney Thomas – an old, broken man in pyjamas, trembling and weeping in self-pity and fear.

She stepped forward, took a breath, and told the solicitor general she was placing him under arrest.

27

They'd taken him to the nick on Esher High Street. The house was being sealed, and two local officers were put on guard – no one, *no one* to be given access. Cox herself had taken photos of the masks.

She'd sat in the back with Thomas; he was silent, withdrawn – maybe suffering from shock. *Well, let him suffer.* It was an unprofessional way to think; she was in an unprofessional state of mind.

She'd made Harrington ride in Wilson's car, despite his protests. The guy was Thomas's fixer; no way was she letting him speak to his boss before she'd had a shot at him in the interrogation room. He was outside now, talking animatedly on his phone as they booked Thomas in with the custody sergeant.

Since they'd arrived, the atmosphere in the nick had been queasy, nervous. Excited, too. Short of hauling in the PM or the lord chancellor, it was hard to imagine how she could have caused more of a stir than by bringing them the solicitor general, handcuffed and still in his PJs.

The sergeant had looked up at her uncertainly when she'd presented the old man at the desk.

'The – the charge, ma'am?'

She'd already told him once.

'Child abuse. Trafficking. Rape. Murder.'

The sergeant had looked doubtfully at the silent, hunched old man; then back at her.

Thomas had finally broken his silence: 'Preposterous,' he'd muttered.

'Just book him in, sergeant,' Cox had said wearily.

While Thomas was being led to his cell, she grabbed a cup of machine coffee and went over to sit beside Wilson on the plastic chairs that lined one wall of the custody suite.

'How're the ribs?' he asked solicitously.

'Feel like I've been through a mangle. But I'll live.'

He nodded towards the cells and the lean, tottering figure of Sidney Thomas, diminutive between two blue-jerseyed young PCs.

'You're sure about this, then?'

Cox nodded firmly, sipped her coffee.

'Dead sure,' she said.

'You won't have much to give the CPS.'

'I'll have enough.' Looked at him. 'I don't have a choice, Greg.'

The local DI, a guy named John Meadowes, called her over; wanted to go over some details of their visit to Thomas's place. He led her into his office – it was neat as a pin, smartly furnished, lined with labelled box-files.

'Nice place you've got here,' Cox said with a tired smile, taking a seat.

Meadowes shrugged.

'Tidy office, tidy mind, so they say. Now.' He opened a cardboard folder. 'We ran the registration numbers you gave us – one match, a grey Merc, bought from a dealership in Newcastle at the end of October. Buyer gave his name as Trevayne.'

'You've put an alert out for the plate?'

'Yep – I'm sure he'll ditch it as soon as he can, but we should at least get a lead on where he's headed first.' He looked up at Cox. He seemed anxious; she understood why. 'What,' he asked, tentatively, 'did you have in mind as the next step?'

Her answer was prompt: 'Search the house. Rip it apart.'

Meadowes looked panicky.

'You do know who you've arrested here, don't you? Sidney Thomas? The solicitor general? Look, I hold no brief for the old bastard – I've no reason to doubt what you tell me – but the guy could get every officer in this nick chucked off the force with a swipe of his pen. Come on, ma'am – give me a break.'

When did the backbone of the service turn to jelly?, Cox wondered bitterly.

'How long,' she asked, meeting Meadowes's pleading gaze with a dour look, 'do you think Thomas will remain as solicitor general?'

'But – if the case falls through, or the CPS doesn't like the look of it, or –'

'I'll nail him.' She nodded, once, emphatically. 'I'll nail him, John, if it's the last thing I do.'

Meadowes gave her a significant look. Sat back, folded his hands on his stomach.

'Careful what you wish for,' he said.

She stood – thanked him for his help.

'Is it okay,' she asked at the office door, 'if I speak to Thomas now? I know his brief's on the way. But I'd like a quick word.'

Meadowes shrugged. 'Sure, but I doubt you'll find him

much of a conversationalist. I'll tell PC George to sit in with you.' Another pleading look. 'Just please – go easy on him. At least for now.'

Meadowes was right. The solicitor general wasn't much of a talker.

He sat calmly, dressed in a police-issue shirt and slacks, while PC George, a keen young constable with a slick side-parting, rigged up the video and sound recorders.

Cox sat down opposite the old man, introduced herself for the benefit of the tape and formally commenced the interview.

'Could you state your full name, please?'

Silence – silence, and a blank, blue stare.

Cox repeated the question.

'I will state nothing,' Thomas said, 'until such time as my solicitor is present.'

Cox looked sidelong at PC George.

'Funny, isn't it,' she said. 'The most senior legal figure in the country – and he needs a small-town solicitor to come and hold his hand.'

George sniggered obligingly.

When she looked back at Thomas, he was looking dyspeptically at her down his nose.

'I'm not accustomed to handling trumped-up charges levelled by unbalanced over-promoted police officers,' he said coldly. 'And, as you will soon learn, Christopher Seaton-Jones is no small-town solicitor.'

Cox nodded, neutrally. She'd figured out one thing for sure: Sidney Thomas was easy to wind up.

She started in on the details of the case. She'd get

nothing but stonewalling from hereon in, she knew, unless Thomas was a bloody fool – and the solicitor general of England and Wales was certainly no fool.

'Do you know the man who was at your house today?' she asked. 'The man who held you at gunpoint?'

Silence.

'Had you ever met him before? We believe his name was Robert Trevayne.'

Silence.

'I would have thought, myself,' Cox mused, twisting a pen between her fingers, 'that these were pretty simple questions. I would have thought that the solicitor general would be quite capable of answering them without any help.' She set down the pen, smiled brightly. 'But what do I know? I'm just an over-promoted police officer.'

Silence.

'I liked your house. Liked what you've done with the place, the furnishings and stuff. Interesting – decorations, would you call them? On the wall, in the drawing room? The masks?'

Thomas's cold, reptilian expression didn't change; his face froze, became rigid, a mask itself.

'From a theatrical production, I expect. Am-dram, is it, down at the Walton Playhouse?' She let the playful tone slip gradually from her voice. 'Lots of fun, I expect. Enjoy performance, do you, Sidney? Being watched? Being on camera?'

Silence. Not a muscle twitched. The old man might've been carved in marble.

Cox talked on.

'He had it in for you, I assume, this Robbie Trevayne.

Any idea why that might be? Why he'd hold a grudge? No? Well, maybe it was a long time ago. I'm the same, terrible memory. God knows what I'll be like when I get to your age. Well, maybe we can help fill in the gaps.' She flipped open her folder, sifted her pages of notes. It was all for show – she knew every detail of this case by heart. 'We know quite a bit about Mr Trevayne. About his childhood – he had a very hard time, you know. Raised in care homes. Abused, sexually abused; betrayed by the people who were supposed to be looking after him. Hard to believe, isn't it? That kind of cruelty. That kind of breach of trust. But it got worse for Robbie Trevayne – his brother died, in tragic circumstances. There was a fire, supposedly. Place called Wolvesley Grange – and at Christmas, of all times.' She sighed. 'Poor kid. Didn't have much of a chance after that.'

Thomas still said nothing – but he was listening, Cox knew it; she could tell, by the look in his glassy blue eyes. He was taking in every word.

But what was he *thinking*?

Let me in, you old bastard, Cox thought, biting back her impatience. *Just a crack. Just give me a glimpse of the monster behind those eyes.*

'Maybe you could tell us what you remember about CARE,' she said. She was getting sick of the sound of her own voice – reminded herself that Thomas must be pretty sick of it too. 'Hampton Hall? The good old days. Your old friends, perhaps. Bill Radley. Verity Halcombe. Reggie Allis. Ian Merton.' She tilted her head. 'All dead and gone now, of course – *such* a shame.' Leaned forward, linked her hands together on the tabletop. 'Such – such good people, weren't they, Sidney?'

He'd blinked at the mention of Ian Merton, aka Euan Merritt; the mask had slipped just a fraction. She could guess why, too.

She sat back. Gave him a hard smile.

'It preys on your mind, doesn't it, what Trevayne did to Ian Merton.' She kept her tone flat, now, rough-edged, no-nonsense. 'You saw the details in the police reports, I expect? The cigarette burns all over his body. The knife cuts, deep, nasty, right where he knew it'd hurt the most. That strange face cut into his chest – a bit like one of those masks of yours, come to think of it. And did you know he cut the poor man's balls off, as well? Christ. It must *haunt* you, Sidney, what he did.' Leaned slightly forwards, right in Thomas's eyeline. 'Imagine what he'd have done to you, if we hadn't turned up. And if you walk out of here a free man – I don't know, if someone upstairs pulls some strings for you, say – well, Trevayne will still be out there. Waiting for his chance.' She sighed, shook her head. 'I don't know how you'll sleep at night, Sidney, I really don't.'

She gave it a minute or so – let it sink in.

Then: 'Interview suspended, 22.19.' She gave George the nod; the young PC switched off the recorders.

Thomas made to rise.

'Just a second,' Cox said, still in her seat, reaching for her bag. 'We're not quite done here.'

He scowled.

'I've heard quite enough offensive nonsense from you already, thank you, inspector,' he said.

Cox smiled.

'It's not me you're going to listen to,' she said.

353

Drew out Colin Carter's mobile phone. Scrolled to the last incoming number; hit the green button. Laid the phone on the table and switched on the speaker.

Two rings. Then:

'What do you want?'

A deep, nasal West Midlands voice, taut with aggression and hostility.

And now Thomas's face *did* change – it contorted, contracted with fear. He shrank back in his seat, staring at the phone as if it were about to attack him.

Cox waited.

'Hello?' the voice barked.

She leaned forwards.

'No, Mr Trevayne,' she said, clearly, crisply. 'It's the woman whose ribs you smashed with a lump of timber, before you ran away.'

A long pause – then a soft sigh.

'You shouldn't have interrupted,' Trevayne growled. He didn't sound angry, Cox thought – he sounded *sad*. 'You shouldn't have stopped me. You've only made things worse.'

'You might like to know I've got Sidney Thomas with me now.'

'*Have* you now?' A faint noise, like the ghost of a laugh. 'Hello, Sidney.'

Thomas's mouth was a puckered 'o' of horror, his eyes wild, his hands white-knuckled on the table edge. Petrified.

'This is over, Robert,' Cox said, simply, as if doing nothing more than stating a fact. 'It's finished. Give yourself up – let us help you.'

'I'm all too familiar,' Trevayne replied grimly, 'with the kind of *help* provided by the British criminal justice system.' An ominous pause. 'Besides,' he went on, 'you can't undo what's done.'

Cox bowed her head.

'No,' she said. 'No, we can't.'

She looked at Thomas; he was still frozen in a grimace of fear, a rabbit pinned by a predator. She hesitated. Trevayne was unstable, unpredictable; she was walking through a minefield here. One wrong step . . .

'I can't bring Stan back,' she said carefully. 'But I can bring the people who killed him to justice – with your help.'

'Be honest, copper.'

'My name's Kerry. DI Kerry Cox.'

'Whatever your name is, don't try and muck me about. Don't try and trick me. And don't tell me you want to help. You don't want to help the likes of me.'

There was a note of self-reproach, even self-loathing, in Trevayne's low, husky voice. *There's something I can use*, Cox thought – then hated herself for thinking it.

For thinking like a copper?

'I know what you've done, Robert. You've done bad things, terrible things. I've seen it with my own eyes – the pain, the suffering you've caused.'

For the first time Trevayne raised his voice a fraction.

'I'll not be judged by you, woman.'

'I'm not judging you. And d'you know why? Because I know what you've been through, what was done to you – what . . . *they* did to you.' She leaned in towards the phone. 'Robert, I understand.'

A long silence. Cox glanced up at Thomas; he was shaking now, all over, the loose skin of his throat trembling, the reflection of the ceiling-light vibrating on the lenses of his glasses. She hoped to God he wasn't going to have a heart-attack, or a stroke – Christ, where would *that* leave her?

At last, Trevayne spoke again. He sounded composed, even polite.

'I'm going to tell you two things, Inspector Cox. Two things I want you to be very certain about. One: you say you understand. You don't. Hear me? You don't. That's one. Two: this, inspector, this is not over.'

'What if I told you that Mr Thomas is here with me because he's in custody? He's under arrest, Robert – for all the things he did back then. He's in a jail cell, and if I have my way –' she glanced up balefully at the trembling solicitor general – 'that's where he'll stay. You can't get to him; you can't touch him.'

Trevayne's response was immediate, faintly amused: 'I wouldn't be so sure about that if I were you.' Then, in a brisk, businesslike voice, he said: 'I want to talk to Thomas. Off speaker. In private.'

Cox hesitated – looked thoughtfully at Thomas. The man had heard what Trevayne had said, that was clear; he was staring at Cox abjectly, lost in fear and bewilderment.

She lifted her eyebrows questioningly. After a long moment, Thomas gulped, tilted his head an inch forwards. She'd take that as a 'yes'.

She blipped off the speaker and handed Thomas the phone. He held it quaveringly to his ear.

'Hello?'

Trevayne's voice was audible to Cox only as a distant mutter.

'Yes,' Thomas said. 'She's here, but she can only hear me, not you.'

Then he listened, eyes downcast, for perhaps ten seconds. Passed the phone back to Cox. She glanced at the screen; Trevayne had ended the call.

'So are you going to tell me what he said?'

Thomas seemed to be coming out of his funk, now he could no longer hear Trevayne's voice. He nodded weakly.

'He said, "There are no innocents," and then Numbers fourteen, eighteen.'

Cox frowned. Didn't ring any bells. Prison numbers? Numbers that signified something back at Hampton Hall?

'And what,' she pressed, 'do you think he meant by that?' To her surprise, Thomas smiled thinly.

'Your ignorance is showing, inspector. That's Numbers with an upper-case "N". The biblical book, fourth in the Pentateuch? Our Mr Trevayne is, you'll remember, a devout Christian.' He clicked his tongue, looked to the ceiling. 'The man's hypocrisy takes one's breath away.'

'That's a bad bloody joke, coming from you.' She looked across at PC George, who'd been sitting silently, bug-eyed and enthralled, while Trevayne had been on the line. 'Stay with him, will you? I'll just be a minute.'

In the corridor she grabbed a passing uniform, asked where there was a computer she could use. The man directed her to a side-room, where four humming PCs were wired up. She sat at one, fired up a search engine. What was it again? *Numbers, fourteen, eighteen.*

It brought up multiple pages of results. Lots of religion

on the web, Cox reflected; lots of violence, lots of porn, lots of hate, lots of religion.

The first link showed her that what she was after was written 'Numbers 14:18' – it meant Chapter 14, Verse 18, of the Old Testament Book of Numbers. She clicked through to an American website that brought up the relevant passage framed in a pop-up box.

Cox read it through. Shuddered – read it again.

The Lord is long-suffering, and of great mercy, forgiving iniquity and transgression, and by no means clearing the guilty, visiting the iniquity of the fathers –

She felt a darkness closing in, cold and malevolent, as she read.

– upon the children unto the fourth and fifth generation.

Cox stared at the final line.

Oh, Christ.

Back to the interview room. Didn't bother to take her seat or restart the tape. She slammed both hands down on the table.

Thomas looked up at her, taken aback.

'Inspector, I –'

'Family,' she snapped. 'Don't you know a threat when you hear one? What family do you have? Any nearby?'

He gaped, completely thrown.

'I, well, there's my son and daughter, of course, Dominic and Ginny, but they're both overseas with their families. Ginny's in the south of France – she's got two children in school out there – and Dominic lives in New York; his boy Jeremy is grown up now, a little girl of his own, although –' He broke up, looked up at Cox – fear, gut-deep terror, once again flooded his lined face.

'What?'

'My great-granddaughter. Abigail.'

Unto the fourth and fifth generation.

Cox gestured at PC George, indicating that he should get ready to put out an urgent call. Snatched up her pen.

'Where is she?'

'She's only five years old,' Thomas whimpered.

'*Where is she?*'

Stammering, Thomas forced out the name of a boarding school, St Katherine's – a high-end place just a few miles to the south-west.

'Jeremy wanted to have her schooled here,' he gabbled. 'He and Anna are only in New York for a short while – he's got a two-year internship with PwC. He didn't want Abi flying back and forth, not at that young age. He thought it would be better, and Mary and I agreed – it's about stability, we said, what a young child that age needs is *stability* . . .'

Cox watched him levelly. Thought of Stevie Butcher, Colin Carter, Robbie and Stan Trevayne – how much stability had *they* had?

Thought of poor little Tomasz Lerna.

Nausea threatened to overwhelm her.

George had already gone to put out the call. She gathered up her things and went out – left Sidney Thomas, solicitor general, sobbing and babbling to himself in an empty room.

28

Four cars, sirens wailing, blue lights smearing the dark sky, streaked through the Surrey countryside. Cox, at the wheel of Greg Wilson's beaten-up Renault, had to drive hard to keep up. As she drove – the little car lurching dangerously on the bends, protesting as she forced it up to speed on the straights – she strained to hear the brittle, refined voice of Mrs Helen Tufnell-Mathers coming over the hands-free.

'I *said*,' the woman repeated fretfully, 'that I shall go and check on the girls now.'

Tufnell-Mathers was Abigail Thomas's housemistress at St Katherine's. She'd been unnerved by Cox's call but so far she was keeping her head – the woman had guts, Cox had to give her that.

'Be careful,' Cox warned, rocketing past a 'Stop' sign. 'Don't take any risks. Check the doors and windows are soundly locked, but don't go outside unless you really have to.'

'Are you on your way?'

'We are. Just a few minutes away.'

It was a half-truth: sure, *they*'d be there soon, with a few carloads of suburban bobbies, but Cox didn't know how much good they'd do. A SCO19 firearms team was what they needed to take down Trevayne, and they'd take a while to scramble out of London.

'Please stay on the line, inspector,' said Mrs Tufnell-Mathers. 'I'm heading up there now.'

'I will, Mrs Tufnell-Mathers. I'm not going anywhere.'

Wilson, holding on tight in the passenger seat, muttered that according to the satnav they were approaching the school grounds now.

'Please, call me Helen,' the woman said. 'It's no time to stand on ceremony.'

Cox smiled. She was starting to like the well-spoken housemistress.

'Okay, Helen. I agree – I'm Kerry.'

'I'm coming up to the girls' wing now. It's blustery outside; can't hear you too well, Kerry.'

'I'm still here.' The car's sweeping headlights picked out a gold-lettered wooden sign on a high stone wall: St Katherine's School for Girls. She braked hard, took a sharp right into the school's driveway.

'There's no sign of anything amiss, here,' Tufnell-Mathers reported. Some of the tension had gone out of her voice. 'I had a quick peep inside, and the girls are all sound asleep, by the look of it. The doors all seem secure. And the windows – oh, but . . .'

She broke off. Cox braked hard, the car skidding sideways in the deep gravel.

'Helen?'

Faint noises – a thump, a clatter; a grunt; a high winter wind, battering on the windowpanes.

Cox looked at Wilson.

'It's happening,' she said, her voice loaded with dread. 'He's here.'

Just up ahead, the Esher coppers were piling out of

their cars. Cox jumped out into the wet, buffeting storm, lifting her injured arm – God, it ached from the drive – to shield her eyes from the lateral driving rain.

She raced up the driveway. The other officers had parked in the shadow of the school, a towering three-storey structure of off-white stone. Tall windows – a modern addition – were spaced across the front of the building. Cox looked up; all across the school, lights were coming on.

The officers were milling, disorganized, talking over one another. She was, she saw quickly, the most senior officer there; time to take charge.

'He's already here,' she said, loud as she could. 'Repeat, the suspect is on the premises.' Turned to face them, blinking in the rain. Wiped her hair from her face. 'I'm DI Cox, from Scotland Yard. Do as I say, and –'

And what? And everything will be fine? A dozen officers, hands on their batons, stared back at her – anxious, jumpy, pumped-up, clueless.

'Well, just do as I say,' she finished.

She dispersed the officers in teams of three, told them to fan out through the school grounds, to cover as much ground as they could – to keep the risks low, to do it by the book – for Christ's sake, to be careful. Robert Trevayne was dangerous. She had the cracked ribs to prove it.

Tense with worry, she watched them move off into the darkness, hi-viz patches glinting in the light from the windows.

There was a scream, from somewhere in the upper storeys, towards the west side of the main building. Cox spun, quickly taking in the possibilities. A narrow, cobbled passageway led into the darkness down that side of the school; an archway in the centre of the building led through, she guessed, into a central courtyard, from which all areas could be accessed.

She squinted through the rain at the cobbled path. Could you, she wondered urgently, get a car down there?

'Hey! You. Sergeant.' She called back one of the officers, a black-bearded man she'd seen at the wheel of one of the patrol cars. He jogged back keenly.

'Yes, ma'am.'

'Move your car across here, quickly.' She half-turned, gestured to the opening of the pathway behind her . . .

An engine roared madly. She saw rain on grey metal. At speed, striking sparks from the school wall with its offside wing, a Merc – Trevayne's Merc – came hurtling up the path – heading straight for her.

She dived, fell, her cheek scraping into the ankle-deep gravel. She *felt* the noise of the car, felt it right through her body, like the noise of shell-fire, as it veered, barely in control, across the driveway, scraping through the gravel barely a yard from her outsplayed feet.

Looked up; saw the Merc fishtail crazily as it spun toward the exit, smashing the wing-mirror from one of the parked patrol cars.

Someone was screaming, a woman. Cox rolled over – felt blood wet and warm on her face, her ear. A woman was running towards her, from the pathway. She was stumbling, limping; there was a dark flash of blood across her brow.

'Helen!' Cox screamed, over the chaos of the Merc's receding engine roar, officers yelling and running, girls screaming as doors banged and upstairs windows were flung open.

The woman stopped, bewildered, lost in the rain and noise. Wrung her hands helplessly. Cox, scrambling to her feet, screamed again: 'Helen!'

This time, Tufnell-Mathers heard. She turned her head towards Cox; her expression was empty, bereft – a face of grief.

'He's got her,' she yelled. Choked on a sob, looked around wild-eyed, looked back at Cox. The blood mingled with the rain and streamed down her face. *'He's got her.'*

If she failed, if she lost Trevayne or pushed him the wrong way, or if Wilson's knackered car gave out now, Abigail Thomas would die. *It's that simple this time, DI Cox.* The Renault howled as she hammered the gas pedal, roaring out of the drive and on to the main road in a clattering shower of gravel.

She'd no radio, no way of contacting the rest of the officers; they were behind her, she knew, somewhere – but she had a visual on the grey Merc and she wasn't going to wait about for them to catch up.

A glimpse was all she'd had: a brake light flaring red a hundred yards down the road as the Merc screeched round a tight left-hand bend.

Now the car was just two dots of light in the distance. Way off. Getting away.

Cox winced, narrowing her eyes, as her rear-view mirror flared with light; one of the patrol cars, siren screaming, hurtled past her, fast and reckless in pursuit.

It'd be the black-bearded sergeant; after Cox, he'd been in the best position to respond.

She wished him luck. The patrol car was already way in front of her and gaining visibly on the distant Merc.

But she wasn't about to take any chances. She kept on at top speed, the needle quivering at seventy, seventy-five – kept on pushing the Renault to its limit.

Up ahead, she saw the twin lights of the Merc vanish abruptly – a bend in the road, Cox guessed. The patrol car, following, close now, within fifty feet, went the same way. Then Cox heard a gunshot, a scream of rubber on asphalt, another shot. What the hell . . . ?

There was a loud, sharp scraping noise, a heavy thump. Someone going off the road. Cox said a quick prayer; hauled the car through the turn at speed, injured ribs shrieking at the effort.

It was the patrol car – out of action, overturned by the roadside. Must've veered up the left-hand verge, overbalanced as it slewed along the kerb; the wall of a concrete culvert had torn away the driver's door. Smoke rose from the crumpled bonnet.

Cox quickly saw why it'd crashed – braked hard, spun the wheel desperately. Another car, unmarked, was parked at an angle across the road. Behind it, she saw lights, uniforms, guns, set, purposeful faces . . .

A SCO19 roadblock. She swore fiercely, wrestling to bring the skidding car under control. *Great work, guys . . .*

What was that, to the left? A break in the kerb, an opening in the steep verge – the armed response guys must've figured it was too narrow for a car. Trevayne had obviously disagreed; he must have come this way – or else he'd vanished into thin bloody air.

One of the SCO 19 officers had stepped out from behind the roadblock, was gesturing at her self-importantly. Cox ignored him. She gunned the engine, bringing the car out of its spin – plunged forwards, down through the opening.

It was narrow, unpaved, barely more than a bridleway, heading steeply downwards through a deep stand of pine-trees. No one in their right mind would bring a car down here. Maybe a desperate killer; maybe a desperate copper.

The Renault bucked over potholes, rocks, ditches. Her arm and ribs ached from gripping the wheel. The windscreen wipers whined back and forth.

Red brakelights flared up ahead.

She had an edge here; not much of one, but something. Off-road, Trevayne had lost his main advantage: the Merc's vastly superior road-speed. On a main road, he could have put his foot down and lost the Renault for good in five seconds flat – he'd already outrun her once. Here, with Trevayne struggling along the muddy, broken-up track, lights glaring full-beam to pick out the way through the pines, they were pretty much on a level footing.

They were also, she realized uneasily, heading away from any place where someone – anyone – might pass by; into empty countryside – into darkness.

If and when the cars stopped, it'd just be the three of them: her, Trevayne and poor, terrified little Abigail Thomas.

She drove on. *Just focus on those brake lights. Just focus on getting it* right.

Up ahead, she saw, the Merc seemed to be faltering, slowing, lurching lopsidedly across the track. Hope clutched at her, hope wound tightly up with a primal, physical fear. A puncture, a broken axle?

Or a trap?

She kept up her speed, closing the gap; the Merc was still moving, still ploughing forward in spite of its difficulties. Cox wondered how she was going to bring the bastard to a halt; there was nowhere near enough room to overtake, and she doubted the Renault had the power to run the bigger car off the road – and how could she, anyway, with Abigail Thomas in there with him?

Trevayne braked, hard, sudden, brake lights bright and terrifyingly close. The Merc skidded sharply through ninety degrees, jolted to a halt, jammed across the track.

Another roadblock. No turning away from this one.

She had a half-second's sight of Trevayne's face framed in the driver's window, grimacing in the white blaze of Cox's oncoming headlights. Cox took her hands off the wheel, covered her face with her forearms.

The Renault bounced over a hump in the path, crunched, off-side first and halfway airborne, into the Merc's driver's door.

Shudder of impact. Scream of crumpling metal. Hiss, bang of the little car's airbag. A dizzying lurch, a hard thump.

Blackness.

*

Cox awoke. Gagged, spat blood. Her right wrist, cramped between her hip and the car door, was twisted, unnatural – the pain of it cut through the fog of her concussion.

'Jesus. Jesus Christ.'

She lifted her head – her neck screamed at her, her vision swam in and out of focus. Fumbled with her left hand to unfasten her seatbelt; reached over, elbowing painfully past the inflated airbag, to unlatch the door.

Freezing cold night air, spatters of sleety rain. She gasped, drew a deep breath. There was light, faint light – how, where? She clambered from the car, clinging to the wet metalwork of the roof, the bonnet – saw that the little Renault still had battery-power, that the headlamps, crushed against the ruptured flank of the Merc, were still gleaming faintly.

She looked up – saw the face of Robert Trevayne, looking straight at her from four feet away.

Cox gasped, stumbled backwards, lost her footing on the mud-slicked path – hit the ground hard, her lower back thudding into an outcropping stone.

Trevayne hadn't moved.

The dim, low-angled light of the headlamps drew out the dark hollows of his face. His nose and mouth were black with blood. As Cox's eyes adjusted to the gloom, she made out a ragged seam, a slash in the skin, running from Trevayne's right eyebrow to the back of his head.

She swallowed. Bile and blood in her throat. Over Trevayne's right ear, the seam split wider, opened out . . . She saw an edge of off-white bone. A dark mess of blood and brain.

The metal frame of the driver's window, she noticed, was drenched with viscous gore.

She let her gaze track downwards. The impact of the Renault had split apart the aluminium of the Merc's door; a sharp-edged horizontal rip had opened in the pit of a deep v-shaped dent.

Thick vertical stripes of blackness cut across the grey on the lower half of the door, beneath the rip. Cox, her belly roiling, squinted through the flickering half-light – then looked sharply away, gulping down vomit.

She'd seen something glistening between the halves of split metal; a bulge, ribbed, glossy with blood. A section of intestine. A good eight inches of Robert Trevayne's gut.

Cox fought her way on to her hands and knees. Scrabbled for purchase; the path was slippery underfoot, gritty and cold between her fingers.

Take nothing for granted. Finish this. Do this right.

On her feet now, uncertain, swaying. A smear of light in the darkness behind her made her turn, narrow her eyes: a car, a patrol car, lumbering down the track. It was maybe half a mile away. Too far off to make a difference now.

She turned back to the Merc, to Trevayne.

Found herself staring down the barrel of a gun.

She took a step backwards. Thick hawthorn, dense and spiny, pressed up against her legs and back. Downhill, the Merc, its nose deep in the hedge, blocked the way; up the slope, in the wet, the dark, she hadn't a hope in hell.

Trevayne was looking at her. There was a defiant gleam in the one eye she could see. The barrel of the gun was propped on the car door. What he must've been going through, she couldn't imagine – just to grip the gun's butt must be causing him agonies.

And for what? What would it achieve? What did he *want*?

She faced down Trevayne, faced down the black eye of the gun barrel. It was all she could do. The only option she had left.

Trevayne cocked the gun.

Cox shook her head – felt helpless, knew it could do no good, knew there was no use in asking Robert Trevayne for mercy – but shook her head, blinking in the rain, and mouthed, 'No. No.'

Trevayne just smiled. The muscles of his jaw tensed. The trembling gun barrel lifted, tilted upwards – and, once it was pressed to the bloodied, sweat-beaded skin of his own forehead, Robert Trevayne pulled the trigger.

Cox hurled herself forward. It was too late to save Trevayne – it'd always been too late to save Trevayne. *But that's not why you're here, Cox.* She threw herself hip-first on to the bonnet of the Renault, skidded across to the near side, stumbled, staggered, found her balance – grabbed for the catch of the Merc's boot, flipped up the tailgate –

A child, a young child, skinny and pale, cold and folded in a foetal curl.

The memory of poor Tomasz Lerna hit her like a physical impact. She bit her lip; reached out a shaking hand.

Abigail Thomas looked up at her. Her dark eyes were wide, her face white and wet with tears.

Took her a second to find her voice.

'Are you rescuing me?'

Cox smiled, felt a hard lump in her throat. Wiped her lank, drenched hair out of her eyes. Christ, what she must look like to the poor kid.

'Yes, darling,' she said. 'I'm rescuing you.'

She bent down. Gathered the child up in her arms.

29

9 September 2015

Cox waited and watched: the kids, smart in matching yellow polo-shirts, running, walking, laughing, scrapping, in twos, threes, fours, out of the gates; and then the adults, waiting for them – some men, mostly women, most in their late twenties, early thirties. Some she knew, some she didn't.

Her phone, on the passenger seat, buzzed. She snatched it up.

'DI Cox.'

A pause – then a laugh, Greg Wilson's laugh.

'Are you sure about that, Kerry? Want to try again?'

She grinned, put her hand to her brow.

'Jesus, sorry Greg – old habits die hard.' Shook her head. 'What's the news?'

'I just left the courtroom. Guilty on four out of seven charges.'

Cox pressed her lips together, nodded firmly.

'That'll do,' she said.

'It'll do for life without chance of parole, yeah. We won't be seeing Sidney Thomas again.' He paused. 'No whooping and cheering? No hallelujah chorus?'

She managed a weary smile.

'I'm happy, I promise. Or anyway, I'm satisfied. It's been a long time coming.'

It'd been a long, wearing trial – but for all the solicitor general's friends in high places, it'd been pretty much a foregone conclusion after the lab matched Thomas's DNA with samples taken from Tomasz Lerna's body.

What should I feel? she wondered. Elated, triumphant? No. Six people were dead, and a jury's 'guilty' verdict wasn't going to change that. There were no happy endings here.

'Surprised you weren't there to see the last act,' Wilson said.

Cox shrugged.

'I kind of lost my appetite for hanging around with lawyers.'

'How about with writers? I want to buy you dinner tomorrow night. I'm celebrating.'

'Finished the book already?'

'I've just rattled off the final chapter. It'll be in the bookshops in the blink of an eye.'

Cox rolled her eyes. You can take the man out of Fleet Street . . .

Still, after everything they'd been through – the horrors he'd witnessed, the dangers he'd fronted up to – she couldn't blame Wilson for wanting a bit of payback. His insider's take on the downfall of Sidney Thomas was going to be a big seller, there was no doubt about that – power, conspiracy, perversion, murder, heroism, it was a great story.

Great to read about, anyway, she supposed. Fucking terrible to have to live through. That was the thing with stories – they were only entertaining from a safe distance.

At least Wilson's version would be true – she'd make damn sure of that.

She was about to suggest that he might want her to read the book before he delivered it to his publisher when she saw a face she knew, passing out of the school gate. Funny how that worked, how that one face – just the same old eyes, nose, smile – stood out in any crowd, like a single lit bulb in a dark room. Unmissable.

'I have to go,' she said to Greg.

'The Met begging you to return?'

'Something like that. I'll call you tomorrow.'

She pocketed her phone, jumped out of the car. Called out his name – and here he came, at a run, sports bag over his shoulder, wad of crayon drawings in his hand. Matthew.

'Mum!'

'Hiya, love.'

She reached down and tousled his messy brown hair. What she really wanted to do was pick him up and give him a proper hug – but she'd been given a proper telling-off the last time she'd tried that in front of his mates.

'What've you been up to today?' she asked as they walked hand in hand to the car.

'We played football in PE,' Matthew said breathlessly. 'I got picked second, only after Jermaine, who's *brilliant*, and I wanted to play centre-forward, but Mr Walsh said I had to play in midfield, and I did and I *still* scored two goals and . . .'

He gabbled on. Cox half-listened, a distant smile on her face, as she manoeuvred carefully out of the busy school car park. Just glad that he was there; just glad that he was hers.

She drove slowly through the new-build estates between the school and the main road back to London.

The tale of his football heroics concluded, Matthew had fallen silent.

Cox glanced at him in the rear-view.

'What're you thinking, love?'

He looked up.

'Am I spending the night at yours tonight, Mum?'

Cox laughed. He'd developed an oddly grown-up way of putting things lately.

'Yes,' she said. 'You are *spending the night* at mine. I've put your Iron Man bedsheets on and everything.'

'Oh.' Matthew looked a bit put out.

'What's up? You like Iron Man, don't you?'

He pouted.

'Not as good as Minions.'

Cox shook her head. Kids. It'd be something else next week. All depended on which TV ads Matthew saw between now and then.

'Pizza for tea?'

His face lit up.

'*Yes.*'

Still, it was never too hard to win him round.

She switched on the radio. It was tuned to Radio Four; the hourly news bulletin had just begun.

'The solicitor general, who is married to the Tory peer Baroness Kent,' a man's voice was saying, 'was given a sentence of life without the option of parole after being found guilty of –'

'*Bo-ring*,' bawled Matthew from the back seat. Kerry smiled.

'Couldn't agree more,' she said. Retuned the radio. The first station she came to was playing a tinny pop song – that'd do.

But Matthew must've picked up an idea of the content of the bulletin, because he piped up again a minute or so later.

'Mu-um.'

'Ye-es.'

'You're not a policeman any more, are you?'

She tutted at him.

'I was never a police*man*, was I, Matthew? I was a police*woman*.' She shifted gear, keeping her eyes on the road. 'But no. No, I'm not a policewoman any more.'

In March she'd taken a job with a charity in southeast London, a small outfit that worked with women who'd been trafficked to the UK. It was fulfilling work – frustrating sometimes, sure, but it felt like it made a difference.

'What are you now, then?' Matthew pestered. 'For example,' he added helpfully, 'Oliver's mum is a decorator.'

'Good for Oliver's mum. I'm – well, I help people, love. People who need help.'

'Do you like it?'

'I do.' Felt the need to throw in a moral lesson. 'It's good to help people.'

'Yes, *but* do you like it as much as being a policeman?'

'Policewoman.'

'Yes, that.'

Good question.

376

'D'you know, love, I'm not sure. It was scary, sometimes, being a policewoman – and it meant I didn't get to see you as often as I wanted to.' Ahead, to her right, the clouded London skyline, dour and doomy, was looming into view. She shifted lanes, ready for the turn-off. 'But then, it was exciting, too – and I got to stop bad people doing bad things, and help people who were in trouble. Sometimes it was really hard, but at other times –'

Matthew cut her off.

'Doesn't really matter, Mum. I like this one.' He was pointing at the radio; the DJ was playing some godawful bubblegum teen-pop track. 'Turn it up. I like this one.'

Cox smiled.

'I like it too,' she lied. What the hell.

She reached for the volume dial. Did as she was told.